Finding
Heaven

Finding Heaven

TALENA WINTERS

MY SECRET WISH
PUBLISHING

Published by My Secret Wish Publishing

www.mysecretwishpublishing.com
Finding Heaven: A Novel

Summary: Sarah Daniels feels trapped in a living hell, but thinks she deserves her life—until a new friend invites her to choose a different future. But is it too late for Sarah to find heaven?

ISBN (hardcover): 978-1-989800-09-6
ISBN (paperback): 978-1-989800-08-9
ISBN (eBook): 978-0-9947364-3-7

Cover and Title Page design by Talena Winters
Edited by Kristin Dyck, familychatter.ca/copyediting
Print book formatting by The Deliberate Page, deliberatepage.com
Author Photo © Amanda Monette. Used by permission.

Printed in the United States of America, or the country of purchase.

Scripture quotations are from the ESV® Bible (The Holy Bible, English Standard Version®), copyright © 2001 by Crossway, a publishing ministry of Good News Publishers. Used by permission. All rights reserved.

To the brave women who shared your stories with me.
You are priceless pearls.

The Spirit of the Lord God is upon me,
     because the Lord has anointed me
to bring good news to the poor;
     he has sent me to bind up the brokenhearted,
to proclaim liberty to the captives,
     and the opening of the prison to those who are bound;
to proclaim the year of the Lord's favor,
     and the day of vengeance of our God;
to comfort all who mourn;
     to grant to those who mourn in Zion—
to give them a beautiful headdress instead of ashes,
     the oil of gladness instead of mourning,
     the garment of praise instead of a faint spirit;
that they may be called oaks of righteousness,
     the planting of the Lord, that he may be glorified.

-Isaiah 61:1-3

one

ALL SARAH WANTED THAT SUNDAY AFTERNOON WAS A LATTE AND SOME PEACE AND QUIET. SHE should have known that she was the one person destined to not get her wish.

She stared at the pastries in the Starbucks display case, chewing her lip absently, hugging her denim blazer closer around her slender frame to protect against the chill of the shop's air conditioning. She had already been in San Francisco for four days and had yet to see anything in the city except a few restaurants and the route to her hotel. Now that the writers' conference was over, she relished standing in line and not having to strike up a conversation with someone. The woman in front of her moved up to the counter, and Sarah automatically took a step forward, still staring into space.

"Excuse me, ma'am, what are you having?"

Sarah jumped. The warm baritone had come from directly behind her. She turned around and was confronted with a tall, lean, muscular man in faded blue jeans and a white T-shirt. His blue eyes crinkled in an easy grin, and sandy hair fell in tousled curls almost to his chin. She blinked. With his height—she was staring straight at his nose, so he was at least six feet tall, maybe more—and stubble-covered cheeks, he looked like he had walked right out of a poster from one of the shop windows in Union Square in order to pop in here for a lunch break. Or maybe out of the pages of one of her novels. She took mental notes—he had the perfect look for her next male lead.

Sarah realized she was staring and dropped her gaze. She brushed aside a wavy blond lock that had worked itself loose from her ponytail, trying to think of an answer to his question. She couldn't even remember what he'd said.

"Pardon me?" She swallowed nervously.

"I never know what to get here. What are you having?"

She frowned. "Haven't you ever been to a Starbucks before?"

The man chuckled. "Not often. There isn't a Starbucks where I live. Well, I guess there are a couple now, but I never go there. What do you recommend?"

"Hmm. I see." She didn't. No Starbucks? Did he live in Antarctica? "I'm having a latte. I like mine sweet, so I add a little sugar and I'm good to go."

"Sounds great. Thanks." He searched the menu for her suggestion.

"Sure." Sarah looked down, then glanced back up, curiosity getting the better of her reticence to make conversation. "Where on earth do you live?"

She couldn't imagine anyone in North America who wasn't familiar with Starbucks. It seemed you couldn't turn a corner in San Francisco without running into another one of the ritzy coffee shops. Sure, there were only a handful in her home city of Edmonton by comparison, and she knew of plenty of places in Alberta without one—but it seemed strange that this man had no idea what to even try.

The man's eyes crinkled more deeply. Did that smile ever leave his face? "Mumbai."

"As in, India?"

He nodded. "Yep. But originally, I'm from Canada. A little town called Miller, in Alberta. No Starbucks there, either."

She gaped. "Really? What are the chances of that?"

He gave his head a confused shake, but his grin didn't disappear. "What do you mean?"

Sarah became aware that the girl behind the till was trying to get her attention. She turned and placed her order, then moved down to the opposite end of the counter to wait while Mr. Tall Blond Stranger placed an identical one. The name the barista jotted on his cup was "Steve."

He came and held up the wall beside her. Sarah focused on the activity behind the counter as she pondered whether to let the conversation die a natural death or risk being friendly. The idea of conversing with this stranger made her throat dry up, but he seemed like he expected her to be the friendly type.

That's what she got for asking a question. She should have known better. This guy wasn't a conference attendee—she was in a coffee shop on one of the busiest tourist corners of San Francisco. This guy could be anyone, from anywhere, with any kind of intentions. He could have stalked her online and was now stalking her in person. Stranger things had happened to people in her profession.

However, he seemed harmless enough. And it's not like they were in a back alley at night. *Geez, Sarah, get a grip.*

She took a deep breath and turned toward him. "I live in Edmonton now. But my mom still lives in Miller. I lived there until I was eighteen."

Now it was his turn to gape. "What are the chances, indeed?" His grin was back with a little snort of amusement. After a moment, he shook his head and laughed.

"What's so funny?"

"I was wondering how we managed to grow up practically next door to each other and yet never meet until the first time I'm in San Francisco. Life is full of funny surprises, isn't it?"

She gave a weak smile. "I guess. I, um, didn't get out much as a kid." She eyed him critically, trying to match his face to any of her former schoolmates. He looked like he was maybe a few years older than her thirty-two years—but she had barely made friends with people her own age when she was in school, never mind a boy several grades ahead of her. And she wasn't at all surprised that he hadn't noticed the awkward girl hiding behind a curtain of greasy hair that had been her junior high school persona.

"Tall caffè latte?" The barista placed the cardboard cup on the counter. Sarah took a step to claim her order, murmuring thanks.

"So what brings you here . . . Sarah?" Steve read her name on the side of her cup. "I'm Steve, by the way. Steven McGuire." He offered his hand.

Sarah shifted the hot beverage to her left hand so she could shake with the other.

"Sarah Daniels. I was at a writers' conference this weekend. Thought I'd catch a bit of the city before heading back home tomorrow."

The barista put a second caffè latte on the counter. Steve grabbed it and followed her as she moved toward the prep station to add her sugars. She grabbed two.

He grabbed five.

Steve laughed when he saw her look. "Coffee gets in my mouth." He wrinkled his nose to emphasize his point. "Unless it tastes like dessert."

She blushed when she realized that she had raised her eyebrows at him, like she had a right to say anything at all.

"Sorry," she mumbled, refusing to ask why he'd ordered a drink he wouldn't even like. She focused on stirring in the light brown sugar crystals. The sooner she finished, the sooner she could escape this conversation. It hadn't been going badly until now, which is why she had to leave before she botched it up even worse.

But he wouldn't stop talking.

"Daniels, Daniels. . . . I don't know any Daniels."

"That's my married name. It used to be Sinclair."

"Hmm. That name's a little familiar, but I got nothin'. Sorry, I'm not great with names."

"Yeah, well, as I said—we didn't get out much." She picked up her cup, gave him a tight-lipped smile that was meant to be a farewell, and turned to leave.

"So, a writer, eh? What do you write?"

He popped a plastic lid onto his latte and followed her out of the coffee shop. Who does that? Shouldn't he just let her walk away?

Sarah looked around, getting her bearings on the busy street corner. Kitty-corner across the intersection a pair of life-sized cement Chinese lions gaped in an open-mouthed roar from either side of the famous Dragon Gate, one paw each held high in warning. She craned her head back and gazed up at the Asian-style arches armoured with columns of verdigrised tiles that marked the entrance to Chinatown. A crowd of tourists of various ethnicities risked their lives on the edge of the curb, holding smartphones on selfie sticks with their backs to the landmark. Cars rushed by only a foot behind them.

Down the street to her right, she saw her salvation in the form of a bright red double-decker tour bus making its way toward them. It was in the opposite lane, so she was going to have to cross the street to board.

Steve was still waiting for an answer.

"Uh, romance. Excuse me, it was so nice to meet you, Steve, but I have to cross. I'm catching that bus." She indicated the crosswalk signal and joined the crowds streaming across the street.

"No worries. Me, too, actually." He stepped off the curb beside her.

Her heart rate jumped again and she took a calming breath. Her friend Erica's voice rang in her head. *If you look like a victim, you'll be a victim.* Of course, no one would ever mistake Erica—beautiful, assured Erica, with her perfect mocha skin, halo of dark, springy curls, and I-dare-you attitude—as a victim. Sarah cleared her throat and kept her voice steady as a rock, trying to emulate her friend.

Confident. Friendly. Interested.

Right.

"You're taking the city tour?"

"Yep!" He flashed her a quick smile. "Excuse me for a moment."

They had stopped beside a row of outdoor tables lining the sidewalk in front of a French-style cafe. Steve pulled his phone out of his pocket and started swiping around the screen, sunlight glinting red in the stubbly growth on his dimpled chin.

Brakes squealed and a man's voice squawked over the bus speaker, calling for people to board and depart. Sarah pulled her own phone out of her purse and opened the lock screen to show the driver her emailed ticket receipt. He squinted at the device in her hand, then grunted and nodded. Steve was only a step behind her.

The bottom of the bus was moderately full, but she hoped the passengers descending from above meant that there was room on the open second deck. By the time she reached the top step, the bus was lurching forward into a right turn. She swayed, almost afraid that Friendly Steve would try to steady her. Almost.

He didn't. She breathed a little easier, felt annoyed at the same time, and wondered what was wrong with her.

There were two seats available—one next to a beefy man with skin the colour of espresso, and another a couple of rows behind him and across the aisle beside a skinny Latina girl with wires trailing from her ears. She sat next to the girl.

As she rotated into the seat, Steve gave her another quick grin and a wave, then slid into the other empty seat. Within seconds, Steve and his seatmate were chatting like old friends.

Sarah grimaced, then tuned in to the tour guide. The short man had a handlebar moustache and was dressed in a 1920s-style straw hat and red striped vest. "Karl," as he introduced himself, was telling a funny story about some celebrity or other, complete with vocal impressions and gestures. The tourists laughed, and Karl grinned back in appreciation.

"Thank you for that. Now, get your cameras ready, folks, and direct your attention to the right where you will be seeing the Transamerica Tower in just a few moments . . ."

Sarah chuckled politely and glanced at the girl next to her. The teen stared over the stainless steel side rail, ignoring everything and everyone on the bus. That suited Sarah just fine.

After four days stuck mostly indoors at the conference, the fresh air and warm sun was invigorating, especially for early October. When she had gone to her doctor's appointment on Tuesday morning, her car had been covered in frost.

Thinking of the doctor reminded her of the outcome of that appointment, and she felt her heart start to squeeze.

No. She wasn't going to go there right now. Today, she meant to forget. Tomorrow, she would be going back home, back to normal—whatever that meant now. She would figure out how to tell Craig what the doctor said, and they would deal with it. She wasn't sure which was more disturbing—the diagnosis or her husband's potential reaction to it. Shaking her head, she took a deep breath, hoping to relax, but her gut remained clenched tight.

Sarah tried to focus on the tour guide, but her gaze kept falling on Steve's blond head. She studied his rugged profile as he chatted with his seatmate or tilted his head to listen to the guide.

Karl pointed out a landmark skyscraper behind them. Steve turned to look at it and caught her staring at him. He cocked a questioning eyebrow at her.

Her eyes darted to the building beside him as though that was where she had been intending to look all along. She was sure he was only being friendly, but she was afraid to encourage him in case he got the wrong impression. She casually draped her left hand over the seat rail ahead of her to display her wedding band and wished again that Craig had agreed to come on the trip. Then she wouldn't be in this situation.

She frowned as she thought of her husband. Other than a few exchanged texts, she hadn't been able to get a hold of him since she'd arrived in San Francisco on Wednesday night. Typical. He worked so much, and had been coming home so late, she wondered if she was going to have to text the doctor's news to him even after she was home.

About half an hour after she had climbed on, the bus pulled into its "home base" on a street near the wharf. The guide explained that they would need to transfer to one of the other buses if they wanted to continue to tour the city, or sit tight until they started their next round of the downtown loop.

Most of the bus emptied out, and by the time Sarah scrounged up a tip for the driver and guide and stepped onto the shady sidewalk, the crowd was migrating elsewhere. She noted with relief that Friendly Steve was nowhere to be seen.

Sarah hesitated and peered down the tree-lined street toward the ocean, wondering what she should do next. A quick check of her map app reoriented her, and she decided to wander along the wharf to take in some of the sights before hopping on the bus tour that crossed the Golden Gate Bridge. She adjusted her purse strap and set off downhill at a quick pace.

Steve McGuire browsed the displays in the athletics store next to the wharf, trying to ignore the feeling in his gut—the feeling that he was supposed to be doing something but wasn't doing it. His thoughts kept circling around to the beautiful woman with the serious blue eyes he'd met in Starbucks over an hour ago.

Sarah. He had gone into Starbucks following a hunch, and when he'd gotten into line he'd sensed that the woman in front of him was the reason he was there. He'd felt that tweak in his gut too often not to know what it meant. He *knew*—in no way he could explain except "God told me"—that he was supposed to talk to her. And he also *knew* that the conversation wasn't over, despite the fact that he had fled the bus hoping not to have to see her again.

He'd been having an argument with God ever since.

This isn't why I'm here, God. She doesn't look like she needs any help. And she's married. What if she thinks I'm hitting on her? Are you sure this is a good idea?

He felt ashamed to realize that he was merely making excuses for his own hesitation. If he'd met a woman in the slums of Mumbai and felt this quiet prompting, he wouldn't have rested until he'd felt he'd accomplished the mission he'd been given. But Sarah was different—she was accomplished, and seemingly-well-off, and completely unlike the women he normally worked with. What could she possibly need from him? And how could he know that—whatever it was he was supposed to do—he wouldn't screw it up?

Guilt and shame needled him as his ex-fiancée's face appeared in his mind. Despite all he'd accomplished since that long-ago disaster, he still felt Vanessa's condemnation and judgement with every new task the Lord set before him.

But he also knew that fear of failure was no reason to run from his duty.

He stared at a display of boxer shorts with "I heart SF" plastered all over them, but wasn't actually looking. He ran his hand through his hair and scratched the back of his neck.

"Okay, God, if this is you, give me another chance. I don't know what I'm supposed to talk to her about, but I'll keep the conversation going until you show me."

"Can I help you?"

Steve jumped at the friendly greeting and glanced toward the male clerk with unruly spiked black hair and large grommets through his ear lobes that had appeared beside him, feeling sheepish. He shook his head.

"No, thanks. I was just looking."

"Mm-kay." The clerk smiled and backed off.

Steve moved toward the door. He wasn't going to go look for Sarah—if he was meant to talk to her, God was going to have to make it abundantly clear.

As he approached the display window, he froze, his breath catching in his throat. Through the logo screened onto the glass and past the life-sized pirate statue he could see the blond ponytail and slender figure of the very woman he was hoping he wouldn't run into again.

"That was fast," he muttered.

The smell of fish and chips mixed with salt water permeated the air. Sarah meandered up and down the street for the better part of an hour, navigating between tourists and buskers and gazing wistfully at small children who trailed along after their parents. A line of those ridiculous Segways being ridden by people in bright orange vests made her giggle. They reminded her of nothing more than ducklings following their mother.

In front of one little shop, a life-sized replica of a pirate that bore a striking resemblance to Captain Hook snarled at passersby. She snapped a selfie next to the rogue and texted it to Craig.

The captain's taking me to dinner tonight.

She feigned interest in the window display while she waited for a reply. As the minutes stretched, her jaw tightened, and she was about to move on when her phone cheeped.

As long as he pays the bill and keeps his hands to himself.

Sarah took a deep breath and smiled to herself. Craig had texted her back.

Don't worry, I'll slap him silly if he starts to get fresh.

Good girl. You tell him that you're MY wench, so he better not get any ideas.

Sarah scowled a little at being referred to as a wench by her husband, but decided to keep running with the joke. He would like that. And it was nice to have him flirt with her. It felt a little like the old days.

You know that we wenches don't care if a customer gets a little handsy as long as he tips well. Maybe he'll lend me his hat for you to wear tomorrow night. ;-)

Her phone tweeted once more.

Gotta run. I'll call you later.

Sarah frowned. That was abrupt.

Okay. Xoxo.

Sarah's brow remained furrowed as she tucked the phone back into her purse.

"Ms. Sinclair?"

Sarah glanced up. Three women stood in front of her, two with hopeful smiles on their faces, the third hanging back, looking distinctly annoyed.

"Yes?"

"You're Devon Sinclair, the writer, right?" asked the redhead in front.

Sarah wasn't sure if she had a "typical" reader, but if so then this was exactly the type of woman she expected her to be—a slightly heavyset house-wife who had kissed the freshness of youth goodbye, and who Sarah imagined never got much excitement outside the pages of books like hers. The woman held a copy of Sarah's latest book in her hands. The look on her face was slightly awestruck.

Sarah repressed a sigh and pasted on a smile. "Yes, that's me," she said, claiming her pen name. "Would you like an autograph?"

The woman's face lit up and she nodded, then handed Sarah the book and a pen. One of her companions rolled her eyes and went to study a nearby shop window, but the other surreptitiously eased another copy of *Black Knight* out of her bag.

"So, were you at the conference this weekend?" asked Sarah as she wrote *Devon Sinclair* in a flowing script on each title page in succession.

"Yes, we were. But there was so much to see! I never seemed to be at your booth when you were there signing."

Sure, you didn't.

In recent years, most sales of her book were digital—she figured it was because an e-reader was much less conspicuous than a brown paper slipcover to hide what you were reading. She was a little surprised that these women had approached her at all, even if the setting allowed more anonymity than the conference crowds.

"Thank you so much for doing this. I'm a huge fan!" The redhead examined the signature as though trying to memorize it.

"My pleasure." Sarah handed the second book back to a mousy-looking brunette, who smiled shyly and thanked her. Sarah wondered what it was like to be her—to be the one reading her dark fiction instead of writing it. To be someone who could enjoy it.

As the two women went to collect their dismissive friend, Sarah guessed what judgemental thoughts were going through the third woman's head—their echoes reverberated in her own skull every moment that she was Devon Sinclair, erotica writer. She bit her lip to keep the grimace of disgust off her face and watched the trio disappear down the boardwalk.

This is the bed I've made. Literally.

She just wished she could have found a more comfortable mattress.

two

"HAVE YOU EVER TRIED GHIRARDELLI'S?"

For the second time today, that warm baritone made Sarah jump. She whirled to face Steve, whose eyes were glittering with mischief. She covered her alarm with a glare and crossed her arms.

"You have a habit of sneaking up behind people, don't you?"

Steve grinned.

"Just today. It's an all-day special."

Sarah's glare faltered and she felt the corners of her mouth lift slightly. Her arms remained crossed, though. She frowned.

"What's 'Gearah Deli's'?"

"I'll give you a hint. There's chocolate involved." He leaned close and whispered conspiratorially. "And ice cream."

She arched a brow. "Keep talking."

Steve stood up. "Tell you what, neighbour. I won't sneak up on you anymore if you visit Ghirardelli's with me. Eating a decadent hot fudge sundae alone seems a little pathetic, even to me. But if you eat chocolate with a friend, it instantly becomes a health food, you know. Even the whipped cream doesn't count."

"So we're friends now, are we?"

"We could be. I'm game if you are."

Sarah gave him a measuring stare.

"How far will it be to walk there?"

Steve unfolded the tour bus map and made a show of studying it.

"According to this, only . . . thirty blocks. We'll have earned the right to eat chocolate when we get there, for sure."

"Wow, you don't ask for much, do you?" She pressed her lips together to suppress a smile. She should not want to go have ice cream with this man. He could be a rapist or a kidnapper or—

Get a grip, Sarah. You know he's just a nice Alberta boy being friendly.

A swipe on her phone brought the map of San Francisco back into view. Ghirardelli Square, the most likely home of said establishment, was clearly labelled only a short distance across the park from where the GPS marked her location in blue.

"Thirty blocks, eh? Will we have to swim out to Alcatraz on the way there?" She glanced up at his twinkling blue eyes.

"If you insist. But it's shorter to go that way." He pointed across the intersection toward a green space bordered with tall trees that marched along the street until they met the water of San Francisco Bay. Barely visible through the lush foliage were some mismatched blocky brick buildings.

Sarah tilted her head and studied his face, then offered him a small smile.

"Okay. Friends." She grinned wider when he raised his eyebrows in mock surprise. "Actually, you had me at 'chocolate.'" Confident.

She fell into place beside him as he took off toward the park.

"Well, who doesn't like chocolate, right?"

"My husband, oddly enough." There. She had mentioned Craig again, in case he had missed the fact that she was married and might be getting any romantic ideas. She glanced up to gauge his reaction.

Steve only cocked an eyebrow. "Huh. Go figure. More for you, right?"

"I guess." She eyed him curiously. Apparently, she had been worrying about her fidelity for nothing. He didn't look the least bit disappointed or uncomfortable that she was married. His intentions must truly be completely innocent. Or completely evil.

Sarah felt a shiver of excitement mingled with fear.

A pretty bohemian busker standing on the street corner caught her attention. The woman strummed a guitar and crooned a lonely tune Sarah didn't recognize. A sign asking for change sat propped in the open guitar case by the woman's feet.

Sarah paused, fished a few small bills out of her purse and tossed them into the case. They landed beside a ten that came from Steve's hand. The young woman beamed at them from a metal-studded face. She kept singing the soul-stirring tune.

Steve glanced at Sarah. "Onward?"

She nodded, wondering what this guy's deal was. Did he throw in the money to impress her?

They passed a shabby-looking man standing on the corner holding a sign that said "Travelling and hungry." Steve tossed a few more bills into the man's upside-down hat and was rewarded with another grateful smile.

Sarah rolled her eyes. If Steve gave money to every homeless person they passed in this city, it might *feel* like they had walked thirty blocks before they got ice cream.

Steve led the way across the street and into the park, sidestepping a little boy absorbed in licking a strawberry ice cream cone. Sarah's eyes followed the boy, who was completely adorable in a ball cap and shorts, with creamy pink liquid dripping down his cheeks and off his pudgy elbows. Sarah smiled at him and glanced at his mother, who smiled back with reflexive pride. The little boy caught her watching, stopped licking for a moment and grinned at her, sticky sweetness covering his face. Sarah melted and felt tears pricking the backs of her eyes.

Don't. Don't do this to yourself.

She shifted her gaze back to the paved walkway, lips pressed together hard.

As they hiked up the hill and across the park, the red arches of the Golden Gate Bridge came into view on their right. Their foundations on this side of the bay were hidden by tall trees on the far side of the park. The bridge stretched above the choppy water to land on rolling hills, barely visible through the afternoon haze that sat heavy on the waves. Sarah paused and pulled out her little point-and-shoot camera to snap a photo, then quick-stepped to catch up to Steve.

"So I thought your name was Sarah Daniels," Steve said as she fell into step beside him. "Who is this 'Devon Sinclair' person?" He grabbed Sarah's arm and pulled her aside just in time for a cyclist to whiz by. "Wait, 'Sinclair' was your maiden name, right? But why the 'Devon'?"

Sarah stared at him. "How long were you standing behind me, anyway?"

"Well, I happened to be right inside the store where your groupies ambushed you." His puzzled expression was exaggerated. "At least, I *think* they were yours."

Sarah frowned, pulled her arm from his grip and kept walking. He caught up to her in one stride. He'd dropped the goofy look, but she could tell he was waiting for an answer.

She sighed. "It's my pen name. I wanted a layer of anonymity and a gender-neutral name. 'Devon Sinclair' seemed appropriate for the genre." It was the story she told to those few who knew both of her identities, anyway. Erica, her sister-in-law Jill, her ex-roommate Abby, Craig—the list was pretty short. They had all asked why she took her father's name for her pen name, but even she wasn't sure she could answer that, or wanted to try—digging for that answer touched raw parts of her soul and she flinched away.

"What genre was that again? Romance, right?"

Sarah nodded. Steve's legs were much longer than hers, and she was struggling to keep up with his long strides. It occurred to her that if she was looking at his back, he probably hadn't seen her nonverbal response.

"Yes, romance."

"Why do you use a pen name?"

Sarah quick-stepped, trying to catch up, but the hill made it difficult. She was beginning to pant a little. "Some of the stuff in my novels I wouldn't want my mother to read, if you know what I mean."

Steve glanced back at her in silence and altered his stride so she could keep pace more easily. She bit her lip to suppress a smile. Was he . . . blushing?

"I just realized why your maiden name was familiar. I'm pretty sure my ex liked to read your stuff. Kinda racy, isn't it?"

Sarah shrugged.

"'Racy' sells. It's a living."

Steve held up his hands. "Hey, I'm not judging. Trust me, I'm the last person in the world to be judging."

Sarah glanced at him in curiosity, wondering what he was hinting at. She was about to ask, but he was distracted by two men that stood off the path to their right. The men had their backs to the bay and arms around each other, trying to take a selfie that included the bridge in the background, and obviously struggling to get one they liked.

"Excuse me," said Steve to Sarah, and stepped toward the men. "Would you like me to take your picture?" He held out his hand to the man holding the phone at arm's length.

The man smiled in gratitude. "Would you? Thank you so much!"

He handed Steve his device and gave him a brief explanation of how to snap the photo.

Sarah shifted her weight and watched while Steve gave them a few instructions about how to stand, then moved around until he had them framed how he wanted. He engaged them in cheerful chatter as he clicked a few photos. They soon volunteered that they were on their honeymoon.

Steve nodded and smiled and offered congratulations as he handed back the phone so they could check the results.

"We actually got hitched back home in Texas right after the ruling in June, but we wanted to wait until the weather warmed up in San Fran before we took our honeymoon," explained the thinner of the two while his husband reviewed the photo. "We'd heard that summers here tend to be chilly."

"Gotta love Indian summers, right?"

Steve stood at ease, hands on hips, while he waited for the verdict. The mild breeze ruffled his hair slightly, and the image of a surfer popped back into Sarah's head.

Sarah realized the other man must be referring to the Supreme Court ruling that had legalized gay marriage in the USA only a few months before. She frowned as she heard her father's voice echo through her memory, ranting against queers and perverts as he quoted Scripture and verse.

She had long ago come to the conclusion that there is no god—she had never seen any evidence of one, especially not the one her father had preached about. He'd talked about his "God of love," but the love she had known from Devon Sinclair had been nothing like the fairy tales about Jesus her mother had read to her as a child.

If God loved her, or anyone, he'd had plenty of opportunities to prove it. But he'd never shown up, no matter how many secret, desperate prayers she'd whispered in the dead of night. If there *was* a God, then he must be a cruel, sadistic tyrant that delighted in the misery of humans. And Sarah wanted nothing to do with him.

"Thanks, man. This is great." The shorter of the two men shielded the LED screen from the sun so he could examine the photos, then smiled and nodded.

Sarah watched her companion shake hands with both men, say his good-byes and congratulate them.

"They seemed nice." She fell back into step beside Steve and they hiked up the last few steps through the park.

"Yeah. I knew they would get a better photo from farther back. You know, with the bridge and all."

"Are you a photographer?"

Steve shook his head. "Not really. I dabble. My partner takes amazing photos, though, and I've picked up a few tips from him."

Partner? Him?

Relief flooded her, and she allowed it to smother a small spark of disappointment.

She could stop wondering if Steve was hitting on her. Of course he wasn't. Steve was gay.

"Of course." She nodded and smiled a little too broadly.

Across the street squatted a large, oddly-shaped complex of brick, glass, and concrete. Large letters labelling the square were erected above on metal framework.

Steve made a beeline for the ice cream parlour which fronted the sidewalk. They joined the queue that trailed out the open door and skirted the crowded cafe tables.

"A lineup. That's promising, if slightly irritating." Sarah stood on tiptoe, trying to see over the heads of those in front of them to get a glimpse of the menu. "What's good here?"

"I don't know. Haven't been here before."

"What? How did you know to come here, then?" She eyed an ice cream sundae that one of the exiting patrons was carrying. It looked sinfully rich. Her mouth started watering.

"My sister gave me very strict instructions when she found out I was coming to San Francisco." He put on an intense look in imitation of his sister. "'Go to Ghirardelli's. Buy chocolate. Bring it to me.'" Steve grinned. "Saying 'no' wasn't really an option. I kind of extrapolated the rest."

"Does she live in Mumbai, too?" Sarah asked the question to be polite, but she was trying to decide how much she wanted to know about this man. Gay or not, he was still a stranger. Why become invested when she most likely wouldn't ever see him again after today?

On the other hand, new people were often interesting fodder for future fictional characters. This guy was definitely walking onto the set of her next book, with a few changes—he'd have to be straight, because those biceps deserved to be on the leading man. Her romances were dark and steamy, but strictly heterosexual. She didn't think she could do justice to a queer romance, since she was wasn't—which, now that she knew he was gay, made her wonder why his ex was so into her books.

"No, she and her husband still live in Miller. I'm heading up there after I leave here. Won't be heading back to Mumbai for a few weeks."

"I see."

They were through the door now and could survey the interior of the shop. Chocolate bars and squares of various sizes and shapes in different-coloured wrappers lined the shelves around the walls and were stuffed into cellophane bags on a central display table, beribboned and ready to gift.

"How much are you supposed to take?" she asked.

"I got the impression that if I had to choose between packing my clothes and the chocolate, I should choose chocolate."

"Your sister sounds like my kind of woman."

Steve laughed and loaded up his arms with several of the cellophane gift bags. Sarah chuckled. "You're a good brother."

"The best." Steve winked. "Of course, it might not all be for her. There's no Ghirardelli's in Mumbai, either."

Sarah laughed, too, watching her companion discreetly. He couldn't be as content as he seemed. Even now—when he was just standing and waiting—a hint of a smile played at his lips, like he knew a joke he was itching to share. She had never met anyone that smiled that much before. At least, not with a smile that seemed so sincere.

Was he truly that happy?

After they got their sundaes—a giant one for him, the smallest size possible for her—they found a table on the sidewalk with hardly any blobs of drying ice cream and took a seat.

Boats sprinkled the bay, pedestrians peppered the park, a steady stream of tourists walked by, and classic jazz music in a woman's contralto voice was being piped over their heads. Sarah guessed that most people would be relaxed here in this lovely setting. But Sarah couldn't relax. She kept glancing at Steve and trying to decide if she should start a new topic of conversation. Her companion was apparently content to eat his sundae and watch the world.

She wished she could say the same for herself. Silence only allowed too much time to think. And wasn't she spending time with a stranger to distract her from all the things she didn't want to think about?

"So, what brings you to San Francisco?" she asked.

Steve swallowed a large mouthful of sundae with a loud gulp.

"My kids." He grabbed his phone and started swiping.

He's got kids? Sarah kept her face blank, but her stomach clenched. Had she been wrong about him being gay? Or maybe he'd adopted? "I thought you were . . . um, are you married?" It was a lame cover for her awkward assumption, but she hadn't been able to think of a better one, and didn't want to ask him straight out about his sexual orientation.

Steve only looked up and laughed.

"Oh, no. No time. Here's one of them." He handed over his phone to show her a beautiful coffee-skinned young woman in a brightly-coloured sari, a red *bindi* dot painted between her eyes. She was smiling stiffly at the camera. "That's Ratna." He rolled the R slightly as he said it.

Sarah studied the girl. Her long black hair was pulled back in ornate gold clips and trailed in a braid decorated with flowers behind her. She looked like she was in her late teens. Sarah still couldn't figure out what relationship this girl was to Steve.

"Is this your . . . daughter?" That seemed to be the safest question, despite the complete lack of resemblance between the two.

"In a manner of speaking." He reached over and swiped to the next photo which showed a group of young Indian women with serious faces sitting around a white man in the centre—Steve. "Nobody there smiles in photos. They actually like me, honest."

"So who are they?"

"Prostitutes."

Sarah was not expecting that at all. She choked and stared at him. His eyes were dead serious for the first time since they had met.

"I work with these girls—women, really—and their children to help them get out of slavery and prostitution. Mumbai has the largest red light district in the world, you know. Over fifty thousand prostitutes live there, and most of them started before the age of nine."

Sarah was in shock. She searched desperately for something intelligent to say. "Slavery? They still have slavery there?"

Steve nodded. "Many of them come from Nepal or north India, where the women are considered very beautiful. It's all a big cycle. Recruiters go and buy these girls from their families, who usually can't make ends meet and welcome the extra cash and one less mouth to feed. The recruiters promise the girls a job and a better life in the city, so their families agree. But what actually happens is that they are sold for a huge profit to pimps and madams who then tell them that they must earn their debt back by working for them."

Steve paused and clenched his jaw. He took a breath and continued.

"The 'debt' only keeps growing, no matter how much they make. They are in slavery until they outlive their usefulness and get released or become madams themselves. But most of them don't live that long." A storm brewed behind his blue eyes.

Sarah swiped to the next photo. The woman in the photo had one good almond-shaped eye the colour of melted caramel that was crinkled in a deep smile. She had a round face, thick, black hair, and an olive complexion. If it weren't for the ugly scar that puckered from under a decorated eye patch to her top lip, she would have been lovely.

"What happened to her?"

Steve glanced at the photo and a fond smile touched with sadness appeared on his lips. "That's Sita. When she was fourteen, a drunk, dissatisfied customer took his anger out on her face with a knife. She couldn't afford good medical care—there was no way to save her eye. She was lucky to live through it. This is her daughter, Aashi."

Steve swiped to the next photo, which showed Sita holding a young girl of about five or six. The child's beatific smile matched her mother's. Judging from the photos, Sita must have been very young when she became a mother.

Sarah stared at Sita's ruined face. She knew she should be appalled and disgusted by what had happened to her. She could see how upset the condition of these girls made Steve. And she was surprised, but inside, she felt—

Nothing.

Almost nothing.

Why couldn't she feel anything? What was wrong with her? But numbness had been her constant companion for so long that she was well-versed in pretending it wasn't.

Sarah handed Steve's phone back to him.

"Why doesn't anyone know about this?" she asked in low voice. "Why aren't we being told?"

"People do know. It's a huge destination for sex tourism. It's bigger than Bangkok." He pocketed his phone and scraped out the bottom of his sundae cup. "There is nothing that isn't complicated in India, especially when it comes to human trafficking and the sex trade. It's such a huge problem that there is no quick fix, and the Indian government doesn't make it easy."

Sarah sat in silence, swirling the partially-melted ice cream in her cup with her plastic spoon. Steve had said that the girls often started at nine years old. She thought of Craig's niece, Tabitha, who would be nine next month according to the note her mother had written on the copy of Tabitha's school photo Sarah had on her fridge at home. She had only met Tabitha a few times, but imagining her sweet face in a brothel, doomed to prostitute herself for life, she felt a small stirring of emotion. It grew and grew, until her stomach churned with rage.

How was it possible that little girls were being sold into sexual slavery and governments were doing nothing to stop it? How could they hide in their bedrooms—uh, boardrooms, and pretend it wasn't even happening?

Why doesn't anyone ever do anything?

Her mother's face flashed through her mind, wrapped in her own little world. *Why didn't she do anything?*

She felt blood rushing in her ears and heat rising up her neck. She glared at her companion. With a start, she realized that she was angry. At Steve. Why? It didn't make sense.

Anger—feeling emotions—was dangerous. In an instant, all the heat froze over in terror. She couldn't be angry. That's how people got hurt. Ice was safer than fire.

Sarah took a bite and held the cold lump against the roof of her mouth until her eyes hurt. She focused her emotion through her spoon, letting the anger drain out of her hand and drift away. Fear of what might have happened still clung like a sheen of frost to her thoughts, but when she could speak calmly again, she continued.

"So, what do you do?"

His tone was somber. "I help run a shelter for women who want to get out, teaching them viable skills so they have options. Them and their kids, who otherwise run a high risk of being trafficked, also. It's not easy—the whole system is set up to keep these women there, forever. Most of them are too scared to leave, or they have nowhere else to go."

He paused, and when he continued, his eyes saw something far beyond the ocean.

"I have seen such unspeakable things in the slums of Mumbai. I had to do something." His eyes focused on Sarah. "That's why I'm here—I'm giving a presentation about my work tonight, raising funds to purchase a building for our child care centre."

Sarah studied Steve, brow furrowed. She had never met anyone like him. He obviously had a lot going for him. And he wasn't even *from* India. Why on earth would he be working with prostitutes in Mumbai? Was this guy really all that he seemed?

"Why do you care about them so much?"

Steve's eyes twinkled mischievously. "Tell you what, neighbour. Why don't you come to my presentation tonight, and you'll find out?"

Sarah gulped, then shrugged. "I'll think about it."

"I guess that will have to do." Steve gave her a broad smile and then licked off his spoon with relish.

Sarah cleaned out the last of her ice cream from the cup. She thought about the haunting faces in Steve's photos, the women—girls!—he fought to free from sexual bondage. Then she thought about the housewives who read the sordid tales that flowed from her word processor, whose favourite escape was a fictional affair. Finally, she thought about the long hours she spent cranking those stories out, inserting names and faces and events around steamy scenes that left her cold as a stone.

"I wish I had even a fraction of your passion for my own work."

She was slightly embarrassed that she had blurted that out loud, but she knew it was the truth. She had a successful career, a handsome husband, and a comfortable lifestyle, yet she felt dead inside. And this man—who never had Starbucks and worked with prostitutes in a developing country—seemed to find joy in even the smallest things and spread it to everyone he met.

She felt a desperate craving to experience that kind of joy. She had hoped that having a baby would let her do that, but now, the chances seemed slim. The diagnosis she had yet to share with Craig loomed in her mind, overshadowing any hope she'd held onto. She thought sadly of the baby that she would likely never hold—the one chance she would have had to break out of her icy existence.

That's not what I deserve. Why bother wanting it? The yearning shrivelled before it had even taken root. *My life is what it is.*

Steve gave her a hard stare.

"It's never too late to make a change. You know that, right?"

Locked in the grip of those blue eyes, Sarah felt like he could see everything she was thinking at that moment. She wasn't sure if the thought was terrifying or comforting.

She also knew he was wrong. Sometimes it *was* too late. Even still, she surprised herself and nodded back.

"Okay. I'll come."

three

SARAH STIFLED A YAWN AND GLANCED AT HER WATCH. SHE SAT NEAR THE BACK OF A HOTEL CON-
ference room, and although she was interested in Steve's presentation, the long
days and short nights were catching up with her. She also had an early flight.
So far, everything he'd covered he had already told her at Ghirardelli's that
afternoon.

Steve was just beginning to share the story of how he and Paul had begun
Love Mumbai when Sarah's purse vibrated in her lap. She pulled out her cell
phone and peeked at the call display. Craig. Excusing herself, she eased past the
elderly gentleman sitting beside her and tiptoed toward the door. She glanced
at Steve and saw him watching her leave, though he didn't miss a beat in his
speech. She returned his subtle smile with an apologetic nod before escaping
through the soft-shut door.

The vibrating stopped.

Figures.

Sarah found an empty section of the hotel hallway. There was nowhere to
sit, but the hallway was wide and carpeted and quiet. She leaned against the
wall and speed-dialled her husband's number.

"Hey, baby," came his familiar voice. "Are you and the captain a little busy?"

Did she imagine the slight edge to his voice?

"Sorry, Craig, I was in a meeting." *Why am I apologizing?*

"I thought the conference was over." His voice definitely sounded accusa-
tory now.

"It was. I mean, it is. I just noticed this presentation happening tonight and
thought it would be an interesting way to spend my evening." She felt a twinge
of guilt for not sharing the whole truth about Steve, but knew that if she did,

it would only require more explanations to calm Craig's jealous concerns. She simply didn't have the energy.

"Really. What is the presentation about?"

"There's this guy talking about the work he is doing with prostitutes in Mumbai. I thought it would be a good opportunity to do some research—you never know what can spark a story idea."

"Oh. Sure." He paused. "This guy a pimp or something?"

Sarah frowned. "Yes, of course he is. And I went to the meeting looking for a new job." She immediately regretted her sarcasm, but it was too late.

"*Or* you could have been looking for ideas for your book, like you said. Don't get bitchy with me." His voice was steel striking granite. He hated it when she was sarcastic with him.

Maybe it was the illusion of safety created by the distance between them at the moment, but she couldn't seem to stop.

"*I* know! In my next book, the spicy scenes will be between a twelve-year-old and her ninth customer for the night!" She snorted in derision at the thought. *As if the things I write aren't disgusting enough already.*

"Well, if it would sell more books . . ."

"Craig." What he had just suggested made her taste bile. She swallowed to control her revulsion. "I write this filth because it sells, and my publisher insists. I only came to this conference because Becky thought the exposure of giving that talk about writing erotica would be a great idea. It wasn't. I hate talking about it. I hate the fans that gush about every bloody scene in my bloody books as I sign them. Don't you ever wonder if I want to do something besides write smut for a living?"

He was silent for a moment. When he spoke, it was the pandering, calming tone of a wise adult to a small child.

"Your agent knows what she's talking about. You should be thanking her for getting you on that panel, not complaining about it. And if she figures writing bleeding-heart literary pieces is a gamble, why wouldn't you want to stick with what you know? We gotta pay for your shopping habit some-how, *honey*."

He was right about Becky Sun, of course. She was a good agent and hadn't ever steered Sarah wrong.

But the way Craig said "honey" made her want to throw her phone at the wall. Never mind that her income easily matched his, and he had invented her shopping addiction out of thin air. She took a slow, deep breath. Getting angry at him wouldn't help her win this battle.

"So, I keep writing smut."

"And you keep selling books. A *lot* of books. Don't the cheques make it all worth it?"

No. Not in a million years.

"I guess we'll live happily ever after in our gilded pigsty." Sarah said it without thinking, spewing it out like a venom-spitting snake. She immediately regretted her brazenness.

Fear pebbled her skin. She might not be within arm's reach of her husband, but his words could sting as much as his hand. Maybe he would let that one slide if she—

"A pigsty, is it? That's what we've got?" His voice was frozen iron.

Too late.

A knot formed in Sarah's stomach and her heart stuttered. She studied a spot on the wall panelling. She put her anger and her fear into the spot and held them there. They couldn't touch her.

"No, of course not." Her voice sounded like it was coming to her own ears from a great distance. "I didn't really mean it." No response. Her gut tightened. His silence screamed at her. "I'm sorry I shouted. I just get so frustrated sometimes, and this weekend has been fairly stressful."

Why wouldn't he answer? What else could she say? What if he was much angrier than she thought? Was he thinking about kicking her out of the home she so obviously didn't appreciate?

Her eyes watered. She swiped fiercely at the wetness and stared at the tears on her fingers like they were foreign objects. How *dare* her emotions betray her right now? She gulped and forced her voice to steadiness. "Craig, you know I love our life together. I sometimes wish I could write something different, that's all."

Craig still didn't say anything. She could hear him breathing hard on the phone.

The knot in her stomach turned to ice.

"Will you forgive me?" she added in a small voice.

An exaggerated sigh blew into her ear. "I guess."

Sarah let out a breath she didn't realize she'd been holding. The knot in her stomach loosened a little, but she recognized that brooding tone. Best to get him thinking of something else.

A porter pushed a tray of covered food down the hallway. Sarah turned toward the wall to shield their conversation from listening ears.

"I got you something." Her voice was low and teasing. "There's a Victoria's Secret near my hotel."

"Really." His voice had a different tone, too. He didn't mind her spending money when it was on lingerie. "What is it?"

She smiled so he would hear it when she spoke.

"You're going to have to wait and see." She pictured his green eyes with the intense, hungry look he always got when she talked that way. "I'll give you a hint. There's red. And lace."

"I can hardly wait." Craig's voice was husky now. "Sounds more like the gift wrap, though."

Sarah laughed, hoping it sounded genuine. "Remember that scene from *The Heart of Darkness?*"

She knew he did. The scene in question was the one that had landed her a publishing deal with Steampressed—and was one of her husband's favourites.

"How could I forget?"

"I was thinking we haven't done that in a while."

She heard a low groan over the phone. The knot in her stomach finally released.

"I thought you'd like that." Her lips curved. She'd managed to turn him on. They were okay again. "Wait, someone's coming."

The meeting was emptying out. She could see Steve standing near the now-open door of the conference room chatting with some of the attendees. She felt relieved that she had an excuse to change the topic to something more publicly acceptable.

"It's getting busy here. So, what did you do today?"

When Craig spoke, his voice was inexplicably strained. "Oh, you know. Work. Erica and I were at the office pretty much all day."

"You made her work through the weekend again?" Sarah thought of the grimace her best friend often wore when she complained about how many hours Craig made her work. Sarah knew that Erica was grateful for the job as his personal assistant, but she sometimes felt caught in the middle between her husband's and her friend's venting.

"She didn't seem upset. She said she was . . . glad of the company."

"Yeah, I guess. I know it's been hard on her going home to that empty apartment." Sarah paused, thinking of how glad she was not to be in Erica's shoes, dealing with the aftermath of a rather ugly break-up. She and Craig might have their problems, but at least they had each other. "Thanks for helping her out. You know I really appreciate it."

"Of course," he said. "She and John are my . . . friends, too." His breathing still seemed disjointed.

Sarah hesitated and decided to broach the subject she had been avoiding for almost a week. "Hey, I was hoping we could have dinner together tomorrow night. There's something I need to talk about."

"That sounds serious. Could you just tell me now?"

"I'd, um, rather not discuss it over the phone. I'll make you dinner tomorrow, okay? Can you be home by eight?"

Sarah heard a dog bark in the background and smiled.

"Nelson wants his walk. You just got home, didn't you?"

"Uh, yeah." His voice sounded gruff. Sarah pressed her lips together. Craig didn't much care for Nelson, and the feeling was mutual. "I didn't mean to be out so late but it just kind of . . . happened." He groaned, then continued. "I have a dinner appointment tomorrow night already."

"Oh. That's fine, I guess. We can talk about it when you get home."

Craig paused. "Actually, there's something I need to talk to you about, too. I'll cancel my dinner date and be home for eight."

Sarah blinked in surprise. What could he need to talk to her about? A lead weight of dread settled in her stomach.

Another bark. And was that a moan or the dog whining?

"Alright then. Give Nelson a pat for me. I'll see you tomorrow." She paused, thinking of the news she would have to tell him soon. A sudden yearning for comfort overtook her. "I love you."

"See you tomorrow. Can't wait to open my present." He was still breathing heavily. "Make sure it's waiting when I get home," he growled, then the phone beeped and he was gone.

The smile dropped off of Sarah's face like a mask coming untied.

Steve started heading in her direction. She pretended not to notice and fled toward the lobby, swiping at tears.

Craig *never* told her he loved her on the phone, ever. She knew he would tomorrow night, though, while they were in bed.

If only she didn't want so badly for him to say it tonight.

Sarah was already on her second glass of wine when she caught sight of Steve strolling into the lounge. He spotted her and made his way toward her at the bar. She ducked her head and dabbed at her makeup with a napkin to make sure that the tears hadn't left her with raccoon eyes. She had no way of telling if she was successful before he reached her.

Oh, well. He was gay, anyway. *And I'm married.*

"Do you mind if I join you?"

Sarah mustered a smile and pretended nonchalance. "Why not?"

Steve slid onto the bar stool next to her and asked the bartender for a soda and a menu. The dark-haired man nodded and disappeared.

Sarah took a gulp of wine and shook her head. "You're persistent, aren't you? How did you find me here?"

Steve studied her for a moment, a quizzical grin on his face.

"What makes you think I was looking for you?"

"Well, you pretty much stalked me all day, though I have no idea why. It seems highly coincidental that you happen to show up in the very lounge where I'm enjoying some private time."

"Not so much when you consider that said lounge is in my hotel."

Sarah closed her mouth, chagrined. *I guess I had that coming.*

"I wasn't looking for you—I only wanted supper. The lounge seemed like a good spot since the restaurant is already closed. Do you want to be alone? I can leave."

Sarah shook her head, then regretted it as the room spun slightly. "No. I'm tired of being alone. Stay."

He gave a small frown and tilted his head. "Alright. If you insist."

She smiled languidly back.

The euphoria of an alcoholic buzz had already set in and made everything seem less urgent. Hard things felt easier. And the pain and fear she didn't want to feel were diminishing by the second.

Perfect.

Steve glanced over the menu sheet. Sarah rested her head on her hand and watched him. She liked to watch him.

The bartender came back with Steve's soda. Steve ordered a burger and handed back the menu, then glanced at Sarah as he took a sip.

"So, why'd you ditch?"

Sarah tried to look apologetic. It was hard to focus on conversation when his dimple was so adorable. "My husband called, and I had been trying to reach him so I didn't want to miss it."

"Huh. I figured you must have had a good reason." He drew lines with his fingers through the condensation on the side of his soda tumbler. "What did you think?"

She gave him a blank look. "Of what?"

"My presentation. Did you get the answer to your question?"

She vaguely remembered asking him something that afternoon, that there was a reason she had gone to see the presentation in the first place—other than something to occupy her mind for the night. Oh, yeah. This guy—this strange, alien man—he cared. About *everything*. Why?

"Uh, no. I don't think so. I left too early." Wow, the wine was good. The bartender came by and she ordered another.

The bartender looked hesitant, but nodded, then turned to Steve and pointed toward the partially-drained soda. "You okay, man?"

Steve smiled and nodded, and the short, Hispanic man left. Then Steve's eyes—his beautiful, sparkly, baby blue eyes—turned back toward her.

"Would you like me to tell you about it now?"

She couldn't get enough of those eyes. Blue, not green. And they cared. She knew it. She rested her head in her palm again and nodded. *Keep looking at me, Steve. I want to care, too.*

She half-listened as he explained how he had just finished his third year of law school—

"Craig's a lawyer, too. Did I mention that?"

"Um, no. And I'm not actually a full-fledged lawyer."

"Well, he is."

"Okay."

—when he took a summer tour with a buddy through Western India. He knew very little about it when he arrived, but what he saw there changed his life.

He fell in love with the people, the culture, and the food. But he was devastated when he saw the way the poor lived. He was drawn to learn more and more, and every step he took into the depths of Mumbai's slums broke his heart into smaller and smaller pieces.

"I didn't know what to do about it, but I knew I felt called to do something."

Sarah swallowed the last mouthful of wine from her third glass and frowned uncertainly.

"Called? Who called you?"

"Well, uh, God did."

Sarah stared at him, waiting for him to laugh at his joke. When he didn't, she did.

"'God did?' You're serious?" She laughed again. "What did he do, dial your cell phone?"

Steve's mouth closed and he just looked at her.

"If God cares so much, why are there children being forced to sell their bodies to survive in the first place? Or parents who break their children's limbs so they'll be better beggars? Why did Sita have her face destroyed? And all that other stuff you talked about? Why didn't he do something about that, huh?" She didn't normally talk this loud.

Steve's reply was quiet and firm. "He did. He sent me."

Sarah blinked at him. For a guy who smiled all the time, she would have thought this would be the biggest joke of them all. But he definitely did not look like he was joking. She tittered and grasped at words like eels.

"Fine. Believe what you want. If you want to think yer some kind of divine instrument, who'm I to tell ya otherwise?" Sarah giggled louder. Then she tilted her head in slow confusion and twisted unsteadily on her stool to face him. "Wait a second. Which god are we talkin' about exactly?"

Steve frowned a little and lifted his hand behind her back as though prepared to catch her. "You know, I'd love to tell you. But I'm not sure now is the right time."

Sarah jabbed at him in drunken slow motion.

"Time? Now is never the right time, is it? Never has been, and never will been." She giggled. "I mean 'be.'" She shook her head at herself and kept giggling, muttering to herself. "'Never will been.' Craig's right again." She cocked the finger and thumb on her right hand as though they were a gun and pretended to shoot herself through the temple, sound effect and all.

The ditch in Steve's forehead deepened. He rubbed the back of his neck.

"Look, you can tell me if this is none of my business, but, um, are you okay?"

Sarah focused on his face with effort and rocked a little on the bar stool. "Why do you ask?"

"Well, you're obviously upset about something, and I know we just met but I, uh, whoa—how are you doing, there?"

Sarah felt the room rock slightly and gentle pressure on her back. She leaned into it, trying to steady herself on the stool back. She kept her eyes on his for a moment longer, then dropped her gaze to the counter. "I've just had kind of a rough week."

When she peeked back up at him from below her eyelashes, Steve's brow was still furrowed, but he nodded and let the subject drop.

The bartender set Steve's burger on the counter, along with a bottle of ketchup. Steve gave the man a glance and a nod in gratitude but never turned his body away from Sarah. He looked like he thought she was the most interesting person in the world.

She smiled at that thought. Then she noticed his neglected burger and frowned slowly.

"Aren't you gonna eat that?" Why did it seem so difficult to speak?

"Maybe. Are you going to stay upright if I let go?"

That's when she noticed that the stools had no backs. A glance over her shoulder showed one of his hands supporting her back, and the other looked ready to grab her if she teetered too far in the other direction. She hadn't even noticed before. Suddenly, the whole situation seemed ridiculously funny. She started giggling and couldn't stop.

Steve frowned at the giggling blonde woman in concern. The hysterical laughing continued as he pulled out his phone. "I'm calling you a cab, okay? What hotel are you staying at?"

"Hotel?" Giggle. "Um, uh, the Windsmere. But I don't need a cab. I'm fine. I'm fine. Eat your burger." She waved a loose hand toward him, then tittered again.

"Hi, I need a cab at the Jade Palace Hotel. Yes, that's right. Thanks." Steve ended the call and asked the bartender to wrap up his burger. The man nodded and swept up the plate, then came back in a few minutes with a white Styrofoam clamshell and the bill.

"Thanks." Steve threw a few bills on the counter and slid off his stool. "That should cover hers, too. Can you send this up to 414?"

The bartender nodded and tossed a glance at Sarah, who was staring mournfully into her empty goblet. He nodded again, then disappeared with the takeout box.

"Where are you going?" asked Sarah. "You didn't even eat your burger."

"*You're* going home. I'm making sure you get there. C'mon." He grabbed her arm and gently urged her off of her stool. It didn't take much—she wasn't staying on it that well anyway.

Steve draped her arm over his shoulders with one hand and wrapped his other arm around her waist to keep her steady, then helped her out to the lobby to wait.

"You don't need to help me, you know. I'm fine."

"Of course you are." Steve's voice was reassuring, but he didn't loosen his hold around her waist.

She smiled up at him. It was a beautiful smile, and after spending most of a day with this too-serious woman, it was nice to finally see it—even if she was drunker than a chickadee in a crab apple tree.

Sarah reached up to touch his face. "You have such pretty eyes."

Steve pushed her hand gently away.

Sarah's blue eyes grew wistful and she sighed. "Too bad you're gay."

Steve's jaw dropped in surprise. He closed his mouth and chuckled quietly. "Well, them's the breaks, I guess. C'mon. Let's get you into the cab."

She hiccupped and giggled.

"Okay, Stevie." She giggled again. "Whatever you say."

He shook his head and helped her to the waiting vehicle.

four

THE NIGHT SARAH MET CRAIG DANIELS, SHE WAS VERY DRUNK.

She and Erica had spent Friday night clubbing around Edmonton, at Erica's insistence. Sarah's boyfriend of two years had just dumped her, and Erica did what best friends are supposed to do—insist that Sarah spend the night obliterating her pain in a euphoria of alcohol and dance therapy.

By 10 p.m., when the charming, ruggedly handsome Craig Daniels swept Sarah onto the dance floor for the first time, she was already well on her way to her goal. The heady sweetness of the club's fog, the strobe lights, the music pulsing like a heartbeat—they all kept her moving, driving her away from the memory of the man who had betrayed her with another woman and into the arms of the dark-haired stranger with the dimpled chin and intense green eyes. Hard-learned inhibitions that were as second-nature to her as breathing dropped to the floor in a trance-like haze—much like the glittery dress she fished off of Craig's bedroom carpet the next morning.

She was trying to be as stealthy as possible to avoid waking him, but he sat up in a rush and swept her half-naked form with an admiring gaze.

"Stay for breakfast? I make a mean omelet."

Sarah felt heat creep up her neck. "Um, I don't think so." She searched for her panties while struggling to zip herself up. "I'm, uh, I've got to—oh, darn this thing!"

Craig leapt out of bed in a smooth motion and moved behind her to help. After a moment's hesitation, she swept her tangled blond hair out of the way with one hand and let him.

Zipper secured, he rested his hands on her shoulders for a moment and laid a light kiss on the back of her neck. She shied out from under his touch and twisted around, wary. He frowned.

"Was it that bad?"

Sarah's face burned, and she dropped her eyes to the carpet to avoid looking at the well-formed nakedness of the man in front of her. "No, it was . . . honestly, I don't remember. But I'm sure it was fine."

"Don't remember? Wow, save the low blows until after breakfast, sweetheart. Of course, I was pretty drunk, too. Maybe it's for the best, eh?"

She spotted one of her strappy heels and dove for it to avoid answering, jumping on one foot to put it on. She felt a moment of victory when she spotted the other one. Deciding to abandon the missing underwear, she scooped up the second shoe and started moving toward the door.

A hand on her arm stopped her.

"Have I done something to offend you?" His green eyes were troubled seas in a perfect, chiselled face.

Sarah couldn't tear her eyes from that piercing gaze. "No, I'm just . . . I've never done this sort of thing before. This isn't me. I'm sorry, but this isn't who I am. I just had a bad break-up and my friend took me dancing and I guess I had too much to drink, and you were so nice and charming and smelled so good, and—"

His hand in front of her mouth and a gentle shushing sound stopped the avalanche of words, but his face was blanketed with amusement.

"I know you might have a hard time believing this, given the circumstances, but I don't usually do this sort of thing, either."

Her face must have revealed her skepticism. He laughed and held up his hands in a defensive position.

"God's honest truth! You can ask John! I'll call him for you right now, if you'd like."

Sarah had a vague memory of the tall dark man that had been with Craig at the club the night before, whom she was fairly sure had accompanied Erica home. She narrowed her eyes.

"What kind of a wingman would he be if he didn't back you up?"

Craig's eyebrows shot up and he laughed out loud, stepping back and crossing his arms. Sarah kept her eyes firmly on his face.

"Well, I guess you're going to have to take my word on it. Tell you what—if you let me make you breakfast, you can ask me anything you like and I promise I will answer you honestly. After that, if you still want to pretend last night never happened, I'll let you leave and never bother you again."

She hesitated. Shame, embarrassment, curiosity, and a definite attraction churned inside her.

"First question, then: When was the last time you had a one-night stand?"

Craig looked thoughtful, like he was trying to remember something buried in the mists of time.

"Last month."

Sarah's heart fell. She gave her head an angry shake, and moved to push past him to the door. He grabbed her arm again and raised her chin to look at him with his other hand. She narrowed her eyes and ground her jaw.

"Let go. I need to go." Her voice barely shook. She was rarely so assertive, but fear was spreading its icy fingers around her heart and beginning to squeeze. This whole mess was definitely one of the dumber things she had ever done.

He didn't loosen his hold. His hand was tight enough to keep her there, but not at all rough.

"Not until you let me finish."

Sarah set her jaw stubbornly, but didn't say anything.

"My girlfriend had just dumped me. I was feeling pretty low, and my excuse sounds a lot like the one you just gave me."

Sarah studied him, trying to decide if he was trustworthy. "How long had you dated her?"

"A year and a half."

"And were you faithful to her?"

"Yes."

Had he hesitated? Did his eye twitch slightly?

"Why did she dump you?"

His jaw worked and he dropped his gaze. "It was becoming increasingly obvious that we were not compatible. We fought a lot toward the end." He looked up, green eyes holding hers. "I honestly don't know what went wrong, or I would have tried to fix it."

He was gazing at her with an expression that was the picture of sincerity, and she decided she had imagined the tells that hinted at lies. Her last boyfriend had cheated on her. No wonder she was seeing liars and cheats everywhere. After a moment, she gave a brief nod.

"Okay, I'll stay."

He relaxed his grip and smiled, caressing her arm as he stepped back.

She repressed a shiver of pleasure and fear. "On one condition."

He tilted his head. "Your wish is my command."

She gave a wry smile and glanced at the door. "Please get dressed."

Out of the corner of her eye, she saw him look down at his nakedness. His face crinkled with amusement. "Deal."

Breakfast turned into the rest of the day, and that night, they met John and Erica for dinner. While she was feeling reserved and curious about the stranger with whom she had so uncharacteristically spent the night, John and Erica already seemed deep in the clutches of infatuation, holding hands through dinner and barely looking at anyone else.

It was at that dinner that the idea of taking skydiving lessons was introduced.

Erica's dark eyes sparkled when the topic came up. "Oh, Sarah! John's been telling me all about it!" she gushed. "It sounds like the most amazing experience. You have to do it with us!"

On almost any day of her life before that one, Sarah would have adamantly rebelled at the idea of participating in an activity as dangerous as skydiving. But something had changed in Sarah—maybe it was her ex's accusations of being an ice queen that still stung like new scratches on her soul, maybe it was the impetus of this relationship that had started without the usual barriers she put in the way, or maybe it was the magnetism in Craig's intense green eyes as he urged her to join them. She felt off-balance and not quite herself, like she could redefine who she was and be someone completely different. She could even be someone who enjoyed living dangerously. It didn't take much convincing to get her to agree.

Two weeks later, staring out the open door of an airplane with only twenty-eight hundred feet between herself and certain death, she thought she had made the worst mistake of her life. Despite the preparation the day of ground school had given her, it wasn't until she felt the wind whistling by the hatch that she began to have serious second thoughts. Hesitating a little too long, her instructors coaxed her out the door with a gentle shove from behind and suddenly she was free falling.

The scream she knew she was emitting was lost in the air whistling by her cheeks. As the seconds passed, terror was replaced by something else—a euphoric sense of freedom. Time seemed to slow down and she became aware of every sensation—the feel of her clothing against her skin, the wind roaring through her ears, the shadows cast by the low slant of the autumn sunlight that threw each tree and building in the landscape below into sharp relief. She felt removed from reality, like she was in a dream. Or like she was finally fully awake.

For years, Sarah's life had been about maintaining control. She struggled to conquer everything she set her mind to, unravelling it until she understood its inner workings and could manipulate it how she wished. It was why she was such a successful novelist—words were tools to be used, and she knew how to use them, though she saw her ability as only mediocre. It was also why her relationships inevitably ended—emotions were unpredictable, and she didn't trust them. She kept her own locked down tight, which is why she knew that her ex's comments were not insults, but truths. She was terrified of situations from which she could see no safe exit.

Free falling, she had never been more out of control—but she felt incredibly powerful. She felt like she had taken the physical laws of the universe and used them against themselves. Gravity pulled her inexorably toward the earth like a predator lying in wait for its prey. It was patient, because it knew its victim was already defeated—had been defeated from the moment the prey was in sight. It was inescapable.

But she was not the victim the predator thought she was. She had the power, a secret weapon that would allow her to cheat death. Within seconds of jumping from the plane, the parachute behind her opened and slowed her descent. Cradled by the chute's harness, she floated down to the drop zone as gently as a babe cradled in its mother's arms.

When Craig, who had jumped only seconds after she had, helped her up from where she had landed and asked her how she had liked it, she experienced a rare difficulty in finding the words to describe her emotions. Breathless, grinning from ear to ear, she kissed him with a passion augmented by the adrenaline rush. It was an amazing kiss, one that curled her toes and left her tingling. She felt Craig's response through the layers of their clothing and flight suits.

They broke apart reluctantly, chests heaving, arms draped around each other's waists. She kept her eyes locked on his, still trying to catch her breath.

"And that didn't even come close." She smiled shyly.

He laughed and took her hand as they walked to the waiting pick-up vehicles.

She had wrestled with the devil of powerlessness and emerged victorious. Hard as she found it to believe, she had fallen in love with skydiving. She squeezed Craig's hand, heart still pounding, and felt a surge of affection when he squeezed back.

Later, they sat sipping champagne in front of the fireplace at his apartment.

"To new beginnings," he toasted.

She hesitated before responding.

"To feeling alive."

Destiny itself seemed to echo in the reverberating clink of their glasses.

five

SARAH LEANED ON HER BATHROOM COUNTER TO STEADY HERSELF WHILE SHE FILLED A GLASS OF water. The hangover headache that had plagued her all the way home from San Francisco was threatening to become something much more horrible. She washed down a couple of painkillers and clenched her jaw while she waited for them to kick in. She couldn't get a migraine—not tonight. Tonight was for Craig.

She took a deep breath and finished applying scarlet lipstick, then surveyed the results. Concealer covered the dark circles a short night and the day's flight had given her. Her lips matched the colour of the teddy she had been teasing Craig with on the phone, but right now his "surprise" was hidden beneath a slim red dress that showed an exceptional amount of cleavage. She knew the way to her husband's heart.

Her thoughts darted back to last night and her face flushed red to match her dress. She dropped her gaze from her reflection and slammed her palm on the vanity, berating her own stupidity.

She couldn't remember much about what had happened, but she knew that Steve had been the one who had gotten her back to her hotel room, put her into bed, and made sure the front desk gave her a wake-up call that would get her to the airport on time.

She remembered trying to kiss him goodbye.

"I'm gay, remember?" he had said, pushing her gently by the shoulders back onto her pillow and chuckling.

She hoped that Craig never found out how much of an idiot she had been.

Sarah frowned at herself in the mirror. She noticed a stray hair and started smoothing her updo.

I wonder if Steve would like this dress.

The thought registered like a slap in the face. Her own accusing eyes stared back at her in rage. "You can't ever just be friends, can you?"

She sneered in disgust, then slammed the vanity drawer shut and strode out of the bathroom. She wished she could leave her shame behind her in the dark, but it followed her as closely as Nelson, and on stealthier feet.

No amount of self-shaming could quench the tingle she felt when Steve McGuire's easy smile flashed before her eyes. And it had nothing to do with his looks, either. He was kind and tender and compassionate—everything she wished she deserved. Her breath quickened and a dreamy smile crept onto her lips.

No sooner had she started to warm, though, than a pillar of ice filled her heart. She hated that every time she met a decent man, her thoughts started to wander. She never followed up on them—quite the opposite. Fear of what might happen usually froze her heart inside an icy shell that others perceived as snobbishness—and effectively prevented a hint of warmth between her and anyone of the opposite gender.

Even still, she hated how desperately she wanted to impress Steve, and how miserably she knew she had failed at it. And she hated that she couldn't seem to be just friends with a guy, even if he was gay.

Which only proved her point—she had what she deserved. Why ask for more? May as well ask for the moon.

Sarah's heels echoed across the spacious apartment as she busied herself with the final dinner preparations. Craig would be home at any moment. She turned from the open wall oven with a hot casserole dish in her hands and tripped on Nelson, who was right behind her. The Pyrex pan fell onto the granite counter top with a cracking sound.

Sarah's heart dropped.

"Nelson! Go lay down!" She shouted it much louder than she needed to.

The dog ducked his head and looked at her with remorseful brown eyes. He tucked his tail between his legs and padded to his dog bed in the living room to watch from there.

With a sigh, she started extracting the chicken from the broken dish. Fortunately, it had only cracked, not shattered. She avoided looking at Nelson. He hadn't meant to cause harm, he only liked to be close to her. And normally, she loved it when he followed her around.

It wasn't Nelson's fault that she was an imbecile.

She arranged the food and the garnishes on the dinner plates, put them in the warming drawer, and lit the candles. She fussed with the table settings. The clock ticked on. She tidied the kitchen, swept the floor, and checked her Facebook messages. Still no Craig.

Finally, at eight thirty, she texted him.

Will you be home soon?

A few minutes later, her phone cheeped.

Something came up. Be home later. Eat without me.

Sarah sighed and looked around at the perfectly-appointed table, spotless apartment, and strawberry-blond dog who sat up and gazed at her with concerned eyes. She retrieved her dinner from the warming tray, then sat and ate it alone.

The doorknob rattled. Sarah slid a bookmark into her book and remained on the couch as Craig came in. The bottle of wine she had intended to serve with supper sat on the side table beside her, half empty. She picked up her glass to have a sip while she levelled her gaze at her husband.

Craig dropped his keys into the bowl on the entrance table and set his briefcase on the floor before he turned toward her. He scanned her outfit, the wine, and her steady stare while he removed his coat. A lecherous smile settled on his lips.

Ten o'clock. An hour and a half late, and he's still hopeful.

Anger bubbled red and hot in Sarah's gut.

She took a deep breath and smothered it with icy purpose. Rising with the bottle in hand, she grabbed the empty wine glass from the dining room table and poured some of the pale vintage into it. This was not the time to pick a fight.

When she turned toward her husband, her face was encased in a seductive smile.

"Welcome home." She sidled up to Craig, wrapped her free arm around him and offered him the goblet while lifting her chin for a kiss.

Craig took the proffered wine and gave her a light peck, then backed away and took a sip. "I should be the one saying that, shouldn't I?"

Sarah adjusted his collar to hide her disappointment at his cool reception, then put on a coy look.

"Maybe, but I was here first. Which means I got to hide all my surprises for you before you got here."

Craig's lips curved. "'Surprises,' hmm? Do I have to hunt for them?" His hand wandered down her back to caress her backside as he bent to nibble on her neck.

"Did you eat?" Sarah kept her arm between them on his chest. "I've kept your dinner warm for you."

"I snacked at the office. What if we skip right to dessert?" Craig's manner was no longer cool, and he definitely looked hungry.

"Good things come to those who wait. Haven't you heard that?" Sarah turned toward the kitchen island and her teasing smile twisted into a hurt grimace. But why was she upset? Had she expected him to starve at work all night? And she'd promised him sex—did she think he wouldn't want it? She hoped her husband hadn't noticed her expression.

"Once or twice. But I'm not a believer." Craig sighed. "Yeah, I guess I could eat something."

Sarah sighed, too, in relief. Maybe they would get their chance to talk after all. She worked her way around the kitchen, grabbing Craig's plate and fussing with the garnish.

The sounds of Craig's briefcase latches releasing, papers rustling, and chair scraping all seemed painfully amplified. She picked up the warm plate to take to her husband at the table. White pain crawled up the inside of her skull and she nearly dropped it. The meds weren't helping as much as she'd hoped, but it was too soon to take more. She clenched her teeth together against the pain and managed to make it to the dining area.

When Sarah set Craig's plate in front of him on the dining room table, his eyes flicked up only briefly, scanning the plate as though going through a mental checklist. He nodded in cursory approval, gave her perfunctory thanks, and then went back to reading the brief as she settled in the chair across from him.

She kept her eyes locked on him while she took a long draught from her goblet. Should she tell him now?

She decided to ease into it.

"What are you working on?"

Craig glanced up at her over the top of the paper. "Nothing you would care about, I'm sure. Bad people trying to get away with bad things, with no one but me to stop them."

"That sounds *very* interesting. Tell me about the case."

Craig let out an annoyed sigh and lowered the page. "I wish I could. But you know I can't, Sarah. Confidentiality." He went back to perusing the document, ignoring the dinner in front of him.

She revived her teasing smile. It was a little tight around the corners—but he wasn't looking at her anyway, so how would he notice? "No rest for the wicked, eh?"

"Sorry, baby, it's only that this case is . . . well, let's just say that if the wicked would rest, I'd be out of a job." He sighed and laid the papers down. "But I'll try to relax for a few hours, for your sake." He reached for his glass. "This ought to help."

He took a sip of his wine, then carefully arranged his napkin on his lap and began eating. Sarah sipped her wine and waited quietly, not wanting to interrupt his meal.

It's not because I'm too scared to tell him. No. We'll be fine. He may as well have supper first, though.

Craig took a bite and studied her, chewing thoughtfully. He swallowed.

"Is that a new dress?" He cut another piece of chicken and popped it into his mouth.

Sarah started. But of course he would notice. He noticed everything she wore. "Um, yes. I bought it in San Francisco."

His face didn't change.

"I hope that's okay."

His green eyes roved over her body. "Looks okay to me." He smiled appreciatively, hunger lurking in his eyes.

A normal woman would feel a rush of heat under that look. She had gathered as much from years of girl talk and romance novels. One of her characters would be melting in a puddle of desire. But it only made her more nervous than she already was.

Because I'm a freak. I get crushes on gay men and can't even be aroused by my own husband.

She jumped when he interrupted her self-recriminating reverie.

"Tell me about your trip."

Sarah fidgeted with her glass. "There's not much to tell that I didn't mention on the phone. Lots of frumpy housewives and long days. Good shopping, obviously. Amazing food." Sarah sighed wistfully as she remembered the gourmet dishes she had been living on for the past five days. "If America has a capital of food porn, I'm sure it's San Fran."

She felt guilty at the rush of pleasure from the remembered epicurean delights. She couldn't let him suspect that the food brought her more pleasure than his company. The coy smile returned. "I may or may not have been inspired to try something new tonight." She winked.

"What, did the captain teach you how to cook last night, too? You two must have been busy." Craig's voice was light, but the words were laden with barbed accusations she had heard too often before. The barbs sank into her heart and burned—more so because for once, there was some element of truth to his suspicions.

Despite his sarcastic comment about her cooking, she noticed that he had been eating steadily since he began. If she told him how much the comment hurt, he would tell her he was only joking, that she needed to stop taking herself so seriously. So Sarah laughed flirtatiously and kept playing the game.

"Wouldn't you like to know?" She rose from her chair to refill his wine glass and trailed her finger up his arm and neck.

He caught hold of her hand and pulled her down so he could kiss her. She let him pull her onto his lap, let him kiss her mouth and neck and keep moving further south as his hands roved over her body. She ran her fingers through his curly black hair and over his neck, responding in ways she knew he liked. Soon, the half-eaten dinner was forgotten as they held hands on the way to the bedroom.

Foreplay was something she did as much by rote as flirting—manoeuvres she had learned to imitate, but not enjoy. As Craig made love to her, she did what she always did—faked love to him. She smiled through the blinding pain in her head, kissed and teased, caressed and moaned on cue.

Feeling was dangerous, as her escapade in San Francisco had once again proven. Her heart froze at the thought of what might happen if Craig discovered what she had actually done last night. All because she had a moment of weakness.

If only she could quench desire, then she would be safe. If you didn't want things, then no one could hurt you by denying them. And having desires met was something only the worthy deserved. Not women like her.

Sarah felt a twinge of regret. Steve had stirred something in her with his joy and passion for life—something that had been frozen solid for years. She thought about her fleeting desire to live a life of passion like Steve McGuire and shook her head. That was fine for him. But now that she had come home and to her senses, she knew it could never be for her. Especially with so much uncertainty in her future.

Her heart, which for a few brief hours yesterday had been deceived into entertaining hope by the warmth of kindness, was locked back into its lonely ice tower, unreachable and cold.

And safe.

Sarah awoke, gulping air into her lungs in raw, jagged gasps. Her heart pounded in her ears. The sheets were drenched. She felt like she had been running for her life.

Beside her, Craig's lean, muscular figure was outlined by a pale green halo of light from his alarm clock. His back was to her. She tried to quiet her breathing, but he stirred and muttered something into his pillow, then was quiet again.

I'm in my own bed. I'm safe. It wasn't real.

Then why don't I feel safe?

With the tentacles of nightmare still clinging to her, she got up and shuffled to the kitchen for a glass of water. The coolness trickled down her parched throat and brought her to full consciousness. She tried to remember what the dream was about, but the images were all jumbled. She could still feel the adrenaline it had released surging through her body.

It had been years since she'd had a nightmare. She used to have them all the time as a kid, but they had all but disappeared after she left for college. With increasing alertness, the cloak of dream's illusion fell from her mind—but the terror that had seemed so real while asleep left her uneasy. There would be no going back to sleep any time soon. At least her headache had subsided.

She grabbed her laptop from the table in the living room, flicked on the lamp, and settled onto the couch. Nelson padded over and jumped up beside her, then lay down with his heavy head in her lap.

She patted the dog's head absently as she opened her browser. Nothing caught her attention on her social media feeds. She sighed, then opened up her author's blog, thinking she might get started on the next post.

After ten minutes of staring at the blank word editor on Devon Sinclair's blog, she cancelled the post. It was no use.

Suddenly, one of the dark shadows of the dream that woke her came into focus. There had been a man coming at her with a knife. He was angry about something—she was supposed to please him, but she hadn't. He had slashed her eye and left a huge gash that trailed down her cheek and split open her top lip.

Sita.

She had been dreaming of her. Sometimes in her dreams, she was other people.

She could still feel the man's dirty hand squeezing her jaw and taste metal from the blood. With her one good eye, she looked him in the face, and—

She caught her breath and her heart rate spiked again.

The attacker's face had been her father's.

Sarah shuddered and tried to push the images away. Nelson looked up at her and whined, and she stroked his head, drawing comfort from his warmth.

"It's all right, boy." She wasn't sure if she was comforting him or herself.

On a whim, she typed "Love Mumbai" into her search engine, then clicked on the organization's website link.

The screen filled with images and stories of the projects Steve had described to her. Sarah studied the faces of the children and women, read about every project, found the page about the current fundraising effort—and then finally got the nerve to click on "Meet our Team."

Steve's bio photo had the familiar, easy grin. He looked almost exactly like he had when she'd met him in Starbucks on Sunday morning. Despite the embarrassing memories that flared to life in her mind as she looked at him, she was mesmerized by his image. Somehow, the contentment and peace that had so quickly become apparent to her in person shone out of his blue eyes, even in this picture.

Her lungs constricted. She wanted to close the computer, go to bed, and forget that she had ever met Steve McGuire. He stirred things in her that she would rather have stayed asleep. For the first time in years, she felt a yearning for something different, something real. Something more than the life she had.

Sarah shook her head at her own stupidity. She rested her hand on the top of the laptop to push it shut. She had no right to yearn for anything. Desire had never done anything good in her life, so she had divorced it years ago.

It's never too late to make a change, you know.

Steve's words echoed in her mind, like they had been spoken into a cavern— the deep, black cavern that existed where passion didn't.

Sarah hesitated and stared at Steve's picture for a moment longer. With sudden resolve, she dropped her hand back to her mouse and clicked on the page's "Donate" button.

When she had sent her gift in support of the care centre project, she opened up her email and started composing a message to Becky.

Maybe Steve was right—maybe it wasn't too late to change. She was going to try to find out.

Finally, she went back to bed—excited, terrified, and exhausted. Before long, she slipped into a restless sleep.

six

THE SOUND OF SOMETHING RINGING DRAGGED SARAH OUT OF THE DEPTHS OF UNCONSCIOUSNESS. She smacked at her side table a few times before she realized it wasn't the alarm clock, it was her phone ringing from out in the kitchen. Just when she was about to jump out of bed to go get it, the ringing stopped.

It took another few seconds to get her bearings. Nelson padded into the room and laid his head beside her on the bed. She petted his soft fur and smiled, and he smiled back, panting into her face. She turned away from his dog breath in disgust.

"I love you, mister, but you stink!"

He bounced happily, tongue lolling and tail wagging, and then licked her cheek.

Sarah chuckled and sat up, then caught sight of the time. No wonder Craig was nowhere to be seen—he must have left hours ago.

Crap. I'm gonna be late.

She started flying through her morning routine, dodging around the dog that kept following her around. She checked the call display as she ran by the phone with her blouse unbuttoned and toothbrush hanging out of her mouth. It was her mother.

Sarah groaned. *I'll call her back on the way.*

Fifteen minutes and a grooming marathon later, she was backing out of her parking space and on her way to the Canuck Cafe. If traffic were clear, she would only be late by a minute or two. She knew Erica would understand.

As Sarah eased onto Whitemud Drive, she voice-dialled her mother's phone number.

"Hello?"

"Hi, Mom. Sorry I missed your call."

"Well, if you're too busy to talk to me, then you don't have to call back."

"I'm not too busy, Mom, or I wouldn't be calling back right now. What's up?"

"Are you talking on the phone while you're driving? That's not safe, you know. Didn't you hear about that accident yesterday where that guy was texting and driving? You should call me back later."

"I'm not texting, I'm talking. It's fine, Mom. I'm using the hands-free set. It's like I'm talking to someone in the car."

"Hands-free, eh? Huh."

With the conversation in a lull, Sarah tried to decide whether to revive it or end it. She gritted her teeth, bit onto her duty, and settled on reviving it.

"I brought you something from San Francisco."

"When were you in San Francisco? That is such a dangerous city. Aren't there car accidents there all the time?"

Sarah rolled her eyes.

"I told you last week I was going on a trip to San Francisco. It's no more dangerous than Edmonton, and quite pretty, too. Lots of old cable cars and delicious food and warm weather. Even a few palm trees. You might like it."

"I doubt it. But if you say so."

Silence again.

Sarah tried one last time.

"Mom, was there something you wanted to talk about?"

"Huh? Oh. Yeah. There was. What was it again? Oh, yeah. Everett and Jill are coming here for Thanksgiving dinner this Sunday. I wanted to know if you and Craig are going to be here, too. It would be nice to have the family together."

Sarah let out a long breath. "Nice" wasn't how she would describe it.

Each year, it was always a toss-up to see which family she and Craig wanted to spend time with the least, his or hers. In their dating days, they had alternated households on the various obligatory holidays. But since they got married, they had always planned a getaway to Jasper or Banff on Thanksgiving weekend to avoid the family politics. However, they hadn't been able to agree on where to go this year—and now here she was, being asked to go to her Mom's and she didn't have a legitimate reason to say no, other than how much she didn't want to see her brother. But Mom never could figure that one out.

Because you've never told her.

Yeah, right. Like I'm gonna tell her.

"I'll talk to Craig about it and let you know. But we can probably come. Call you tonight?"

"Sure. I'm not going anywhere. Bingo's not until Wednesday."

"Fine, Mom. If we come, I'll bring your present then."

"What present?"

"You know, the one I got you in San Francisco."

"Oh, yeah, right. Okay, talk to you tonight."

"Bye, Mom."

"Yup."

Sarah sighed again and tapped the button to end the call. She was fairly certain that her mother was developing memory problems, but then, Ellen Sinclair had always been a little uninvolved in reality.

A few minutes later, she had parked at the Canuck Cafe and was searching the dining room for her friend. She spotted Erica giving her a little wave from across the room and made her way toward her.

Despite its rather low-brow moniker, the Canuck Cafe was a favourite lunch spot for when someone wanted a little more "character" than what Denny's could offer. The dining room had a very rustic-outdoors theme, with hand-hewn maple-stained log pillars and walls and round wooden cabin tables. A large log carving of a rearing black bear that was a little too cute to be realistic greeted guests, and various pieces of antique outdoor sporting equipment decorated the walls and hung from the vaulted ceiling. A stone fireplace dominated the wall near the table where Sarah joined her friend, but the flames flickering behind the glass were gas fed.

Sarah had barely settled into her seat when a waitress in a red plaid flannel shirt and long white apron over blue jeans came by for her drink order. Seeing Erica's white wine, Sarah said she'd have the same.

They were soon chatting about the weather and traffic and Sarah's new handbag, which she had bought at Coach in Union Square. It felt nice to have her fashion-conscious friend admire one of her purchases for once—the envy usually went the other way.

The small talk helped Sarah ignore the anxiety-inducing topic she really needed to discuss—the very topic she had managed to not tell Craig yet again last night. She wasn't sure she was ready to bring it up with Erica, either. She was trying to decide how best to broach the subject when her friend diverted her with a question.

"So?" Erica sounded like a twittering bird. "Tell me about San Francisco."

Sarah had been expecting the topic to come up, but she did *not* expect to blush when it did. "I, uh . . ." she stammered.

Just then, the waitress came back with her drink and asked if they were ready to order. Sarah shook her head and the girl left. She took a sip of the wine while she collected her thoughts.

Erica stared at her, dark eyes wide. "What happened? Why are you blushing?" She gasped and covered her mouth. "Did you"—she raised her eyebrows meaningfully—"you know?"

Sarah straightened. "No! What? Oh, no. Nothing like that. Geez, girl! It's just that something happened, and I'm excited about it." She took a deep breath. She wasn't sure how much to tell Erica. Erica might be her best friend, but she also worked with Sarah's husband, and Sarah didn't want Craig to know about her diagnosis until she'd had a chance to talk to him. Or her burgeoning career plans until something official happened. She also didn't want Craig to know about what had happened with Steve, ever.

She wasn't even sure what *had* happened with Steve. But that was something to think about later.

Erica was leaning forward in anticipation, her dark skin glowing even more than usual. In fact, although Erica always looked beautiful, she looked better than Sarah had seen her since she and John broke up, like she was making an extra effort to look nice. Good for her. It was about time she put herself back out there again.

"Okay, spill the beans—" Erica nudged Sarah's elbow. "What's got you hemming and hawing?"

Sarah decided to take the plunge on at least one of the secrets that had her gut roiling. She smiled nervously, clenched her fists, and dove in.

"Okay. But don't say anything to Craig yet. I want to talk to him about it once I know more."

Erica nodded eagerly. "Of course."

"So, I met this guy named Steve in San Francisco."

"I thought you said you didn't"—Erica's voice dropped—"'you know.'"

"I *didn't*." Sarah tapped her fork on her plate in irritation. "It's not like that. He was just super-friendly, and when he found out that we are both from Miller, it was like I couldn't get rid of him. Anyway. We ended up hanging out together for a bit and I found out that he was giving a presentation that night, so I went."

"A presentation?" Erica rolled her eyes. "Wow, this is hot stuff. You weren't kidding about it being exciting."

The waitress came back and took their order. Sarah echoed Erica's order of chicken Caesar salad because she hadn't even glanced at the menu.

"Where was I?" Sarah asked herself.

"Presentation. Exciting. 'You know.'"

"Right. Okay, it wasn't so much what the presentation was about, which was human trafficking and the sex trade in India—"

"Sex trade? Finally." Erica winked at her.

Sarah frowned slightly and continued. "It was—well, it's hard to describe. Steve is not like anyone else I've ever met. I'm still trying to figure out if he's a complete phony or the real deal."

"What do you mean?"

"So, he completes three years of law school and goes on a trip to India and then decides to give up all of his life plans to help prostitutes in Mumbai."

"Whoa." Erica picked up her glass and took a sip. "This guy must be a real goody-two-shoes. Probably eats Shredded Wheat three times a day and thinks donating blood is a fun night out."

"You would think so, right? But Erica, he is honestly the most down-to-earth guy I've ever met. And he is so happy with what he does. It made me wish that . . ." Sarah stopped and shook her head, closing her eyes at what she was about to say.

"You have a crush on him, don't you?"

"NO! He's gay, for Pete's sake! And I'm married, in case you've forgotten." Sarah dropped her gaze. "I just wish I could be like him."

Erica froze, wide-eyed. She cleared her throat and blinked.

"What, you want to go live in a box downtown this winter and give all your stuff to homeless people now?"

Sarah sighed. "Not like that. I wish I could—you know—be happy."

The words were out before she could stop them. Sarah gasped and stared at her friend in fright. She hadn't meant to say that. Now Erica would want to know why she was unhappy, and she might tell Craig about it, and this lunch date just got a whole lot trickier.

But Erica surprised her.

"Girl, I'd say you're about as happy as anyone else I know. He must be a phony, and he wants something from you. Are you sure he's gay?"

"Um, fairly sure." She had a foggy memory of him saying as much. No straight guy would ever do that. And he'd mentioned his partner Paul a few times. But what if Erica was right? What if Steve had had an ulterior motive, and she'd been too stupid and naive—and let's face it, desperate—to notice? She racked her brain to figure out if he had asked her for anything other than a little bit of her time and company and came up dry.

"Well, maybe he simply wanted a friend." Sarah knew it sounded lame. But it was no more lame than the reason she had agreed to wander around a strange city with a strange man—a move that any sane person would question. She needed to get the conversation onto another topic, fast.

Thankfully, the waitress came back with their salads at that point.

Saved by the salads.

"So, Craig made you work all weekend, did he?"

Erica unwrapped her cutlery from the napkin and arranged the square of red cloth on her lap. "Mm-hmm. My boss is a real beast." She seemed very absorbed in selecting the perfect salad constituents for her first bite. "Not much to talk about there. But you never told me why you are so excited."

Sarah wasn't so sure she *was* all that excited anymore. Erica's comments about the situation had cast a shadow on her intentions, and now she thought that she might be chasing a genie that didn't exist.

"Well, it might be dumb. I don't even know what I'll say if she agrees. But this morning I sent an email to my agent with a pitch in a completely different genre for me."

"Because that's always turned out well before."

"Well, I think she might go for it this time."

"What's the pitch?"

Sarah hesitated. "I want to write Steve's biography." She took a bite and focused on her plate.

Erica swallowed, fork hanging in mid-air. "Steve the phony?" It was a statement more than a question. "Sarah, have you lost your mind?"

"Well, it would depend on a lot of things. Even if Becky agrees and can find a publisher willing to take it, Steve might not. And I'll have to go to India—I doubt Craig will want to come with me, though. So he will have to be okay with all of it. Who knows? It might not happen. But I have to try."

Erica slowly chewed another bite, obviously struggling with what to say next. "You really want to do this, huh?"

Sarah nodded. "And after writing the man's biography, I'll have a pretty good idea of whether he is Phony Steve, Friendly Steve, or something else altogether." She took a breath and stared at the flickering gas flames in the fireplace. "You know, whether this book project exposes a fake or profiles a truly amazing human being, it will be the first thing I've ever written that means anything."

She looked up at her friend to gauge her reaction.

Erica gave a slow nod. "Well, if you get the go-ahead, let me know. I can probably help you convince Craig to let you go to India." She smiled. "It's not every day someone gets to follow their dream. I'll help you in any way I can."

Sarah smiled back and nodded. "Thanks, Erica. Thank you so much."

Sarah was about to take another bite when she felt a gentle touch on her arm and looked up in surprise.

"Be careful, okay?"

Sarah's jaw tightened. She would normally say she was more careful than anyone she knew. But she had to admit that she had been a little bit reckless over the past week or so. She smiled reassuringly at her friend.

"Of course."

When Sarah got home, she rushed to her laptop to see if Becky had written her back. A thrill of excitement surged through her when she saw her agent's name in the list of new emails. It was short-lived, though.

Becky said that there was absolutely no way that Sarah would be able to substitute the bio for her last contracted book. Her long-standing publisher, Steampressed, only produced fiction and specialized in romance and erotica. However, since her contract allowed her to publish elsewhere for other genres as long as she used a different name, Becky said she would run Sarah's proposal past a few other editors but that she shouldn't get her hopes up. Sarah might be an established brand in erotica under her pen name, but as Sarah Daniels, none of these editors were likely to have even heard of her. And with the publishing industry tightening its belt collectively these days, most houses weren't prone to gamble on an unknown author.

Why do you want to write a biography anyway? This guy isn't a celebrity—he's just a guy. Who will want to read a book about him? Erotica is where the money is these days. Why not stick with that?

Sarah reread the final line of the email once more, her heart dropping. Resigned, she typed a quick reply confirming that she would finish her contract and then write the biography, as long as Becky could find a buyer. She sighed and pressed her fingers against her temples, choking down disappointment at her agent's lack of support. Becky was just looking out for her. And what was one more book she would hate writing when she had already written a dozen others like it?

She hit send, then went to make some tea in preparation for her afternoon writing session.

She had just put the kettle on the stove when she heard the chime of an instant message come in. She returned to where the laptop sat open on the kitchen island and opened her Facebook app.

It was a message from Steve.

Hey, wanted to say thank you so much for your very generous donation! Wow, $3k is going to help a lot! Also, I'm glad to see that you made it home from SF in one piece. Cheers, Steve.

Sarah chewed her lip. Her heart pounded in her ears and heat crept up her face. She hadn't in a million years expected to hear from him again. She hadn't thought through how she was going to approach him about the book, and it never occurred to her that he might be the first to reach out. Now what should she say?

I was hoping it would be enough to buy another chance. I am so embarrassed. And sorry. I'm not usually that much of an idiot. Are we still friends?

She hit enter on her keyboard and waited. Of course, it would take a minute for him to reply, if he replied at all. She kept chewing her lip and tried to remember to breathe. The notification bell chimed and she caught her breath.

You don't need to "buy" anything. We all have rough days. I'm just glad you're okay. . . . You're okay, right?

Sarah felt a rush of relief, but the knife of embarrassment twisted a little deeper. How could she have let him see her like that? And how could he not think her a complete hussy now?

His question teased her. She thought about all the things in her life that she wished were different—her marriage, her career, her family relationships, her health—and sighed. Okay? She was as okay as anybody. Which was to say, not really. But since her life didn't have a writer, this was as close to "happily ever after" as she could expect. She had come to accept that long ago.

Fine. Thanks for checking up on me. She hesitated over whether to say more, then shook her head. *I'm glad we're cool. Take care.*

Yeah, you too.

The kettle started squealing and Sarah jumped. She twisted the burner knob to "off" with one hand and poured hot water over the bag in her mug with the other, but her thoughts were still on the conversation with Steve. Once again, he had done nothing more than be respectful and kind to her, not demanding anything.

Yeah, well anyone would be nice to someone who just gave them three thousand dollars.

Erica's assessment of Steve as a phony coloured the memories of the congenial stranger in a sickly yellow light. Which was more likely, after all—that he was unique among humans and truly did care about something besides his own interests and concerns, or that everything he did was to further his own ends? Sarah shook her head at her own stupidity.

Should she have asked him about her book idea?

No. She would wait to see what Becky came up with for offers.

Still, she wasn't sure if she was glad she had shut the conversation down, or regretted not finding a reason to keep talking. If she was going to write a book about the man, she needed to find out as much about him as possible.

Once she had doctored her tea up with honey and cream, she settled down in front of her laptop to outline her next novel. If she was going to have to write it, she may as well get it over with. Becky had already been bugging her for the synopsis for three weeks, and she knew time was ticking away for both of them.

In the past, this part of the project was very easy for her—her stories followed a definite formula, one that had proven popular. All she had to do was think of new, exotic scenarios, characters, and settings into which to weave explicit sex scenes and she could start pounding out the story into her word processor. She was a master at raising tension throughout the story until her reader was worked into a thorough frenzy, releasing it at the last possible second to ensure they kept turning pages through the whole book. And buy the next one.

Today, the blank screen stared at her, mocking her. She made a few false starts, then deleted the words in distaste. Nothing seemed to be working. After an hour, all she had were the names of her two main characters and the setting—a small prairie town. A lot of good that did.

Frustrated, she went to rinse out her empty mug and paused to bathe in the sun streaming in the kitchen window.

Nelson woke up from his nap and came and sat beside her, looking up at her with hopeful brown eyes. She turned her head toward him and he whined a little.

Sarah laughed.

"You want a walk, boy?"

He jumped to his feet and started panting, his tail wagging—and his whole back end with it.

"Well, I'm not getting anything done here. Why not?"

She threw on her scarf, light gloves, and wool coat and grabbed Nelson's leash, and then they headed to the nearest dog park by the river.

As was typical of an early October afternoon in Alberta, the air was warm but with a crisp feel to it. A slight breeze rattled the drying brown leaves that still clung tenaciously to the poplar and birch trees. Underbrush flashed a brilliant array of fiery colours, and yellow poplar leaves covered the ground in a golden carpet, smelling sweet and musty.

They reached the off-leash area, and when Nelson was released he took off in a sprint. His eager nose explored tree trunks and nooks, startling a blue jay from a low-hanging branch. He let out a few joyful barks at the retreating bird, his tail wagging in wide semicircles. Then he turned to his mistress with a big doggy grin on his face.

Sarah laughed. She loved to watch him revel in his freedom with such abandon. She sometimes envied the fact that he was able to find pleasure in so little. Or at all. Her times with Nelson were some of the few moments in her life where she felt safe enjoying herself. Nelson loved her regardless of what she said or did. There was no intricate dance required to try and please him. His only expectation of her was regular attention—and he was happy with whatever she could spare.

Why couldn't people be as easy to please? Why was everything such a game?

She had once made the mistake of believing that people were good and trustworthy. It was so long ago, the memory was covered in cobwebs and clouded with shame. How could she ever have been so foolish?

And yet, hadn't she told Erica this very morning that Steve seemed to be a truly good person? Maybe she *had* lost her mind. How many times must it be proven to her that no one really cared for anyone but themselves?

Even me.

And why not? That's all anyone did. Sarah bet that if she examined Mother Teresa closely enough, even she could be accused of having some self-serving motivation for her life of service.

You know that's not true.

She and Nelson were now in the leashed area near the play park. A child's soccer ball bounced across the trail in front of them and landed in a wild rose bush. Sarah stepped off the trail, carefully dug out the ball and threw it toward the young boy who was coming after it.

He caught it and waved. "Hey, thanks!"

"You're welcome," she called, but he had already rejoined the game.

Sarah watched him run back to his playmates and smiled. It was such a small thing—but it had felt good to help the boy by doing something as simple as throwing his ball to him when there was nothing he could do in return to help her.

And couldn't that be why people like Mother Teresa—and Steve—do what they do? And isn't that why I wanted a baby to love? Isn't that what living a happy life is about—to feel good about what you do? Or is it just as selfish to do something unselfish for selfish reasons—to serve so you feel good?

Sarah felt a twinge of guilt—is that why she wanted to write Steve's story? So she could feel good about herself? What made her think she deserved that?

Sarah watched the children for a few more minutes, then turned back to her dog. Nelson stood at the length of the leash watching the soccer game. He barked happily at the boys as they kicked the ball around the field, yelling back and forth. His wagging tail showed the pleasure he got in watching the game. But to Sarah, the sun seemed to have dimmed and gone cold.

She tugged on Nelson's leash and headed back to the apartment.

Maybe she should write to Becky again and tell her to forget her earlier message. She probably wouldn't be able to write a book about a guy like Steve that did him justice, anyway.

Why had she even thought she could try?

It's never too late to make a change, you know.

The words popped into her brain and stayed there. She wanted to shake them off. She wanted to shout how wrong they were. But her mind couldn't stop thinking about the man who had said them. What made him so sure?

When she got back to the apartment, she opened up the Facebook conversation with Steve again.

Are you in the Edmonton area? There is something I want to discuss with you and was hoping to do it in person. Maybe next week sometime, if it works for you?

She waited for a few minutes, but no response came. She sighed and re-opened her book idea document.

A change. Maybe she didn't have to do the same exact kind of book she always wrote. Could she make this erotica book that she was obligated to write mean something? Would that even be possible?

The title came to her in a flash. *Her Father's Daughter.* She typed it in. Then she glanced at the clock. She would have to hurry to get ready on time for her dinner out with Craig. She scurried off to the bedroom to change.

seven

CRAIG BREEZED IN AND DROPPED HIS BRIEFCASE ON THE COUCH.

"Hi, honey." Sarah gave him a bright smile that completely belied the turmoil in her stomach and leaned in for a kiss, one earring still dangling from her fingers. His responding peck was wooden, and there was a furrow between his brows that stopped her in her tracks. "Tough day?"

"You could say that." He assessed her appearance with a glance. "You're wearing that?"

Sarah froze. She thought he would approve of the slim black dress she had chosen, especially the plunging neckline. He had purchased it for her, after all. "Don't you like it? I can change."

Craig scowled, his green eyes dark like the bottom of the ocean. He shook his head. "It's fine. It'll take you half a frickin' hour to decide on something else, and we don't have that kind of time. Are you ready to go or what?"

Sarah hesitated. He might be mad at her, or at something that had nothing to do with her—past experience told her he wasn't likely to explain soon. Great. Not an ideal way to start their evening together.

"I'll, um, get my coat and then I'll be ready to go. Do you need to do anything before we leave?" She hoped to placate him enough to make the evening go smoothly—or at least be bearable.

He scowled in return. "No, I'm fine. I've invited Doug Fenway, by the way. Him and his wife. They're meeting us at the restaurant at six thirty." Craig glanced at his Rolex. "Hurry up, for Chrissake. We're gonna be late!"

Sarah grabbed her black woollen pea coat with one hand while fumbling with her second earring with the other, cowed by the shouting and hiding her disappointment behind blank features. She couldn't talk to Craig about her doctor's visit in front of his colleague, and she didn't want to ruin the evening by mentioning it on the way to dinner—especially given his current mood. Maybe when they got home.

She finally got the earring into her ear and started pulling on her coat—but not fast enough to please Craig.

"Come *on*, woman. Do that in the car! My great-grandmother is faster than you, and she's been growing worms for twenty years."

Sarah ducked her head on the way through the door he was holding open so he wouldn't see her hurt look and moist eyes. She hated it when he yelled at her. It was her fault, really. She should have been completely ready when he got home. But no, he had already seemed upset when he got here. She racked her brain to see if there was something else she had done to put his mood off.

It must have been something at work. She wished her husband could find a way to leave that kind of garbage at the office.

The ride to Chilton's was quiet. Sarah watched the cityscape go by in the lengthening shadows of twilight. Now that they were past the autumn equinox the days were noticeably shorter with each one that passed. While parts of Edmonton seemed somewhat ungainly, as though the city planning had been done by a small child with some randomly-placed blocks, the river valley was lovely, and so was the skyline. It was one of her favourite parts of this drive.

The chill in the car strung her nerves tighter than violin strings. She decided to try and ease the tension. Maybe if she got Craig talking, he would get over whatever was bothering him so much.

"I had lunch with Erica today." She offered him a faltering smile.

He didn't even glance at her. "She told me."

"Oh."

The silence was too uncomfortable.

"Well, she seemed to be doing great. She looked great. It's nice to see how she is picking herself up. Have you noticed?" Sarah stopped. If she kept talking about Erica, she was going to have to tell Craig what they had talked about, and he wasn't nearly mellow enough for that conversation yet.

Craig glanced at her. "Not really."

They rode for a minute in silence.

"Mom called today. She wanted to know if we would be there for Thanksgiving. Everett and Jill are coming."

Craig grunted. "Did you tell her we would be in Banff?"

"I never booked the hotel. Did you?"

Craig grunted again. More like growled. "No, that's *your* job. You're supposed to plan these things. Apparently, you've been too busy? Or have you developed a sudden craving for your mother's mashed potatoes?"

"I asked you where you wanted to go, and you never gave me an answer. So it didn't get booked. And now here we are."

"Here we are."

More silence.

"Do *you* want to go for Thanksgiving dinner?" he asked.

"What do you think?"

Craig sighed. "Then call her back and tell her we already have reservations in Banff. Book the hotel first, if you want, so you don't have to lie."

"My mother can't tell when I'm lying, but she'll know I just booked it since I didn't mention it this morning. She'll take it personally now, and then I'll have to endure a six-month guilt trip."

"Do you want to go for dinner or something?"

"No. You know I don't. Like I want to see Everett." She kept her voice low-pitched to avoid provoking him.

Craig shook his head and said nothing. She had never told him the specifics of her antagonism for her brother, and he had never enquired too closely. Which was fine by her. They each had things in their past that were "no-fly" zones for conversation.

He flicked his eyes at her. "I'll call Ellen and tell her for you."

Sarah jerked her head in his direction. "What?"

"I'll tell her I want to surprise you so you don't know about it yet, and ask her to help keep the surprise."

Sarah stared at his grim-set profile, fearing to trust his sudden altruism. "Really? You would do that?"

Craig glanced at her, then back at the road.

"Yeah, of course. You're my wife. It's my job to help you out. And it's not like I'm in love with Ellen's mashed potatoes, either." He gave a sardonic smile.

Sarah watched him, confused. "Thank you."

"Don't mention it."

His jaw still radiated tension, but the smile on his handsome face helped to drain some of hers. They rode the last few minutes to the restaurant in silence.

Sarah smiled politely and faked enjoyment through dinner with the Fenways, watching her husband and Doug talk nothing but shop. She tried to strike up a conversation with Doug's wife, but the woman was painfully shy. Every conversational ball Sarah threw was immediately dropped. Eventually, she gave up and focused on drinking wine and trying to decipher the source of her husband's angst.

Sarah watched the way Craig's strong jaw moved as he spoke, completely at ease and in charge. She noticed the way his dark hair curled behind his ear in waves, and how his green eyes flashed when he laughed.

It had been too long since he had laughed with her like that.

Sarah sighed. Even though he appeared to be having the time of his life, the occasional cool glance and clamped jaw aimed in her direction was a reminder that whatever was between them from earlier was still there. She just wished she knew what it was.

Their first real date had been in a restaurant like Chilton's—fancy, with linen tablecloths and glittering silverware and a *maître d'* named Pierre. She remembered being swept off her feet by Craig's charms—handsome, funny, great smile, very chivalrous. She could hardly believe that a man as dashing and suave as Craig Daniels actually wanted to spend time with her. It wasn't until after they were married that she noticed how generously he shared those same charms with other women.

Craig cracked a joke about Sarah's cooking skills and Doug burst out laughing. Craig's eyes twinkled and he winked—at Christine, who blushed the colour of the Cabernet. Doug didn't notice, but Sarah did.

She always did.

"Harmless flirting," Craig called it.

Sarah had tried to tell him that it bothered her.

"Oh, no you don't! Don't you dare turn into one of those women who is all clingy and needy now that we're married," he had admonished, glaring at her. She could always feel his glare—like coals burning her skin. "I did this the whole time we were dating and you didn't say a thing. I'm not going to change now."

His adamant assertion that this behaviour wasn't new made her doubt her own memories. Maybe she had been too love-blind to notice? Her resolve weakened in the face of his scowl, but she didn't back down.

"Aren't . . . Isn't marriage about respect and compromise?" Sarah's voice had barely trembled as she'd asked.

"Respect you? How can I respect you when you're trying to change who I am?"

"I don't want to change you, Craig. It's only that when you flirt with other women, it makes me feel . . ." She trailed off.

Craig grabbed her arms—gently, though.

"Hey, it's you I married. It's you I want. The flirting is a game, just for fun. Let me have my fun, okay?"

Pinned beneath those burning green eyes, Sarah's words were gone. She nodded. He crushed her lips with his and she kissed him back, melting under the weight of gratitude that Craig Daniels, who could have had any woman he desired, wanted her at all.

That gratitude dimmed a little further with each successive encounter, however. As she watched her husband give her the cold shoulder and flirt with the wife of the oblivious man he was entertaining, her heart iced over. He was right—he had always behaved this way. And she had become an expert at tiptoeing around his volatile mood swings and petulant silences, pretending not to see the things he did that ripped at her soul, accepting that this is how her life was, and would be. This was how marriages worked. One gives, the other takes, and so it goes until death do you part.

But she had been dead when they started. So where could she go from here?

Craig's voice penetrated her thoughts. "That's a lovely ring, Christine. I'm a bit of an amateur geologist, you know."

Craig held his hand across the table toward his colleague's wife. Christine hesitated a moment, glanced nervously at Doug and Sarah, then held out her own hand for him to inspect the wedding band. He cradled her hand delicately but with his thumb clasping her fingers as he admired the diamond.

Sarah's eyes narrowed. Her husband had absolutely zero interest in geology. "You have good taste, Doug. A fine stone for a beautiful woman."

Christine tried to pull her hand back, her face turning pink as she mumbled her thanks. Craig kept the hand captive a moment longer, then released it with a charming smile at its owner. Doug didn't seem to notice, only rambling on about his search for a very precise stone, top-quality, nothing but the best for Christine.

Sarah's gut boiled, but she kept her face placid and sipped her wine. He was trying to provoke her. Experience had taught her that the slightest reaction on her part and he would simply intensify the heat, so she did her best to ignore him.

Wasn't this what you wanted? Taunted a voice in her head. Her father had paid too much attention to her—in private and in public. She had hated trying to explain away the flirting comments he made in front of her friends.

But was being shamed and ignored by the man she had married any better?

Christine caught her eye, her face awash in sympathy and embarrassment.

Sarah couldn't take it anymore. She stood and smiled apologetically at their guests, ignoring the sudden chill on her husband's face.

"So nice to meet you, Christine, Doug. I'm not feeling well, so I think I will go wait in the car. No rush, baby." She smiled sweetly at Craig.

Craig's glare went from a cool autumn day to the depths of winter. "You can't be feeling that bad, Sarah. Why don't you stay?"

"I feel a headache coming on. There's too much talking going on in here." She twisted her smile from sweet to pained and rubbed her temples to emphasize her point.

Craig jumped up to help her put on her coat and leaned in close as he held it up behind her. His low voice was like icicles on the back of her neck.

"Don't you have your meds?"

Sarah glanced over her shoulder and kept her voice low to match his. "Yes, I just took them, but they're not helping." She shrugged into the coat and turned around to face him, adjusting her scarf.

"I want you to stay, then." The dangerous look Craig gave her made it clear that his words were a command, not a request. She saw the promise of a screaming match with plenty of name-calling—and probably worse—in his eyes if she didn't do as he wanted. He raised his voice so the others could hear, coating it with molten honey. "I'll miss you if you're gone. Are you sure you want to wait in the car?"

Sarah stared up at her husband's hard eyes. She could feel her will weakening, and her knees buckled. Her knuckles were white on her beaded handbag.

"Okay, I . . . I guess I could stay a little longer. Those meds do seem to be taking effect now." She sank back into her seat and began shedding her outdoor layers, keeping a firm grip on every coat button to conceal how badly her hands were shaking.

"Are you sure?" Doug frowned. "If you're not feeling well, please don't let us keep you. Craig, we could finish our chat at work tomorrow."

Craig had slid back into his seat and was watching with satisfaction as his wife disrobed her winter clothes again. He smiled at his friend and waved off his concern.

"She's perfectly fine, but thanks." He glanced at Sarah in victory, then leaned toward Doug and whispered at a pitch that concealed nothing, "She often gets these pseudo-headaches. Thank goodness for modern medicine or I'd never get lucky!"

Craig laughed. Doug chuckled uncomfortably. Christine blushed and glanced at Sarah before dropping her gaze.

Sarah met her husband's triumphant sneer with a placid expression.

Craig turned to Christine. "So, Christine, Doug tells me that you are quite an accomplished cellist. You play with the Edmonton Philharmonic, isn't that right?" He captured the other woman's eyes and maintained contact through the intensity of his gaze. Of course Christine was blonde, like Sarah. Her husband did have a "type."

Sarah knew that look, how mesmerizing it could be, and how hard it was to tear your eyes away from a man who was looking at you like you were the most fascinating woman in the world. She knew all too well.

Doug bragged about his wife's musical achievements, seemingly unaware of the silent signals being passed around the table.

"Last season, Christine was promoted to first cello. She can do things with that bow that some might consider scandalous. Honestly, sometimes I get jealous." Doug winked at his wife.

Christine smiled shyly and waved his flirting away with a pleased grin. "Oh, Doug, stop. You're embarrassing me."

Doug's cell phone rang. He fished it out of his pocket and glanced at the screen.

"Excuse me, I have to take this. Be back in a few minutes." He got up and headed toward the lounge as he answered the call.

Craig chuckled and leaned toward Christine. "Hey, if I got to spend every night between your legs, I could make beautiful music, too. Couldn't I, Sarah?"

Craig casually dropped his hand onto Christine's forearm. She blushed furiously and edged her arm away, but didn't turn away from Craig's smokey stare for several long seconds. Then she glanced at Sarah and dropped her gaze.

Craig gave his wife a gloating smile.

Sarah stood.

"Actually, I think I'll wait in the car after all." She started pulling on her coat again.

Craig paused with his wine glass in mid-air. "Sarah, sit. I'm not quite ready to go."

"Please give my regards to Doug, honey. Come when you've *finished* here."

The sight of Craig's stone-cold face lingered in her mind as she turned and walked away. A satisfied smile curled her lips.

She knew she would pay for this later. But right now, the small victory was worth it.

Craig exploded the moment he opened the car door and slid in behind the steering wheel. "What the hell was that?"

Sarah winced, but kept her voice calm.

"I told you, my head hurts. Would you mind keeping your voice down, please?"

"Mind? Hell, yeah, I mind! You made me look like an idiot in there." Craig slammed the car into reverse and peeled out of the parking space.

Sarah's heart was pounding. Maybe defying him had been a stupid idea after all.

But maybe it was too late to stop.

"I didn't need to. You were doing a fine job all on your own."

Craig jammed on the brake at the parking lot entrance and glared at her, face contorted with rage. He raised his hand, and she flinched. A spark of triumph flickered in Craig's eyes. He lowered his arm slightly.

"How dare you?" he seethed. "If I tell you to stay, you stay, and if I tell you to jump, you jump, and if I tell you to dance, you dance. You understand?"

Sarah stared at him in disbelieving shock. She knew he hated when she disagreed with him, but did he really want an automaton for a wife?

"You—you're joking, right?"

He backhanded her across the cheek, and she screamed.

"I said, 'Do. You. Understand?'"

Sarah touched her lip gingerly, and her fingers came away red and wet. She looked back up at her husband with moist eyes. His chest was heaving and his face was red. It was like looking at a stranger—but a stranger whose face she had seen before.

"Craig—"

He raised his hand again. She nodded, hands up in defence.

"I understand. S-sorry. It won't happen again."

He glared at her for another moment. A car honked behind them.

"Good." He flipped the bird to the driver behind them in the rear-view mirror and then roared out of the parking lot.

Sarah stared out the window all the way home and wept.

eight

THE FIRST TIME CRAIG HIT HER, IT WAS BECAUSE OF SALT.

The plastic grocery bag containing the heavy paper-packaged salt had stretched to capacity and torn on the way up to the apartment. The paper bag had split as it hit the elevator floor, spilling its contents around her and Craig's shoes like snow.

Sarah stared at the mess in dismay. The burning slap across her face caught her completely by surprise.

"You stupid bitch. Look what you've done! You think I make so much we can throw food away, now?"

Shock left her speechless long enough for him to exit the elevator and lock their apartment door behind him. Since she didn't have her keys, she was forced to knock and beg through the door to be let in, and he said she had to learn her lesson, which would start with cleaning up the mess.

"When hell freezes over," she muttered, fury stifling shock. Back down in the lobby, she informed the doorman of the mess in the elevator and called her friend Abby, who gladly came and picked her up when she'd heard what had happened.

Abby commiserated with Sarah over margaritas and let her crash on the couch for the night. The next day, Craig showed up with flowers and a tearful, heartfelt apology, begging Sarah to come back. He succeeded in convincing her that the slap was a one-time thing, so she went.

Abby shook her head and watched her go.

The next time and the next, Abby let Sarah stay at her place, but became increasingly more vocal in her opinions about Craig. Sarah knew that Abby could never understand the kind of love that she and Craig shared, nor why she kept going back to him. How could she? Abby was single. She had never needed someone as much as oxygen.

The blows became more frequent, but were always followed by several days of sweetness that almost made up for it. Sarah stopped calling her friends for help, resigning herself to enduring the storm at home rather than having to explain herself to anyone. In fact, Sarah eventually stopped calling Abby at all. Abby had refused to rescue her again, saying she couldn't watch Sarah let Craig destroy her anymore. Abby didn't call her, either. Life seemed easier that way.

One day Sarah found a photo of her and Abby on her phone and realized that they hadn't spoken in nearly a year. In fact, she hadn't seen any of her old friends, except Erica, in nearly as long. The reasons seemed individual with each, but in her heart, she knew it all boiled down to Craig.

Which made her even more thankful for Erica's loyalty.

Sarah never told Erica the real reasons why she needed a place to stay every so often. She was too embarrassed to explain it, and feared losing one more friend. She simply said they had had a fight and needed time to cool off.

Erica never questioned why Sarah went back. Or why she stayed. She simply held Sarah's hand and even tried to help work things out between them at times.

Sarah thought she knew why.

Despite how well Erica seemed to be adjusting to single life, Sarah knew it was a sham. A bad marriage? That's not hell.

Hell is being alone.

When Craig and Sarah got home, Nelson was sitting patiently on the carpet, staring up at them with his gentle brown eyes. Sarah was glad for an excuse to escape her husband's presence.

"I'm taking Nelson for his walk, okay?" Her voice trembled slightly, and she cursed herself for the sign of weakness. She cursed herself more for feeling the need to ask permission before she went.

But she did need it, didn't she?

Craig grunted and nodded, so Sarah grabbed the dog's leash and headed out the door.

As Sarah walked, she kept half her mind alert for potential after-dark dangers, but the rest of it chewed on thoughts of her marriage.

How could Craig be like this? She couldn't understand how a man who had once been so charming and attentive could become so callous and cruel.

When they were dating, Craig had doted on her, gushing over things that no other guy had even been interested in. He had been curious about almost every area of her life, giving advice on everything from her career to her fashion sense. He'd reviewed every manuscript she'd written since they met, noticed every item of clothing she'd purchased, and had even been interested in what she was eating and who she was hanging out with.

If it weren't for his constant affirmation of her writing talent, she may never have had the guts to approach her agent, believing Becky to be too high-profile and unattainable. He'd known Becky's husband, though, and that connection had been Sarah's "in."

Sarah thought she was the lucky one, especially after listening to her friends complain that their husbands or boyfriends never noticed anything they did for them.

What happened to that guy? When did he go from interested in her life to dictating it?

When had she gone from pleasure at his approval to craving it?

As time passed, his approval had seemed harder and harder to come by. She wished she knew what she was doing wrong. She wanted their relationship to be like it used to be when they couldn't keep their hands off each other—when she had felt like the centre of Craig's world.

Now, he slapped her for having a headache. Never mind that the headache was faked—what kind of a guy does that?

Was that really the kind of man she wanted to spend the rest of her life with?

The questions had been roiling through her brain since they left the restaurant. As she'd walked out of the apartment with Nelson, it had been so tempting to simply hop in her car and drive away.

But where would she go? She had no friends left on whom to call except Erica, and pride forbade her from asking Erica—perfect, self-sufficient Erica— for help this time. Not with her face bleeding. Sarah couldn't bear for the woman she idolized to see how messed up her life was.

That left a hotel, or her mother's. But she couldn't take Nelson to a hotel. And it would be a cold day in hell before she would go to her mother and tell her that her fairy-tale marriage was much less ideal than advertised.

In her parents' household, divorce was one of the worst sins that could be committed. It didn't matter how bad the marriage was, or for what reason—every time news of another dissolution reached their ears, Devon Sinclair had lectured about the evils of divorce while Ellen had shaken her head and clucked her tongue in agreement. Even since Devon's passing, Ellen had made it clear to her daughter that she would not be the safety net if Sarah and her husband had issues to work out—she would have to figure out how to handle it on her own.

Not that she wanted to divorce Craig. She needed Craig. Before him, she hadn't even known who to be. He was the reason she got up in the morning, the definition she gave herself in her own mind. "Craig Daniels' wife." Even when she introduced herself as a writer, she knew her success was because of him.

She knew exactly what she owed him. And the thought of tearing free to start again on her own filled her with terror much worse than the fear of having to weather his current stormy mood. She just wished she knew how to fix what had broken between them. Or that she even knew what it was.

When Steve had talked about making a change, she was sure that leaving her husband wasn't what he'd had in mind.

Sarah felt calmer after her walk, but anger and hurt still simmered in her belly. She stood and stared at the apartment door, trying to muster the courage to walk through. Craig's muffled baritone rumbled from inside the apartment and she wondered if he was already doing damage control with Doug Fenway. Nelson sat obediently beside her, one small whine his only expression of impatience.

"I guess it's time to face the music, huh?"

Nelson blinked his swampy brown eyes.

She sighed and put her key in the door.

By the time she opened it, Craig had finished on the phone and was making noise in the kitchen. She hung up her coat and put Nelson's leash back on its hook by the door before turning to face her husband.

Craig was pouring himself a drink at the kitchen counter, his back to her. She took a breath, wrapped her arms around herself, and then headed toward the bathroom to inspect the damage while keeping a wary eye on him—an injured gazelle watching a lion.

Craig turned around, drink in hand, and winced. She must look pretty bad.

"Hey," Craig said softly.

Sarah stopped at the hallway entrance, but didn't turn. She kept her eyes on the floor.

He lifted his glass. "You want something to drink?"

She shook her head.

"You, uh, got a Facebook message." He indicated her open laptop on the dining room table.

"Okay." She gave a slight nod. She didn't know why he'd brought that up. Had he looked at it? Was it from Steve? Her grip on her arms tightened.

"I talked to Ellen."

Sarah frowned and dared to look at him. "You called my mom already?"

"Yeah, just now. I took care of Thanksgiving."

"Uh, okay. Thanks."

Craig broke into a sudden flurry of activity.

"Here, let me help you clean up." He ran cool water through a fresh dishrag.

Sarah watched him with her jaw set. What was this sudden show of kindness for? Was he trying to apologize? Did he think she would just forgive him if he pretended they were okay? There's no way she was going to let it be that easy.

He came over and took her hand. She narrowed her eyes, but let him lead her to a bar stool at the island. At his gentle push, she sat down stiffly. Her shuttered gaze never left Craig's face as he dabbed at the blood on her lip, then rinsed the cloth again and instructed her to hold it to her puffy cheek. Her muscles were so tense they ached.

Craig sat down on the stool facing hers. He stared at his hands for a moment, looking like he was trying to find the words to say.

"Look, I'm . . . I'm sorry." He looked up. "It's only that sometimes you make me so . . . *frustrated*, and you won't listen to me, and so I"—he looked back down—"I hit you. But you didn't deserve that."

She stared at him, her face hard. But he had found a chink. He actually recognized he was wrong to hit her? That was new. Most of his apologies were only promises that there would be no repeat performances and he would do better if she could only pretend it hadn't happened.

He leaned toward her and locked her eyes with his.

"Sarah, I promise I will never, *ever*, do that again. Just don't be mad."

There it was. Her eyes narrowed. "You said that last time. And the time before. And all the times before that. Why should I believe you now?"

Craig sat up. "I know. And I'm sorry. I don't know what comes over me sometimes. You're like my drug—I need you, but you also make me crazy." He cupped her cheek with his palm.

She resisted the urge to pull away.

"When you do something like tonight . . ." He frowned. With an exaggerated sigh, he let his hand drop. "Why don't we compromise? You promise to listen to me from now on, and I won't hit you again?" He leaned in close so his face was only inches from hers. His voice was tender. "Sarah, we love each other. Let's not fight. You don't need to argue with me about this. Let's just pretend it didn't happen and move on."

Sarah wavered. He needed her? She lapped at the praise like a stray puppy in a drought. He genuinely loved her, didn't he? And he was right—she didn't want to argue. It took too much energy. She spotted the crusty, dried blood on the rag crumpled in her hand.

Of course she would forgive him—he had already put up with so much from her, after all. She knew he'd had a difficult past, and if anyone got how that could leave a mark on someone, it was her. And she loved him.

The fight melted out of her. "Okay, forgiven."

He smiled and sat up, visibly relieved.

One last survival instinct kicked Sarah in the gut, a small spark of petty defiance born of too many trips down this road before. She refused to let Craig walk away from this without paying some kind of price.

So she bluffed. She laid a hand on his thigh.

"But, Craig, if you ever do that again?"

He froze and met her narrowed eyes. "I'm walking out that door"—she jerked her head toward the entrance—"and the next time you see me I'll be with my lawyer."

Craig looked stunned for a moment, then his face darkened.

"You wouldn't dare leave. You don't have the backbone." He leaned back and crossed his arms. "And how are you going to pay for a lawyer, exactly?"

Sarah pressed her lips together and said nothing, meeting his steady gaze. She had no backbone? That's what he thought? She refused to be the first to look away.

He scowled more deeply. "More backbone than I realized before today, though. Exactly how much money do you have socked away in that account you've been keeping secret from me?"

Sarah stopped breathing. How did he know about that?

She gulped. "I . . . I, uh, only have a little. I was saving up for a, a special trip for us. I wanted it to be a surprise for you, so I opened my own account."

"Well, I feel *super*-special knowing that my 'surprise' went to whores in India." Sarah scowled. "How did you find out about that?"

"Oh, 'Steve' told me. We're not quite as chummy as you two, but I'm sure if I was on Facebook he would have messaged his gratitude to me instead. And hey! What's a few thousand dollars between 'strangers?'"

Sarah looked at him blankly, unsure of how much he knew. She felt completely out-manoeuvred. Panic started to rise in her throat and clench it shut in vice-grips.

"I . . . I was going to talk to you about it. Tonight. But then you invited the Fenways, and embarrassed me in front of them, and . . ."

As soon as the words were out of Sarah's mouth, she regretted them. Craig leapt up and grabbed her arm in a grip of iron. He bent down and snarled in her face.

"*I* embarrassed *you*? You have no idea what kind of embarrassment you've caused me, woman."

Her arm burned where his fingers gripped her. She tried not to let the pain into her voice.

"What are you talking about?"

He heaved her up off the stool and began dragging her toward the bedroom. Nelson whined after them.

"You lied to me about your writing. You made me look stupid in front of Erica. And you defied me in front of Doug—someone I *work* with! You completely crossed over the line. And now, you will find out what happens when you cross the line."

"Craig! You're hurting me. Ow! Craig, let go!"

Sarah pried fruitlessly at his fingers as she stumbled after him.

He didn't let go until he shoved her backward onto the bed and pinned her with a knee.

Her eyes widened as she realized what he intended. No! He wouldn't dare! She wouldn't let him! She screamed and writhed as he tore off her pantyhose. She beat at his leg and tried to knee him, but couldn't make contact with anything that would cause pain.

He shoved his knee harder into her abdomen until she had to fight to breathe. He kept shouting at her to shut up, that this is what she got for embarrassing him and keeping secrets. He spun and grabbed her flailing hands, then pinned them above her head as he tore off her undergarments and started working on his own belt one-handed.

She couldn't believe this was happening. She had never denied Craig anything in the bedroom—had never dared. It wasn't ever something she found great pleasure in, but she feared that if she said no, even once, he would leave her and she would be alone once again. Why did he think he needed to force himself on her?

He must have finally seen her for who she was—a dirty, worthless whore. Any self-respect she had garnered from being the wife of Craig Daniels, successful prosecution lawyer, evaporated like mist in the desert.

Sarah wasn't strong enough to push him off. The truth of it drained all the fight from her. She became still and started weeping.

She had never been strong enough.

"Why are you doing this? Craig, stop. Please, stop. Why are you doing this?" she sobbed.

He leered at her and leaned in close, keeping her arms pinned. His eyes were filled with hate.

"Not so sure of yourself now, are you? You're going to learn how a wife should behave, one way or another."

He crushed her lips with his, nearly suffocating her. Then he forced himself into her.

It was uncomfortable, but it didn't hurt—not physically. But in that moment, Sarah felt like her soul was being flayed—that part of her soul that she could never quite kill, never quite numb, the part that screamed to be loved by someone, anyone. The part that she thought was loved by Craig Daniels.

It was too much. She couldn't think about it or she would implode. So she did something she had done thousands of times before.

Sarah found a spot on the ceiling and stared at it. It was a smear where a mosquito had been squished, or maybe a bit of plaster had pulled free and a shadow remained. She focused all of her attention on it, closing her mind to everything else. The spot was her whole existence, her whole being and awareness. No room for anything but the spot. The pain, the heartbreak, the fear, none of it could touch her, not while she was the spot.

This isn't happening. I'll be okay. This isn't happening. I'll be okay. This isn't happening.

Suddenly, the lust-filled face of her father filled her mind, juxtaposed over her husband's contorted features. She felt her father's hands pulling up her dress, pulling off her underwear and spreading her legs.

She whimpered, but it was a small child's whimper.

Her name was Sarah. She was four years old. And her entire being was being eviscerated by the man she loved most in the world.

"No, please, no!"

Devon Sinclair put a hand over her mouth and growled at her. "Quiet, girl. You're going to like this."

Her head thrashed. "No, not again," she moaned, pleading.

But, as usual, the man above her didn't listen.

nine

SARAH LAY BACK, SUSPENDED IN TIME AND SPACE. HER CHUBBY CHILD ARMS AND LEGS KEPT HER afloat in the tub. If she relaxed and held still, she could almost believe that she floated somewhere far away, outside her body, where nothing could touch her.

Her eyes were closed, and sounds were garbled and amplified by the water covering her ears. The scent of the bubble bath—strawberry—filled her nose and made her nauseated. Bubbles popped loudly next to her head.

I'm dreaming.

But it was a dream with the taste of memory.

She swooshed her head in the bubbles to drown out the other noises. As the man in the room—the man she knew was her father, even though her father was dead—began bathing her, she left, rising up and out on the wind of dreams, far away.

She floated through clouds, over the ocean, on rainbows through blue, blue skies. Somewhere far below her she could see her body, floating in a tub full of bubbles. She could see Daddy, touching her like Mommy never touched her. She could see the little girl who was too stupid and weak to tell him to stop, to scream—the little girl who loved her Daddy so much that she would agree to anything to make him happy.

She hated that little girl with all her heart.

Like a spectre suspended above a bubble bath lake, she watched the little girl as she aged. Snippets of her life appeared on the water's surface, distorted by dream and refracting a thousand times from the skin of every strawberry bubble. She tried to turn away, to close her eyes, but no matter what she did, the vision was firmly in front of her.

She watched her father offer her a glass and, in the way of dreams, *knew* that whatever was in the drink was bad for her.

"Call for Mommy, you idiot!" she shouted at the girl, or tried to. But something was wrong with her mouth—it was full of strawberry cotton candy and no sound came out. Instead, she watched helplessly as her father gave the child the glass and the girl drank it all. It was brackish and sour, but it made her feel special for Daddy to give her something.

She handed the glass back. "It's salty, Daddy. It makes me thirsty."

"Let me get you some more," he said.

So he gave her another glass of water that left her thirstier than when she started. And did it again. And again.

She watched while her child self did nothing but guzzle it down, not realizing that the tainted water only made her crave more.

Her brother appeared beside her father and started giving her glasses of salt water, too. She couldn't drink them fast enough.

Last of all, Craig appeared beside the other two and gave her a glass of cloudy, salty water. She drank it, feeling her throat parch with every swallow.

She was back in her body, her grown-up body, surrounded by water. Her skin was hot, crackling, dry. She felt herself shrivelling. The bubble bath did nothing to hydrate her. She watched the bubbles melt and the water disappear as though it had been sucked into her own flesh.

She stood up, naked, surrounded by a salt plain for as far as she could see. The heat was like the blast of an oven. Her skin developed fissures and cracks as it dehydrated, mimicking the dried mud she stood on. She needed water, but there was no water anywhere.

Her father, brother, and husband appeared and circled around her, laughing and touching her with hands coated in slime. The slime was the most disgusting thing she had ever seen, but when they touched her with it, the brief reprieve from the scorching heat felt like heaven. She couldn't bear the thought of them touching her with the slime, but the ravenous dehydration won. She stood with her arms out and let them slather her all over until she was completely covered in the goop. The slime was absorbed almost as fast as it was applied, but eventually, they were finished, and she stood before them.

Craig angled a full-length mirror so she could see herself. She stared at her reflection in horror.

The slime hadn't only coated her—it had transformed her. Gone were the blond curls and blue eyes of the little girl and the feminine curves of the woman.

Instead, black hair as coarse as twigs protruded in patches from a misshapen green skull. Black piggy eyes perched above a potato-shaped nose and blubbery lips. Her head was too big for her ponderous body, and her arms and legs were too short.

She had become a troll.

"This is who you really are, you ugly wench." It was Craig's voice.

Or was it Daddy's?

Or Everett's?

Somehow, it was all three at once.

"I'm the only one who could ever stand to touch you. No one else can bear the sight of you. You would only suck them dry and turn them to dust."

Sarah's fear and hatred consumed her. She had only let them put the refreshing slime on because of how thirsty she was. And she was only thirsty because the only drink they had given her was salt water, and she needed to drink *something*. How could they have made her so ugly and made her like it even the smallest amount? The three men stood around her, leering and laughing. She screamed in rage, and the mirror shattered.

"Now look what you've done!" shouted her father. "You'll pay for that."

He grabbed a jagged shard of the glass and started to come at her with it like a knife. She tried to defend herself, but her limbs felt like lead—she couldn't move at all. He cut her face from her eye to her lip.

The deadness on her body lifted. She grabbed the shard and stabbed him in his eye. Blood streamed down his cheek, but he still smiled and leered at her with his other eye like one of those movie villains that just won't die.

"Trust me," he said. "Daddy loves you." The other two men laughed and nodded approval.

She lashed out with the shard, hating them, wanting to make them pay for what she had become. She jabbed blindly, eyes shut, flailing and hoping to make contact, a wordless scream of rage ringing from her chest—

And then she woke up, still screaming.

A moment later, she saw the blood in the tub and screamed again.

Her heart was pounding in her ears, and the jumbled images of her dream drifted through her mind like cobwebs as she tried to understand what she was seeing.

She must have fallen asleep in the bathtub. Why? Where was the blood coming from? Her father . . . it had been a dream.

Then the reality of what had happened with Craig fell on her like a breaking wave. The slap. The ra—She still couldn't even think it. Was it rape when it was your husband who did it?

She cringed as she remembered the disgust on Craig's face as he noticed the blood on himself.

"Why didn't you tell me you were having your period?" he had snarled. "You know how I feel about that."

She stared at him, then turned her face back to the spot on the wall and said nothing.

Craig swore at her and went to have a shower.

When he was gone, Sarah sat up, looking blankly at the spots of blood on the sheets.

She wasn't having her period.

She drew her legs up to her chest, covered herself with a sheet, and waited for the bathroom to be free.

Now, sitting in the tepid pinkish water, she wondered if Craig had damaged something when he . . . because of what had happened. Or was this because of what the doctor had said?

She frowned. It must be. She had rarely even bled when her father and brother had—

She stopped, realizing how dangerously close she was coming to focusing on memories that she usually kept at the periphery, where the emotion of them couldn't touch her. But it had been harder to do that this week, with the roller coaster ride of hope and fear and disappointment and, and . . .

The dam of memory burst all at once.

Daddy. Bathing her, touching her, making her feel good and special and dirty. Everett. Sneaking into her room and waking her up at night. Trying to stop it but she couldn't, she wasn't strong enough, there was nothing she could do. Begging her mother with her eyes to save her, but her mother never seemed to see what was happening.

The images flowed and swirled and covered her with slime and got in her nose and down her throat and she couldn't breathe she couldn't breathe she couldn't—

Sarah saw a spot. It was where some soap scum had dried onto the wall from an evaporating water droplet. She traced its descent with her eyes, thinking that she should wash the tub soon. She would do that tomorrow.

Her breathing returned to normal. She stood, rinsed off with a quick shower, dried herself, and put in a tampon.

She tiptoed back to the bedroom and stood at the door, listening. Craig's even breathing confirmed that he was asleep. To be sure, she stage-whispered his name. No response.

She slipped into her side of the bed, turned her back to her husband, and stared at the wall. She wanted to forget what had happened, like she had managed to forget the details of so much of what had happened when her father and brother were abusing her. It hurt too much that Craig finally knew how awful she was, how dirty. Why would he even want to be married to her? Maybe he wouldn't, now. The thought chilled her to her bone.

When she closed her eyes, she could still see snippets of her dream. She hadn't thought about those things in years. She remembered the stupid little girl who had let herself be turned into a troll.

She really did feel like a troll. Maybe she deserved what Craig had done. *Obviously.* Why else would he have done it?

Why else would any of them have done it? It was her fault, somehow. She just wished she knew how to make it stop. How to make them happy.

She should have listened to Craig. She never should have sent the money to Love Mumbai. She never should have kept secrets from her husband.

She should do better. Starting tomorrow, she *would* do better. He wouldn't believe how good of a wife she could be.

Her thoughts started to fuzz, and then she remembered the mirror shard. Her face had been cut. And she had tried to kill them all.

Sita.

Sita hadn't deserved it. But that was different. How could I have tried to kill them? It was only a dream. But it came from me somehow. I'm sorry I'm sorry I'm sorry . . .

Finally, sleep claimed her.

Sarah was up long before Craig, making good on her silent vow. She went through her morning routine as silently as possible, trying not to wake her husband. She curled her hair, applied makeup to cover the bruising as much as possible, took a bathroom break—relieved to see that the bleeding had stopped—and then tiptoed out to the kitchen to make a hot bacon-and-egg breakfast.

The coffee had just finished brewing when Craig came out, straightening his tie. He looked around in surprise.

"What's all this?"

Sarah gave him a quick peck, wiping her hands on a frilly red gingham apron—a memento of her grandmother.

"I wanted you to know how much I appreciate all your hard work. So I made you breakfast."

Craig studied her for a moment, then nodded slowly. "Okay, thanks."

"You're just in time." Sarah transferred some sunny-side up eggs onto a plate next to the still-sizzling bacon. With a flourish, she set the plates on opposite ends of the small dining room table and finished the settings with cutlery and cloth napkins.

Craig looked like he didn't know what to make of everything. He watched Sarah settle herself across from him and begin to eat.

She glanced up when she realized Craig wasn't eating.

"So? Go on! I know this is your favourite. And even I can make bacon and eggs." She flashed a perky smile and stuffed another forkful into her mouth.

"Uh, okay." Craig hesitated, then spread his napkin on his lap and started cutting up his eggs. He only took a couple of bites before he let his arms rest on the edge of the table, cutlery suspended above his plate.

"Listen, Sarah, about last night—"

Sarah froze, fork in midair. Was he actually going to apologize for what happened?

Craig cleared his throat. "I'm glad you got the message." He avoided her gaze and took a bite of bacon.

Sarah watched him for a moment more, then slowly resumed eating. She should have known better.

Craig stopped again. "There's something else I've been meaning to tell you."

She looked up, and he hesitated.

Sarah's heart fell. "You have to work over Thanksgiving, don't you?"

"No, it's not that." Craig paused, obviously uncomfortable. "It's, well, worse than that."

He was still mad about the money, she knew it. Angry enough to leave her? Maybe. She couldn't bear the thought of that right now. She needed him. She didn't even know who she would be without him.

"Craig, I have cervical cancer." The words exploded out of her before she could stop them. The stunned look on her husband's face looked like *she* had slapped *him*.

"Excuse me?" He sounded choked.

"The doctor, he told me last week. Remember how he called and asked me to come back in after my PAP to go over the results?"

"You have . . . cancer?"

Craig looked like he was flailing through a dense fog. His Adam's apple bobbed convulsively. "So, now what? How serious is it?"

Sarah swallowed, too. "I don't know yet, but Dr. Mahmoud referred me to an oncologist. I have my first appointment today. I guess I'll know more after that."

For the first time since she'd received the news, she teared up a little.

"I'm so afraid that I'll have to have a"—she choked on the word—"hysterectomy."

The reason she had gone to get her PAP smear done was because Craig insisted on it before they started trying for a baby—a baby that she desperately wanted. Now, she might not even be able to bear children. The thought had been her constant companion since Dr. Mahmoud had told her the news.

Craig took a deep breath.

"Well. We'll figure this out, Sarah. Do you need me to come with you to the doctor?"

Sarah blinked in surprise.

"You'd do that?"

"Yeah, of course, whatever you need. I could get Erica to clear my schedule. What time is your appointment?"

Sarah hesitated. She didn't want to be a burden to him, but it was so unusual for him to give her this kind of priority that she wanted to take advantage of it.

"Um, ten o'clock."

Craig was already pulling out his cell phone and sending a text.

"Okay. I've got an early meeting I shouldn't skip, but I'll be back here at nine thirty to pick you up." He met Sarah's skeptical gaze. "I promise."

She gave a hesitant nod.

He stuffed his last bit of breakfast into his mouth, gathered his things, and kissed her on the mouth.

"Wait—" she said. "What did you want to tell me?"

"What?" Craig shrugged into his jacket.

"You had something to tell me, remember?"

"I did?" He paused, frowning, then shrugged. "I don't remember now. Okay, I'll see you soon."

He kissed her again, then breezed out the door.

Sarah watched him, her stomach roiling with conflicting emotions.

Craig never, ever, forgot what he was going to say. And what he said always made sense. That's one of the things that made him such a good lawyer.

The icy serpent of fear that lived in her belly stirred and started to wrap itself around her heart. She stared at her eggs.

Whatever it was, Craig had changed his mind. He was going to help. Maybe they would get through this.

I'll be okay. I'll be okay. I'll be okay.

The serpent receded and settled. She could feel its wary eyes, waiting to attack.

With trembling hands, she finished her breakfast.

ten

SARAH STOOD NEXT TO CRAIG ON HER MOTHER'S SHADED CONCRETE STOOP, CHEWING HER LIP AS her husband rang the doorbell. The house was much like any other in this quiet subdivision, built in the sixties when the town of Miller had experienced a bit of a population boom after the new plant had gone in. Her parents had purchased it brand new, but the gypsum siding seemed horribly dated now.

The gift paper on the package in her arms crinkled as she shifted her weight. She held the flat, rectangular parcel like a shield, as though to deflect the oncoming tide of family togetherness. She studied the fading blooms of the sunflowers next to the stoop and took deep breaths of sweet prairie small-town air to calm her nerves. The October afternoon held a hint of crispness, and the breeze that kept tickling her face with some wayward strands of hair smelled of dry leaves and cut fields and savoury cooking.

She heard her mother hollering and footsteps approaching from within, and then the door was thrown open to frame her brother's hulking figure. His wide face broke open in a grin.

"Craig!"

Before Craig could react, Everett crushed him in a bear hug like they were long-lost bosom friends. Craig patted his brother-in-law's back awkwardly and then dropped his arms, pushing past the bulky blond man—who looked every inch the softened ex-soldier that he was—and forcing him to step back from the door.

Sarah followed her husband into the small entrance—merely a corner of the living room near the door on which the contractor had thought it sufficient to lay linoleum and call the job done. With Craig in front of her removing his coat and shoes and her brother pressed against the wall near the stairs, the space felt very crowded.

"Sarah!" Everett's face maintained its garish smile as he tried to give her the same treatment he'd given Craig.

Sarah deflected his hug by shifting the package a little further in front of her chest with her left hand and grabbing his hand with her right.

"Everett." Small handshake. Weak smile.

Everett's short, slightly heavy-set wife hovered at the edge of the lino behind him, a warm smile on her round face. She'd cut her medium-brown hair into a blunt, chin-length bob since Sarah had seen her last, and she was dressed in her typical uniform of faded jeans and sneakers. She'd traded in her typical graphic tee for a plain black one, her one concession to the holiday. Sarah shifted the package to her hip and embraced the plain-faced woman with one arm.

"Hi, Jill." Sarah's smile was genuine now. As much as she dreaded family gatherings, she had a soft spot for her sister-in-law. She sometimes wondered how her brother had managed to convince such a kind person to marry him.

Jill came out of the embrace and frowned as she scanned Sarah's face. "What's that?" She indicated Sarah's bruised cheek with her eyes. Sarah had been able to cover most of the remaining damage with make-up, but not enough to escape Jill's keen observation.

Sarah glanced at Craig, who had moved onto the living room's brown shag carpet with Everett. The men were standing by the couch, chatting about hockey, but her husband kept what appeared to be a concerned gaze on her.

Ever since she had told him the news the other morning, his entire demeanour had been different. He had almost been doting on her, checking in on her by text or phone throughout the day while he was at work. Yesterday, he'd surprised her with a true romantic dinner out, just the two of them. The massage and gentle love-making that had followed belied the wounds left by the violence of only days earlier. It was like he was a different person—but it gave her hope. Maybe this cancer diagnosis wouldn't be all bad. Maybe it would fix what was wrong between her and Craig.

She turned back to Jill with a terse shake of her head. "Nothing. I whacked my face on a door frame the other day. You know, another one of 'Sarah's classic moves.'"

Jill's frown didn't disappear, but she nodded uncertainly, glancing toward their husbands in doubt.

"Is that Sarah?" came Ellen Sinclair's voice from the back of the house.

Sarah raised her voice so she would be heard. "Yes, Mom."

Her mother bustled toward her from the kitchen, her pear-shaped figure clothed in a lavender skirt suit Sarah had never seen before that was mostly obscured by a clashing faded cotton-print apron she had seen many times. The apron was Ellen's favourite, and she had used it on family holidays and Sunday dinners since Sarah was a child.

Her mother gave her a brief and distracted hug, then turned back in the direction of the kitchen.

"Hurry up. I need your help."

Sarah sighed. "I'm coming."

Jill had a sympathetic look on her face. "Here, let me help you with that." She took the paper-wrapped package from Sarah's hands.

Sarah smiled gratefully. She shrugged out of her coat and hung it up, then took the package from her sister-in-law before heading to the back of the house where she knew her mother would be working to prepare dinner. Jill trailed after her.

Sarah knew Jill would already have offered to help in the kitchen, and Ellen would have turned her down. Having learned from past experience, Jill wouldn't have pressed the issue. In Ellen's mind, Jill was a "guest." Everett was the "man of the house," not to mention her favourite child, which automatically exempted him from anything resembling domestic duties. But Sarah was the daughter—so she had to help.

"Here." Ellen tossed a frilly apron covered in faded flowers at her.

Sarah caught the wadded cotton, set the package down on the peninsula, wrapped the apron's ties around her waist and set to work on the salad Ellen directed her toward. Jill tried once again to get involved, but Ellen shooed her away like a child that was interfering where she shouldn't. Jill gave a small shrug, then settled herself at the peninsula on a stool so she could at least visit with Sarah.

"So, how was your trip to San Francisco? Did you enjoy the conference?"

As soon as Jill mentioned Sarah's trip, Ellen slammed the oven door closed, whirled to face her daughter, and frowned.

"San Francisco? You were in San Francisco? When?"

"Yes, Mom. Remember? We were talking about it on the phone a couple of days ago. I was at a writer's conference. I was one of the presenters."

"Really. Huh. I do remember that, now."

Sarah wondered if Ellen actually did remember the conversation or not. She indicated the paper-wrapped package with the chef's knife in her hand.

"I brought you your present. Do you want to open it?"

"I'll get to it a little later, Sarah." Ellen's voice and face reflected impatience that her daughter could think there was time for frivolous gift-opening right now.

Sarah sighed, but decided to let it drop. She turned back to Jill.

"It was okay, for the most part. I'm sure I put on ten pounds. The food there was to die for."

Jill laughed. "Well, you look amazing, and I'm glad to hear there was something there you enjoyed."

Unlike Sarah's husband, Jill empathized with Sarah's distaste for the genre in which she had made a name as a writer. And unlike Ellen, she knew what the genre was.

"So, you were there for a conference, were you?" Ellen fussed with some pickles and cheese on a tray as she talked. "What were you presenting on?"

"I was talking about, um, how to write romance successfully."

"You know, I was looking for one of your books in Walmart the other day, and I couldn't find one. But did you know there is an author with the same name as your father?"

Sarah's heart caught in her throat and she met Jill's gaze. Her sister-in-law looked almost as alarmed as she felt. "Really? What are the chances?"

"He writes the nastiest books, though. I'm not surprised if you haven't noticed them there. Anyway, I thought you said you were a pretty good writer. Why weren't any of your books there in Walmart?"

Sarah cleared her throat and tried to find her voice. When she finally got it working, it sounded squeaky.

"I—I guess my publisher hasn't made a deal with Walmart. How do I know, Mom?"

"Well, why haven't you ever brought me one of your books to read? How many books have you published now, anyway?"

"I, um, I'm sorry, Mom. I didn't know you wanted to read one. I'll try to remember for the next time I see you, okay?"

Ellen frowned and nodded, then jabbed a piece of boiled potato from a large pot to test for doneness. "It's almost like you don't want me to read them. I'm your mother, for goodness' sake."

Sarah cringed at her mother's hurt tone. She had always managed to distract her from this conversation before, but while Ellen Sinclair's mind may not be a steel trap, she had a habit of remembering things Sarah had said at the most inconvenient times. Sarah replied carefully. "That's not it at all, Mom. You never read romance novels. I didn't think you'd like it."

"I'd read yours."

Oh, the horror of the idea.

"Okay, Mom. Sorry."

Jill came to Sarah's rescue.

"How did your garden do this summer, Ellen?"

Ellen's face lit up. This was among her favourite subjects. "Well, that early frost got a bunch of my tomatoes and all my summer squash, but the potatoes and peas did quite well."

Sarah tuned out as her mother went on about vegetables and the Farmer's Market where she sold them, focusing her energy on chopping tomatoes and carrots and mixing dressing. Despite her best efforts, she couldn't block the sound of Craig's and Everett's raucous laughter from the next room. It sounded like they had moved off hockey and were now discussing movies—actresses, to be precise. Craig's voice dropped, and she could hear only the low rumble of men's voices between snickers. She frowned slightly, not sure she wanted to know what was being said, anyway.

When she had first found out that Craig had arranged for them to come here for Thanksgiving instead of bowing out as he'd promised, she had been upset. In response, he had gently explained that in light of her news, he thought she should spend some time with her family.

She was perfectly well aware that he had arranged it before he knew about the cancer—probably as part of her punishment for defying him. However, he was being so nice to her now that she let it drop. Their only disagreement in the last several days had been whether or not she should tell her mother about the diagnosis—Craig insisting that she should, and her own heels dug in hard against the idea, ostensibly because she didn't want her mother to fuss.

If she was honest, she didn't want to appear vulnerable to her family—not to any of them. However, as usual, it didn't take long for Craig's reasons to start making sense and she had acquiesced to going to the dinner, at least. Now that she was here, she wondered if it was fair to her mother and sister-in-law not to tell them what the doctor had said. If the situation was reversed, wouldn't she want to know?

She chopped green onions fiercely, barely even seeing what she was doing. Pain shot through her finger.

Sarah stared at her bleeding index finger in dismay, then went to the sink to wash it off so she could inspect it. It could have been worse, but it would still be a major inconvenience and make typing painful for days.

"Jill, would you run to the bathroom and grab me a bandage?"

Jill glanced at her, continuing to nod in commiseration with Ellen about the neighbour's invading hops plants even as she took in the blood on the cutting board and Sarah running water over her hand. She jumped off her stool without a word.

Ellen didn't even look up. In fact, it seemed likely she hadn't even noticed what had happened. She kept right on talking as she scooped a large blob of butter into the drained potatoes and opened the fridge. She scanned the contents and went silent, looking puzzled. After poking around for another few seconds, she stepped back with her hand on her hip, staring into its depths in dismay.

"Oh, good grief. I forgot to buy whipping cream." Ellen turned to her daughter. "Sarah, you're going to need to run to Duncan's Market."

Sarah had dried her hand and was holding her finger out for Jill to wrap in an adhesive fabric bandage.

Ellen finally noticed the injury. "What happened to you?"

"The knife slipped a little. I'm fine."

Jill finished patting the ends of the bandage down and smiled. "Good as new."

"Thanks, Jill." She flashed her an appreciative grin and started removing her apron. "Do you want anything else while I'm there, Mom?"

Ellen frowned uncertainly. "You're sure you're fine?"

"Yes, perfectly." Another chorus of laughter burst from the living room. Sarah frowned. "Would you like to come, Jill?"

Ellen waved her hand. "No, no. She doesn't need to do that for me. Jill, honey, you go on and relax in the living room with the men."

"How about I finish Sarah's salad instead?" Jill moved to clean up the bloody cutting board.

Ellen pressed her lips together, then gave a short nod. "I guess it's got to be done. As long as you truly don't mind?"

"Of course not. It's my pleasure." Jill set the clean board back on the counter and began peeling carrots. She flashed a small, secretive smile of victory at Sarah, who covered her own with her hand.

Ellen turned back to her daughter, who was waiting by the kitchen entrance for a response. "Only the whipping cream. Everett will be so upset if I don't make these mashed potatoes the way he likes. And what about the pumpkin pie?" Ellen's face was covered in horror as she contemplated the consequences of serving pumpkin pie without whipped cream. She couldn't bear to disappoint Everett in anything. "Hurry, okay?" She paused. "And drive safe."

Sarah rolled her eyes after she turned away so her mother couldn't see. "I think I can make it to the store and back, Mom."

"You know it's my job to worry about you, right?"

Sarah blinked and glanced back at her mother, who was standing with her hands on her stout hips. The frown on Ellen's face seemed meant to show concern for her daughter.

Sarah knew her mother worried—constantly—but she had never for a second thought that it was ever about her. Everett, bingo, her garden, her house, her neighbours, even her dead husband, but never her daughter.

"When did that start?" Sarah regretted the words as soon as she said them.

Ellen blinked, then turned away, but not quickly enough for Sarah to miss the hurt look on her face.

"Mom, I didn't mean—"

"Buy some gouda, if they have any." Her mother's voice was tight.

Sarah sighed and retrieved her coat from the front closet.

"Where are you going?" Craig demanded, reclining in an easy chair.

"To the store. Mom forgot whipping cream."

Everett folded his meaty arms and leaned back into the couch, watching the exchange with interest.

Craig frowned slightly. "I told you to call her this morning to see if she needed anything. Didn't you do it?"

Sarah frowned as she shrugged into her coat and arranged her scarf. Everett and Craig both stared at her like she was a small child whose forgetfulness had caused the greatest inconvenience possible.

"I *did* call, remember? She didn't realize it until just now."

Craig jumped up. "I'll come with you, then."

Sarah's throat squeezed. She had been looking forward to a few minutes to herself. Even though Craig had been more civil recently, she still felt like she was walking on the edge of a knife when they were together, and it was exhausting. But she didn't want to discourage the changes she was seeing, either. She kept her tone even. "If you want. But I'll be right back. I'm only going to Duncan's."

Craig's phone beeped, and he peeked at the display. His lips flattened in an annoyed line and he glanced up at her.

"Whatever. Forget it, I'll stay here. The keys are in my coat pocket." Craig turned back to Everett and rose. "I gotta make a call." He headed for the back patio.

Everett nodded, then turned back to his sister. Alone at last, he let pretence dissolve into a look no brother should ever have. It was hungry.

Sarah gulped and tried to quickly fish the car keys out of her husband's coat pocket. Not fast enough. When she turned around again she bumped into Everett's chest. She yelped involuntarily and he smiled unpleasantly.

"Jill's expecting." Instead of being proud, his smile looked predatory. His breath smelled like something dead.

Dread sunk talons into Sarah's gut and began shredding her insides. Her brother was the very last person in the whole world who should have a kid. And yet, he was. But right now, she feared more for her own safety than his unborn child's.

"Congratulations." Sarah forced a steadiness into her voice that she didn't feel. She glanced sideways around her brother's bulk to see if anyone had noticed the two of them in such close proximity, but the stairs blocked the view of the kitchen from here. She could see Craig through the dining room's glass patio doors, standing on the deck in his socks and shirtsleeves with his back to them. "She hadn't mentioned it."

"She wanted to wait and tell everyone at dinner. But after Craig told me you two have been having a bit of a hard time of it, I thought you should know."

Sarah eased backward, flattening herself against the coat closet doors, surreptitiously trying to put some space between them.

"Hard time of what?" She glanced at the front door and eased in that direction.

Everett shifted his weight to match her movements and barred her path with a hand on the wall by her head. His smile was that of a cat playing with a mouse. "Getting pregnant."

Sarah frowned. They hadn't actually tried to conceive yet. Why had Craig brought it up? Maybe he'd been trying to get Everett off of a touchy subject. But had Craig mentioned the cancer, too?

She pressed farther into the wall and tried to twist away as Everett leaned in close to her ear, but his other hand held her arm fast now and there was nowhere to go. He was close enough that she could smell sweat and cologne, the same musky scent her father had used. Her throat burned with bile.

"Maybe he's not doing it right." Everett let go of her arm to rub the back of his fingers down its length.

Sarah's heart was flinging itself at her ribs like a caged bird. With her arm free at last, she smacked away his hand, ducked under Everett's other arm and fled out the door, not even closing it behind her. Scrambling into the car, she closed the door and locked it, breathing hard. She couldn't see the front door of the house from here, but she held her breath, wondering if Everett would be rounding the corner of the garage at any moment. The car engine revved to life and she slammed it into reverse.

She promptly had to put it back into park. Opening the door, she leaned out and deposited her breakfast onto the gravel driveway.

Sarah closed the door and sat there for a moment, engine idling. When she was sure she was under control, she began easing backward onto the street.

Glancing back at the front of the house before she pulled away, she could see her brother standing in the picture window, watching her leave.

It looked like he was laughing.

eleven

"STEVE, YOU WANNA HIT DUNCAN'S WITH ME?"

Steve glanced up from his paper at his sister. Joanna stood poised at the top of the half-flight of stairs leading to her front door, opposite his position on the couch, with an infant carrier hanging from one hand and her thick brown hair pulled back into a sleek pony tail. With her olive green sweater that skimmed her slim figure, knit scarf, and skinny jeans tucked into tall boots, she looked as though she were ready to go for coffee with her friends instead of waiting around for Thanksgiving dinner.

"What did you forget this year, Jo-jo?"

"Nothing. I'm making something up so I have an excuse to help you get a date. Supermarkets are one of the best places to meet women, I've heard. I'll let you hold Sophie. You'll be a shoo-in."

Steve rolled his eyes.

"If I wanted to meet someone, I would. But I don't. For all kinds of reasons. You know that."

Joanna gave an exaggerated sigh. "Fine, I confess. I'm just tired of feeling useless in my own kitchen." She raised her voice and aimed it at through the door to the kitchen from where the sounds and smells of cooking emanated. "We're going to get ourselves out of Daddy's hair!"

"Great idea!" hollered the intended listener.

"That's okay." Joanna wrinkled her nose at her daughter, whose elfin features peered up at her mother from the carrier. "We'll have more fun at the store with Uncle Steve anyway, won't we Sophie?"

Sophie cooed from the infant carrier hanging in Joanna's arms and let out an infectious baby giggle.

Steve laughed and stood, laying the paper on an end coffee table and taking a step toward his sibling. Despite Sophie being only seven months old, Joanna retained hardly any of her pregnancy weight. She'd definitely inherited their mother's metabolism and height, though her chestnut hair and grey eyes were all their father's. In fact, no one in the McGuire clan was very tall. Except Steve. And he wasn't sure that he counted.

"Okay, Sophe, we'll humour your mom. I'm sure Duncan's Market is crawling with attractive single women who want to leave everything for a life of charity work in India. On Thanksgiving Sunday. I mean, why wouldn't it be?" He leaned toward his niece's curly red mop and whispered conspiratorially. "Besides, I know you just want to hang with the coolest uncle on the planet. Right, kiddo?"

Sophie giggled again and chewed on her fist, eyes locked on her uncle's face. He kissed her forehead and stood.

Joanna handed him the keys.

"You remember the way, right?"

"Um, I'm not sure." He stilted his language like one of those automated voice recordings as though he had no intelligence of his own. "You might have to pull it up on the map for me." He grinned, letting his voice relax to its normal cadence. "Besides, you sure you trust my driving? All you crazy Canadians drive on the wrong side of the road, you know."

Joanna chucked her brother in the shoulder with her fist. "I don't want you to forget how and have your license revoked."

"Ah, so that's it. I'm glad you're looking out for me."

"Someone has to." Joanna laughed, then took a step into the kitchen. "Be back in ten, hon."

"You're sure they're open?" came Derek's voice. His wiry frame appeared in the doorway of the kitchen behind Joanna, holding what looked like a rose made from a red pepper in his hands. Derek liked to pull out the full chef's outfit for special occasions like this—"to keep the dream alive," he said—and was garbed from head to toe in white. His close-cropped dark hair was hidden beneath a tall white paper hat.

That was one thing about Thanksgiving dinner at Joanna's—since Derek was a trained chef, it was never a disappointment.

"Yep, I'm sure." Joanna gave her husband a peck on the lips. "Only the cranberries, right?"

"Yeah. So sorry. Can't believe I forgot cranberries, of all things." Derek shook his head, presumably at his own forgetfulness, and disappeared behind the partition wall once more. After a moment, the opening bars of a Bruno Mars song emanated from the kitchen, Derek humming along.

Joanna rolled her eyes in long-suffering amusement and headed out to secure Sophie's infant carrier into their van.

Steve slipped into his shoes and jacket.

"Bye, Derek!" he called from the landing by the door, aiming his voice upward at the kitchen entrance.

Derek stopped singing and leaned over so his head appeared in the opening. "You're going too? Yeah, bye!" He disappeared, and Steve was sure Derek was right back to creating his masterpiece before Steve had even turned around.

Steve chuckled and shook his head, then closed the door tightly behind him, cutting off his brother-in-law's voice nailing the chorus.

October had been unseasonably warm this year—for Alberta, that is. He wasn't complaining, as he was the first one to admit that eight years in Mumbai had thinned his blood. He would prefer not to have to dig out a winter coat before heading back to India in a few weeks. He took a deep breath of bracing autumn air and sent up a prayer of thanks for the gorgeous day before hopping into Joanna's gold minivan.

Steve relaxed and laughed with Joanna as he drove the short trip to the store. They so rarely got to see each other anymore. There were many things he missed about his home, but none so much as his sister. No one knew him better than she did. An hour with her was more relaxing than a massage. It was nice to simply take a load off and forget about the number of people that were counting on him for their livelihood at that very moment—and about how far short he still was of his fundraising goal for this trip.

When they got to the store, Joanna kept her word by handing him the infant carrier. She then proceeded to tease him mercilessly about every woman they passed.

"Look, Madge is working the till today. Pretty sure she's available at the moment. Those goods will move fast, though, so don't let her slip through your fingers. Oh! And there's a looker over in the bakery. You should go get her number." Joanna giggled and indicated the appropriate directions with her head.

Steve glanced from the apple-shaped, middle-aged cashier in a "Duncan's Market" apron—with ties that barely reached around her extensive mid-section—over to the bread aisle. An iron-haired woman in polyester slacks stood picking over the plastic-wrapped loaves.

"Madge doesn't strike me as a cougar. And Mrs. Peterson? Really? Don't you think Mr. Peterson might have something to say about that?"

Joanna's face grew serious.

"Oh, I'm sorry. You haven't heard. Of course you haven't. Mr. Peterson died of a heart attack three years ago."

Steve glanced back at the elderly lady who lived just down the street from his sister. He remembered cutting Mrs. Peterson's lawn when he was a kid. She had always been a generous tipper—even the time when he'd set the blade a little low and ended up making her front yard look like a balding golf green.

"That's too bad," he said.

"Hi, Mrs. Peterson," Joanna sang as they approached. The old lady glanced up and her face broke into a smile that instantly made her sparkle.

"Joanna, Happy Thanksgiving. How's your little one?"

"Great. You can ask her yourself." Joanna beamed and pulled back the blanket from Sophie's face a little.

Steve obliged by lifting the carrier to a more accessible height. Sophie obliged by letting out a delighted squeal.

Mrs. Peterson smiled even wider. "She's so precious. She looks exactly like your mother, doesn't she?"

Joanna nodded. "The red hair definitely gives her a resemblance. Hey, Mrs. Peterson, you remember my brother Steve?"

Steve smiled and nodded as she made eye contact with him for the first time. "Happy Thanksgiving, Mrs. Peterson. It's been a while."

The woman's watery green eyes seemed to dance. "Well, where on earth have you been hiding, boy? My lawn hasn't had a proper shave in twenty years."

Steve cleared his throat. "Right. Your lawn might be glad of that. I live in India now. And I was sorry to hear about Mr. Peterson."

Mrs. Peterson waved him off. "George is better off now, even if the rest of us are worse off without him. Yep." She glanced heavenward, then back at him. "You mark my words, he's got some poor lady angel do-si-doing circles around the streets of gold to stay limber 'til I get there." She raised her voice a little as though talking to someone in the rafters. "And I'm sure I'll get there soon enough."

The old lady chuckled, a little sadly. Steve and Joanna chuckled, too, not quite sure what to say.

Thankfully, Sophie chose that moment to throw her toy on the floor and give an attention-getting squeal.

"Sorry, Mrs. Peterson," said Joanna, bending to pick up the duck-shaped teether, "We better get moving. Sophie will need to eat soon, and then it's bye-bye Beauty, hello Beastie."

The grandmotherly woman laughed. "Yes, yes, deary, I remember those days well. Happy Thanksgiving to both of you."

They smiled and nodded and wished her the same. Steve tucked the carrier back into the crook of his elbow, turned around, and froze in his tracks.

Browsing the dairy section at the back of the store was the stunning blond woman whom he had met only seven days ago—and who had rarely left his thoughts since. He stood rooted, torn between going to say hello and ducking down the cereal aisle to hide.

Joanna, who had been marching right toward the object of his confusion on her way to the frozen foods section, stopped nearly adjacent to Sarah's position and spun, obviously noticing that she had proceeded alone.

"Steve? Are you coming?"

"Uh, what? Yeah, of course."

Sarah looked up. Straight at him. Too late for the cereal aisle.

"Steve?"

Sarah looked as stunned as he felt. He knew her family was from his home town—but what were the odds of running into each other in the market while they both visited on Thanksgiving Day?

"Hi, Sarah! Wow, what are you doing here?" He shifted Sophie's infant carrier to his left arm so he could offer Sarah a hand. She already seemed to be going in for a hug, then realized what he was doing. After a couple of missteps, they gave each other awkward pats on the back, bodies barely making contact.

Joanna hesitated, glancing between them, mouth quirked in half a grin. "Steve? Who's your friend?"

"Joanna. Um, this is, uh, I met Sarah last weekend in San Francisco. She came to my presentation, but her family is from here. What are the chances, right?"

Joanna watched him fidget and smiled knowingly. "What, indeed?"

Oh, he was so going to hear about this later.

Sarah shifted her weight and glanced nervously at Joanna. She seemed to be avoiding looking directly at him, ducking her head away from them to one side. Seeing her discomfort made him realize how rude he was being. Now that the initial shock of seeing her was passing, he managed to get a grip on himself.

"Sarah, this is my sister Joanna."

Sarah nodded and smiled—yep, it was as dazzling as Steve remembered—and offered her hand to Joanna, head still bowed slightly. "Uh, hi, Joanna, nice to meet you." She paused, recognition and confusion flickering on her face. "Do I know you?"

Joanna tilted her head. "You do look a little familiar. Did you grow up here?"

Sarah nodded. "Yeah. Hey, I think you graduated the year after me. My maiden name is Sinclair."

Joanna's face registered recognition. "Sarah Sinclair! You have an older brother named Everett, right? I see your mom at the Farmer's Market sometimes. She has the best carrots."

Sarah nodded and cleared her throat. "Yup. That's me. Joanna McGuire—were you on the basketball team?"

Joanna nodded. "Such a small world, isn't it? But it's Larson, now."

"And this," Steve turned the infant carrier to face Sarah, "is Sophie. Her mom let me borrow her. Say hi to Sarah, Sophe-meister."

Sophie's blue eyes locked onto Steve's face and she cooed, gnawing a pudgy fist.

Sarah turned to the baby and smiled even wider, the way women always did when they talked to babies. She bent toward the infant carrier and tickled a slipper-clad foot that was peeking from beneath the blanket. "Hi, Sophie. Are you keeping Uncle Steve out of trouble?"

Sophie gurgled.

"Good for you." She squeezed a toe and laughed, but the laugh seemed weak.

As she stood up and faced him directly, Steve noticed the fading bruise she had been trying to hide. He had thought she was simply being reserved. Now he noticed that there seemed to be a tightness around her mouth today, and she kept darting her eyes over her shoulder as though she was ready to flee. And was she a little pale?

"Sarah, is everything okay? I mean, are *you* alright?"

Sarah's eyes snapped to his—the bluest of big blue eyes, bigger than Sophie's, more beautiful than—

Steve dropped the thought like a hot potato. Sarah was married. Completely off-limits.

Sarah hesitated, mouth open like she wanted to tell him something. She glanced at Joanna.

"I'm—I'm fine," she stammered. "I, uh, better go. I have to get this whipping cream back to my mom's." She smiled weakly at Joanna. "It was very nice to meet you again, Joanna. Steve." She turned away, then swivelled back like she'd just remembered something. "I'll reply to your Facebook message soon. I've been . . . busy. Okay, bye."

Sarah spun and headed up the aisle toward the register.

Joanna turned to Steve with a gloating grin. "So . . . 'Sarah' seems nice. What did I tell ya about meeting women at the store, eh?"

Steve resumed their trajectory to the freezer section at a quick walk, hoping Joanna wouldn't see his flushing face.

Joanna kept up, ticking points off on her fingers as she spoke. "Attractive, single, likes to travel."

Steve spotted the cranberries and grabbed three bags, not letting his sister pause to peruse for the best ones.

"Well, two out of three ain't bad. She's married."

"Really? Oh." Joanna frowned at her brother. "Right, she said Sinclair was her maiden name. So, how did you guys meet?"

"We ran into each other at Starbucks, then she helped me pick up your Ghirardelli's chocolate."

"Sounds like you guys spent a lot of time together—Starbucks, Ghirardelli's, presentation, *Facebook*." She put a hand on Steve's arm and stopped him short. "Hey, bro. Are *you* okay? You're being careful, right?"

Steve hesitated. He could see the shadows of his past failures hovering like a storm cloud behind his sister's eyes. He frowned. He knew Joanna was only looking out for him, but he couldn't help feeling annoyed at the reminder.

He shook off her hand. "Yup. I'm being a friend. Nothing more."

There was no doubt that he found Sarah Daniels attractive, with her golden angel's tresses, forget-me-not eyes, and a strange mix of vulnerability and self-sufficiency that he found both intriguing and troubling. However, he had zero interest in striking up a romantic relationship with a married woman, no matter what kind of marriage it may be. As if his last relationship hadn't ended badly enough.

But Steve knew a lost and wounded soul when he saw one. That's what he did, after all. He frowned and shifted the infant carrier on his arm, then turned toward the till. "Something tells me she could use a friend right now."

Joanna arched a brow at him, then gave a terse nod. "Okay. Good."

Sarah had just finished paying for her cream when they got up to the till. She glanced at them once more, smiled, and then turned to leave. Steve barely had time to nod his head in a return salutation before she dashed out the door. He didn't think she even saw it.

As he and Joanna exited through the sliding glass door, Steve stood for a moment to let his eyes adjust to the bright autumn sunlight. When they did, he noticed Sarah sitting in a black Audi in the parking lot. She seemed to be crying.

He squinted to make sure of what he saw. She rubbed her eyes with the back of her hands, shoulders heaving. She was definitely upset.

"Joanna? Can you take Sophie? I have to go do something."

Joanna glanced up at him in confusion, then followed his line of sight to the blonde woman in the car. She nodded and reached out to take the infant carrier.

Just then, Sarah noticed them standing there and gave a smile and a wave as though nothing in the world was wrong, then pulled out of the parking space and drove away.

Steve pressed his lips together and watched the car turn out of the lot. That woman looked like more trouble than a bag of cats. He should probably walk away and let whatever trouble she was in be someone else's problem.

Only problem was, he had never been very good at that. The consistent tugging at his spirit said that this meeting, like the one last week, was no accident. For some reason or other, his path and Sarah Daniels' were meant to cross, and until he had fulfilled whatever purpose it was the Lord had in mind for him, he had a feeling they would be doing so again, soon.

When he turned back toward his sister to take the infant carrier back, Joanna was watching him with a concerned frown.

He shrugged, trying to ignore the pressure in his chest. "I guess she didn't want to talk about it."

Joanna pursed her lips. "I guess not." She gave him a worried glance as they made their way to the minivan. "She'll probably be fine."

He nodded and grunted noncommittally, opening the van's side door with the key fob and clicking the infant carrier into the base behind the driver's seat. He chucked his giggling niece under the chin with his finger, then rose and closed the sliding door.

His hand was on the driver's door handle when Joanna stopped him with a piercing gaze over the top of the vehicle. "You know it's not your responsibility to fix all the problems of the world, right?"

He nodded again. "Trust me, I know. I've got enough problems on my plate already."

She gave him a pointed look. He felt his hackles rise a little more.

"Don't worry, okay? As I said, we're just friends. And barely that. I'm not going to get any more involved than I have to."

Joanna studied him a moment longer, gave a decisive nod, and slid into the passenger seat.

Steve schooled his expression to jovial content as he fastened his seat belt. By the time they pulled out of the parking lot, his sister would never have suspected the inner turmoil he was wrestling with.

Not going to get any more involved than I have to.

Than I have to.

Lord, do I have to?

twelve

SARAH PULLED HER FEET UNDER HER AND TUCKED THE SOFT THROW BLANKET A LITTLE TIGHTER around her bare legs, regretting that she hadn't thought to put on her robe before she had snuck out of the bedroom. This short nightgown didn't offer much protection from the midnight coolness in the living room. She balanced her laptop on her thighs and wiggled back into the couch cushions, waiting for the leather to warm.

Nelson raised his head from where he lay on his pillow and gave an inquisitive whine. She smiled and patted the cushion beside her. He padded over and leapt up, then settled down again with his heavy head on her thigh where the laptop left a little room. She petted him absently, staring at the nearly-blank screen.

It had been a long time since she had had this much trouble deciding on a plot for a book. Normally, she was reliably prolific, with ideas that bubbled out of her like an Artesian spring fed by years of reading adventure romances and watching rom-coms on TV. Her characters usually came to her almost fully-formed, or as much as they needed to be. If her critics accused her of writing the same cardboard people into her stories again and again, she could care less—what author didn't, after all? As to their flatness—this was erotica. These people could be stick figures, and as long as she could figure out a decent love scene between them, the books would sell.

Still, her editor, Yolanda, had been encouraging her to branch out lately. With erotica becoming more mainstream, readers were coming to expect a higher standard of storytelling than the dime-store books that had been the genre's staple for years. Maybe that's why this story seemed to be so elusive—to create a character with depth, one must be willing to explore the depths of oneself.

Sarah wasn't sure she was ready for that.

She gave her mouth a wry twist.

On the other hand, if she were to tell Steve's story, she would get her feet wet exploring a real character completely unlike any other person she knew, all from the safe perspective of an outside observer.

Thinking of Steve made her stomach clench. She still found it hard to believe that she had *happened* to run into him at Duncan's Market that afternoon. If he hadn't looked as shocked as she had felt, she would have begun to think he was stalking her. For what purpose, she couldn't imagine, but the coincidence seemed to stretch credulity.

She should have asked him about the book at the store. But with how shaken she'd been by her recent encounter with Everett and the shyness she felt in the presence of Steve's sister, she had decided to wait. She still wasn't even sure she should try to write the book about Steve at all. What if the Boy Scout persona turned out to be an act after all? The thought unsettled her. She desperately wanted to believe that he truly was as altruistic as he seemed.

The rest of the afternoon at her mother's had been about as bad as she'd expected. She had managed to steer clear of a close encounter with Everett for the rest of the day, and if anyone noticed that she seemed jumpy, no one had mentioned it. Everett had announced Jill's pregnancy during the dessert course, and Sarah had been duly congratulatory, despite her personal misgivings. When Ellen had immediately begun prodding about when she could expect a similar announcement from Craig and Sarah, she'd evaded the topic with vagaries about timing.

Everett snorted. "'Timing,' eh?"

Craig frowned at him from across the dining room table. "What's your problem?"

Everett stabbed another mouthful of pumpkin pie, a wicked grin on his face. "From what you told me earlier, 'timing' has nothing to do with it."

Craig's jaw worked, but he was well-practised in courtroom restraint.

"What on earth are you talking about, Everett?" demanded Ellen, eyes clouded with confusion.

Everett flicked his eyes at his mother and back at Craig, then over to Sarah. The smirk remained in place. "Seems to me that if you've been sowing a field and nothin's coming up, you can either blame the dirt, the equipment, or the quality of the seed." He quirked his eyebrows at Sarah, and she cringed. "Which one seems to be the problem here?"

Sarah saw her husband's hand clench. When Craig argued a case in court, the attacks were rarely personal. Cold aloofness disappeared in the face of this assault on his manhood.

"Sarah has cervical cancer."

Sarah froze. Craig had agreed to leave the decision about whether or not to say anything today up to her. Apparently, though, if it was his fertility or hers on the altar of ego, he wasn't about to let his own suffer the flames of ill-repute. Craig merely glanced at her sideways, jaw tight, before paying close attention to the pie he was eating.

Sarah glanced around the table. The frozen expressions on the faces of her family members ranged from stunned disbelief on Jill's and confused denial on her mother's to smug victory on her brother's. Craig avoided her gaze.

Sarah finally fixed her eyes on Jill. "Sorry, Jill. I wasn't going to say anything yet. I didn't want to steal your thunder."

Jill cleared her throat. "No, it's alright. I mean, it's not alright, but I'm glad I know now." She cast a scowl toward her husband for the way he had elicited the news, but he didn't notice. "Do you know how bad it is?"

Sarah sighed. Time for both feet, now. "Well, it could be worse. I have to have surgery, but my oncologist is optimistic that I may still be able to have children once all this has been dealt with."

Jill smiled encouragingly. "That's a relief."

Ellen found her voice at last. "What kind of surgery? When is it? How long have you known?"

"Well, um, we only found out recently," Sarah began, starting with the easiest answer first.

"Why didn't you say anything?" Ellen demanded, her voice rising in pitch, her eyes wide. "For crying out loud, Sarah, you never tell me anything!"

Sarah blinked, then laid her fork on her plate and placed her hands in her lap. When Ellen Sinclair got hot under the collar, Sarah found the best response was icy calmness. She studied the autumnal polyester tablecloth for a moment, hoping to appear chastened, before meeting her mother's eyes.

"I'm sorry, Mom. I wanted to tell you in person, and we only did find out a few days ago." Well, she had only told Craig that long ago, anyway. "I didn't want to distract you before Thanksgiving. We meant to tell you all today, but when we found out about Jill's pregnancy, I thought maybe it could wait." She twisted her hands into her skirt to keep them from fidgeting. Ellen's screaming didn't make her upset, but the thought of a pregnancy that may or may not be possible for her now certainly did.

"So my only daughter has cancer and you thought I wouldn't want to know?" Ellen's voice had taken on a screechy, agitated tone. "You didn't want to *distract* me? Good Lord, Sarah, what on earth is wrong with you?"

Sarah gulped, trying to think of a response that wouldn't bungle the situation worse.

"It was my fault, Ellen." Craig's quiet words cut through Ellen's hysteria like a knife through butter.

Sarah looked up at her husband in surprise. He met her gaze with a small, apologetic smile. Well, she hadn't expected a rescue, but he definitely owed her one. He turned back to his mother-in-law, who was gulping water like a dehydrated fish. She caught his gaze over the top of her glass and put it on the tablecloth with a trembling hand.

Craig kept his tone conversational. "I told her to wait until after dinner today. She was only doing what I asked. We meant to tell you a little later."

Ellen looked like she was about to begin haranguing Craig. She frowned and opened her mouth to say something and was met with his gaze of iron— one that had unnerved many an opponent in the courtroom. After a moment, Ellen glanced away and fussed with the edge of the table runner.

"Well, if that's the case, then, I'm sorry," she mumbled to no one in particular.

Craig's mouth quirked in satisfaction. Sarah let out a breath she hadn't realized she'd been holding.

Jill shifted in her seat. "So, what does that mean for you now?" Her voice was gentle and encouraging.

Sarah glanced at her mother's closed face before fixing her attention on her sister-in-law's open one. Jill's wide-set round eyes and round face framed by straight brown hair would never be on the cover of a magazine, but Sarah had known for years that its beauty shone from deep inside. At the moment, she was thankful for one person who was an ally. It was to Jill that she gave her answer.

"I have what's called a LEEP procedure scheduled for Wednesday," she said. "It's a fairly minor surgery to remove the affected tissue. The oncologist—Dr. Strickland—doesn't believe that the cancer has metastasized, and thinks that this one treatment ought to do the trick."

Ellen turned back to her daughter. She seemed to be avoiding Craig's gaze.

"They can remove all the cancer with a minor surgery? And you'll still be able to have kids?"

Sarah sighed. She was torn between being strictly honest and putting on the best face so they could hopefully move on. She decided on a best-face scenario.

"Yep, she's fairly confident. Within a few weeks I should be good as new." Sarah rose, eager to change the topic. "I'm going to put on the kettle. Does anyone want coffee or tea?"

There was a round of hot beverage orders from the men and Jill. When Sarah turned back to her mother for her drink preference, Ellen was regarding her with a troubled expression.

"How do you get cervical cancer, anyway?"

Sarah pressed her lips together and stared at her mother. She had never expected her to ask something like that, and didn't dare reply that her own had likely been caused by extremely early sexual activity—fourteen years of rape by her father and brother from the age of four years old. A quick glance at the wicked delight on Everett's face told her that he knew—God, how did *he* know?—and was waiting to see what she said. The bastard didn't seem to be even slightly nervous that she would tell the truth.

She hated that he was right.

"I don't know, Mom. It's just one of those things."

She hurried toward the kitchen to start the hot water kettle and hide.

Nelson licked Sarah's hand, bringing her back to the present. The blank screen taunted her.

She chewed her lip, mulling over the dozens of skeletons in her closet. She had been running from those demons for so many years, but with this cancer diagnosis, they all seemed to be catching up with her. As they gained strength, she could practically hear them scratching at the door behind which she had shoved them—or maybe the door was weakening.

A picture flashed in her mind of Joanna and Steve and little Sophie in the aisle of Duncan's Market. The warmth and camaraderie between them had been obvious. Is that how normal brothers and sisters acted?

The only time Everett had ever been warm toward her was when he had come sneaking into her room in the middle of the night to play under the covers—an idea he had surely hatched when he had walked in on her and her father before school one morning. He was already old enough to know what was going on, thanks to Sex Ed class at school.

For a tiny soul starved of affection, the physical warmth and touch of a father and brother who otherwise ignored her was like a spring in the desert. The hatred that she felt toward them was matched only by the craving she felt for the only kind of love she knew—and the loathing of herself for wanting it.

She used to stare at her mother over the breakfast table, boring into her with her eyes, willing her to see what was going on and rescue her. She felt totally powerless to do anything about it herself and was too scared to tell her mother. After several years, she thought that there was no way that Ellen could *not* know about it, and came to the crushing realization that her mother was going to do nothing.

Sarah had no protector. She was on her own.

Ellen had wept openly when Sarah moved out of the house to move into the college dorm. Sarah had only rejoiced that she was finally free and hoped that she could find a way to obscure the pain of all those years of humiliation. When Devon Sinclair had been killed by a drunk driver on his way home from Wednesday night prayer meeting only one week later, she hadn't shed a single tear. Her mother had accused her of being made of ice, to which she hadn't replied.

Made of ice? If she was, she had been formed that way by the relentless shaping of a childhood of neglect and twisted affection.

Weep for the man who had made her?

What kind of a tribute would that be?

Sarah sighed, tapping her fingers lightly on the keys, but not depressing any buttons. This train of thought didn't exactly inspire creativity. She flipped over to her browser and found it open to the page on Love Mumbai's site that shared Sita's story. She had watched the video interview with the scarred young woman at least three times already. Each time she did, her emotions ranged from disbelief to yearning to despair—and something else that she was afraid to name.

In only slightly-broken English, Sita talked about her life as a prostitute, how she had been sold to the recruiter who had visited her home in Nepal when she was eight. Her father thought she would be getting a job as a domestic in a good place to live and hadn't questioned too closely after the money had changed hands. When she had arrived in Mumbai, though, she had been sold to another woman for more money than Sita thought existed in the world. The woman told her that she would have to work for her until Sita had paid back what was "owed." The "work" meant serving men sexually, usually eight or nine per night.

The footage from a hidden camera swayed along a darkening street at the bearer's knee level. It showed images of barefoot, unkempt, dark-faced girls in brightly coloured clothing sitting or standing along the edges of dusty roads in an urban neighbourhood steeped in squalor. Stone buildings in various states of disrepair hunched over rows of small booths that lined the street. Many of the booths had girls standing in front, waiting. Garbage lay in random heaps, and dirty children whose clothes hung off of them played among it.

Teen girls called out to the camera holder, trying to interest him—had it been Steve?—in spending some time with them. A girl and a john disappeared into one of the dilapidated stone buildings. A child of about two peeked out from behind a ragged curtain on the second floor, then disappeared.

A strong but pleasant female voice with a clipped Indian-English accent narrated. "Sita is one of over fifty thousand prostitutes who populate Mumbai's red light districts. Many of these girls start at the age of eight or nine, like Sita. A great many of them will not live past twenty-five years old, victims of sexually transmitted diseases like AIDS."

Sita came back onscreen and went on to tell how, after she'd lost her eye, no men wanted her so her madam put her out. With no skills to speak of, a new baby, and nowhere to live, she feared she and her daughter would end up dying of starvation. That was when she found Love Mumbai.

"They take us in. They give us medicine, and food, and help me get an education. They tell me about Jesus, how he forgives me and loves me and die for me. No one else ever die for me. No one else ever love me.

"Now I work at Love Mumbai to help others like me. I no longer worry that my daughter will have to work for a madam when she is older. She will be able to get a good job, and have a good life. I am so happy for Uncle Steve and all my friends at Love Mumbai."

The narrator came back on. "At Love Mumbai, we are changing lives. Will you join with us?"

The screen faded to contact information and an invitation to donate.

"Isn't 'Uncle Steve' the world's biggest frigging hero?" Sarah muttered to herself. Nelson whined and glanced up, and she patted his head to soothe him.

Staring at the screen with the now-frozen video, she felt her blood surge in a sudden, irrational jolt of adrenaline. Why had Sita earned a rescue, when she herself had not? What had Sita done that had deserved the intervention of a God that had only neglected Sarah? Where had her own "Uncle Steve" been?

She clicked over to the Bios page and stared at the image of Steve McGuire. She scowled at the photo, focusing her hatred and loathing on him for a minute—then realized what she was doing. The raging heat froze around a spike of fear in seconds. She couldn't be angry—anger was dangerous. Especially at a man who had been nothing but kind to her, however little she deserved it.

What if this guy was a phony? What if this whole Love Mumbai thing was a front to lure donations from unsuspecting and gullible people like herself while at the same time profiting off of the prostitutes they purported to help? She knew that she would be disappointed, but only slightly. After all, wouldn't that simply mean he was the same as everyone else—looking out for number one?

She chewed her quickly-chapping lip again, dancing around the other niggling thought—what if he wasn't?

What if he was for real?

With sudden resolve, she opened Facebook to send him a message.

Becky be damned. She definitely wanted to write this book.

Steve rolled over again, struggling to find a comfortable position. After eight years of sleeping mostly on the hard, lumpy mattresses so ubiquitous in India, he would have thought that sleeping on a pillow-top would be like resting on a cloud. He squirmed around again, stubbornly refusing to believe that he couldn't sleep comfortably on the most advanced mattress technology offered by man.

He woke with an abrupt jolt, jarred by Sophie's muffled wail somewhere on the main floor above him. He must have at least dozed for a while—long enough that the surge of adrenaline from waking so suddenly meant he wasn't likely to do so again soon. He took a deep breath and laid flat on his back, staring straight up at the ceiling. Joanna's footsteps made the floor joists above him creak as she went to soothe the baby.

Grabbing his cell phone, he woke up the screen to check the time. 12:40 a.m. He sighed, lay back, and closed his eyes. His mind started to wander a bit, and he realized he was thinking about Sarah.

After leaving Duncan's that afternoon, he had tried to push her to the back of his mind, with little success. Every moment when he wasn't engaged with something else, she had popped unbidden to his thoughts. He was worried about her. She had obviously been upset, and the bruise on her cheek suggested that she had reason to be. He had seen far too many bruises like that on the women he worked with to be unaware of what caused them.

More than likely, Sarah's husband had beaten her. Steve couldn't say so with certainty, but his gut knew it for truth. The question is, what was he supposed to do about it?

What would you have me do, Lord? She obviously doesn't want help.

Hard experience had shown him that if someone didn't want help, they wouldn't thank you for forcing it on them.

Not that he even could, in Sarah's case.

The dark room was quiet, lit only by an orange trapezoidal patch of light on the wall that remained as unmoving as the street light that cast it. Sophie must have settled down. He heard Joanna's light tread making her way back to bed.

He checked the time again. 12:55. Grunting, he was about to lay his phone on the nightstand when it vibrated in his hand. The screen lit up for a moment to indicate an incoming instant message. It was from Sarah.

Steve frowned in curiosity. He unlocked the screen so he could read the message.

Nice to see you today. I have a weird question for you, but would like to ask you in person. Are you busy on Tuesday? We could meet for lunch somewhere—Edmonton or Miller, you pick.

Steve read the message again, pondering. She probably didn't expect him to be awake to read it now, so he could wait until morning to answer. But he already knew what he would say.

Okay, Lord, I give in. You don't need to have a whale swallow me for me to get the picture.

He began typing with his thumbs.

Sarah went back to staring at the all-too-blank word processor document that was meant to be her next novel. She rubbed her eyes, wondering if she might finally be able to sleep if she went back to bed. Her browser chimed with an instant message and she jumped.

She blinked at the laptop dumbly. Steve was replying to her already? It was one o'clock in the morning!

She hesitated, nervous about his response. She wasn't sure if she was more scared of him saying no, or saying yes. She bit her lip and opened the browser window. It was still open to Facebook.

Colour me intrigued. I could meet you in Edmonton. I have to head up there, anyway. When and where?

Sarah held her breath and thought fast.

Canuck Cafe. 12:30.

She added her phone number for good measure.

The reply was a thumbs-up symbol.

She let her breath out in a rush. The first hurdle had been crossed. Now she had a day and a half to stew about what he might say to her proposal.

Nelson raised his head and gave a small whine, sensing her mood.

Sarah smiled and patted his head. "Whatever he says, I'm still stuck with this other book, aren't I?"

Nelson's swamp-brown eyes flickered in commiseration. She chuckled and clicked her laptop closed. She *was* tired, and if she didn't want to sleep away Craig's holiday Monday, she should get some rest soon.

She was rising from the couch when she heard the text message notification from Craig's cell phone. It seemed to be coming from somewhere inside the couch. The phone must have fallen out of his pocket before they went to bed. She slid her hands along behind and between the cushions until she found it, then set it on the kitchen island.

The jar of setting the phone down woke up the lock screen, which displayed a preview of the text he had just received. She didn't mean to spy, but Erica's name caught her eye. A glance was all it took for the words to register.

I miss you. Come over tomorrow, okay?

Odd. Erica saw Craig at work every day. This was the first weekend in months that he hadn't forced her to work overtime with him on at least one of the weekend days. Tomorrow was a holiday because of Thanksgiving, and Sarah had a hard time believing that Erica couldn't figure out something to do with her time for three days in a row away from the office.

Unless . . .

The most likely truth loomed ugly and red in front of her, but she refused to look at it. Her mind shied away from even the suggestion that her husband

and best friend might be having an affair—the possible ramifications were suffocating. She shook her head.

It couldn't be true. There had to be another explanation. She would find out what the real reason was tomorrow.

Sarah crawled back under the covers next to her husband's sleeping form. She watched him for a moment, wondering, then rolled onto her other side to face the wall.

Exhausted or not, it was hours before she found relief from her anxious thoughts in the oblivion of sleep.

thirteen

SARAH AWOKE TO THE SMELL OF COOKING BACON MIXED WITH COFFEE—A HEAVENLY BLEND OF aromas. She rubbed her eyes and stretched, glancing at the clock. It was late in the morning already. Nelson padded in through the open door and licked her face. She flinched away.

"Yeah, yeah, I'm awake. I have to say, the bacon is a much more pleasant alarm clock than you are, Stinky-breath."

Nelson just blinked at her in contentment, wagging his tail at the sound of her voice.

The sounds and smells of her husband cooking made her smile, but then she remembered why it had been so hard to fall asleep last night. In a flash, she was fully alert, a fist of dread clenched around her stomach. Reluctantly, she rolled out of bed.

Craig had her breakfast on the table by the time she got dressed and emerged from the bedroom. Sunny yellow yolks, crispy bacon, and buttered rye toast were arranged on a plate next to a steaming mug of dark roast mellowed to a caramel colour with cream. An exploratory sip confirmed that it had exactly the right amount of sugar, too.

She looked up at Craig, who smiled widely. She smiled back, pleased but uncertain. Yesterday morning, the sight of a breakfast prepared by her husband would have given her a thrill. Confusion blanketed the dread, and she hoped desperately that her suspicions were wrong.

Craig had not been this attentive since they were dating. She had thought he had reformed his behaviour because of the cancer, out of concern for her. But niggling doubt whispered that it could be because of guilt.

He came around to pull out her chair. She gave a tight-lipped smile as he helped her be seated.

"Thank you, honey."

He bent and pecked her cheek, his breath warm on her ear.

"My pleasure. Would you like anything else to go with that?"

She shook her head. "This looks great."

He gave her a pleased smile, then settled himself into his chair on the other side of the table to sip coffee and read the newspaper. She cracked open a book to read while she ate but kept glancing up at him, studying his handsome features—the thick shock of black curls, the intense green eyes, the sensual mouth. He glanced up and caught her looking, then flashed her a smile and a wink that should have made her insides melt.

If it weren't for the shadow now growing in her heart, it probably would have.

Craig's text notification chimed, and he glanced at his phone, then sent a quick message back to the sender.

Sarah chewed slowly, pretending to read, but surreptitiously glanced at her husband as he texted. He looked up and she studiously bent her nose to her book.

"I have to go into work for a while this afternoon. Is that okay with you, sweetheart?"

Sarah glanced up. His expression was the picture of sincere affection. She wished she could forget the invitation from Erica, but now he was "going to work?" How convenient. She smiled as warmly as she could.

"Sure, no problem. I'll head over to the Bean Bin and write while you're out."

"Great idea. How's the new book coming along, anyway?"

Sarah shrugged. "I'm having a rough time getting started on this one, but I'm working on a few ideas. Maybe today will be my breakthrough."

Craig nodded absently, then went back to reading the paper.

Sarah left the apartment as Craig was changing into his suit, laptop bag slung over her shoulder to sell her supposed intentions of an afternoon spent writing. She eased her silver RAV4 out of the lot, drove around the block, and parked on the street far enough away from the apartment that Craig wouldn't see her when he left but close enough that she could follow him. Before long, his black

Audi sports car glided out of the lot and headed downtown. She shifted into gear and followed at a distance.

Since it was a holiday Monday, traffic was light, but still heavy enough to keep several vehicles between her little SUV crossover and his tail lights. She followed him the few blocks to his office and pulled over when he entered the parking garage.

She chewed her lip. What was she doing? Tailing her own husband? He had been telling the truth—he was going to work. After how nice he had been since her horrible news, this was the kind of gratitude she had!

She continued to berate herself as she put her car into gear and signalled to re-enter traffic. As she was checking for a clear lane, she caught sight of Erica's little red coupe entering the parkade.

Sarah clicked off the signal light and put the car back into park, biting her lip again. It could be nothing—it could be that Craig figured he needed Erica's help with whatever he was working on.

Or it could be evidence of Sarah's worst fears. She tapped her cell phone with her forefinger, trying to decide whether to fish for more evidence. Did she want to go there? Did she want to push this?

Did she actually want to know this answer?

She sat and argued with herself for another minute. Shaking her head, she opened her messaging app. Seconds later, she pushed send on the text inviting Erica to join her for coffee at the Bean Bin.

Sarah sat waiting for an agonizing few minutes with no response. Maybe Erica hadn't heard the text? Or else she was ignoring her?

An elderly parking enforcement officer in a yellow vest was making her way up the sidewalk toward the RAV, chalking car tires. Sarah watched the woman's progress, flicking her eyes to the Expired flag in the parking metre beside her. She was going to have to make a decision soon or she would get a ticket.

She was about to pull out of the parking spot when her phone tweeted.

Sorry, sweetie. I'd love to have coffee, but I'm visiting my mom today. Rain check?

Sarah stared at the screen, not wanting to accept it. She read the text again, willing it to say something else. It was like the entire world was reduced to the words—the deceitful, lying words—on her phone.

A rap at the passenger side window roused her. She gulped for air, not realizing until that moment that she had been holding her breath.

Sarah glanced over to see the creased face and short curly grey coif of the metre lady standing outside her vehicle. The woman frowned and pointed at the metre, her intentions obvious.

"Sorry," yelled Sarah, hoping the woman could hear through the glass. The matronly woman put her hands on her hips, clearly not mollified. Sarah gave a quick smile and a wave and pulled out into traffic.

The sharp blare of a horn behind her jolted her back to the task at hand. "Sorry."

The man flipping her the bird in her rear-view mirror couldn't hear her muttered apology and scowled ferociously. She scowled too, fight-or-flight response augmenting the anger forcing adrenaline through her veins.

A small part of her was thankful that he'd seen her mistake in time to stop.

Another part—the part that was huddled inside her icy fortress for protection against the earthquake of reality—couldn't care less.

Sarah eased down the lane between hangars at the Westbank Regional Airport. Dull metal Quonsets were connected by wide asphalt alleys, some with small planes, helicopters, or other airport machinery sitting on them. Beyond that, thin October sunshine cast slanting rays on tawny fields and distant stands of poplar trees, their yellow leaves clinging stubbornly in the mild temperatures of an abnormally mild autumn.

She pulled into the parking lot of the Skydiving Club office, put the RAV4 in park and turned off the ignition. She hadn't really intended to come here—she had only wanted to take a drive to clear her head. When she'd realized how close she was to the west end of the city, the idea of taking a dive to clear her head instead had seemed more appealing, since the driving hadn't helped.

Sarah grabbed the bag containing her flight suit from the hatchback where she always left it—just in case—and headed toward a man door in the front of the metal hangar. She could see a small airplane on the strip behind the building with several people working around it and people in jump suits filing up the stairs. Good, they had a flight about to go up. Maybe she would be able to dive today.

The office was a smaller space inside the building's large frame that was enclosed to human dimensions. It looked like it hadn't been updated since the seventies. Fake wood wall panelling and cheap wood veneer doors surrounded a couple of desks hosting stacks of papers and dusty computers. One of the desk chairs was occupied by a stocky middle-aged man in a polo shirt and a ball cap that read "The Ground's the Limit."

Murray glanced up when she entered, adjusting the grungy cap on his round head with both hands, a pencil protruding from between his fingers. The gesture was likely meant to make the tufts of iron grey hair behind his ears lay down, but only succeeded in making them stick out more crazily than before. His wide face broke into a gap-toothed grin when he recognized her, and he hefted his paunchy frame out of the rolling chair to give her hand a pump.

"Hey, little lady! Haven't seen you in a while."

He sat back down with a *fump*.

"Hey, Murray. Don't suppose you have space on that jump this afternoon, by chance?"

Murray clamped the pencil crosswise between his teeth as he rolled his chair over to reach his keyboard, the sound of rolling wheels on grit amplified on the hard tile floor. He clicked a few keys, then smiled and removed the pencil from his mouth so he could talk.

"You're in luck. This one was s'posed to be full, but the group that's rented it had one of their members cancel. I'll check with them to see if they'd object to ya joining in."

She gave a nod, trying not to fidget impatiently. Her nerves were wound tighter than violin strings. Craig would be furious if he knew she was here.

Screw what Craig thinks.

Sarah studied a photographic wall calendar advertising the local Treasury Branch to steady her nerves while Murray radioed the pilot to present her request. A few monosyllables later, he turned back to her with a grin.

"You're in!"

Forty-five minutes later, she was in free fall over a familiar landscape. The sixty seconds after jumping when she was screaming toward the earth were exhilarating. Time seemed to stretch as wind whipped past her cheeks and she spun and twisted in the air. For a few moments, there was this and nothing else.

At twelve hundred feet, Sarah pulled the cord, her chute opened, and the ear-splitting speed of her descent was abruptly slowed to a gentle drift. She knew she was still moving fairly fast, but once again, gravity had been cheated of its prize. She allowed herself a grim but victorious smile.

She could have seen the Edmonton skyline to the east if she had chosen to look, but she didn't. She scanned the patchwork quilt of fields, some dark and tilled, some green or golden, with shadowy lines cast by rows of trees between them. She picked out squares and rectangles in circles of pale earth that she knew were buildings—farmhouses or businesses. Her gaze followed the line of the highway, cars reduced to the size of match heads at this height, but with more detail becoming apparent every second.

Sarah relaxed into her parachute harness, expertly guiding herself toward the landing zone as the earth continued to expand to meet her.

It had been years since she and Craig had gone diving together, and almost as long since she had gone alone. When they were first dating, it had been a favourite shared activity. She earned her solo skydiving license and the two of them went out whenever they could. In a life where she had so often been powerless, skydiving made her powerful. When she was skydiving, she could outsmart gravity, defy the elements, and overcome nature. She could be free.

Craig had lost interest in skydiving soon after they were married, but Sarah had continued to go alone . . . until he found out and insisted she quit. He said he was concerned for her safety. Reluctantly, she had agreed to stop, secretly wondering why he would deny her the one thing that made her feel alive.

Now she wondered if it was *because* it made her feel that way. Her forehead tightened.

All afternoon, she had tried to weigh her options rationally, distancing herself from the emotional entanglement of the situation so she could decide what the most logical thing to do would be. If she confronted Craig and he repented, could they go back to the way they used to be? Would she ever be able to trust him again?

She thought of the way he had made love to her on Saturday night and wanted to curl up on herself in shame. She had believed that she was the centre of his world that night—but it had been a lie. Could she ever trust a man who lied as easily as he breathed?

No, the most likely results of a confrontation were that they would either separate, or they would remain together, reduced to roommates propagating a facade of marital bliss while he continued to carry on however he pleased. Neither option appealed to her.

Maybe she could pretend she didn't know. Maybe, if Craig kept being so sweet, he would realize he didn't want to be with Erica at all, and they could fix what was wrong between them.

And maybe the grass would be pink when she touched down.

Without warning, she felt the crush of agonizing grief inside her chest, like her heart might implode. Craig had been the first man she had trusted fully, or as fully as she was capable of. How could she have been so blind and stupid?

Why was this happening to her?

She and Craig had been so great together at first. He was a daredevil, and he inspired her to try things she had never thought to try. With him, she could pretend to be someone exciting—dangerous, even. Being with him was as close to feeling alive as she got outside of skydiving. He had looked at her like she had never thought a man would look at her, like she was the most desirable creature in the whole world. She knew he was wrong, but still, it was nice to think someone believed that.

Then he'd begun beating her. But every time he hit her he would be so sweet and gentle afterward, blaming the fact that his dad used to beat the living day-lights out of him, and promising it would never happen again. Like an idiot—a desperate, love-blind idiot, at that—she had believed him. She wanted so badly to believe he loved her that she had stayed as the situation got worse and worse.

And then, last week . . .

Last week, he had raped her. She acknowledged it as rape at last. Though he hadn't done it since, she knew to her bones that he would do it again if he felt provoked. Not only that, he had been unfaithful to her for who knows how long, and—the chilling thought suddenly occurred to her—with who knew how many women.

She had been stupid enough to think that his doting behaviour was a sign of hope for their relationship, that maybe things would go back to the way they used to be. With the perspective offered by knowing the truth about the affair and dangling hundreds of feet above ground, she realized it was simply a repetition of the same worsening cycle of abuse and remorse that had been developing for the last two years. Unless a miracle happened, they could *never* go back to the way they used to be.

Sarah clenched her fists around the chute's risers so tightly that her hands started to cramp. She had long since stopped believing in miracles.

Craig was not just a troubled soul that occasionally succumbed to behaviour he couldn't help because of his past. He was an abuser. He was abusing her. He was an adulterer. He was cheating on her. And he was a rapist. It absolutely counted as rape even if it was done by her husband. He made her feel small at every opportunity, and she had accepted it both as her due as a worthless whore, and as understandable on his part based on what he'd been through. She had thought that if she could love him enough, and please him enough, he would change—truly change. Just like she had hoped that if she could excel enough in school, her father would find her pleasing enough as a daughter to stop using her for his twisted, selfish pleasure, and her mother would notice her and stand up for her.

"Damn."

She had growled it, but the wind snatched at the word and threw it away as though it were inconsequential. Gathering all the defiance she could muster, she drew a deep breath and yelled at skies dotted by other divers too far away to hear.

"Damn, damn, DAMN!"

In a flash of clarity, she realized she had married a man who treated her exactly like her father had. And the woman she thought was her best friend had betrayed her exactly like her mother had. And here she was, dangling above the earth, alone, trying to figure out if she could pretend that she didn't know so that her life could go on as it had before. Just like she had pretended that she lived in a perfectly normal family for eighteen years.

"*I don't want to pretend anymore!*"

No one even looked her way. The only response was the wind in her ears.

The ground was very close now. The blurred tops of a row of poplar trees swept by only a few hundred feet beneath her. She blinked furiously, trying to clear her vision and prepare for landing.

Health, career, marriage—she was still in free fall. Only she didn't know where to find the ripcord that would save her life. She did know, beyond doubt, that the way her life had been before was no way to live, not really. But the uncertainty of a future filled with unknowns terrified her just as much as the first time she had stood in the door of that airplane, trying to work up the courage to jump. She felt the fight drain out of her.

"I don't want to pretend anymore." She slumped in her harness, tears collecting inside her goggles. "But I don't know what else to do."

She lifted the mask away from her cheeks to let the moisture escape. Salt water tracked down her cheeks and dripped upward off her chin, carried on the wind.

The target was directly ahead of her. She got into position for a running landing. Her right leg made contact first, then her left foot hit awkwardly and rolled.

Jolting pain seared through her. She managed one more fumbling step, allowing her to throw up her hands and keep her face from being dragged through the grass. The parachute sailed over her head and dragged her for another few feet before collapsing in a flaccid heap of yellow nylon.

Gingerly, she rolled over and sat up, disentangling herself from the cords. Her leg throbbed as she probed gently with her fingertips. She could see Bernie, the jump master, humping it toward her, but she didn't need his analysis to tell her what she already knew—she had sprained her ankle badly. Maybe broken something.

So much for keeping this a secret from Craig.

"Damn."

fourteen

SARAH EASED INTO HER PARKING STALL NEXT TO CRAIG'S CAR AND HER STOMACH CLENCHED. ANY remaining hope she had of getting home before him evaporated. The anger that had pulsed through her veins all afternoon now crystallized into icicles of fear. She would do a lot of things to avoid having to confront her husband, but frankly, she didn't see what other options she had besides disappearing for the night.

The thought was tempting—check into a hotel, turn off the phone, and wallow with a bucket of ice for her ankle and a bucket of Breyer's for her miserable wreck of a life. In fact, she had almost decided to do just that at least three times on the way home. But she figured that disappearing would only make Craig angry, maybe even tip him off that something was up.

Sarah had no intention of sleeping in the same house as her husband tonight. But she needed time to think, and she had hoped that she could deal with Craig from the safe distance offered by a telephone. That could have worked—if she had been home first.

She scowled at Craig's Audi and pondered her options. If she was patient and sneaky, she thought she could still get into the house to grab some things and get out without violence. She could save the ice cream therapy for afterward, and at least have a clean nightgown to do it in.

Sarah gingerly eased her swollen ankle to the side, mentally working herself up to stepping onto the asphalt.

After Bernie determined that her ankle was merely sprained, he had iced it in the office and wrapped it in a tensor bandage. Then he had tried to insist on driving her home. She had a momentary fantasy of letting him, then somehow coercing him to come into the apartment with her to face Craig. But the scenario always got messy after that, and she couldn't see any advantage in a near stranger being there. So she had made light of the pain she was in and adamantly refused.

Sarah's foot had been immobile while she drove, but much lower in elevation than her heart. The blood had pooled and her ankle had swollen even more. Since she had no cane or crutches or support of any kind, she was going to have to put weight on it to get into the building.

Sarah tested its weight-bearing capabilities with a light touchdown and white-hot agony shot up her leg. An involuntary cry made a neighbour walking by with a small dog eye her curiously. Sarah bit her lip so she wouldn't do it again.

She hopped into the foyer, clumsily buzzed the doorman, and made it into the lobby, then the elevator. Her foot touched down to steady her several times, eliciting small grunts.

She opened the door to their apartment, clutching the door jamb to avoid lowering her injured ankle. Craig was sprawled on the couch with his feet up on the coffee table watching the news.

Although Sarah was exerting heroic effort to not let her discomfort show, he jumped up as soon as she came in, his face a picture of concern as he put out his hand to help her. She had expected to flinch at his traitor's touch, but the flames in her ankle temporarily pushed aside reflexive revulsion. Still, she resented that she was grateful for his help.

"What happened to you?"

She had decided in advance that there were some truths that would only make this harder.

"I rolled my ankle off a curb this afternoon and sprained it. It's nothing, really." Just then, Nelson came over and brushed her ankle, panting and smiling. She sucked in her breath and held it to keep from crying out.

Craig shook his head.

"'Nothing?' You're white as a sheet! Here." He supported her arm and helped her hop-skip over to the couch, then eased her down onto it. "I'll get you some ice."

Sarah rubbed her arm as though she could erase the searing warmth his hands had branded there. The leather cushions she sat on still radiated his body heat and his cologne hung in the air. "Thanks."

Sarah let him prop her swollen ankle on the coffee table and arrange a bag of frozen peas around it, then dutifully swallowed the ibuprofen he handed her with a glass of water. "Thanks," she mumbled again.

"Sure, sweetheart." He planted a light kiss on her cheek, then took the glass.

She watched his athletic form retreat to the kitchen and put the glass in the dishwasher. While he was there, he loaded up the few dirty dishes and wiped down the counter.

He was being so kind and considerate. Was this the man she had convinced herself was cheating on her? He wasn't perfect, but who was? Okay, he lost control of his temper, but did that make him an adulterer? What if she had misunderstood what she had seen this afternoon?

Why was she so damn suspicious all the time?

Craig glanced up at her, scrubbing at a stubborn spot.

"Did you at least get some work done before the 'Big Accident'?" He paused his work to use air quotes, obviously trying to distract her with some humour. His face was the picture of earnest interest, mouth quirked in a grin. That ridiculously handsome face—so easy to look at, so hard to resist—was a good part of the reason she was in this mess to begin with. His firm biceps rippled beneath the sleeve of his grey T-shirt as he leaned on the counter, and his green eyes glinted at her beneath wet, dark curls.

Wait . . . why was his hair wet? He could have worked out and showered at the office, like he did most regular work nights, but on a holiday?

Yeah, he would do that.

Or maybe he always came home freshly-showered for another reason—like trying to hide tell-tale evidence of intimate encounters. The realization made her catch her breath.

She hated wondering. She had to know the truth, one way or another. She felt her stomach lurch at what she was about to do.

All this passed through Sarah's mind in a split second. She met Craig's light-hearted gaze with a level stare, careful to keep her voice calm.

"I did research. It was . . . enlightening." She took a sip of water, her eyes locked with his. "How about you? Get any 'work' done?"

Okay, maybe not so calm.

He froze momentarily, then went back to his wiping.

"Yeah, enough." His voice was nonchalant, but he avoided her gaze as he scooped up the cloth, methodically shook it out into the garbage can, rinsed it out, and laid it flat to dry. She watched him take a deep breath, then paste the charming smile he usually reserved for his flirtations onto his face as he came over to sit on the coffee table in front of her, oozing indifferent ease.

She wasn't buying it.

"Why did you call Erica in?"

The smile faltered, but didn't drop. "What makes you think I did?"

"I happened to see her pull into the parkade and assumed you had called her in. Why else would she be there on a holiday?" Her belly knotted as she waited for his response.

"I, um, I . . . you know. I'm working on a big case, so I needed her help."

Sarah nodded and shifted her position so she was a little more upright. She still felt defenceless with her foot up, but at least it didn't feel like the soft couch had trapped her in irons.

"I had texted her to join me. If she was working, why didn't she just say that?"

Craig's smile disappeared. He frowned and crossed his arms. "I don't know, Sarah. She's my assistant, but she's your friend. What did she tell you?"

"She said she couldn't meet me because she was at her mom's."

"Well, she never mentioned it to me."

Sarah clenched her jaw.

"No, I suppose not, since I assume the whole thing was a lie because she was about to have sex with you. You two are having an affair, aren't you?"

Craig bolted erect. His face flushed and his jaw dropped slightly. "What? You're insane! You know I would never cheat on you! I'm insulted you would even suggest it! Why would you think that?"

Had she been wrong? He looked so authentically wounded. Maybe she had read the facts wrong, after all.

"I saw her text last night." Sarah fidgeted with her sweater hem. "It said she missed you and wanted to see you. Then I saw that you had called her in on a holiday and she lied to me today when I asked her for coffee. What else do you think I would suspect?"

Craig seemed to be searching for words. "Oh, that? Well, um, she has been behaving a little too familiarly lately. I've spoken to her about it several times, but I guess I'll have to do it again. Just because we're friends doesn't mean she can act that way at work. I'm sorry I never mentioned it. I guess I didn't want you to worry about something that I thought I had handled."

Sarah searched his face, trying to divine the truth. He looked completely sincere. She hesitated.

Should she believe him? It was plausible, and if it were the truth, the massive dilemma she had been wrestling with since yesterday would be reduced to having a husband who hits her sometimes but not one who cheated on her. The first was still a problem but came without the deep sense of personal betrayal that an affair would. Why would she automatically assume the worst—especially when doing so could be so devastating for her future?

She suddenly felt exhausted. She had been running on adrenaline and suspicion since last night, her ankle pulsed with pain, and with the realization that all of her fear may have been for nothing, all the fight fled from her. She was too tired to worry about this anymore.

"If that's the case, then I'm sorry for doubting you." Her vision blurred with tears as she realized she had nearly thrown away the most solid relationship in her life. How could she have done such a thing? And how must Craig be feeling under her false accusations? She had to fix this. "I'm such an idiot sometimes. Can . . . can you forgive me?"

She expected him to continue to be angry and defensive, but he surprised her.

Craig rested his elbows on his knees so their eyes were on a level, and tenderly brushed a tear from her cheek. "Of course I will. You know how much I love you. Trust me, you are my one and only."

She nodded slowly. He cupped her jaw and gave her a lingering kiss. As he pulled away, she sniffled and wiped her face, amazed at his gentleness—and grateful for it.

"Look, Sarah. I don't know why Erica lied to you, but I certainly haven't. Sounds like you two have some stuff to work out. Would you like me to talk to her about it?"

Sarah shook her head. "No, I'll deal with it. Thank you for being so understanding. I don't know what I did to deserve you."

"Got lucky, I guess." His sudden grin belied the arrogance of his words.

She chuckled through her tears. Relief and remorse flooded her with warmth toward the man she had married, and she yearned to feel him close to her, to show him that she was truly sorry for her suspicions and to know he still desired her. She reached a hand toward him. "Come here, you."

Craig obligingly bent to kiss her again, long and deeply. She closed her eyes and let the kiss chase away the doubts that had been plaguing her since last night. Yes, Craig had his problems, but then, so did she. They could get through it. That's what you did when you were married—you worked through it, right?

Craig made a trail of small kisses toward her ear, then down her neck. His fresh aftershave left a musky scent in her nostrils. She opened her eyes to run her fingers through his hair—

And there it was.

A smudge of plum lipstick behind his ear. A colour that Sarah didn't even own—but that Erica wore every single day.

He had been pushing her back toward the couch again, but she stiffened and pushed him away. He sat back on the coffee table, brows drawn together in concern. "Did I hurt your ankle?"

Sarah shook her head and sat up, leaning on her arms for support. Blood rushed through her ears. "No, I just have one more question." Her voice sounded much calmer than she felt. "How did Erica's lipstick get behind your ear?"

Craig's eyes widened and his jaw started opening and closing like a fresh-caught fish.

"Sarah, I—" His voice broke and he stopped, speechless. The man who always had something to say was mute.

Caught.

It was the confirmation she had been dreading. She saw in his eyes that he knew she knew. A dagger slid into her heart, and it should have killed her—and would have, if she hadn't been undead for years. Instead of buckling, she felt something inside go very still and hard.

For once, she let the anger take her. Today, anger felt safer than fear.

"You bastard." Her voice was the slow cold of a glacier on granite.

Craig pulled back as though struck.

She felt the rage build in her chest, growing from somewhere primal and gathering intensity as the words ripped out of her throat.

"You *bastard*!" She leapt up as she said it, the bag of peas falling unheeded to the floor. "You made me believe you! I *believed* you!"

For some reason, she barely noticed her throbbing ankle. Craig leapt up, too, stepping back. She must look pretty wild to make Craig give ground.

"How long?"

Craig stared at her blankly.

"How long have you been sleeping with Erica?"

Craig blinked and closed his mouth, face hardening. Sarah's chest heaved as though she had run a mile.

They stared at each other for a moment in silence.

Craig's jaw worked and he crossed his arms. "You really want to know?"

Sarah wasn't sure she did, but she gave a tight nod.

"Over a year."

Sarah blinked. That was longer than Erica and John had been separated.

"And has there been anyone else?" Her balled fists were hot and sweaty at her sides. Her heart sounded like a freight train in her ears. Her knees shook and she tensed her legs to keep them from buckling, touching only the ball of her injured foot down for balance.

Craig narrowed his eyes. "Yes. And I'll tell you right now, you don't want to know how many."

Sarah rocked back as though she had been fisted in the gut. Her calves hit the sofa and she collapsed onto it, feeling dazed.

This seemed to be the opening Craig needed. He sat down on the stuffed leather chair facing her and rested his arms on the sides, suddenly casual. He smirked.

"It's your fault. You know that, right?"

Sarah pulled in her scrambling thoughts and focused them on Craig's words. "*What?*"

"You heard me, you frozen bitch." Craig scratched his chin. He might have said that it was cold outside, or that the Eskimos were playing this weekend, for all the emotion in his voice.

Sarah felt her own fury rise in response and swallowed convulsively, trying to work some moisture into her chalk-dry mouth.

"I never could figure out how you could write a sex scene that could make the words melt off the page but be such an ice cube in bed. Sometimes I wondered if you were even awake. Tell me honestly—did you think that would satisfy me?"

Sarah felt like she had been punched again. She shook her head in denial, trying to make his words make sense with her memories of their life together.

"I—I never once turned you down. I gave you sex whenever you wanted it. I did whatever you asked of me." Sarah cringed at some of the things she had done at his request. She had told herself it was okay because Craig was enjoying it, and if it made her feel dirty, well, that was nothing new. "What more did you want?"

"Oh, I don't know—maybe some hint that you were enjoying yourself? Some spark? A little *passion*?"

"But—you married me! We were going to have a baby. You said you *loved* me! Didn't you mean any of it?"

Craig's eyes didn't soften a bit. "Of course I love you. Love has nothing to do with it. And honestly? I never wanted a baby—that was your idea. I only agreed because it meant you would be travelling less, and I'd know where you were."

Sarah stared at the stranger she had married. It had been lies. All of it. He said he loved her, but the things he said seemed far from loving.

His accusations of her being frozen echoed in her ears. How could this have happened again? First her father, then her last boyfriend Chris, now Craig. No matter what she did, she couldn't make a man happy.

And they always lied.

Maybe he was right. Maybe this *was* somehow her fault. And she probably deserved it—her own conscience constantly told her she did, so it was no surprise that Craig agreed. But she knew she couldn't bear to look at his cheating, lying face for one moment longer. Her ice castle was already splintering.

Sarah struggled to stand up, but the pain that speared her ankle made her bite her lip and she sat down involuntarily.

Craig stiffened. "What are you doing?"

"Leaving. I can't deal with this right now." She reached for the coffee table to use as leverage.

In a flash of motion, Craig crossed the space between them and smacked her across the cheek. "Like hell you are."

Her hand flew protectively to her stinging face. It felt like her head had been ripped from her body.

Craig grabbed Sarah by the hair and dragged her to sit upright. She gave a small scream as all her fury evaporated instantly into fear.

"Craig, stop it! You're hurting me!"

He grabbed her jaw and squeezed, forcefully caressing it with his thumb. His face was only inches above hers, a wicked grin marring his features.

Sarah's breath came fast and shallow. What was he going to do now?

"You want to know why I married you?"

Sarah's eyes rolled sideways to see his face. He seemed to take her silence as permission to continue.

"I married you because you needed me to." His hideous smile widened. "You were a mess before you met me. You didn't even know how to dress. I made you what you are. That's how I know that you aren't leaving. Because you're nothing without me, and I won't let you go."

He pulled on her hair, dragging her face up toward him, and used his free hand to pin her chest to the sofa. He kissed her so hard that her lips hurt. She squirmed and pushed on his shoulders, trying to break free, but he didn't budge. Her head was swallowed by the soft couch cushions. She felt like she was suffocating.

She bit his lip, hard.

Craig broke away swearing, still pinning her to the couch by the chest. She started beating at his stomach, but he caught her wrists in one hand and forced them above her head, immobilizing her. With his other hand, he released her chest and touched his lip. When he saw the red smearing his fingers, he swore again. Without warning, his left fist connected so hard with the side of her face that she felt her neck crack. A dark red curtain dropped in front of her vision for a few moments. Her cheek burned, and she tasted metal.

"That's it, you whore." Craig's spittle landed on her face. "I wasn't going to do this, but you asked for it."

What was he doing? She struggled to make sense of what she saw as the stars cleared from her vision. He seemed to be struggling with his belt buckle. He got it loose and unzipped his fly. Sense started returning to her addled brain and with it, horror.

As soon as he began dragging at her belt, she screamed and started bucking and writhing. She would fight until her last breath before she let him rape her again. She kicked at his backside with her knees, her ears full of cruel laughter as he worked the belt loose.

Without warning, Craig let out a howl of rage and leapt backward off of her. Sarah blinked and struggled upright. Nelson's jaws were clamped onto Craig's calf. He growled ferociously as he strained to pull Craig away.

"Let go, you filthy mutt!" Craig swung his fist around and caught Nelson behind the eye. He yelled as the dog snarled and bit harder.

Sarah used the distraction to struggle off the couch and away from her attacker. She snatched her keys from the coffee table. The pain in her ankle momentarily deadened by adrenaline, she eased around the writhing mass of man and dog toward the apartment door, never taking her eyes off of her husband. She grabbed Nelson's leash from its hook, backed against the door and used her most commanding voice.

"Nelson, drop it! Nelson, come!"

The dog hesitantly let go and came to her, keeping an eye on Craig and still growling low in his throat. Craig tried to dive for the dog and Nelson snapped at the man's hand. Craig snatched it back and scowled. He noticed the blood seeping through his jeans and bent to stanch the flow, glaring at Nelson. The dog kept growling at Craig while Sarah clipped on his leash.

"I'm going to kill you, you rabid, good-for-nothing mongrel!" Craig sounded like he meant it, but he stayed put in his awkward crouch, wincing in pain.

Sarah fumbled with the doorknob behind her back, keeping a wary eye on her husband. Finally, it opened, and she backed into the empty space.

"Craig, you might think I am nothing without you. But I'm nothing with you, either. I'm going to take my chances without you for a while."

His hurled obscenities were muffled by the slamming door.

She limped past the curious neighbours standing in their doorways, Nelson padding along beside her. She kept looking straight ahead, heart pounding, until she managed to get into her vehicle, out of downtown and had pulled off the freeway into the parking lot of a big block store mall. All the stores were long since closed because of the short holiday hours, so it was nearly deserted.

She sat there staring straight ahead at nothing for several minutes. Then the shaking started. She shook, and screamed, and realized she was crying when Nelson started licking tears off her face. She wrapped her arms around his neck and buried her face in his soft fur.

Sarah held on until the shaking became imperceptible and her wracking sobs reduced to hiccups. She sat up, wiped her face and blew her nose, dabbing at the blood that had crusted at the corner of her mouth. The lights in the parking lot flickered on, electric orange against the gentler watercolour hues of dusk.

She had no idea what to do next.

Her husband's ring tone sounded from the floor. She glanced down and realized she hadn't taken her purse into the apartment. She pulled the phone out of the side pocket and turned it off.

Sarah looked around and took stock. She had her phone. And her purse. And laptop. But other than those, her vehicle, and her dog, she had nothing. No clothes, no toiletries, no dog food, and very few options.

She patted Nelson's head. He gazed back at her with sad brown eyes and whined. She hadn't planned on bringing him, but after he had attacked Craig, she knew it would be too dangerous for him to stay.

"Guess we won't be staying in a hotel tonight, will we?"

He just looked at her.

Sarah sighed and put the car into gear. She only had one other option, and it was not one she relished.

"Settle in, boy. It's a long drive."

She pulled onto Calgary Trail South—toward Miller.

fifteen

ELLEN SET THE MUG OF CHAMOMILE TEA IN FRONT OF HER DAUGHTER ON THE KITCHEN TABLE ALONG with a teaspoon and a little plastic honey bottle in the shape of a bear. Sarah never could understand that marketing tactic—bears eat honey, not produce it. Right now, she didn't care. Wrapping her hand around the bottle made the shaking less noticeable, and the motion of stirring honey into tea soothed her frazzled nerves.

Ellen settled herself across from Sarah with her own mug and gave her daughter a measured stare. She had barely said a word since she'd opened the front door and took in Sarah's dishevelled appearance, brought Sarah in, sat her down and started the tea. The searching gaze Ellen was giving her now unnerved Sarah more than the silence, and she dropped her eyes to her mug.

"So, Craig hit you." It was a statement of fact.

Sarah nodded in response. There was nothing to say.

"And your ankle? Did he do that, too?" Ellen took a sip, her eyes never leaving Sarah's face.

Sarah shook her head. Her ankle was throbbing dully, despite being propped on the chair next to her smothered with a towel-wrapped ice pack.

"I rolled it this afternoon."

Ellen nodded, and they both took a sip of tea. "Do you want to tell me what happened?"

Sarah fidgeted with the mug, the teaspoon, the honey. Eventually, she sighed.

"I found out that Craig has been cheating on me. With my best friend. When I confronted him, he . . ." She waved a weak hand at her swollen eye and cheek and cut lip, not having the strength to go into details.

Ellen nodded. After a few minutes more passed in silence, she set her mug down with a decisive thud.

"You can stay here tonight, Sarah, but tomorrow, you need to go back and deal with this mess."

Sarah's head snapped up. "You can't be serious!"

"You bet I am. When your father and I had problems, do you think I went running home to mommy? Absolutely not. We worked it out."

Sarah snorted. "Sure you did."

Ellen frowned. "What is that supposed to mean?"

"Can you truly be that clueless about what went on in this house?"

"What are you talking about?"

Sarah threw up her hands. "Me. Dad. Everett. You have to know. All those years, you can't have been that oblivious."

"Sarah, I don't know what you're insinuating, but you better not say a word against your father. That man was a saint."

"A saint? Really? Just like Everett is now, I suppose? You know that Everett made a pass at me yesterday?"

"Sarah!" Ellen's hands slammed down on the table and made Sarah jump. "How dare you! I know you're not thinking clearly, but be careful you don't say something you'll regret."

Sarah probably should have stopped right there. She could have smoothed it all over and walked away. But she knew she couldn't stuff it back into the bottle. Not this time.

"Mom, you think you had a good marriage? Well, you didn't. And I *know* I don't. I'm not even sure what a 'good marriage' is. I've made excuses for my husband for years, but I'm through. He's beaten me, repeatedly. Last week, he raped me, and tried to do it again tonight. He *raped* me, Mom. Just like Dad and Everett used to do."

"Sarah!"

Sarah took a long, shaky breath. Her mother's eyes were as round as saucers in a face gone ghostly white.

Sarah met her mother's gaze with a pleading one of her own. "You can't tell me you didn't know. What mother doesn't know something like that about her own kid? Dad wasn't a saint. He was a child molester and a rapist." Tears flowed freely down Sarah's cheeks now. "And you let him do that to me."

Ellen stared at her, seemingly dumbfounded. After a few moments she stood up in deliberate slow motion, her fingertips tented on the tabletop.

"I think you'd better leave."

"Mom, I know you don't want to hear this, but it's true." Sarah's voice shook and she gripped her spoon so hard her knuckles went white. "What did you think Dad was doing in my room all those mornings before school? What did you honestly think?"

Ellen was shaking now, too.

"Sarah, leave."

Sarah put down her spoon and stood, bracing herself against the table to avoid putting weight on her injured leg. She tried to look her mother in the eye, but Ellen stared at the wall behind her.

Tears streamed down Sarah's face, and desperation clawed at her insides.

"Mom, are you seriously kicking me out right now, when I have nowhere else to go?"

Ellen didn't budge, just stared straight ahead of her.

Sarah shook her head in disbelief. Sobbing, she slung her purse over her shoulder and limped to the front door where Nelson lay on the rug. He jumped to his feet and wagged his tail. Sarah pulled his leash off the closet door knob and clipped it onto his collar, opened the door, then turned back to face her mother.

"All those years, all I wanted you to do was to protect me, to save me. But you didn't. I guess I should have known that nothing has changed."

Ellen didn't even glance at her.

The door slamming behind her sounded like the lid of hope's coffin falling into place.

Steve pulled Joanna's minivan off the highway onto the Miller exit ramp. He'd spent the day reconnecting with old friends from his college days. There weren't many left, which made him all the more thankful for the ones who kept in touch. Kallie and Sam were among the few who didn't reject him after his ex-fiancée, Vanessa, had publicly dragged his reputation through the proverbial mud.

His shoulders slumped in remembered shame. He took a deep breath and straightened them. No sense revisiting that. It was water long gone under the bridge. And he'd forgiven her—and himself—years ago. Mostly.

Stuff like that shows you who your real friends are.

He sent up a prayer of thanks that Kallie and Sam had stuck with him through it all. They had remained loyal friends, and were now avid supporters of his work in India. Today, they had surprised him by mentioning that they were hoping to come visit him there sometime in the near future. The prospect of showing his friends what he'd accomplished warmed him.

When Steve had backpacked through India after his third year of law school, Sam had been the one who had gone with him. Sam had been one of the few who didn't think Steve had completely lost his marbles when he decided to quit law school to work in Mumbai. Even Joanna had been skeptical of his intentions, pointing out his lack of connections and experience in running that sort of project. Thankfully, she had come around eventually and was now solidly on board with Love Mumbai.

A small chime sounded, and he glanced at the dashboard. The gas tank was on empty. Well, he had intended to fill up before bringing the van back anyway as a courtesy for his sister letting him take it. He pulled into the 24-hour Tags Convenience Store and Gas Bar that was the first building to greet him as he approached town.

He pulled up to an empty pump, then hopped out and started filling up, whistling to himself. At nearly 11 p.m. on Thanksgiving Monday night, Miller was deserted and mostly dark, but he was certain that the fluorescent lights of the gas station were visible from space. He absorbed the quiet, something he had rarely experienced in the last several years. Odd. He had missed this and often yearned for it, but now he found himself looking forward to the hustle and bustle of Mumbai.

A dog barked at him. He popped his head around the pump and saw a beautiful Golden Retriever on the front seat of the silver RAV4 opposite. He smiled.

"Hey, boy. Don't worry. Your owner will be back soon, I'm sure."

The dog barked a couple more times, then panted at him, obviously unconcerned.

Steve finished filling up, then decided that the iced tea he'd had before he left Sam's and Kallie's place an hour ago couldn't wait until he got back to Joanna's. He closed up the gas tank and headed inside to use the toilet.

Steve washed his hands, threw the paper towel into the bin and opened the door of the washroom just as the occupant of the other washroom across the narrow hall emerged.

"Oh, sorry." He stepped back to allow the woman by. Her head was down and she was wearing a slouchy white toque, but a second glance at the blond waves flowing down her back and the curve of her jawline as she turned away sent a jolt through him. She wore the same tailored black coat Sarah had worn in Duncan's yesterday. Could it really be her?

"Sarah?"

Sarah jerked her head around.

"Steve."

Of friggin' course Steve was here. Friggin' perfect.

She knew how she looked. She had spent the last five minutes trying to tidy herself up, but there wasn't much that could be done. Her right eye was already turning deep shades of purple and had swollen grotesquely, making it difficult to see. Her cut lip had bled again after she left her mother's. She had managed to wipe off most of the blood, but there was no hiding the wound. She had tamed her snarled locks with a comb, but her bloodshot eyes were a dead giveaway of all the tears she had cried today. She leaned against a pop rack to avoid putting weight on her ankle, which another round of ibuprofen had only made bearable, not pain-free.

To his credit, Steve's only reaction was a slight widening of the eyes and a small intake of breath. After a moment, he found his voice.

"What, uh, are you doing here? Do you need help?"

Now it was her turn to stare.

Do I need help? Her husband abused her, her mother rejected her, her brother bullied her, and her best friend betrayed her. Now a man she barely knew was asking her if she needed help?

Part of her screamed that she shouldn't trust him, that trust was what had always gotten her into trouble before.

But right then, she was too exhausted to care.

Man, I hope this guy is the real deal.

She nodded, unable to speak. Embarrassed, she ducked her head and wiped away a fresh batch of tears.

"Have you gone to the police?"

She shook her head, looking at his shoes. "I hadn't even thought of that yet. I was going to stay at my mother's, but she kicked me out." Her voice cracked at the end. She hated that she was crying in front of him, that she appeared so weak.

She hated that she *was* so weak.

The middle-aged Filipino man behind the till hollered over at them. "Everything okay, ma'am?"

Sarah buried her face in her elbow to absorb the tears, unable to speak. Steve cocked his head at the till.

"Yeah, it's okay. She's my friend. I'll take care of her." He hooked his arm under Sarah's and helped her hop toward the door.

I'll take care of her. The words echoed in Sarah's mind, and she looked up at Steve in wonderment. With all of Craig's meticulous attention to the details of her life, she couldn't say he had ever "taken care of her." No one had *ever* taken care of her. She didn't know what to think of it.

"Ma'am?" asked the cashier uncertainly.

Sarah wiped her dripping nose on her sleeve and met the man's eyes, nodding confirmation. He looked slightly relieved.

Steve held the door open and helped her hop through. "The RAV is yours?"

Sarah nodded, and they headed toward it. She protested as he opened the passenger door. He shooed Nelson into the back and helped her sit down.

"I can drive, you know." She grabbed his arm for support, which felt reassuring and solid beneath the denim of his jacket.

He looked at her sharply, but smiled kindly. "I know. You've gotten yourself this far. But now you can rest. I'll get you home."

"Home?" Her heart rate spiked. Was he going to try to force her to go back, too?

Steve pried her hand from his arm and held it, wrapping it in both of his. "*My* home. My sister's place. Not yours."

Sarah breathed again, and nodded. She let him lift her legs into the vehicle. He took extreme care with the swollen ankle. She felt a wave of relief as he eased her shoe off.

"Why do you keep rescuing me?"

Steve glanced up and the familiar grin lit up his face.

"'Cause I'm the one who will." He squeezed her arm, then stepped back, hand on the door handle. "I'm going to move the van. I'll be right back."

She nodded again, and he closed the door.

She laid her head against the seat and stared into the darkness beyond the gas bar's fluorescents. Home? Not her home.

But at least at Steve's sister's place, Craig would have no idea how to find her. That was home enough for tonight.

sixteen

THE SOUND OF AN INFANT CRYING DRAGGED SARAH OUT OF EXHAUSTED SLUMBER. SHE BLINKED AT the unfamiliar room, trying to get her bearings, and started to push herself to sitting. White pain from the vicinity of her ankle flashed behind her eyes and she winced, muttering a curse word under her breath. Carefully, she slid herself upright and oriented herself.

A trapezoidal patch of orange light from a street light reflected from one wall and provided gentle illumination. The pillow-top mattress of Joanna's basement guest room held Sarah in feathery comfort. Steve had been using the room, but he opted to sleep on the rec room sofa for the night so she could have privacy. The sheets still smelled faintly of his spicy aftershave and man sweat.

Slow, shuffling steps moved above Sarah's head and in a moment, the baby's crying ceased.

Exhaustion still dragged at her. Between the unfamiliar surroundings, the pain in her ankle, and the agony in her heart, she had slept fitfully. It felt early, but the sun rose so late at this time of year it was difficult to tell—dark was dark.

She felt around on the bedside stand for her phone. It wasn't there.

It must still be in my purse.

A feeling of helplessness swamped her, like she was floating at sea with nothing to grab hold of and no way to find shore. She glanced around the room in alarm, searching for her purse. What had been charming country-style decorative vignettes in the light when she had come into the room were now shapeless grey blobs without any distinctive features. She felt panic tighten her throat. She *had* to know what time it was. She *had* to have her phone. She had to have one thing in her life that was not completely out of control right now.

Where the heck did I leave my purse?

She spotted it on a chair across the room with her coat and laptop bag and took a deep breath to slow her pulse. Using the bed and bedside table as support, she manoeuvred to her feet. As soon as she tried to put weight on her ankle, her leg buckled and she knocked over the lamp. Swearing to herself, she set it upright and listened to see if anyone had been disturbed. There was a small wail from the baby, then nothing.

Holding her breath, she tried again with better success. She gingerly held her injured leg in the air and hopped over to the dresser where her belongings sat, hands extended to the walls and bed for support.

She reached the chair and perched on the edge of it while she rummaged for her phone. When she pulled it out of her purse, the screen was black. Dead.

Crap. Her charger was at home. She had a car charger in the RAV, but she didn't want to go outside and charge the phone right now—all she wanted was to know the time. She tried turning it on, hoping to get a few seconds to glimpse the clock before it died again.

4:15. Wowza. No wonder she was tired.

The battery also showed eighty percent power. Then she remembered—she had turned it off in order to avoid calls from Craig while fleeing the city.

Now that it was connecting with the cellular network, notifications started chiming. She covered the speaker with her hand while dropping the volume, cursing again. When she checked the screen, Sarah was shocked to see five voicemail messages waiting for her.

Nelson's faint whine reached her from somewhere far away. Steve had thought it best that her pet stay in the garage, as he wasn't sure how Joanna would feel about having a dog in the house. Sarah hadn't wanted to appear ungrateful, so she had agreed. Now, sitting here with a throbbing ankle and an aching heart in a stranger's house, she felt a desperate pang of longing for Nelson's company. But what if she ran into Joanna, still soothing her baby, and had to explain her presence? On the other hand, Joanna would probably be freaking out about a dog whining in the garage. Better that Sarah explain it, if necessary.

She tossed the phone onto the bed and hopped to the door, then silently inched it open. She ended up mostly crawling up the stairs and over the landing to the garage door. Nelson's whining became more desperate.

"Ssh, shh, boy. I'm coming."

She reached up and grabbed the knob, used it to pull herself to standing, and opened the door. As soon as it swung open a few inches, Nelson's soggy snout pushed through, snuffling and anxious and whining. She shushed him and forced herself into the space as the door opened so he wouldn't be able to push himself into the house.

As soon as she was through and the door was closed behind her, she collapsed on the rough carpet in front of the door and let Nelson slather her with affection. She threw her arms around his neck and buried her face in the soft fur, feeling like she had found her only anchor in the storm that was her life. After a few more doggy kisses, Nelson just sat there and let her hold him until she was ready to let him go.

When her butt cheeks had started to lose all feeling, she reluctantly released the dog—with a few whispered reassurances—and rose to return to bed. When she crept under the covers, the phone's display read 5:02 and the voicemail indicator still blinked at her impatiently. She chewed her lip, pondering whether or not to listen to the messages now.

After a moment, she put the phone on the night stand and turned her back to it, snuggling under the down duvet. She would bet that every voicemail was from Craig, and she wasn't interested in anything he had to say at 5:02 in the morning. After a few minutes, she dozed off again.

Steve lay on the couch and held his breath as Sarah slid down the stairs and snuck quietly into the guest room. He had been wide awake since she had gone up, listening, waiting . . . for what, he didn't know. To make sure she was coming back? Ridiculous. He hadn't been able to see her in the dark, but she hadn't seemed about to disappear into the night.

While he'd waited, he'd prayed. He prayed for this stranger, this friend by divine appointment, and all she was going through. He prayed for wisdom in how to help her. Above all, he prayed for her ravaged heart to heal.

The guest bed creaked as her weight settled into it. For some reason, tension he hadn't realized he'd been holding drained out of him. He couldn't do anything for her tonight—but at least he'd have the opportunity tomorrow.

Sleep crept up on stealthy toes and he sank willingly into its arms.

Sarah rose instantly out of the depths of a dream-stuffed sleep, her heart racing and the pillow wet from tears. She breathed hard, blinking in the lightening gloom.

In the dream that woke her, she had been a small bird in a cage. Everett was poking a stick through the bars, laughing as he tried to skewer her with it. Her father stood beside her brother, telling her what a special little bird she was as he honed an ax. In the background, Craig sat on the couch in their apartment, Erica on his lap. They were already at second base. He broke off sucking face with her former best friend and looked straight at Sarah.

"This is your own fault," he had said, a wicked grin on his face.

The evil laugh of dream-Craig still rang in her ears as Sarah stared at the stucco ceiling of a stranger's house. Her breath came in ragged, shallow gasps.

In her mind, she knew that Craig's cheating wasn't her fault. How could it be? Yet some part of her actually believed what he'd said. After all, if she had been a good enough wife, what need would he have had to cheat?

She wiped the remaining tears from her face, blowing her nose with a tissue from the nightstand.

The orange patch of man-made light on the wall was gone, replaced by the pervasive dull grey of October sunlight that struggled to pierce through the clouds. The room was cozily appointed with country-style dried flowers and a painted wooden sign that read "Welcome Home." She felt inexplicably comforted by such warm surroundings.

The sounds and smells of cooking emanated from the floor above, but the only voice she could hear sounded like a woman's, with an occasional happy squeal from the baby. Maybe Steve wasn't awake yet. She was in no hurry to explain her presence to Joanna without him.

The phone now read 8:17 a.m. Strange that, aside from the adrenaline rushing through her veins, she didn't feel any more rested than the last time she had checked the clock. Sighing, she decided she may as well get the voicemail ordeal over with and dialled her mailbox number.

Unsurprisingly, the first call was from Craig. The time stamp meant he'd probably left it immediately after she turned off her phone. She listened, horrified, as he raged and left her a litany of threats if she didn't come back, ranging from making sure she never had another penny to her name to killing Nelson. Silent tears started leaking down her cheeks again, wetting the inside of her ear. She almost deleted the message but decided that she better save it for now. She didn't know whether she would need it or not, but it might be evidence of the kind of abuse she had endured.

The next message was also from Craig. He sounded calmer, but the gist was still the same, if more subtly worded—come home, or there would be dire consequences.

The third message was from her mother. In a strained voice, she apologized for kicking Sarah out and told her that if she wanted to come back to stay the night, she could, and to please call her right away when she got the message.

It's a little late for that, Mom. Sarah grunted and frowned as she deleted the message. She still had a hard time believing that her own mother had turned her away. What mother does that? Was Sarah truly so worthless? She had almost as little desire to speak to her mother right now as she did Craig.

The next two messages were Craig and then her mother again. Craig's voice in this message was completely different. He sounded contrite and almost like he'd been crying as he apologized for what happened, begged her not to go to the police and to call him back so they could work this out and she could come home.

Her mother's voicemail had been left only fifteen minutes ago. She was "just trying to get in touch with you again since I hadn't heard back." Her voice was tinged with worry.

Good. Let her worry. Sarah would be damned if she would care about that right now.

She let the phone rest on her chest and stared at the ceiling. Her mind was so clouded with thoughts and emotions, it was difficult to make sense of much of anything. There was anger, definitely—anger at her mother, at Craig, at Erica, even at herself. Mostly herself. Also, a sense of betrayal that she recognized as an old companion.

Why was she surprised at what had happened? Why was she even grieving? Had she *ever* had a relationship that had worked?

Fear spiked through her thoughts, scattering the other emotions to dusty corners for a moment. What if this was it, her only shot, gone? What if her marriage to Craig was her last chance at happiness?

She remembered Steve asking her last night if she had gone to the police, and now Craig was begging her not to. She didn't understand all the repercussions of what would happen if she filed a domestic violence report, but she knew that Craig's entire career might be put in jeopardy. Was that what she wanted? Maybe there was another option—she could call him back and see if there was any hope for their marriage before going ahead and doing something drastic, right?

He had hurt her so badly, though. For some reason, she was much more willing to put up with his rages than his cheating. The rages and results of them were at least partially deserved because of all the mistakes she had made. But she knew she hadn't ever done anything that would deserve being cheated on. Even if he apologized and meant it, broke up with Erica, and never hit her again, could she ever trust him? His words about his past affairs rang in her ears—*you don't want to know how many*. How does a man with habits like that simply flip the switch? And would Craig even want to?

He'd tried to rape her again! If not for Nelson, he would have succeeded. She was no match for his strength, especially with her injured ankle. Could she stand to go through the rest of her life wondering when he would do that to her again? Could she survive it if he did?

She felt broken, more broken than she had ever been before. The little girl she had never been was curled into a corner of her heart, weeping uncontrollably. She felt as though Craig had crushed her very identity and sense of worth into the dust, and, like Humpty Dumpty, she didn't think repair was possible.

Sarah was hit by a wave of grief—for her marriage, her life, and that little girl. She buried her face in her pillow to stifle the noise and shook with body-wracking tears for several minutes. Eventually, the tears ran out with a few hiccupping sobs.

She wiped moisture from her stinging eyes and winced. Her right eye was extremely tender, and she could barely see through it. She turned her phone camera on to the selfie side and gasped as she examined the damage to her face. The swelling had gone down some in her eye since last night, but it was still puffed nearly closed and saturated with the most hideous shade of dark purple. The bruise extended down her face and mottled the skin near the scabbed-over cut on her still-puffy lip. There were several bruises on her wrists, too.

She cringed at the image on the screen, then snapped several photos of the damage. She hadn't been with a lawyer for four years without learning that you gathered evidence when you had it, because every scrap could be useful someday. She didn't know if she could go through with destroying Craig's life because of what he did—but she wanted to make sure she had evidence, just in case.

The phone rang in her hand, and she nearly dropped it in surprise. When she saw that it was her agent, she decided to answer it. She cleared the frog from her throat and hit the answer button.

"Hi, Becky."

"Sarah? Oh, thank heavens!"

Sarah wondered why Becky sounded so relieved.

"Are you all right? Craig called, asking if I'd seen you, saying that you never came home last night. He sounded very worried."

Sarah frowned. That explained it. "Of course he is." Man, that guy knew every trick in the book.

Or maybe he had become genuinely worried about her after he calmed down. Becky didn't even like Craig, and he knew it. She wondered who else he had called first, trying to track her down. Maybe he still cared for her a little after all.

"*Are* you all right?" Becky repeated.

Sarah sighed. "I'm fine. Craig and I had a fight and I stayed at a friend's. I'm sorry he dragged you into this. Sorry, and embarrassed. He never should have called you."

"It's fine, Sarah. Really. After all we've been through, I'm surprised *you* didn't call me if you needed me." She hesitated. "If you don't mind me asking, are you honestly going to be okay?"

Sarah's turn to hesitate. Okay? What a laughable idea. It would be laughable, anyway, if she could find anything funny at the moment.

"I'm sure I will be eventually. Things could be touch-and-go for a while, though. But I'll be sending you your chapters in a few days. I nearly have them finished." She cringed at the lie—she had nothing but a title, but wanted to put Becky off before she bugged Sarah about them again.

"Never mind about that. Take as much time as you need. And if you need anything else from me, call. Seriously."

Sarah blinked in surprise. "Thank you," she said, and meant it.

They exchanged goodbyes and ended the call.

Sophie's delighted giggle drifted down the stairs, muffled by the closed door and floor between. Still no sound from Steve. With a resigned sigh, Sarah decided she may as well get up.

She glanced into the rec room as she limped by on her way to the bathroom. The couch contained only folded blankets and a pillow in a neat stack at one end. Where was Steve?

The aromas of fresh coffee, cinnamon and oatmeal met Sarah as she struggled up the stairs. Her stomach growled, reminding her that she hadn't eaten at all since her late breakfast yesterday. She was ravenous.

Sarah entered the kitchen and saw Steve's sister sitting at the dining room table feeding his copper-haired niece. She stopped, feeling self-conscious.

Joanna looked up. Her oval face broke into a welcoming smile without a hint of surprise.

"Good morning." She set down the small bowl of mush she had been spooning into Sophie's mouth and stood to greet her guest. Sophie planted a chubby fist in her mouth and gurgled, whacking her other hand on the tray of her high chair.

"Hi." Sarah smiled shyly as they briefly clasped each other's hands.

"I hope you're hungry. Steve hardly ate a bite before he went to get the van." Sarah nodded. So that's where he was. "I'm starving."

"Go ahead and sit down while I get your breakfast." Joanna indicated a place at the dining room table.

The house was a typical eighties split-level. Sarah limped around the peninsula that separated the bright, well-appointed kitchen from the dining room and skirted the table, sitting down near the far wall. To her left, French doors opened onto a deck, and to her right she could see straight to the front door beyond the living room. The clouds must have lifted, because October sunshine streamed in through the south-facing living room picture window and bathed everything in an inviting glow.

"You like oatmeal?" Joanna asked.

Sarah nodded again. "And I *love* coffee," she said, gaining confidence.

Joanna grinned. Before Sarah could have counted to three, her hostess had placed a steaming cup of coffee before her, followed quickly by a spoon, a sugar bowl, and a carton of cream.

Sarah lifted the mug, waved it under her nose, and inhaled deeply. She took a sip of it black to steady herself.

"Heavenly," she breathed.

Joanna laughed.

"A fellow java junkie. Excellent."

Sarah smiled, then began spooning sugar into her coffee.

Joanna brought over a large bowl of cinnamon oatmeal and a small pot of honey and other fixings to go with it. She enquired whether Sarah wanted anything else, and when Sarah assured her that it all looked perfect, she sat down and resumed feeding her daughter. Unfortunately, Sophie seemed to have lost interest in the remains of her breakfast and kept spitting it out while making a scrunchy face. Joanna sighed and went to the sink to grab a cloth to clean up the mess.

Sarah practically inhaled the oatmeal, and soon the entire bowlful disappeared. Joanna scooped her a second helping as she made small talk, keeping the conversation light.

"So, Steve says you're a writer. What do you write?"

Sarah didn't bother dissembling. "Erotica. I recently released a book called 'Black Knight.'" She stirred honey into the hot cereal until it melted, then scooped a large spoonful of butter on top and repeated the process.

Joanna didn't appear phased. "Really? Do you enjoy it?"

Sarah froze. Her friends didn't usually ask her that question.

She blinked to cover a flicker of anger as she realized that thanks to Craig, Erica had been her only remaining friend. And now that friendship was gone, too—also thanks to Craig.

"Um, no. I keep trying to get my agent to let me write something else, but apparently she thinks I'm a sure paycheque in the erotica genre. Maybe it's all I'm any good at." She shrugged, trying to blow it off, but felt the implied criticism of Becky's explanation etch further into her core, like a groove that has been worn deep by repeated tracing.

Joanna lifted Sophie out of the high chair. "I'm sure that's not true. What would you prefer to write?" She set her daughter down in a sitting position on the living room carpet and surrounded her with a soft blanket.

Sarah chewed slowly, wondering how much she should tell Joanna. She seemed nice enough, but right now Sarah had no idea whom she could trust. However, the fact that Joanna had been raised with Steve and he seemed to think highly of her marked up several points in her favour.

"I'm hoping to write a biography next."

"Really," Joanna repeated, this time an exclamation of interest more than a question. Her task done, she grabbed her coffee and sat down across from Sarah but kept an eye on her daughter. "Good for you."

Sophie blew spit bubbles from the centre of a nest of toys. She seemed more interested in making an undulating whooping sound with her hand moving back and forth against her mouth than playing with any of the dolls and balls and brightly-coloured plastic whatsits around her.

"So what do you do?" Sarah asked between mouthfuls.

Joanna took a sip from her mug and made a wry face. "Mostly drink cold coffee and change dirty diapers." She got up and retrieved a small pot from the cupboard, pouring in the tepid brown liquid. Sarah wondered why Joanna didn't simply pop it into the microwave, then realized she couldn't see one in the kitchen anywhere.

"I mean, do you work outside the home?"

"Not right now." Joanna stirred the coffee with a spoon. The metal-on-metal of the spoon swirling in the pan made a rhythmic silvery swooshing sound. "I'm on maternity leave. In my previous life I was a bookkeeper for an office here in town. Can't say I miss it, so I haven't decided what I'll do when it's time to go back." The coffee began to steam. Joanna clicked off the burner and poured the coffee back into her mug. She took a sip and smiled. "Much better."

Sophie squealed and threw a teething ring as far as she could, then reached out a grasping hand to pick up something else and fell over onto the blanket ring. She rolled from her side to her stomach, lifted her wobbly head to look at her mother and let out a low wail.

"It's okay, sweetheart." Joanna set her mug on the table and picked up her daughter. She kissed the baby's cheek with a loud squelching noise that made Sophie giggle before setting the little girl down amidst the toys again. Sophie began happily smacking at the playthings, and Joanna sat back down at the table.

Sarah admired the child's fair, chubby cheeks and cap of red curls and felt her stomach clench. Would she ever have a chance to hold her own child, or was she doomed only to admire other's babies forever? It was so not fair! Why was her life so hard, and other people's lives so blessed? Even if her marriage hadn't been on the rocks, the cancer could still have stolen any chance she had to—

Cancer! Surgery! In all of the other drama, she had completely forgotten that her LEEP procedure was scheduled for tomorrow. She rested her elbows on the table and held her head in her hands, feeling the beginnings of a headache coming on.

"What's wrong?" Joanna's brow furrowed in concern.

Sarah opened her mouth to reply, but right then the front door opened and admitted a blast of fresh autumn air and Steve, his arms full. Standing on the landing as he was, Sarah couldn't see what he was carrying. He set his packages down and glanced around the room through the gaps in the railing. When he saw Joanna and Sarah, his face split into a grin.

"Sarah, I hope Nelson likes fish, because that's the flavour of dog food I got. Jo, would you grab me some scissors and a bowl for his food?"

Sarah's jaw dropped. "You bought dog food?" She gingerly stood and limped over to the top of the stairs to see it for herself. Sure enough, a large bag of dog food sat by Steve's feet. "You really didn't have to do that."

Steve grinned. "Who said anything about 'have to'?"

Joanna appeared beside her with a plastic Tupperware dish and some scissors. She handed them down to her brother, who thanked her and then set to work opening the bag. "Do you think he'll want a walk before or after he eats?"

Sarah hadn't been able to take Nelson for a walk the night before. She chewed her lip, wondering if it might be too late for a walk and she would need to clean up a mess in the garage.

"Um, he hasn't had a walk since yesterday morning, so I should probably take him out first."

Steve glanced up at her, a "don't-be-ridiculous" frown on his face.

"You're not going anywhere, Missy. Where's his leash?"

Sarah blinked and felt a sudden, idiotic urge to cry at the kindness of these strangers. "It's, um, in my coat pocket."

Steve opened the small closet and rummaged around in her coat until he found what he was looking for, then turned back to her in mock sternness.

"Now, go sit down and drink your coffee, young lady. Nelson and I will be back soon."

Sarah gave a tight smile, not trusting herself to say anything at the moment.

"Hey, Jo, can you start some tea for when I get back?"

Joanna nodded, already heading to the kitchen. "You bet."

Then Steve disappeared through the garage door and Sarah stood there staring after him in gratitude and amazement.

She wasn't sure why these people were being so nice to her. Part of her kept waiting for the other shoe to drop.

But mostly, she had never felt so thankful.

seventeen

BY THE TIME STEVE GOT BACK, SARAH WAS BEGINNING TO FEEL AT EASE. SHE AND JOANNA SAT IN the living room—Sarah in an overstuffed chair, Joanna playing with Sophie on the floor while they visited. Sarah had found out that Joanna's husband Derek was a bank manager by day and a chef by training, with dreams of opening his own restaurant. They were still saving up for that dream.

The garage door opened and Steve appeared. He grabbed the bowl of dog food and disappeared through it again momentarily, then came in empty-handed and took off his things.

"Everything go okay?" Sarah asked. From her chair in the front corner of the room next to the railing, she could easily see down the stairwell. Steve's rugged features were ruddy from the cool morning air, his ears pink against his sandy blond curls.

"Of course. Nelson and I are old buds, now. He's happy as a clam in sand with his breakfast, too."

Despite her inner turmoil and uncertain future, Sarah couldn't help but smile at Steve's perky banter. He came up the stairs and plopped himself down on the couch. Joanna brought him his mug of tea and sat back down on the floor with Sophie.

The little girl squealed with delight when she saw Steve, stretching out her arms toward him and making a grunting sound that seemed designed to get his attention.

"Well, how can an uncle say no to that?" Steve grinned as Joanna lifted Sophie over her head and into his arms. He held his niece upright with one arm and tickled her round belly with the other. Sophie giggled and squirmed.

Steve laughed, then bounced her and turned toward Sarah.

"So," Steve began. This already sounded serious. "Would you like to tell us what happened last night?"

Sarah's gut clenched as she tried to decide how to respond. "Um . . ." She stopped and fidgeted with her shirt—the same one she'd been wearing yesterday.

Steve tucked Sophie into the crook of his arm and entertained her by letting her grab at his fingers, but his attention was all on Sarah. Joanna quietly began picking up toys and putting them into a bucket. Sophie reached for one, a teething ring in the shape of a duck, and Joanna put it in her pudgy fist. The baby shoved it into her mouth.

Sarah studied all this as she formulated her words. What should she tell them?

"It's okay, Sarah. You're safe here." Steve's face and voice calmed her. How she desperately wanted to believe him. With surprise, she suddenly realized that she did.

"I, uh, found out my husband has been having an affair. It was stupid to confront him alone, especially with a sprained ankle. I know what he is capable of."

Joanna looked surprised. "How did you sprain your ankle?"

Sarah didn't know why, but she felt compelled to total honesty with these two.

"Botched a landing while skydiving yesterday afternoon."

Steve cocked an eyebrow.

"Well, aren't you just full of surprises?" He grinned appreciatively.

Sarah blushed, and continued.

"Anyway, I did confront Craig. He admitted to the affair and said that there had been others. When I tried to leave, he attacked me. He . . . he tried to r-ra—" She couldn't get the word out.

Joanna put the toy bucket aside and shifted closer to Sarah, laying a comforting hand on her knee.

"It's okay, honey. We get it."

Sarah nodded and drew a shaking breath. "If it weren't for Nelson, I wouldn't have gotten out of there before he succeeded." She smiled grimly as she remembered Nelson's jaw clamped around Craig's leg. She lowered her gaze to her hands and whispered, "It wasn't the first time."

Joanna took her hand and squeezed, and Sarah was grateful for the comforting warmth of it.

A tear tracked down the side of Sarah's nose and dripped off the tip. "I don't know what I'm going to do."

Steve stood, still holding Sophie in the crook of one strong arm, and squatted beside her chair. He took her free hand in his.

"It's going to be a tough road for a while. But I want you to know that you won't be alone. We'll help you out."

"Yes." Joanna nodded in confirmation. "You can stay here with us for as long as you need until you get stuff settled. Do you want one of us to take you to the doctor to get checked over?"

Sarah looked from one to the other in amazement.

"You barely know me. Why are you doing this?"

Joanna smiled kindly. "You need help. We can give it. That's all the 'why' we need."

"But what about your husband?"

"Derek and I already talked about it before he left for work. He's okay with it."

Sarah's jaw dropped. She hadn't even met Derek and had only seen Joanna for a few minutes in the grocery store when this couple decided to let her stay in their home, despite having a seven-month-old baby. Tears of gratitude started flowing freely down Sarah's face.

"I—I don't know what to say."

"Say you'll let us help you." Steve gave her hand a gentle squeeze. His large hand felt warm and rough compared to Joanna's small, cool one.

Sarah nodded, sniffling. They let her have her hands back so she could wipe her face. Joanna handed her a tissue.

"Now. Should we take you to the doctor? That eye looks pretty bad, but I'm mostly worried about your ankle."

Sarah shook her head. "I'm fine, as far as that's concerned. Only . . . I'm scheduled for a procedure at the Cross Cancer Institute tomorrow. Craig was supposed to come with me, but . . ."

Both Steve's and Joanna's eyes widened.

"You have cancer, too?" Steve sounded a little choked.

"It's cervical cancer. My oncologist is optimistic that we should be able to get all of it with this procedure, and that I won't need more drastic intervention. It's only a day surgery, thankfully."

Steve nodded. "Well, I'll go with you, no problem. I don't have much scheduled until the weekend. Now, what about all"—he indicated her facial injuries with his hand—"this? Do you want to go to the police?"

Sarah opened her mouth, but no sound came out. She still wasn't sure what she should do about that.

Joanna cocked her head. "Do you hear something?"

They grew quiet, and Sarah heard her phone's ringtone—Craig's ringtone—drifting faintly up the stairs.

"Shoot. That's my phone. I left it downstairs this morning."

"Do you want it?" asked Joanna, already rising.

Sarah hesitated. She wasn't sure she did. But Joanna was halfway down the stairs already.

"It's on the nightstand."

"'Kay."

By the time Joanna got back upstairs, the phone had long since stopped ringing. Just as Joanna handed it to Sarah a voicemail notification chimed.

Sarah stared at the phone. "That was Craig."

Steve's mouth pressed into a thin line.

"Do you want me to listen to it for you?"

Sarah shook her head. "No, I can do it."

Joanna and Steve gave her some privacy by retreating to the kitchen.

Craig sounded frantic, almost begging her to call him and let him know she was okay. He mentioned that he'd been calling everyone he could think of trying to find her.

When she finished listening to the message, she stared at the phone for another few minutes. She decided that she wasn't ready to talk to him just yet, but thought it wouldn't hurt to let him know she was all right. She opened her texting app.

Got your messages. I stayed at a friend's last night. I'm fine.

It was only seconds before his reply came in.

Thank God! I've been worried sick! Which friend?

Sarah chewed her lip. If Craig knew where she was, she knew that the feeling of safety she had right now would immediately go away.

No one you know.

It was almost a minute before his next text came.

When will you be home?

Sarah frowned. That was brazen. Like she would go back to living with that man, just like that. Did he think they could pretend that nothing had happened and that life could go on as it had before?

When will you apologize for beating me, raping me, and cheating on me?

His response was so long in coming, she thought maybe he wouldn't send one. But after several minutes, the phone cheeped.

Sarah, I want you home, but not if you are going to spew such nonsense. Yes, I cheated. I've already talked to Erica and told her we're done. As for the rest, I can't believe you'd accuse me of lifting a finger to you.

Sarah gaped. Was he really denying everything that had happened, as though she wasn't sitting here with a black eye and a swollen cheek and a mouth that hurt to move? And although she was glad he'd ended things with Erica—if that was even true—she noticed that he still didn't apologize. Her nostrils flared and she slammed her fist onto the arm of the chair.

Steve strolled into view, crossed his arms, and leaned against the dining room wall.

"You okay?"

"Not really," Sarah growled, still staring at Craig's last message. "But I've decided what I want to do today." She looked straight into Steve's eyes. "Would you come with me to the police?"

The rest of the day was long and exhausting. After being interviewed by a policeman, Sarah wrote out a statement about what had happened the night before in as much detail as possible. When that ordeal was done, Steve agreed to take her to the apartment to get some things. Even though she was sure Craig would be at work (or maybe in jail, as the officer said he would be arrested and held for at least twenty-four hours—the thought made her smile, and then she felt guilty for being happy about that), she still felt very relieved to find he wasn't at home.

The apartment had been trashed. It looked like Craig had taken out his unspent anger on everything breakable that the two of them owned. She shed a few tears when she found an heirloom teacup her grandmother had given her in shards behind an overturned spider plant.

She resisted the urge to tidy up. Instead, she packed her clothes—some of which she found in the garbage—anything else she treasured and didn't want to leave to Craig's tender mercies, Nelson's dog dishes, toys, and brush, and then they left.

By that time she and Steve were both hungry, so they went for a very late lunch at the Canuck Cafe. Sarah was glad she had found some big sunglasses while packing, which she used to conceal some of her injuries.

"Hey, I guess we didn't miss our lunch date after all," Steve joked as they were seated.

Sarah chuckled. With everything else that had happened, she had forgotten about their lunch date. Ironic.

"So, since we're here, what was it you wanted to talk to me about?"

Sarah chewed her lip and scanned the menu. Now that she was staying in the same house as Steve, she was nervous about asking him about the book. What if he said no? Would that make things awkward between them?

But what if he said yes? Was she even up to the challenge?

The waitress stopped by for their drink order, giving Steve an appreciative glance. Sarah noticed, but Steve didn't. The waitress also gave Sarah's face a double-take, but didn't say anything.

When the woman left, Sarah faced Steve.

"This might sound presumptuous. And I hope it doesn't make things weird between us."

Steve's mouth quirked in a quizzical smile.

"Whatever it is, I'm sure it will be fine."

"Okay." Sarah fidgeted with her napkin and cutlery and cleared her throat. "I, uh, I was wondering if you would consider letting me write your biography."

Steve's eyes widened. He leaned back and ran his fingers through his hair.

"You want to write a biography? About me? What on earth for?"

Too late to take it back now. There was nothing to do but keep going.

"Your work in India is extremely interesting. I thought it might be a way to spread the word about Love Mumbai. And to be honest, I'm hoping that once my agent sees what else I can do she will finally stop forcing me to write erotica."

Steve rested his elbows on the table and clasped his hands.

"Has she truly been forcing you?"

"Pretty much."

"What, gun to head? Blackmail? Lien on your firstborn child?"

Sarah chuckled at his ridiculous suggestions. "As good as. My publisher has me on contract. When my first contract was up, they said they wouldn't sign me for anything but erotica again, which makes sense, because that's pretty much all they do. Besides that, my agent didn't seem to think I should even try to change genres. She always told me that I'm such a superstar in this one that I'd be crazy to change to something different. I felt painted into a corner."

"Hmm. And do you think your agent was right?"

Sarah shrugged uncomfortably. "Why wouldn't she be? I'm sure she knows what she's talking about."

"Did you ever consider going to a different agent?"

Sarah shifted in her seat, avoiding his eyes. "No, I guess not. Craig—" She swallowed a lump in her throat so she could continue. "Craig found her for me, and he wouldn't have wanted me to change. But you know, she *is* pretty sought-after. I doubt I could get another agent as high-profile as Becky on my own. Besides, after being with her for almost four years, wouldn't it seem a little ungrateful to ditch her for someone else?"

"I don't know." Steve frowned slightly. "If a professional isn't fulfilling their end of a contract, I don't think you need to continue paying them simply out of loyalty. Wouldn't a lower-profile agent who is on your side be better for your career than a high-profile one trying to make you do things her way?"

Sarah frowned. She couldn't think of any rebuttals she liked. "It's not as simple as that."

"It's not?"

"No. There are plenty of other factors to consider. You're not a writer. How would you know?"

Steve blinked. "You're right. I'm not. And I wouldn't. Sorry for putting my nose where it didn't belong."

Sarah's stomach twisted. He hadn't deserved that. "It's okay. You didn't know."

"I think we just established that. Along with the reason you are stuck writing material you would rather not write. I'm clearly very ignorant of the publishing industry."

"Clearly."

The drinks came, and Steve asked for a few more minutes before ordering. When the waitress left, Steve became very absorbed in squeezing the lemon wedge into his iced tea and testing the results. Then he studied his menu intently—and very quietly.

Sarah chewed her lip unhappily. She didn't know him well, but she did know it was unusual for him to have no further comment. He was being too deliberate about avoiding her eye.

Guilt pecked at her, and she scowled at the tablecloth. She felt bad for turning the conversation around on him. He'd only been curious, after all. And she *had* sometimes felt uncomfortable with Becky's insistence that the erotica genre was her best bet, but Craig had always backed her agent up. And she knew Craig would have been furious if she'd fired Becky—who was the wife of one of his colleagues—and gone looking for someone else.

All that aside, though, why *hadn't* she ever tried writing in a different genre? She'd done very well writing advertising copy for her college courses, but after she'd published her first novel in her second year—to instant success—the only professional work she had turned out had been erotica. It had always been easy to blame Craig and Becky and even Yolanda for keeping her stuck in the genre, but as she struggled to answer Steve's line of questioning, she had to admit the truth.

"I wasn't brave enough to try," she blurted.

Steve looked up. "What?"

"Until I met you, I was never brave enough to put my foot down and insist that I wanted to write something different. I was afraid that I wouldn't be able to write anything else, that this is all I was good at. That day in San Francisco, you told me that it's never too late to make a change. I haven't been able to get that out of my head since. That's why I want to write your biography. I want to believe you're right, that it's not too late."

Steve looked thoughtful. "That was what? A little over a week ago? You certainly seem to be taking my words to heart. Look at all the changes you've made since then."

Sarah took in a breath to deny what he said, then paused. Other than pursuing a different direction in her career, she didn't consider the other changes to be her choice. But in retrospect, she could have pretended she didn't know about the affair. She could have stayed with Craig and continued to endure the abuse. She could even have left Craig but not reported him to the police. But that's not what she did.

While the Victim Services liaison had been telling her what to expect if they went forward with filing the assault claim that morning, Sarah had realized that this choice was about more than revenge or keeping herself safe. It was almost as good as serving Craig divorce papers. His pride would never allow her to come back after he had been suspended from his job—which seemed likely—and if he did, it wouldn't be for love. The public humiliation alone would make him hate her, and he would never, ever forgive her. He was also the type to hold a grudge—regardless of the choice she made about filing, he would punish her for leaving him in any way possible for a long, long time.

She had gone ahead and filed the claim. It was up to the police to determine if there was enough evidence to press charges, but she'd made her choice. She had endured abuse and injury at the hands of all the men in her life who were supposed to protect her, and she was done with it. She was protecting herself, now.

It was difficult to feel good about anything in this screwed-up life of hers, but she realized that, for the first time, she had done something to make a positive change in it. She smiled.

"Yeah. I guess I have made a few. Some of them were hard changes, but I'm glad I made them."

Steve lifted his iced tea glass in a toast. "To new beginnings."

Sarah picked up her wine glass and clinked his. "I'll drink to that."

They ordered their meals, then the conversation shifted to more mundane topics until the waitress returned with large plates of food. The woman flirted shamelessly with Steve as she slid his entrée onto the table in front of him.

Sarah wasn't sure whether to be offended or amused.

Again, Steve seemed oblivious to the young woman's attentions, returning her comments with politeness, nothing more. When she'd left, he opened up his napkin and put it in his lap.

"So I take it this wouldn't be an officially-sanctioned project?" Steve arched his brows at Sarah over the turkey bacon club he held in both hands, not eating.

Sarah shook her head as she buttered a warm roll. It had taken her forever to choose what to eat, mostly because she had never fully examined the menu here before. For years, she had either let Craig order for her in restaurants or simply ordered whatever the friend she was with was having, unless it was something she detested. She had decided to be as adventurous as seemed wise with a cut lip—which was to say, not very. But she had never had the roasted red pepper and Gouda soup before, even though she had thought of ordering it several times.

Look at that. Another change.

She smiled to herself as she replied.

"I'd be writing it on spec. I'm still under contract for one more erotica novel. I already checked to see if I could wiggle out of it to write your bio instead, and the answer was no."

Steve clasped his hands casually together above his plate, bowed his head and closed his eyes for a few moments. Was he *praying*? Then he took a large bite.

"Mmm, delicious. Have I mentioned how hard it is to find a good club sandwich in Mumbai?"

"No." Sarah shook her head.

"They put cucumbers in theirs. Cucumbers! And they think fried eggs are the same as chicken or turkey. And bacon? Ha!" He analyzed the sandwich's layers appreciatively. "*This* is what I'm talkin' about."

"Cucumbers and fried eggs?" Sarah shook her head, amused, and stirred her soup to cool it.

Steve ate ravenously for a few minutes before continuing.

"So what if your agent doesn't find anyone interested in taking the book?"

Sarah paused in raising a spoonful of soup to her mouth, nonplussed. "I, uh, don't know. I guess I'll query other agents. Or self-publish." Just considering those ideas made her realize how much had changed in her life in the last week. She had always been too terrified of failure to pursue other avenues before. Smiling to herself, she took the bite. Tangy, savoury, and sweet flavours exploded in her mouth. The soup was delicious.

Steve chewed thoughtfully, then swallowed.

"You know, if what you really want is to write something more meaningful, you could try writing a different kind of book *this* go-round."

Sarah tilted her head. "What do you mean?"

"Well, I know you have to write your last contracted book. Would it be possible to do that and still make the story mean something in some way?"

Sarah's heart fell. He seemed to be trying hard to find reasons to refuse her request. But the truth was, she had already had the same thoughts about her upcoming book.

"I had wondered that myself. I think that's why I've been struggling so hard to begin this one. I have a title and a setting, but I'm not sure how far I can push my typical envelope before my publisher fires me. I guess I'm still not sure I'm brave enough." She watched him cautiously as she decided to take another risk. "I think what I want to do is to make it somewhat autobiographical."

His expression was bland. "What's the title?"

She swallowed. Moment of truth. "*Her Father's Daughter.*"

Steve stopped chewing and looked at her for a long moment. She could almost see him putting the pieces together—erotica novel, autobiographical, *Her Father's Daughter.* The man was no idiot. Other than her mother, he was the first person she had ever disclosed this part of her past to. She waited for the horror and revulsion she expected, the body language that would indicate that the doors of friendship were closing, but they never came. He simply nodded and looked thoughtful.

"Sarah, I think you already know what you need to do." His blue eyes met hers without blinking. She wanted to look away, but his gaze held her. "You think you're not brave enough, but you're wrong. There is strength in you that I don't even think you know about yet."

Sarah blinked at him, not sure what to say. The compliment was ludicrous, but also so sincere and unexpected that she sat frozen for a moment. For the second time today, she had the sudden, ridiculous urge to cry.

He leaned forward as though to make sure she wouldn't miss what he said next. "If you write that book, I think you might be the bravest person I know." He leaned back and took another bite.

Sarah knew it couldn't possibly be true. If only he could see how afraid she was of everything, even him, he would never say that.

But for a moment, it was nice to entertain the thought.

"So, what do you think?" Sarah scraped the last bite of soup from her bowl, scared to look up at Steve in case she didn't like the answer on his face. She had been on tenterhooks for the whole meal, waiting to see what Steve would say to her request.

Apparently, it hadn't weighed quite so heavily on his mind.

"About what?" Steve wiped his mouth with the napkin and took a big gulp of iced tea.

Sarah glanced up and frowned, brushing a stray piece of hair out of her eyes. "About the biography? Or do you need some time to think about it?"

Steve sat back in his chair and crossed his arms, a summer storm behind the ice-blue eyes. Finally, when she thought he might not answer, he spoke. "Sarah, I would love to help you. I think it's awesome that you want to do something that you believe in and make a difference. Trust me, I'm a big believer in following your passions. But . . . I can't." He sighed. "I'm going to have to say no."

Sarah's heart felt like it was being crushed. "But—"

"I'm sorry, Sarah. I'm just not ready for that."

She studied him for a moment, surprised when he dropped his eyes and fidgeted with a napkin. She'd never seen him look unsure about anything.

"You're sure I can't convince you to change your mind?"

"Yes. Please don't ask me again."

Disappointment throbbed through her, and she felt her eyes grow moist again. She pressed her lips together and nodded her head. "Okay."

Now what was she going to do?

eighteen

SARAH SHIFTED POSITION ON THE PADDED METAL CHAIR, TRYING TO GET COMFORTABLE. THE CHAIR wasn't all that uncomfortable—she was just so nervous that she couldn't seem to get settled.

The OB-GYN's waiting room was crowded. She tried to ignore the curious glances at her bruised face from the other patients, and wondered how many other people were here to get a LEEP procedure today. Then she wondered how many were here to get something more extreme done and felt a little better.

Next to her, Steve looked up from his paper, caught her eye, and gave her a reassuring grin. She gave him a tight smile in return and he went back to his crossword puzzle. She looked away, the annoyance she had felt toward him since yesterday's lunch bubbling beneath the surface. Being annoyed didn't make sense, and she kept trying to tell herself so. But her emotions weren't listening.

She still had a hard time accepting that Steve wasn't on board with the book. Maybe Erica had been right—maybe what he was doing in India wasn't as above-board as it seemed. That idea didn't jive with the man she had been getting to know for the last week and a half, but really, how would she know? She'd married a sociopath. Obviously, she wasn't the best judge of character.

A nurse in wildly-patterned scrubs and a pony tail of tight, glossy, black braids came into the waiting room, glancing at her clipboard.

"Sarah Daniels?"

Sarah's heart leapt into her throat. She stood, slinging her purse over her shoulder.

"I guess this is it."

Steve stood with her. "Do you want me to come with you?"

Sarah hesitated.

The nurse must have overheard his question.

"It's fine for your husband to come with you, ma'am. We're only doing pre-surgery prep."

Sarah felt heat start to creep up her neck. "Oh, no, he's not my husband," she blurted at the same time as Steve said, "We're just friends."

The nurse shrugged. "Well, either way, he can come for this part if you want him there."

Steve cast a questioning glance toward Sarah, and she responded with a slight nod.

They followed the nurse down a hallway and into a room that looked a lot like a typical examination room, except on a larger scale. There was a large light on a flexible arm attached to the ceiling above the exam table, a long counter with a sink and medical supplies on one wall, and several chairs along another wall by a window. Steve and Sarah settled themselves on the chairs. The nurse leaned against the counter opposite, a clipboard resting on her abdomen.

"You're pregnancy test was negative, so we're clear to proceed."

"Okay." Sarah was unsurprised, but the words still made her a little sad. Not that she and Craig had started trying yet, but would she ever have a different result? All she could do was hope—hope that this procedure worked and that she would eventually be able to carry a child to term, which may or may not be possible even if it went perfectly.

The nurse handed her a clipboard. "You've been told what the procedure entails?"

Sarah nodded, remembering too well the description of the hot wire that would be used to slice off part of her cervix. She shuddered.

"All right, hon, I need you to sign these papers. You can leave the clipboard over on the counter when you're finished. The doctor will be in to see you in a moment."

"Sure."

The nurse bustled out, closing the door behind her.

Sarah picked up the pen and scanned the form. It was a waiver that said she gave permission for the procedure to be done and understood the risks. She swallowed and fidgeted with the pen, tapping it on the clipboard.

Steve put a hand on her bouncing knee to still it.

"Hey. It's going to be okay." His voice was as soothing as his words.

Sarah glanced at him, then frowned and dropped her gaze back to the form. His perky attitude was usually one of his best features. Today she found it unbearably irritating, and she knew she wasn't doing a good job of hiding the fact.

"You don't know that for sure."

Steve let out a long breath and released her knee. "You're right. But I've got a good feeling about this."

Sarah looked into his face. He had a warm, reassuring smile. After a moment, she gave a small smile in return.

"Thanks for that."

"Hey, it's what I'm here for."

She signed her name in her neat hand, then put the clipboard on the counter and sat back down to wait. She realized she was bouncing her knee again and stopped.

Doctor Strickland—a small, redheaded bundle of energy in a white lab coat—bustled in a few minutes later. She stopped short when she saw Sarah's bruised face, studying her through gold-framed glasses. Her eyes flicked over Steve and she looked mildly confused. She had met Craig only the week before. Despite how busy the doctor was, Sarah was sure she would have remembered him and might be coming to conclusions already.

"Hello, Sarah. Good to see you again." Her vowels were clipped and her consonants precise, with the exception of an undefined quality to the "r"s and very open "a"s. She turned to Steve and extended her hand. "Hello. I'm Dr. Strickland."

"Steve," he replied, returning her gesture firmly. "I'm the designated driver."

Dr. Strickland smiled and turned back to Sarah.

"Did you do some boxing over the weekend?" While her words made light of it, the doctor's expression was all seriousness.

"Only as a punching bag. I'd rather not talk about it, if you don't mind."

Dr. Strickland nodded hesitantly. "Would you like to talk to someone else about it? I could get you some resources."

Sarah smiled politely, knowing that the doctor's intentions were good and she was being a good caregiver.

"Thank you, but I spoke to Victim Services yesterday and they have already given me some very helpful resources."

Doctor Strickland nodded and moved on to a checklist of questions to make sure Sarah had followed the pre-surgery instructions. Then the doctor told Sarah to take off her clothes, put on the faded mint-coloured gown, and wait on the exam table for her to come back.

"That's my cue to leave." Steve gave Sarah's shoulder a gentle squeeze and stood. "You'll be fine."

"'Kay." Sarah nodded, not feeling very fine.

Steve tailed the doctor out of the room.

Sarah did as she had been instructed, doing her best to tie the split-backed robe closed behind her, but only managing to secure the top ties. Giving up, she sat on the table and gingerly lifted her swollen ankle onto it so she could lay flat. Her feet protruded off the end so the flannel sheet she had spread over her lower half dangled around them.

She laid back and stared at the pockmarked white ceiling tiles. Fear chewed at her gut like a caterpillar on a leaf. She worried about how much the procedure would hurt. About how long it would take her to recover. About whether it would be enough to get rid of the cancer. About what she would do now that she couldn't write Steve's biography.

Anger flared like fireworks, and she started cursing Steve out in her mind—then felt guilty. What right did she have to be angry at a man who had done so much for her, and with no personal agenda? Why was she even angry with him at all?

Maybe it was because he had told her she could make a change in her life. Well, she'd tried, and the only thing she had to show for it was that she was homeless, friendless, and husbandless. Her mother didn't even want to talk to her. Sarah's gut twinged with more guilt—her mother had left two more messages, which Sarah hadn't returned. *Okay, maybe I don't want to talk to my mother.*

But could anyone blame her? In her hour of direst need, her mother had abandoned her. Again. The only people to show her any kindness were a family she barely knew.

Joanna. Derek.

Steve.

And now she was angry with him. It didn't make sense.

Dr. Strickland came back into the room, followed by the nurse with the braids pushing a strange-looking machine that resembled Johnny Five, the robot star of the old movie *Short Circuit*. While the nurse set about laying out equipment and setting up the machine, Dr. Strickland explained what each device was for. Then she pulled some plastic stirrups on metal arms out from under the exam table and locked them into place, instructing Sarah to place her feet into them.

Sarah winced as she eased her sore ankle into the left stirrup. "I sprained my ankle two days ago, so please be careful."

Dr. Strickland glanced at the ankle appraisingly, nodded, and nudged her stool slightly away from the limb.

"Have you been icing it?"

Sarah nodded, and Dr. Strickland gave a perfunctory nod in response. "Excellent. I'll send you home with a tensor bandage."

"Thanks. I've got one."

Dr. Strickland arched a brow slightly.

"I forgot to put it on this morning," Sarah explained.

Dr. Strickland nodded and turned to her work.

The process was reminiscent of having a PAP exam. The nurse stood off to one side, handing over instruments as they were required. She caught Sarah looking at her and gave her an encouraging smile.

"Try to relax, if you can."

Sarah nodded, but felt like she could relax as easily as a cat could swim or a fish could fly. She clenched her hands into tight fists as the doctor inserted the icy metal speculum and opened it to allow access to the cervix.

"I'm going to inject the anaesthetic now. You might feel a pinch." Dr. Strickland was being very gentle and professional, but Sarah got a flash in her mind of when Everett had violated her with a cold curling iron when she was about seven. Her heart rate spiked and she started breathing fast. Everything inside her screamed that she needed to get out of there.

She had to calm down. She had to stop this. Her eyes roved the room, desperate for something to think about besides what was happening in her nether regions.

The nurse had the most lovely skin tone. It almost seemed like she glowed, light shimmering from the deep ebony like—Sarah cast about for a comparison—starlight on a lake.

Sarah felt an uncomfortable tweak and her panic rose. She knew that the anaesthetic must be working, but she felt disconcerting vibrations and pressure inside her belly. She tried to find a spot on the ceiling to concentrate on, but the panic kept rising.

The nurse turned on the machine, which whirred loudly. It sounded much like her mother's vacuum cleaner. She used to hide in her closet when the vacuum cleaner turned on, but Everett had always found her there anyway. He had used the noise as both a way to track their mother and a cover for what he did to her next. She had been such a stupid, weak little girl. Why hadn't she figured out the pattern earlier and hidden somewhere else?

She looked for a spot on the ceiling, intending to focus all her fear and anger there. However, the doctor seemed to notice her agitation and struck up a conversation.

"So, did you see your family for Thanksgiving?"

Sarah was thankful for the distraction, but would rather talk about almost anything but her family at the moment. However, she tried to concentrate on the question and ignore the fact that this woman's hands were in Sarah's most delicate location.

"Um, yeah. On Sunday. Big dinner, family drama, the whole shebang."

"Mmm-hmm," Dr. Strickland replied vaguely. "There's nothing like family."

"Thank God." Sarah didn't want to go there right now. Time to get the conversation off of herself. "How about you?"

"My husband and I had a few friends over. Both of our families are still in London."

Sarah grunted. "Ontario?"

"England."

Duh. The woman's accent had already told her she was from England. Sarah was having a hard time thinking about much right now, though. She kept staring at the spot on the ceiling.

"Do the English celebrate Thanksgiving?"

Dr. Strickland didn't answer for a moment, probably concentrating on her task. "Not really. Some people are starting to celebrate American Thanksgiving, which is odd, since there is absolutely nothing British about it. Ah, well. Each to their own."

Sarah grunted as she felt something else tweak inside her, unable to think of a reply. She always had a hard time carrying on a conversation while a doctor was working on her privates.

The doctor's stool creaked. "That'll do it," she said in her precise tones. "We're nearly done. You are doing great, love."

"Okay." Sarah tried to relax her tense muscles. Her heart still pounded in her ears. She forced her panting through her nose. She felt the way she imagined a woman in labour might, trying to control her pain and panic through her breathing. It was difficult when a smell like burning meat filled the room. *Is that from me?*

After what seemed like an eternity—but was probably only another minute or two—Dr. Strickland rolled her stool backward. The nurse unplugged the machine and pushed it to the wall. By the time Sarah propped herself up on her elbows, the nurse had bundled up the smaller tools and left the room.

Dr. Strickland stood and smiled. "It went well. I think I got everything of concern, but I'll call you in a few days with the results of the biopsy. You can rest here for the next ten minutes or so. The nurse will pop back to check on you in a bit."

Sarah finally relaxed slightly, panting and exhausted. She felt like she had just survived a car crash. "Thank you."

Dr. Strickland smiled, then left.

As Sarah lay in the exam room staring at the ceiling once again, it occurred to her that Steve's hesitancy about having the biography written might have nothing to do with exposing a fraud, and a lot to do with exposing difficult pieces of his past. She certainly wouldn't want someone to write a biography about her—it would require digging way too many skeletons out of closets. After the conversational aerobics she had just gone through with her doctor to avoid talking about the recent holiday, she didn't think she could survive that kind of scrutiny.

The revelation made her sad. She had hoped that she could find a way to convince Steve to change his mind about the bio, but now she knew she couldn't, in good conscience, pressure him to do this. She was going to have to think of a different project.

Steve tried to concentrate on his crossword puzzle, but the words kept blurring before his eyes. He'd received word from Paul that morning that the landlord for Prakaash House, their children's care centre, had evicted them. Not immediately—Paul had been able to negotiate a sixty-day grace period to allow them to find another place to go. When Steve had asked Paul the reason, Paul's answer had been "What do you think?"

Steve knew. This wasn't the first time that the organization had been discriminated against by landlords and neighbours because of the population they served. In India, image was everything, and sex workers bore a tarnish that no amount of rehabilitation and polish could ever remove—much like ex-cons in the West. Their children were often branded with the same iron. It was one of the many challenges Love Mumbai faced as they tried to reintegrate their charges back into society.

Steve sent up a prayer of thanks for the grace time and asked that the Lord would soften Vijay Paresh's heart toward the care centre so they would not have to move. While he was at it, he sent up yet another prayer for Sarah, that the operation would go smoothly and recovery would be swift.

After lunch yesterday, Sarah had seemed to retreat from him, becoming quiet and withdrawn. He thought he knew why. She had been through so much recently that she was probably exhausted in every way. This morning, Sarah said she hadn't slept well again. Steve wasn't surprised, and thought maybe the rough night and fears about the surgery were the reason she was so quiet on the way to the clinic. He hadn't pressed her, letting her keep her thoughts to herself.

However, he had caught her glaring at him a few times when she thought he wasn't looking. Was she angry with him? Why would she be?

The more he learned about her, the more he was amazed at what she had survived—sexual abuse, an abusive marriage, a cancer diagnosis. Any one of those would be enough to flatten most people. Yet he saw a spark in her, the will to keep fighting, keep trying. To keep moving forward.

He had to admit that he admired her. In the short time he had known her, she had already proved her strength and bravery, although he knew she didn't see it in herself. That made him sad.

Steve worked with many women—and a few men—with horrific pasts. Some of them let those pasts rule them, blaming every failure in their lives and relationships on the wounds that still festered like open sores on their souls. Others wandered through life, unaware that those sores still existed, confused as to why they never seemed to have a fulfilling relationship with anyone.

But others knew they were wounded and were willing to let those wounds heal. All they needed was a little help and support, someone who believed in them and would root for them as they walked the difficult road to recovery.

Like Sarah. Steve hadn't understood why he had felt compelled to talk to her that afternoon in Starbucks. But now that he was getting to know her better, he knew. She had been ready.

Sometimes, he wondered why these women's lives seemed to get so much worse before they got better. In his experience, it almost always seemed to be the case. He thought of Sita, Ratna, Joy, and Priya, all girls who had left the brothels of Mumbai and found some sort of healing through Love Mumbai and the grace of God. Each of them would carry their scars—both emotional and physical—for the rest of their lives. But he found them all to be incredibly beautiful in a way that went far beyond how they looked.

He was still pondering this when Sarah appeared in the waiting room, shaky and pale. He jumped to his feet.

"That was fast! You're ready to go?"

Sarah nodded. "Almost. Let me book my follow-up."

A few minutes later they were heading out to the parking lot. Steve stayed close beside her in case she fainted or something—by her looks, that appeared imminent. However, she made it to the car, still upright.

Steve opened the passenger door of the RAV and helped Sarah inside, making sure her feet were clear before closing it and heading around to his side. After he had the vehicle started and his seat belt on, he turned to her. She was staring straight ahead, looking a little shell-shocked, but some colour seemed to be coming back to her cheeks.

"Was it as bad as you thought?"

Sarah glanced at him and shrugged. "Well, it wasn't any worse, I guess. The doctor said she'll call me in a few days to let me know what the results are."

Steve nodded. "How are you feeling?"

Sarah looked thoughtful. "Surprisingly okay. I'm supposed to rest a lot for the next couple of days. But I'm feeling good right now." She chuckled. "I'm sure the Tylenol 3 isn't hurting."

It was nice to hear her laugh again. In fact, other than being a little pale, she was decidedly more relaxed than the woman he'd brought to Edmonton that morning.

Steve looked at her sideways. "Wanna go for ice cream?"

Sarah gave him a look of mock incredulity. "Dessert before lunch?"

"It's a bit early for lunch. Besides, once in a while you gotta have dessert first. Especially any time body parts have been removed."

Sarah looked wistful. "Know anywhere that serves wine with their ice cream?"

Steve cocked an eyebrow, a teasing grin on his lips. "Wine? At eleven a.m.?" He shrugged. "Nothing springs to mind. Do you?"

Sarah's smile faltered. "Never mind. How about coffee?"

"That, we can do. The place I have in mind is in Miller, so feel free to nap on the drive if you need to."

"Mm-kay." She laid her head back against the headrest and turned toward the far window.

After Steve navigated through Edmonton and finally pulled onto the long, flat straightaway of the Queen Elizabeth II highway heading south toward Miller, his thoughts returned to their circling.

When he had found out that Sarah intended to explore her past through her next book, he was floored. He knew instinctively that writing about what had happened to her would be an amazing tool for her healing—but the fact that she would write a book about it while fully intending to publish it afterward stunned him.

As much as he admired her guts, when she had asked to write his story too, he'd clammed up.

That reaction had been bothering him ever since. Especially since he knew why he had said no. Fear. Fear of rejection, about how the truth would affect his ministry.

He had good reason.

He had been in university when he had finally made contact with his birth grandmother. She had revealed the truth about his parentage—something he had always yearned to know, but immediately wished had remained a mystery. Stunned and overwhelmed by what she had told him, he'd confided in his then-fiancée, Vanessa, whom he was crazy about. It had been more than Vanessa could handle. She had dumped him and had then proceeded to expose his darkest secrets to the world. After that, he watched person after person disappear from his life. Confused and hurt, he had sworn never to let that piece of his puzzle see the light of day again.

He felt so torn. A book about him and Love Mumbai would be such a benefit to his work. Instead of only being able to spread the word through speaking engagements and the much less effective solicitation letters, he would be able to spread the same message with a book, connecting with people on a level not otherwise possible. But knowing that Sarah would be exploring much more than current projects—that she would want to know the root of the reason why he began Love Mumbai in the first place—left him in a cold sweat.

All at once, it hit him how letting this incredible opportunity pass would hurt his girls. He thought of Sita again, and her daughter Aashi. He worked for them, and all the others like them, not himself. What right did he have to turn down an opportunity like this because of fear, when they had already pushed through so much fear to get to where they were?

"Steve?"

Steve jolted out of his reverie. Sarah was staring at him, biting her lip. He knew it meant she was nervous, but he couldn't help but find the gesture strangely endearing. "Yeah?"

"I, uh, I've been thinking."

He sat up straighter and looked at her. This sounded serious. "Yeah?"

"I was angry with you yesterday for turning me down when I asked about the book. Since you were the one who told me I could make a change in my life, I thought you would be more willing to help me with this." She dropped her gaze. "But I realized today how intimidating it must be for someone to ask to write your biography. I might be asking you all kinds of personal questions, and I know how uncomfortable I'd be if someone were doing that to me. So, uh—"

"Sarah—"

"I just wanted to tell you that I'm sorry I put you in that position in the first place."

Steve glanced at her. Her face was tight in concern and pain. It was uncanny how she had guessed his reasoning. Now she felt bad simply for asking him? He felt his heart grow tender toward her. Surely a woman like that would be sensitive enough not to print something he didn't want written.

"I've decided to do it."

Sarah's eyes widened. "Are you sure? Because after yesterday—"

Steve turned toward her. "I said I'm going to do it."

Sarah's face split in an uncertain smile.

Steve stared at the road, feeling his throat clench. He gulped.

"But I do have a condition."

Sarah's smile disappeared. "What is it?"

"You're right. There are some things in my past that I'm not too keen to talk about. So if I tell you to back off on something, you need to respect that. Okay?"

Sarah nodded, frowning. "Of course."

Steve grinned. "So, where would you like to start?"

Sarah's face brightened and she looked like she was about to respond, but she abruptly grimaced and placed her hands over her lower abdomen. "I'm not so sure I'm up to starting research at the moment. I mean, there are limits to what even Tylenol can do right now. How about we put that on hold for a day or two?"

"No problem." He paused. "Say, do you think you would like to come visit my project?"

Sarah blinked. "In Mumbai?"

Steve winked mischievously. "That's the only one I've got. Everything is there—the women's shelter, the child care centre, the vocational training centre. You really need to see what we're doing to do it justice in the book."

"I'd already thought of that, but Craig would never have let me. Now—" she broke off and frowned. When she spoke again, her voice was low. "I guess I don't need to worry about that now, do I?"

Her eyes were bright with unshed tears. Steve wished there were more he could do to help her during this difficult time. After all he had been through, he still felt so inadequate in the face of another's pain. He knew all too well that there were some things that people needed to work through on their own.

But not alone.

He reached for her hand, which was resting on her lap, wrapped his around it and squeezed. She squeezed back.

There was nothing more to be said.

nineteen

FOR THE NEXT COUPLE OF DAYS, SARAH SPENT MOST OF HER TIME LOUNGING OR NAPPING AT VARious locations around the house—mostly the basement, because it was quieter—between frequent trips to the bathroom to change her absorbent pads. The discharge was completely normal, she had been told, but she still got grossed out every time she had to deal with it.

Sophie had a good two-hour nap each afternoon, and Joanna took Sophie out for several hours in the mornings. Sarah thought it might be solely to leave a quiet house for her to rest in, which made her feel guilty but grateful.

Steve went out, too, but never for long. He took Nelson for his walks morning and night, ran some errands for Joanna, and told Sarah he even went to have coffee with his old pastor. In between comings and goings, he checked in on Sarah to see if she needed anything or simply to keep her company.

Joanna also checked on her frequently, but only as a brief foray to the basement before going back upstairs. Steve was the one who seemed to consider the basement space as joint-use with her. Probably because the couch on which Sarah lounged watching TV and napping during the day was the same couch that Steve used as a bed at night—and all of his things were piled in a corner of the room.

At first, Sarah felt obligated to try to make conversation with him, but was too exhausted to keep it up for long. Her brain felt like it was floating in soupy fog, and latching onto conversational ideas was like trying to catch a goldfish in hands coated in dish soap.

Thursday afternoon, she woke up from a nap on the rec room sofa and blinked at her murky surroundings. Steve lounged in a nearby easy chair, feet up on the coffee table and laptop perched on his legs, typing rapidly. The TV, which she had fallen asleep watching, had been turned off. The waning afternoon light of early winter seeped in from the high basement windows, washing everything in desaturated tones. A slight bluish tinge from Steve's laptop monitor illuminated his face, casting defining shadows on his sensual mouth and deepening the blue of his irises.

Sarah watched him from under heavy eyelids for a few minutes, trying to muster up the energy to begin a conversation about something. She couldn't think of anything but the obvious.

"What are you doing?"

Steve glanced up at her and a wide smile cracked his face.

"Hey, look who's awake!" He tilted his head. "Not *very* awake, though."

She tried to smile, but it took work, and her muscles would rather be slack, so she let them be.

Steve chuckled. "To answer your question, I'm writing to the director of Love Mumbai, Paul Ramashankar."

That piece of trivia surprised Sarah enough to rouse her slightly. She eased herself backward on the couch so her body would be propped more upright against the arm.

"I thought you were the director."

"Well, Paul and I are equal partners in running it, but we have different roles. My title is more like 'assistant director.' I do the PR work and also the 'people stuff' work—that's called HR, isn't it?—so when I'm away I sometimes need to weigh in on things. As far as the Indian government is concerned, though, Paul is in charge of the whole show. It is much easier for the country's own citizens to run an NGO like this, as India does not like foreign interference of any kind."

"NGO?" she asked. She felt like she should know what that meant, but couldn't quite access the data.

"Non-governmental organization."

"Oh." That seemed like as much information as her tired brain could assimilate.

Something about the "partner Paul" part tweaked her memory. She had thought that Paul was Canadian, like Steve, and was his romantic partner. Paul's last name indicated he was either Indian or of Indian descent. Steve and Paul could still be in a relationship, but maybe not. Perhaps she had misunderstood what Steve meant by "partner" in this case. At any rate, she was too tired to ask about it now. She let her head fall back on the arm of the couch and closed her eyes.

After a moment, she heard Steve begin typing again.

"You don't have to stay here with me, you know," she told him, her eyes still closed.

The typing stopped. After a moment, he said, "I know." The sound of clicking keys resumed, then stopped. "You don't have to entertain me, you know."

Sarah cracked one eye open at his face and caught the teasing delight dancing in his eyes. How had he known what she had been thinking?

She mustered a smile. "I know." Or she did now. She was thankful he'd let her off the hook so her inner critic could relax.

He chuckled and went back to work.

Sarah slid down under the multi-coloured afghan and let her eyelids droop closed and stay there. She dozed off listening to the quiet tattoo of Steve's fingers on the keys.

Other than Wednesday, when she ate very little and barely moved from bed, Sarah joined the family for evening meals. By Friday night, she even insisted that Joanna let her help do the dishes—then regretted it as her ankle began to throb after ten minutes of standing. She took a couple of painkillers and mentally thanked whichever scientist had invented them. Repeatedly.

"Your face is looking better," Joanna remarked as she rinsed out her rag in the sink.

Sarah glanced up from the other side of the open dishwasher where she was trying to find space for one more glass. She hadn't been bothering with make-up since the surgery, so Joanna's assessment was based on a naked face. "Thanks. It feels better, too."

"And how are you feeling otherwise?" Joanna asked.

"My energy is good, but I guess it ought to be after all that sleep. My ankle is still punishing me."

Joanna glanced up in alarm. "Do you need to sit down?"

Sarah had just finished rearranging the dishes to tuck in the last glass. "There, I think that does it. And yeah, I should probably go sit, if that's okay."

"Of course." Joanna gave her a don't-be-silly look. "You only do what you feel you can. You don't have to help with the dishes at all."

"Yeah, but I want to."

Joanna nodded. "I know. I'd feel the same way in your shoes. But you go rest now. I'll finish wiping everything down and get the dishwasher started and I'll join you."

"Okay." Sarah grabbed a glass of water and took it with her to the living room. Steve sat on the couch visiting with Derek, who was sitting across the room bouncing Sophie on his knee. Sarah took the other chair.

Thanks to her invalid status, Sarah hadn't had much chance to get to know Joanna's husband. So far, she had gathered that he seemed equally comfortable in the three-piece-suit in which he went to work and the plaid flannel shirt and jeans he wore at home. She imagined he was also equally at ease with directing affairs at the bank as he was with hunkering down on the floor and playing with his baby girl or creating masterpieces in the kitchen—in fact, he often came home and prepared the evening meal, which left Joanna or Steve on cleanup. Tonight, he had made baked white fish with mushroom risotto. Sarah couldn't remember the last time she had eaten so well.

Physically, Derek was an average specimen—brown hair cropped short, slight build, medium height. But watching him interact with his family in a way Sarah had never experienced from either father or husband, Sarah decided that "average" was completely erroneous. Seeing how Joanna joked with him and Sophie squealed in delight as he blew raspberries on her stomach, Sarah felt envy curdling her insides.

She liked Joanna, and was completely grateful for all that the woman was doing for her. She just wasn't sure if she was glad for this glimpse of what her own family would never be like.

What Joanna had—close relationships with her brother and husband, loving support from her parents, even if she rarely saw them, and a beautiful baby—was what Sarah had always wanted. But Sarah knew the chances of getting it were slim. Derek respected Joanna, but Joanna was also *worthy* of respect, not "damaged goods" like Sarah was—a woman with a marked past and a potential-ly-ruined reproductive system.

After about fifteen minutes, she excused herself to spend a few minutes with Nelson in the garage, then descended to her room. They didn't need the resident fifth wheel—especially one thinking such dark thoughts—intruding on their family dynamic.

She spent the evening watching Netflix on her phone, holding her cloud of gloom and misery tightly to her chest.

twenty

WHEN SARAH WOKE UP THE NEXT MORNING, HER ANKLE WAS LESS SWOLLEN THAN IT HAD BEEN the previous two mornings, which she took as a good sign. Her abdomen also felt pretty good. In fact, she felt better than she had in days and was going a little stir-crazy. She decided that she had to get out of the house for a while today, even if it was only to take Nelson for a walk.

When she climbed the stairs, Joanna was feeding Sophie at the dining room table. Derek sat beside her reading the Saturday paper. Steve relaxed in one of the living room chairs holding a heavy stoneware mug on his knee. He glanced at Sarah and smiled.

"Good morning, Sunshine. That's a distinct lack of hopping you have going on there."

Sarah chuckled. "You noticed that, did you?" She limped into the kitchen and poured herself some coffee from the pot. Scrambled eggs and a few strips of bacon sat in a cast iron skillet on the stove. "Is it okay if I help myself?" she asked Joanna.

"Absolutely. There's some fresh orange juice in the fridge, too."

Sarah gathered her breakfast items and sat down in her usual spot next to the dining room wall. Her melancholy of the night before had been dispelled by a good night's dream-free sleep. Her new, shiny outlook augmented the bright sunshine that suffused the living space with a golden aura.

She sat quietly eating for a few moments, listening to the conversation her hosts were having about mundane things and smiling at the silly faces Sophie made at her mother. She was struck by how at-home she felt here. No one was trying to entertain her, and she didn't feel the need to make conversation for conversation's sake. It was like she had transitioned from guest status to being one of the family.

Which part? she wondered. *The crazy aunt? The down-on-her-luck cousin?* The golden bubble burst, and the moment passed.

"So, what do you folks usually do on a Saturday?" Sarah asked in a silence made suddenly uncomfortable. She glanced down at her plate and covered her self-consciousness by taking a bite.

Derek put his paper down, leaned back, and stretched.

"Oh, this and that. We usually like to go to the Farmer's Market, but that's all finished for the season."

The mention of the market made Sarah think of her mother, and her stomach pinched in a guilty tweak. She had sent Ellen a text to let her know that she was safe and staying with a friend, but had ignored her mother's subsequent messages and voicemails. Sarah told herself that she had been too tired and drugged up to deal with her high-maintenance parent, but wondered if she should make time to call her today. Sarah could ignore her mother for only so long before the amount of work required to assuage Ellen's over-hypersensitivity to her silence was no longer worth the peace and quiet of ignoring her.

Joanna placed a hand on Derek's arm. "Honey, your parents asked us to go out to the farm today, remember? Your dad needs you to help him with something, and your mom said we could stay for lunch. It sounded like the project would take awhile."

Derek pressed his lips together. "That's right. The barn loft repair. I forgot."

Joanna glanced at Steve and Sarah. "Are you two going to be fine here for the day . . . alone?"

Sarah thought her tone was odd, and couldn't decide if Joanna's concern was more for her comfort or Steve's. Her feelings toward Steve were complicated, but she was sure he saw her as a friend. And in the nearly five days she had stayed here, she had grown familiar enough with the house to fend for herself.

"We'll be fine," she assured Joanna. "Maybe Steve and I can go for a walk or something."

She hoped he would like to join her, anyway. She found that she enjoyed his company more than was probably safe.

Sarah had never known anyone like Steve, although Derek seemed to be cut from a similar cloth. If only she had met someone like Steve—or Derek, who was straight—before she had become entangled with Craig. Before she had become so damaged that she almost wanted to swear off men forever.

As it was, she was thankful for the friendship she and Steve had begun. She was surprised to realize that she was looking forward to spending the day with only him.

Which is why his next words left her with a crushing sense of disappointment.

"Actually, I won't be home much today, either. Sam and Kallie asked me to meet them in Red Deer this afternoon for coffee."

Joanna cast a concerned frown at her guest, but before she could say anything, Steve turned to Sarah and spoke.

"I'd love it if you could join me. Do you think you're up to it?" His voice held only warmth—not a trace of hesitation.

Sarah's disappointment melted into uncertain pleasure, and she smiled.

"Yeah." She nodded. "I think I could handle that."

Steve beamed and gulped the last of his tea. Joanna nodded in satisfaction. Sophie squealed in delight. Derek excused himself from the table to prepare for the trip to his parents'.

Sarah sipped her coffee, hoping it would land on the butterflies that had appeared in her stomach and drown them.

Sarah got up to clear her dishes and noticed Steve getting bundled up in the entrance, Nelson's leash in hand.

"Wait," she said, frozen with dishes in her hands as she tried to catch his attention.

Steve glanced up.

"What's up?"

"I wanted to take Nelson for his walk this morning." She thought that may have sounded ungrateful, so to soften it she added, "If that's okay?"

Steve smiled. "Of course. I'm glad you're feeling well enough to do it. Would it be alright if I come, too?"

Sarah nodded, smiling uncertainly. "Sure. Thanks."

They were soon bundled up against the chilly October morning. Nelson jumped in excitement when he saw her with the leash in hand, and she had to keep telling him to sit so she could attach it to his collar.

Steve chuckled. "I think he missed his mom."

Sarah finally felt the leash click into place and scratched the dog behind his ears, relishing the soft fur between her fingers. "I missed you too, boy."

Steve showed her the trail on which he had been taking Nelson—a paved walking path that ran behind the back fence of the Larsons' home. Grassy ditches on each side left a wide buffer between the rows of similar back fences. At the end of the block, the walkway opened out to an undeveloped partially-treed meadow at the edge of town. The pavement ended, but a well-worn network of pathways looped around and through the dried brown grass.

Once they reached the meadow, Sarah removed Nelson's leash. He ran here and there, excitedly following his nose and rooting around at interesting scents. Every few minutes, he would raise his head and smile his doggy smile at her or come over for another pat.

Sarah limped along, breathing deeply of the crisp prairie air. Bright sunshine with a thinness that hinted winter was coming cast everything in stark relief, drawing lines where a golden summer sun would blend them out. Dried leaves rattled on dry bone branches in a gentle breeze that carried earthy scents of sweet poplar bark, musty dried timothy grass, and leaf mold. Frost laced its way over everything the sunlight hadn't yet touched and spiked the air with its sharp signature.

Sarah and Steve walked in companionable silence, as though in mutual agreement to not mar this perfect morning with words. She glanced at him and thought he seemed to be enjoying the walk as much as she was. He cut quite a striking picture, with a plaid wool scarf wrapped around a freshly shaved chin, unruly sandy blond curls escaping from the brim of a knit toque emblazoned with the Farm Co-op's logo, and lined work-gloved hands tucked into the pockets of his denim jacket. He looked so picturesquely "Alberta farm boy" that for a moment she questioned whether her gay-dar was off.

She reviewed the evidence in her head and gave it a shake. If he was straight, she would know by now. And gay men could look rustic, too. If "all the good ones were gay or taken," as the saying went, Steve was one of the good ones. No way would he still be single without some kind of excellent reason.

She was glad he was gay, actually. Her friendship with Steve was the first one she'd ever had with a guy that didn't leave her wondering what he truly wanted from her—always looking between the lines for the sexual innuendo or the hidden demand.

Being with Steve was so easy. Come to think of it, she couldn't remember the last time she'd had a friendship with *anyone*—male or female—who placed so little expectation on her, someone who simply was who they were and expected nothing more nor less from her. Her heart bobbed in momentary content. Impetuously, she stuck her hand through the crook of Steve's arm. He smiled at her and they kept walking.

The past week had been among the hardest of her entire life, but despite that, she couldn't help but feel that she was someone different than she had been a week ago. She imagined last Saturday's Sarah as trapped in a locked stone tomb with no light, no air, no help, and no hope, her life decaying in rotting pieces around her.

But this Saturday, there was a hint of hope and a freshness in the air that suggested anything was possible. She limped through the vast austere beauty of a landscape battened down for a frozen onslaught with someone she considered a friend beside her, and with her heart wide open. Nature was ready for winter, but Sarah was ready for spring.

This Saturday's Sarah had pushed the door of the tomb open and was breathing in the light of day for the first time in years. She stood on the threshold, peering into a blank and uncertain future, but felt like she could glimpse for the first time what was possible beyond the stone prison she had always known. All she had to do was step into it.

She shivered. The idea was both terrifying and invigorating.

Steve strolled at the pace Sarah set. The morning was beautiful, and the company more-so. It did his heart good to see Sarah so at ease and relaxed, a hint of a smile playing on her lips. At her shiver, he pulled his arm from hers and wrapped it around her shoulders.

"Are you cold? We could go back."

She looked up at him. "I'm not cold, but my ankle is starting to hurt. We probably should turn around."

"No problem."

Steve searched for Nelson, spotted him on the far side of the meadow, and took a step away from Sarah to protect her hearing. Removing a glove, he stuck a couple fingers in his mouth and gave a long, piercing whistle.

Nelson's head popped up and the canine bolted at them full-tilt, practically skidding to a halt when he approached—but not quickly enough. In his doggy joy, he collided with Sarah's legs and she toppled to the ground, crying out in pain. He began to lick her face in apology.

"Nelson, sit," she commanded in a strained voice between shallow, panting breaths, hands raised to ward off the doggy kisses.

Steve bent over her before she could even finish the command, a hand on Nelson's collar to ensure he obeyed, the other hand supporting Sarah's back. Her face contracted in pain.

"Are you okay?" Steve scanned her from head to toe, taking in her pale expression, moist eyes, the lip she was biting down on hard, and her injured left leg, which she held off the ground with her hands to keep it from touching down. "Silly question. Can you stand?"

"Just . . . give me . . . a minute."

She seemed able to sit without his support, so Steve grabbed Nelson's leash from the ground where it had fallen and snapped it onto the Golden Retriever's collar. Then he and Nelson both crouched beside Sarah, waiting.

A few minutes later, Sarah's breathing became more normal and the colour began creeping back into her face. She gingerly put her foot down on the ground with only a slight grunt of pain, which was a good sign—but her jaw was clenched tight and she looked like she was steeling herself for the next step.

Steve stood and clasped her forearm, bracing her good foot with his boot. "On three. Ready?"

She nodded, keeping her injured leg off the ground and clasping his arm with both hands.

"One. Two. Three." He heaved her up to standing and caught her so she didn't over-correct. When she seemed balanced, he released her waist, held her hand steady for support and stepped back a few inches.

She put her injured foot down experimentally, then transferred some weight onto it. Her leg gave out and he caught her once again. She crumpled against his chest, panting.

"I don't know if I can walk back," she said into his jacket.

The frustration in her voice was plain. He could only imagine what it must have been like being cooped up in a strange house all week, eating other people's food, life pretty much in chaos, and not even getting to keep her canine companion close. The joy he had seen on her face on the way to the meadow had revealed how much she had needed this walk, this symbolic step into her future—and now last week's injury had brought her down again.

"Here." He jammed Nelson's leash into her hand.

She looked up at him, confused. "What are you doing?"

He bent down, placed his arms behind her back and knees, and scooped her up. "You don't have to walk. I'll get you home."

She tensed and looked like she was about to argue, but he simply began walking. After a few minutes, he felt her body relax and she rested her head on his shoulder. Nelson padded along behind them.

By the time they got back to the house, Derek and Joanna were gone. Steve told Nelson to stay in the entrance, then carried Sarah right up the stairs and laid her on the living room couch. He helped her slide her boots off—which wasn't so easy on the swollen side—and they examined the damage.

Sarah probed the swollen joint with her fingers, frowning and wincing. "Would you get me some ice?"

"Yes, of course." Steve leapt into action, wondering why he hadn't thought of that. Soon, he had Sarah's ankle cooling with an ice pack and the rest of her wrapped in a blanket to keep her warm. Before long, he put a cup of hot coffee in her hand, too.

Sarah took a sip and smiled. "This is just the way I like it."

"I know." He grinned, then knelt by her ankle and removed the ice pack to check it. He caught her blush from the corner of his eye and wondered if she was also remembering their meeting in Starbucks. It had only been two weeks, but it felt like a lifetime ago. He pulled out the tensor bandage he had retrieved from her room and carefully started wrapping the swollen appendage.

She swallowed. "I guess I shouldn't go with you to Red Deer today. It would probably be best if I keep weight off this darn thing as much as possible."

Steve frowned. His coffee date with Sam and Kallie had temporarily slipped his mind. He didn't want to leave Sarah here alone all day, especially not now that she would barely be able to move. He snapped on the bandage clips and gently worked her sock over it.

"What if I don't go?" he suggested, sitting back on his heels.

"What?" She blinked at him. "Why not?"

"I don't want you to be alone. I'll call Sam and cancel. I saw them on Monday, after all. They'll understand."

Sarah was already shaking her head. "No, don't cancel your meeting with your friends because of me. I'll be fine. Really. I'm a big girl."

Steve looked at her doubtfully, wrestling with himself.

"Look, I know my way around the kitchen and I could use some time to work on my book." When he didn't say anything, she gave him a mock glare and a shooing gesture. "Go! See your friends. You can bring me back some fancy coffee or something."

Reluctantly, Steve agreed. She wasn't a child, after all. He didn't want to offend Sarah by trying to babysit her if she didn't feel the need for company.

Now, he only had to deal with his own disappointment and an unexpected sense of rejection.

twenty-one

SARAH HAD THE BEST OF INTENTIONS TO GET SOME WRITING DONE WHILE STEVE WAS GONE. AS WAS becoming the norm, that wasn't how things worked out.

She stared at her blank word processor, typed in a few sentences, and then deleted them. After twenty minutes of frustration, she decided that her brain would be much more creative if she stopped trying to force it and focused on something else for a while.

Ordinarily in this situation, she would go for a walk. Or clean something. She flexed her ankle experimentally and tensed as pain shot up her leg. On the pain scale, it was maybe only a five. She could manage getting around the house okay, but taking another walk was out of the question. And since Joanna was one of those new moms who managed to retain house cleaning superpowers, no tasks that required doing jumped to Sarah's attention.

She decided to take a drive. She needed to clear her head, and it would get Nelson out of the garage, too.

After a fair amount of hopping and careful manoeuvring, she got herself and Nelson into the RAV4, which was parked on the curb in front of the lawn. Since driving through town would take all of five minutes, she decided to go the other way, out onto the highway heading east to the open prairies. Shorn wheat fields dotted with round bales or with white plastic-covered snake-like rows of the same lining their edges whizzed by the window. It was only three thirty in the afternoon, but the sun was already dipping toward the south-western horizon, stretching long shadows from every poplar tree and farmhouse on the landscape of rolling hills.

As intended, her thoughts began to wander, but not around the topic of her book.

She hadn't wanted to admit to Steve how much it rankled that she couldn't go with him today. Just when she thought that her life was changing for the better, just when she had a little bit of hope and was feeling optimistic about her future prospects—just when she could finally get out of the house, for Pete's sake!—she'd re-injured her ankle. While walking her dog, of all things.

She glanced at Nelson in the rear view mirror. He lay on the back seat, head erect, watching her and the passing scenery by turns.

She didn't blame him for the accident. He was simply so excited to be out with her and hadn't been able to control himself. He didn't intend to hurt her.

But she badly wanted to blame someone. Unfortunately, there was no one left to blame but herself. She should have been more careful. Why was it that any efforts she made to move forward with her life were continually sabotaged by her past mistakes? Would she ever truly heal from all her past wounds and be able to move on?

First, there was her chronic inability to choose a partner who would remain faithful to her, or even respect her. Thinking of how her ex-boyfriend Chris and now Craig had cheated on her filled her with an overwhelming sense of betrayal—followed by a yearning to talk to her husband. Not the man who had betrayed her, beaten her, and bullied her, but the one she had married—the one she had been in love with, whom she had once viewed as her lifeline.

She frowned. After all that Craig had done to her, how could she miss him? She hated him, but she felt incredibly lost without him. She had stopped herself from calling or texting him several times in the past week, knowing that no good would come of it—but craving the familiar voice, the warm body to cuddle with in bed, the opinion she had once come to believe she couldn't live without.

"Like a bad habit I need to break," she muttered, and smacked the steering wheel with her palm.

She *could* live without him, dammit, and she was determined she would. *But it's so freakin' hard.*

As much as she appreciated the Larsons' and Steve's generosity, she knew that the past few days had been an escape from reality. It had been like living in a bubble, though one she had desperately needed. It had given her the chance to rest both physically and emotionally after the literal beatings she had taken. But she also knew that bubbles were temporary, transient things. She couldn't ignore the mess that was her real life indefinitely. She wondered bleakly how she was going to face it alone. The future that had looked so bright and optimistic only that morning now seemed terrifying, filled with uncertainties and pitfalls and loneliness.

Sarah had set out from Miller with no destination in mind, but by the time she had been on the road for thirty minutes, she had made a wide loop and was pulling into the parking lot of Lucky's Liquor Store on the west side of town. She slammed the RAV into park and stared at the blinking neon signs in the barred front window, suddenly aware that some part of her had been aiming this direction from the moment Steve had left the house.

She assured Nelson she'd be right back and left him in the RAV. Glancing across the lot, she could see the gas station where Steve had found her on Monday night. She faltered, then turned back toward Lucky's with determination. Hobbling as fast as her injury allowed, she roved the store aisles on a mission. Lucky's didn't carry as much variety as her favourite store in Edmonton, but she knew it would have white wine of some kind, even if it was boxed. At the moment, she wasn't feeling picky.

As it turned out, she didn't have to settle for boxed. She was soon pulling away from Lucky's with a bottle wrapped in brown paper on the passenger seat and a powerful thirst in her soul. It felt like she couldn't get back to the Larsons' fast enough. Guilt pricked her at the idea of spending her afternoon in their house drinking, but not hard enough to quench the voracious need that only increased with each passing second.

She parked in front of the house, left Nelson in the garage on her way through, and crawled up the stairs, cradling the brown bag like an infant to protect it. Her laptop sat on the dining room table, a condemning reminder of the chapters she hadn't made any progress on writing—the real work she needed to do if she wanted income to help her out of her current bind. Her desperation increased, and she began searching around in the cupboards for a wine glass.

Steve would be going back to India soon. She didn't know when, exactly, but he would leave.

Didn't they have any wine glasses in this house?

And she couldn't stay here forever—she already felt like she was pressing her welcome. Wasn't there some saying about fish and guests stinking after three days? She was already well over that. And where were the damn glasses? There didn't even seem to be a clean tumbler in the house.

The dishwasher. She cracked it open to a face full of steam, then grabbed a hot tumbler from the top rack and set it on the counter.

Better let it cool for a moment. Don't want to crack it and waste the wine.

She needed to get a divorce lawyer. And a place to live. And probably a roommate, so there was the hassle of finding one she could get along with. She'd had more bad roommates than good ones, and didn't relish beginning that search.

She couldn't find a wine corkscrew, either, but managed to find a screw and a screwdriver in the kitchen's all-purpose drawer. Didn't these people drink, ever? Maybe she should have gone with the box.

After several minutes of frustration, cursing, and the creative use of a roasting fork, she managed to get the cork out and poured a good eight ounces into the lukewarm tumbler. She raised the glass to her lips with trembling hands, then gulped down half of it without taking a breath.

Damn Craig the Abusive Control Freak, with his wandering dick and superiority complex. Damn Erica. And Everett. And even her mother. Damn them all to hell.

The second half went down the hatch.

Her phone rang, and she nearly dropped the glass.

She fumbled in her coat pocket and pulled it out, already feeling a spreading euphoria numb the hysteria that had propelled her. The call display read "Joanna Larson".

After a moment, she answered it.

"Hello?"

"Sarah? It's Joanna. I wanted to check in with you because it looks like Derek will be working on the barn for a couple more hours, so we're staying for supper. Steve said you stayed home, so I wanted to make sure you'd be okay there on your own until we all get back. There are leftovers in the fridge, or you can make yourself at home in the kitchen if you're up to it."

Sarah hesitated. There was a large framed mirror on the dining room wall opposite. She caught her hollow-eyed reflection staring back at her and saw what Steve would see if he were here—a desperate drunk who couldn't handle being alone for two hours without falling back into her old ways.

She despised that woman in the mirror.

"Sarah? Are you there?"

"Yeah, I'm here. And I'll be fine. Thanks for calling to check. I'll see you guys when you get home."

"Hey, are you all right?"

Sarah glared at her reflection, as though the woman in the mirror would betray her, too.

"Absolutely. Why wouldn't I be?"

"I—okay, great. We'll see you in a few hours, okay?"

"See you then."

Sarah ended the call and stared at her doppelgänger.

What am I doing?

Was this who she was, now? A woman who handled all of her problems with a bottle of wine?

She had realized that she had been drinking more for the last several years— Lord knows, she had needed the alcohol to numb the pain of what Craig did to her—but for the first time, she realized that it had become her default setting. She hadn't eaten since breakfast, and the cup of wine she'd downed so fast seemed to be hitting her system equally hard. But she suddenly didn't want to have her senses numbed with wine.

What if Steve came home and she was sloshed out of her gourd? What would Joanna think of her if she found out?

She limped to the toilet, stuck her finger in the back of her throat, and retched the contents of her stomach into it. It was the first time in her life she had made herself vomit, so it took a couple of tries to get it right. As the sickly-sweet acid burned her throat, she promptly decided that this would also be the last time it would ever happen.

She was using her hand to splash water on her face at the bathroom sink when Nelson began barking and a vehicle's engine cut out in the driveway. She limped to the front window and saw Steve open the driver's door of Derek's BMW.

"Shit."

twenty-two

SARAH HURRIED TO THE KITCHEN, SCOOPED UP THE HALF-EMPTY BOTTLE AND GLASS AND TURNED on the faucet, rinsing the glass and dumping the wine simultaneously while trying to stay perched on her good leg, using a knee against the cupboard door to maintain balance.

The front door opened. Pulse racing, she opened the garbage can under the sink, but there wasn't room for the bottle. Besides, someone would notice it as soon as they opened the lid. Did they have a recycling bin here somewhere?

"Hey," came Steve's cheery greeting from the out-of-sight entrance.

"Hi," Sarah called back, panicking as she looked around for a place to hide the evidence of her indiscretion.

She spotted the large garbage can on the back deck through the kitchen window. The door to the deck was in a direct line of sight from the front entrance, though. She took a few hobbling steps toward it, trying to position the bottle so Steve wouldn't see it as she stepped outside. However, she had only gotten to the short hallway leading to the back door when Steve rounded the corner into the kitchen behind her, still wearing his denim jacket and carrying two plastic bags full of take-out containers.

Sarah froze, bottle in plain view.

Steve halted and looked her over, assessing the situation.

"I, uh, I was about to throw this out," she stammered.

"Okay." Steve didn't move.

She wobbled on her good leg.

Steve set the containers on the counter and held out his hand. "Would you like me to do that for you?"

He didn't wait for an answer, but gently took it from her, went out to the back deck for a moment, came back in, and closed the door. Then he descended to the front landing to remove his coat as if nothing had happened.

Sarah limped over to the table and sat down in the closest chair. Guilt gnawed at her and she wondered what Steve must be thinking right now. She watched him ascend the stairs, the pressure building with every step he took toward her.

"I dumped it out," she blurted as he reached the top step.

He glanced up at her, a quizzical expression on his face.

"What?"

"I didn't drink it. Well, no, I drank some of it. But then I changed my mind, and I dumped it out." Her hands fidgeted in her lap, and she stared at them.

Steve sauntered over to the table and pulled out the chair at the head, dragging it to within a foot of hers, then sat down. He leaned forward and grabbed her fidgeting hands in both of his, holding them gently.

"Sarah, it's okay. You don't have to explain yourself to me."

She frowned and blinked back sudden moisture.

"I know, I guess. But—" She bit her lip and looked away. "I want you to—to not think badly of me. I want you to know that I didn't drink a whole bottle of wine this afternoon. That I don't want to be that person who handles all her problems with alcohol. That's what I used to do, but . . . that's not who I want to be."

"Well, that's good to know. But let me ask you—who *do* you want to be?"

Sarah froze, her mind racing. *Who do I want to be?*

She had no definable answer to that question.

She thought about all the people she knew, about the ones she had truly admired. To some degree, she had tried to become all of them. When she was with Abby, she had emulated her outgoing vivacity. When she was with Erica, she had hoped to gain some of her friend's confident assurance and fashion sense. Only last night, she had been lamenting that Joanna's "perfect" life was not her own.

If she could, she would be the best of all of these women. But she had heard all the self-help platitudes about "being yourself" often enough to know that she couldn't admit that out loud. What kind of independent woman of the twenty-first century admits to craving to be anyone but herself?

"I—I don't know. Someone better. Someone who doesn't rely on crutches to help her through her problems." She hung her head.

"Hey," he said gently. Steve still held her hands with one of his own, but the other lifted her chin until she looked at him. "We all need help through tough times. None of us is meant to be the Lone Ranger, you know."

Sarah glanced down again and nodded, lips pressed together to keep her emotions contained. "Even he wasn't alone, was he?"

Steve frowned. "He wasn't?"

Sarah shook her head. "Tonto, remember?"

Realization dawned, and Steve's face cracked into a grin. "See what I mean?"

Sarah tried to grin, but couldn't put her heart into it. "I know you're right about me needing someone. But the thing is, if I'm the Lone Ranger, every person who has auditioned for the part of Tonto has failed to show up for the call-back."

Steve's gaze became intense. "Not me."

Sarah caught her breath. "Not you." *I'll be damned if I know why.*

Steve continued. "And for what it's worth, I'm proud of you. You have already done so much to start becoming that 'someone better.' You should be proud of yourself, too."

Sarah nodded because he expected a response. But she wasn't sure what to make of what he said. He was proud of her? Her heart warmed, melting the icy crust of fear that had gripped it only moments ago. Instead of rejecting her or even chastising her for her moment of weakness, he was proud of her? It didn't make sense. She felt a giddiness quite different than one brought on by alcohol permeate through her. She didn't know if she was proud of herself, but she was relieved, and grateful, and confused.

She looked up at him shyly and smiled. "Thanks."

Steve's face cracked into his familiar smile, too. "You wanna know what I do when I'm feeling like a failure?"

Sarah blinked. "You feel like a failure?"

Steve leaned back and stretched. "Not all the time, but sure. There are plenty of times when I get overwhelmed by my work or difficult situations, and a little voice tells me that I'm no good and I'll never make a difference so why do I even bother?"

Sarah digested this. Even Steve felt overwhelmed sometimes? Maybe she wasn't such a lost cause, after all.

"So, what *do* you do?"

"First, I pray. Then I usually call up a friend to talk or hang out. Or go for a run or do a workout. Or I make a list of things to be thankful for and try to think about that for a while." He leaned forward, his smile compassionate. "There are positive ways to cope with stressful times, you just have to find out what works for you."

Sarah sat straighter. Pray? Steve had mentioned God before. Was he a Christian? His other advice seemed good and simply made sense, but why would someone as strong as Steve need religion? She was trying to be more like him, strong and independent, and here he was admitting that he had a crutch of his own. She frowned, considering.

Steve stood and went to bring the takeout boxes from the kitchen counter to the table. "It so happens that you have someone to hang out with tonight, Ms. Daniels. I hope you like Chinese food. And Tom Hanks."

Sarah tracked him with her eyes as he brought over the plastic bags and began pulling out sauces and plastic cutlery.

"Tom Hanks?"

He reached into the bag and pulled out a five-dollar-bin copy of *You've Got Mail*. Sarah grinned uncertainly, pushing her confusion aside for later. Her stomach was growling, and she rearranged her chair to face the table where he was setting a plate for her.

"I love Chinese. And Tom Hanks." She looked at her friend.

Friend. He really was, wasn't he?

"Thank you, Steve." Her voice was full of emotion.

He kept setting up the table and opening boxes, releasing savoury puffs of steam that made her stomach growl. "My pleasure. Couldn't have you going hungry, after all."

Sarah placed a hand on his so he would stop and look at her. "No, not only for supper. Thank you, for everything you've done for me. I don't know what would have happened to me if I hadn't met you."

He turned his hand under hers to clasp her fingers, then gave them a squeeze. "You're welcome. I would do it all again in a heartbeat." He lifted her hand to his mouth, planted a quick peck on the top, then released it. "So, ginger beef or kung pow chicken?"

Steve quietly slid the remote control through his fingers until he could reach the power button. Blanking the TV, he shifted his body under Sarah's warm, dead weight. She had fallen asleep on his shoulder while they were watching the movie, and he didn't want to disturb her. She needed the rest.

She stirred when he scooped her up. "Is it over? What are you doing?"

"Sh. I'm putting you to bed."

She put a hand on his chest and didn't argue.

He laid her on the bed, removed her socks and pulled the covers up to her chin.

"Thank you," she mumbled.

"You're welcome."

He stood and looked at the sleeping angel for a moment more, her hair fanned out in waves over the pillow like a halo. A piece of hair lay across her cheek, and he reached out and tucked it behind her ear.

Sarah sighed deeply and rolled to her side.

Steve tiptoed out of the room and closed the door.

twenty-three

SARAH SURGED FROM THE DEPTHS OF SLEEP LIKE A DROWNING WOMAN PUSHING HERSELF TO THE surface, gulping air, heart pumping, fighting for survival.

She bolted up in bed, arms flailing. After a moment, she realized where she was—the guest bedroom in Derek and Joanna Larson's basement. It was dark. That orange trapezoid of light faithfully alighted on the same spot on the wall, partially illuminating the "Welcome Home" sign. Her staccato heartbeat slowed, and her heaving chest calmed like the sea after a hurricane.

Only a dream.

They were getting worse, the nightmares. In this one, she had been chained to a rock while wolves came and tore pieces of her flesh from her bones while she was still alive. The wolves had the faces of her brother, father, and husband. No matter how much she screamed and begged, no one showed mercy, and no one came to save her.

Doesn't take a psychologist to figure out what that one's all about.

A gentle knock sounded on the door, and Steve called softly from the other side.

"Sarah? Are you alright?"

She must have cried out in her sleep. She got out of bed and shuffle-limped to the door, not wanting to rouse Sophie by raising her voice to be heard through it.

She opened the door a foot or so and leaned against it. Steve stood on the other side, hair rumpled, but otherwise fully dressed, wearing a button-down shirt for the first time since she'd known him. A light from the bathroom down the hall backlit him in a halo of light.

Like an angel of mercy. She smiled at the thought. Someone *was* looking out for her.

"I'm okay. What time is it?"

"About seven thirty. I thought I heard you scream." His eyes were full of compassion. She didn't respond. "Wanna talk about it?"

Sarah shook her head. "Not really. Just another stupid nightmare." She felt shaky with the last wisps of dream still stuck in her hair. She absently finger-combed her locks. "Why are you up so early on a Sunday?"

"I have a speaking engagement at a church in Edmonton this morning. This is my last one before I head back to Mumbai on Tuesday."

"What?" Sarah stared at him blankly. Her first thought was surprise that he would be speaking in a *church*. Her second was shock that he was leaving in two days.

Of course, she knew he was going back soon, but she hadn't realized how very soon it would be. A sense of impending loss settled on her, and she blinked back tears.

Don't be ridiculous, idiotic girl. You're protecting yourself now. You don't need him, or anyone else.

She wanted to believe what she told herself, but her heart mourned at the thought. She had so very few people she could trust, and Steve and Joanna—mostly Steve—made the short list. She didn't relish the thought of facing whatever Craig would be throwing at her alone.

Steve crossed his arms and leaned on the door jamb. "How are you feeling this morning?"

Besides terrified? Sarah looked down to give herself a moment to collect her thoughts. She was surprised to see herself in yesterday's clothes—then a dim memory of Steve putting her to bed after the movie warmed her insides. She flexed her ankle and was pleasantly surprised that yesterday's re-injury hadn't left it more tender.

"All things considered, I'm alright. Even my ankle. Why?"

"I was wondering if you'd like to come with me. Derek and Joanna will be going to church here in town, so if you want to take advantage of the quiet house to stay home and rest, that's fine. But if you're up to coming with me, we could go out for lunch after. My day tomorrow is going to be fairly busy getting ready to go, so this is probably our last chance before I leave. Besides, you haven't heard my whole spiel, yet. It might help the book."

Sarah shifted her weight, pondering her answer. She would rather do almost anything than go to church. However, after the dream she had just had, she didn't want to be alone, either. And Steve was right—if she was going to get started on gathering information for his bio, it had to be soon. Person-to-person contact relayed information that was difficult to gather via email or text messaging, and it would be months before she would be able to take a trip to India herself.

"Okay," she said.

"Great!" Steve grinned and pushed himself upright, looking much more enthusiastic about her answer than she would have expected.

She heard Nelson's whine drift down the stairs, muffled by the door to the garage.

"I'll get him," Steve said. "You go take your time and get ready to go. We have to leave at nine."

Sarah smiled gratefully and stepped away from the door, getting ready to close it. "Thanks, Steve."

"Don't mention it."

With a parting eyebrow wiggle that seemed to indicate he was looking forward to an adventure, he patted the door jamb and tiptoed up the stairs.

The church was big—way bigger than the small congregation she had grown up in. With dimmed lights above the semi-circle arrangement of pews and spotlights on the musicians, it reminded her more of a rock concert than a church service. And that wasn't the only surprise.

She may have turned her back on her religious upbringing, but she was sure she could still sing every hymn in the traditional repertoire by heart. These songs were completely unlike the ones she had cut her teeth on. Instead of a wheezing organ and a song leader singing slightly off-pitch and off-tempo, the stage was cluttered with modern rock instruments—drums and an electric guitar and a keyboard. Several singers stood in a line behind a woman with one of the most amazing voices Sarah had ever heard. And while the lyrics of the songs—which were projected on a screen above the band's heads—were overtly Christian in content, the rhythms made her want to dance.

She remembered getting a U2 CD when she was a kid. When her mother had found it while vacuuming Sarah's room, she had reported it directly to her father, who had made Sarah burn the CD and watch. He had called it "the devil's music."

She could hardly believe that "the devil's music" was regular Sunday fare in this church.

Beside her, Steve sang along with every song, clapping and even moving his feet a little. Sarah clapped half-heartedly, feeling completely out of place. Of course, no one was looking at her, and even if they were, it was too dark to see her. Still, she was so far out of her comfort zone that she wished they were sitting in the very back pew so she could take everything in without being seen, rather than halfway to the front on the edge of a centre aisle. She got the feeling that Steve had picked the location as a compromise—being a speaker, he would probably be in the very front if it weren't for her.

The tempo came down several notches on the next song—*like a slow dance*. She almost giggled aloud as she pictured the staid elderly couple beside her locked in an embrace and swaying back and forth to the music. The piano beat out a slow, mournful chord progression, but when the lyrics of "Amazing Grace" started, she was startled to realize she recognized this song.

Steve's strong baritone rang in her ear. He had a surprisingly good voice.

"Amazing grace, how sweet the sound, that saved a wretch like me."

See? That's what's wrong with religion. Who wants to be told that they are a wretch? Why would you want to sing that about yourself? Still, she had certainly been feeling wretched lately. And she had desperately needed saving not that long ago. She glanced at Steve, wondering how she would have made it through this past week if he hadn't been at the gas station last Monday night. It *almost* seemed more providential than coincidental. Almost.

"I once was lost, but now am found, was blind, but now I see."

Lost and found. Very poetic, but what did it even mean? She wasn't lost. She knew where she was. But she had to admit, it was kind of tough to see where she was going these days. Her entire life had been turned around in less than a week, and there was absolutely nothing in her future that was certain right now. Lost? Okay, maybe she felt a little lost. And blind. But some pretty words in a song did exactly squat to find and illuminate her.

The song shifted into a chorus, one that she had never heard before. As Steve sang gustily about broken chains and being set free, her nightmare exploded through her mind in living colour. She gasped and gave a heaving sob as yearning filled her heart. The next lines explained how the writer had been ransomed by God, and talked about mercy like a flood.

Mercy. That was a concept that was so foreign to her, she wasn't even sure she knew what the word meant. She remembered a scene from one of her favourite movies—a gladiator stands in the middle of the ring, clearly the victor over the man at his feet. They both stare up at the petty, selfish emperor above them as the crowd calls for the death blow. The emperor, trying to curry favour with his subjects, gives the thumbs-down—the vanquished man must die. But the hero—a man carrying a personal grudge against the emperor—throws down his weapon and walks away in defiance, refusing to kill on the lesser man's whim.

Was that mercy? Letting someone live to make a political statement?

That didn't seem right, but she didn't know what else to think. And that didn't seem like mercy that floods, or unending love, or amazing grace.

What did she know about any of those things? Love always ended, if it even existed at all. And grace? That *would* be amazing. She didn't know what that looked like, either. Was that what Steve did for her yesterday, with the wine bottle? She wasn't sure.

Her parents had certainly never shown her any grace or mercy. Every mistake she had ever made was taken out of her flesh for her father's pleasure, justified with scripture. Could it be possible that the religion her father showed her was not the same as what other Christians believed? The beautiful words seemed like a code, one she couldn't quite crack but was desperate to understand.

The song continued to wash over and around her, returning to the familiar poetry of "Amazing Grace." Some lines made her wistful, and some made her angry. The Lord has promised good to me? Well, that didn't exactly work out, did it? He will my shield and portion be? Sarah snorted. Fairy tale words about a fairy tale God who did absolutely nothing about the misery on earth.

The tears she had been fighting evaporated in the derision that now filled her. This time, the refrain about broken chains was revealed for the illusion it was. How could any intelligent person believe this garbage? Were they so desperate to escape reality that they couldn't see how unreasonable the whole charade was?

The final strains of the song faded away and the pastor came up onto the stage. Sarah crossed her arms and glared at people in the dark. It had been a mistake to come here. She could have met Steve for lunch somewhere. She thought about going out to wait in the car, but then remembered that Steve hadn't even spoken yet, which would defeat the purpose of why she was here at all.

She gladly sat when instructed to do so, crossing her legs as well as her arms. This ordeal couldn't be over quickly enough.

Steve was called to the front. He turned to her and gave her a reassuring smile before he strode up to the platform and accepted the mic the pastor held out to him. The pastor cracked a joke, which got the crowd laughing. Steve returned it easily, as though they had planned the repartee in advance. Then the pastor went and sat down on the front pew.

Steve's presentation was almost exactly as Sarah remembered it—for the first five minutes. He talked about Love Mumbai and his work there, showing PowerPoint slides of the slums and his staff, as well as several of Love Mumbai's success stories. She recognized the photo of Ratna and the one of Steve and his "girls" that he had shown her in San Francisco.

Then he began explaining the day and night care centre they ran to protect and educate children of sex workers. A photo of a group of young children with their arms around each other and wide smiles appeared on the screen.

"Prakaash House is our newest project," Steve said. "Rather than leaving their children unsupervised while they work, sex workers can bring them to our day-and-night care centre to be cared for, fed, and educated, on either a per-day or permanent basis. Without initiatives like this, these children have nowhere to go, and stand a very high probability of being trafficked. Our goal with Prakaash House is to break the cycle and prevent second-generation trafficking. 'Prakaash' means 'beacon' in Hindi. We want this facility to shine a beacon of hope into each child we serve."

The image on the screen changed to show a tall stone building with scrolled cast-iron grills covering the windows and a fence in front.

"This is the building we are currently using for Prakaash House. Recently, our landlord discovered that our ministry serves the children of sex workers and has severed our lease."

Sarah started in surprise. She didn't remember Steve saying anything about that before.

"Many of you will remember that this is not the first time we have had to deal with discrimination from neighbours and landlords. Our women's shelter moved three times before we finally purchased the property we now use. Thank you very much for your part in creating a stable home for these women."

The screen now displayed a smaller, squat brick building that looked like a beauty parlour but must be the women's shelter. Steve's warm smile and gesture at the photo was returned with a short burst of applause from the audience.

"Now we are working to raise the funds to purchase a permanent property for Prakaash House."

He brought up the photo of Sita holding Aashi. The little girl had shining brown eyes, a straight black bob and a smile that would melt the hardest heart.

"This is Sita and her daughter Aashi." Steve shared Sita's story, how she had escaped sexual slavery and now led a meaningful life because of Love Mumbai, managing their women's shelter and working to help others like her. He explained how Aashi was able to receive first-class education without discrimination because of Prakaash House.

Sarah smiled wistfully. There was something about Sita that drew her in. Even though she had never met the woman, she felt a connection to her, like they had something in common.

Which is probably why what Steve said next landed like a blow to the face.

"Unfortunately, Sita has AIDS. Like so many of the victims of human trafficking in Mumbai, her health was at the mercy of her customers, and she has been fighting the disease for several years. Medicines are expensive and not easily available for someone in her position. As an employee of Love Mumbai, we have been helping her get the care she needs, and God willing, she still has many fulfilling years ahead of her. She's one of the lucky ones. If a sex worker gets ill, they are often still worked until they are too weak to do so, then put out onto the street to die."

Sarah felt a tear slide down her cheek and swiped at it. She truly must be exhausted. Her ice castle was melting out of her tear ducts.

Steve cleared his throat, as though he was having difficulty speaking. "Thanks to Love Mumbai, Sita has a place where she will always be welcome, and should the Lord take her home early, she need not fear that her daughter will be trafficked in order to survive. But to make sure that Aashi's future—and that of many children like her—remains secure, we first need to secure the future of Prakaash House."

Steve went on to outline his fund raising needs. The remaining number still sounded very high to Sarah.

The screen showed contact information, and Sarah was sure Steve was finishing up. Abruptly, he flipped back to the slide of Sita and Aashi. He rubbed his chin as though trying to decide what to say next. Then he looked up, resolve clear on his face.

"A friend recently asked me a question. She wondered how a God of love could allow such heartbreaking atrocities to occur on this earth."

Sarah squirmed, and her heart beat slightly faster as she realized he was replying to a question she had asked the day they met in San Francisco. Although she was sure the darkness must conceal her from the vantage of the brightly-lit stage, he seemed to stare right at her.

"Here's the thing, friends. God doesn't create misery. And yes, he 'allows' it, but only because of the amazing gift he gave us at creation—free will. God doesn't do *this*." He indicated Sita's scarred face. "People do this. Evil does this. But God *does* do something about it. He sends people like you, and people like me, to care for the broken-hearted, the orphan, and the widow. Please, friends. Consider partnering with me to bring hope and healing to the broken-hearted widows and orphans of Mumbai."

As he set the mic down and made his way off the stage, the congregation clapped. Sarah could see a few wet faces. She clapped, too, but inside, her gut roiled.

Steve stared into the face of horror almost every day. He seemed to be an intelligent person. Yet he still, very obviously, believed in this religious nonsense whole-heartedly.

None of it made sense to Sarah. As the pastor gave some closing remarks and the band came back onstage for a final song, Sarah kept glancing at Steve. She realized she was trying to make all the pieces she knew of him fit into the same puzzle, but no matter how hard she tried, they stubbornly refused to meld.

This biography was going to be very interesting, indeed.

Sarah stood at a self-serve coffee counter in the brightly-lit church foyer and stirred sugar and cream into her mug, trying hard not to look approachable. The last thing she wanted right now was to be trapped into a conversation and have to explain what she was doing there and how much she'd rather be elsewhere.

The coffee bar was another difference to what she remembered from her childhood. It appeared that the after-church potluck social had been replaced by socializing over coffee. She thought it was an improvement. *If you like socializing at churches, that is.*

Sarah turned and glanced at Steve as she took an experimental sip. He stood near the sanctuary doors, chatting with people and shaking hands as they streamed past him and through the foyer, getting his money's worth out of that million-dollar smile.

Sarah noticed a middle-aged couple moving in her direction, so she casually drifted away from the coffee bar.

Peeking through an open door, she was pleased to discover an uninhabited room that was obviously some sort of library. It was a fair size, with shelves lining the walls, a circular table surrounded by padded chairs in the centre, and a couple of overstuffed chairs beside a gas fireplace on the other side. An unoccupied desk sat near the door.

Blowing across the top of her cardboard cup, Sarah sauntered around the room, scanning titles. There were Christian books on every topic, it seemed— marriage, addictions, apologetics—whatever those were—Bible studies, history, even home education. She got to a shelf entitled "self-help" just as a middle-aged woman in a flowing skirt and a silvery pixie cut entered the room. Sarah turned to the shelves to avoid making eye contact, pretending to study the titles intently.

The spine right in her line of sight was a title about healing from Childhood Sexual Abuse. In spite of herself, she pulled it off the shelf to read the blurb on the back. It had never occurred to her that she might be able to find a book that would help her deal with the flashbacks and nightmares she was having, but this one looked interesting.

"That book helped me a lot."

Sarah jumped, and hot coffee slopped onto her hand. She dropped the book and hurriedly set the cup down on the floor while the other woman apologized profusely and scrambled for some tissues on the librarian's desk. With no other immediate options, Sarah licked the burning liquid off her hand and patted it dry on her skirt, wincing in pain.

"I am *so* sorry! I didn't mean to startle you." The woman thrust a wad of tissues at Sarah, keeping a couple to soak up the coffee drops in the carpet. Sarah accepted the offering and bent to pick up her cup and the book, dabbing at brown streaks on the cover and the outside of the cup and assuring the woman that she was all right, no harm done. Still, it was several minutes before the mess was cleaned up and the woman rose to stand awkwardly before her.

"You're visiting today, aren't you?"

The woman's cheeks were slightly flushed in what Sarah guessed was embarrassment. Sarah felt a twinge of guilt that her clumsiness had made the other woman so distraught. She thought that the least she could do was talk to her for a few minutes to put her at ease that she truly was fine.

"Yes. I came with Steve McGuire to hear his presentation. Do you attend here?"

The woman nodded. "I'm Kathy." She stuck out her hand with a broad smile.

Sarah shifted the coffee cup to her left hand and gingerly took Kathy's hand with her right, trying not to wince as it brushed her stinging skin. "Sarah."

"That book helped me a lot," Kathy said again, indicating the book that Sarah had tucked under her arm.

Sarah glanced down at the book and heat started creeping up her neck. Kathy probably assumed that Sarah was interested because of her past. Never mind that it was true, the last thing she needed was to bare all her dirty laundry to a stranger she met in a *church*.

"I'm, uh, a writer. I thought the topic looked interesting." This woman hadn't asked for an explanation, but Sarah felt the need to distance herself from the subject of the book in her hand.

"Oh?" The woman's eyebrows lifted. "What are you writing?"

This topic wasn't any better. Sarah squirmed at the reaction she knew she'd see if she mentioned she wrote erotica. She decided to offer the response she thought would be more socially acceptable to a church-goer.

"I'm writing Steve's biography. That's why I came."

"I see. How does CSA relate to that?" She tilted her head, not in shock, but as though a thought had just occurred to her. "He wasn't a victim, was he?"

Sarah gasped and shook her head. "Oh, no! Lord, no. Nothing like that. I'm also writing a fiction book and the character experiences sexual abuse."

"Oh? I hope your focus is on the healing, and not the abuse?" Kathy tilted her head in hopeful interest.

Sarah nodded. She hadn't thought about that part yet, but she liked the idea of her pseudo-fictional character finding healing—even if she didn't believe it was possible for herself. The beauty of writing fiction was that she could create the ending she wished for, not the one she got.

Kathy shifted her weight and adjusted the purse strap over her shoulder, looking Sarah directly in the face with a friendly smile. Sarah knew that her bruises barely showed any more, especially under her makeup, and the cut on her lip was nearly healed. However, the intensity of Kathy's gaze left Sarah sure that the woman missed very little. She shifted uncomfortably, wondering how to politely extricate herself from this conversation.

Kathy spoke before Sarah could say anything. "Steve gave such a great talk today, didn't he? What an amazing project! Will you be going to India to see everything close up?"

Sarah nodded, relieved at the abrupt switchback in the topic. "Eventually. I have some other things to take care of first. I . . . it's been a rough couple of weeks."

That felt lame, even to her. She wasn't sure why she felt the need to explain anything to this woman, but Kathy's openness seemed to encourage a like response, and Sarah wanted to deflect the questions she had seen forming in the other woman's eyes after her scrutiny.

Kathy nodded, her dangly feathered earrings swaying against her cheeks.

"Well, if you're around, maybe you'd be interested in coming to our CSA Survivors support group. I would have to check with the members to see if they would be comfortable having you there, and you'd have to maintain the confidentiality we expect of everyone, but some of them may be willing to talk to you. You would be more than welcome. Our next meeting is a week from Wednesday."

Sarah stared in shock. A support group? Where people were talking about being sexually abused? She wasn't sure she wanted to endure that. Bad enough that she had her own past to contend with, the last thing she needed was to hear how someone else was brutally used. However, she didn't want to seem rude to this nice woman.

"I'll, uh, think about it."

Kathy dug in her purse and pulled out a business card with her personal information. "Well, give me a call if you decide to come. We'd love to have you. The more people who are aware of childhood sexual abuse, the more chance we have to effect cultural change to prevent it."

Sarah nodded and accepted the card. She felt numb, and wasn't sure why. "Thank you," she murmured.

Steve stuck his head in the door. When he saw her, he stepped into the room, his face splitting into a grin.

"There you are! I wondered where you were hiding. Are you ready to go?"

"Yes!" Sarah started toward him, trying to conceal the relief she felt.

Kathy called after her. "Did you want to borrow that book? You just have to fill out the card with your name and number."

Sarah realized that the book was still in her hand. "Oh, I better not. I probably won't be back again."

"Do you live in Edmonton?"

Sarah wasn't sure how to answer that one. "I'm in the city fairly often."

Kathy waved a hand as she took the book from Sarah and flipped open to the library card pocket. "No problem, then. Simply drop it off during the week sometime after you're finished with it. It's definitely one of the best books I've read about CSA. What's your last name and phone number?"

Sarah meekly told her, and Kathy jotted them down on a library card which she dropped in a box on the desk, then handed the book back to Sarah.

"Enjoy. And I hope we get to see you next week."

Sarah nodded again, a weak smile on her face, then hurried out of the library before Steve could even open the door for her.

She didn't stop walking until she was standing beside her car.

twenty-four

SARAH HAD ALREADY CLOSED THE PASSENGER SIDE CAR DOOR BY THE TIME SHE SAW STEVE EMERGE from the building. She tossed the book on the dash, kicked off her shoes, and wiggled her toes in relief.

With so much standing and walking, her ankle was beginning to throb dully, and she was relieved she could let Steve drive. The Tylenol she had taken this morning to subdue the pain in both her leg and her abdomen was wearing off. She rummaged around in her purse until she found the small bottle of pain killers and washed down a couple tablets with the help of a bottle of water sitting in the console. The bottle had been left in the RAV for several days, and despite the sun that had warmed the interior of the vehicle while they were in church, there was a rim of ice clinging to the plastic where the water's surface had been. The near-frozen liquid made her teeth ache.

Steve hopped into the driver's seat as Sarah was putting on her seat belt. He clicked his own into place and started the ignition. His eyes flicked over the cover of the book on the dash, and then he turned to Sarah, a study in casual.

"What was that all about?" He jerked his head toward the church.

Sarah knew exactly what he was referring to. She probably wouldn't have lit out of there faster if the building had been on fire.

"Do you know that woman I was talking to?"

Steve shook his head. "I only come through here every year or two to give updates about what I'm doing. This church is way too big to meet everyone in a single morning. Who is she?"

Sarah frowned and began fidgeting with her skirt. "She said her name is Kathy. She, uh, invited me to attend a CSA support group."

Steve looked at her blankly. "CSA?"

"Childhood Sexual Abuse."

"Oh." He gazed at her for a moment, tapping the steering wheel with his thumb, then shoulder checked and backed out of their parking spot. "I take it you don't want to go?"

Sarah chewed her lip. "Are you kidding? I'm not big on strangers in the first place, and going to talk to them about all the crap that happened in my life? Sounds like as much fun as sleeping on broken glass."

Steve nodded, looking thoughtful, but kept his eyes on the road. "Aren't you writing a book about it, though? It might be easier to tell a few trusted people than a bunch of strangers."

"I'm not so sure. For one thing, the book will be marketed as fiction. No one will know that this was my real life. For another, what if I meet them and tell them what happened and they can't take it? What if they flip out, like my mom did?"

She felt a twinge of anger combined with guilty dread as Ellen's face flashed into her mind. Sarah hadn't called her yesterday. *Tonight*, she promised herself, stuffing her anger into a box to be dealt with later.

"It's a support group. They have all been through the same thing, right? I'm pretty sure talking to each other about stuff you can't talk about with anyone else is the point."

Sarah looked out the window as streets zipped by. They were in an older suburban neighbourhood. Late-falling leaves from birches and poplars littered grass that was still surprisingly green after the dry summer. Some people were out bagging them up, others getting in the last mow of the season. Several yards sported cheap plastic pumpkins and witches and other kitschy Halloween decorations. The thin blue backdrop of the October sky made the scene very picturesque—completely unlike the turmoil that roiled within her.

"I suppose you're right. I'm just . . . scared."

"Why?" Steve's voice was gentle and quiet.

Sarah shook her head. "I don't know."

Steve glanced at her, then back at the road. After several minutes, he spoke again. "When we have a new girl come to the shelter, it usually takes a great deal of time to convince her that she is truly safe. Many of them have nightmares and are terrified of going outside in case their previous owner sees them and makes them go back to sex work. They are deeply distrustful of me and our other male staff. Nearly all of them spend years dealing with Post Traumatic Stress Disorder. Wanna know what one thing seems to help most consistently, though?"

"What?"

"Telling their stories. No, they don't always want to, and no, they don't tell all of it. But for those who do, sharing their stories with each other, realizing that they are not alone, and knowing someone cares and can understand what they went through makes all the difference in the world." Steve paused, then cocked his head at her. "Remember Sita?"

Sarah nodded. She was beginning to feel like she knew the woman, though they had never met.

"Sita became a counsellor, and she now helps girls that have come in off the streets. Although it might seem strange that she is willing to take on their pain, she can, because she understands it. And they trust her far more quickly and easily than they would if I tried to talk to them, because Sita has been where they are."

Sarah stared at him, not sure what to say.

"The sooner they can begin to process their pain, the sooner they can begin healing. Those that don't—or can't—never truly stop being victims, even if they don't end up back on the streets." His gaze met hers. He didn't have to say the obvious—she knew he was talking about her, too.

"So, you think I should go." It was a statement, not a question.

"I think you should do whatever you're ready to do. And if you're ready to get involved with a support group, that's what you should do."

Sarah gulped. "I'm still not sure why you care so much about these women you work with." *Or me.*

Steve laughed, but it sounded brittle compared to his normal belly laugh. "Sarah, we all have our own wounds. We're all broken in our own way. Mine might look different than yours, but they were deep enough to enlarge my heart." He grinned, back to his upbeat self. "Besides, that's what being a Christian is supposed to be all about. Loving people."

Sarah shook her head. Despite having spent a whole morning in church with this man, she was still trying to wrap her head around him being a Christian. He was so unlike any other Christian she had known.

"Why are you shaking your head?" He squinted in amused curiosity.

Sarah gave a half-smile. "I'm trying to figure you out."

Steve laughed again, and this time it reached his eyes. "I'm not that tough to figure out, am I?"

"You're not like any man I've ever met before."

Steve glanced at her and his smile faltered. Something on her face must have betrayed what she was feeling right then. This man was gay, and Christian, and way out of her league even as a friend, and she had a past that gave her every reason to distrust men. Even still, she couldn't help but feel warm and tender toward Steve whenever she thought of him. He made her feel like she was a somebody, that she mattered. He showed her what it felt like to be respected as a person.

He left her completely flabbergasted. She didn't think she would ever feel worthy of his kindness. She'd spent a fair amount of time in the last week wondering why on earth he kept helping her when she could do so little to repay him.

They had reached the restaurant, a little brunch place called Cora's. Judging from the lineup out the door, it was a popular Sunday spot.

"Have you eaten here before?" Steve asked.

Sarah shook her head. "I've thought about it, but never managed to go."

Steve gave her a huge grin, his anticipation obvious. "You're in for a treat." He was out the door and opening hers before she even managed to get her shoes back on.

"Such a gentleman," she teased as he helped her out of the vehicle.

"When the lady is crippled, special consideration must be shown."

"I see." She gladly accepted the arm he offered to steady her as they went to stand in line on the sidewalk. She managed to walk normally and hoped he wouldn't realize how much pain she was in. "Thank you."

"For what?"

She kept her arm through his as they stood there. Besides needing the support, the extra warmth protected her hand from the crispness in the air.

"For being you. For saying 'yes' to the book. It lets me have a chance to repay you in some small way."

He had a puzzled smile on his face. "You don't have to repay me for anything. Everything I have done I have been glad to do. There is no debt owed."

"But I feel like there is. So, thank you."

Steve nodded. "Well, if it makes you feel better, okay. You're welcome."

They stood there for a few minutes in silence, moving only a few steps toward the door as the line inched along.

"You know, I've been thinking." Steve's eyes were dancing with mischief. "You're going to be learning all this personal stuff about me, and I won't be learning anything about you."

Sarah frowned. "Is that a problem?"

"Well, it's hardly fair. I don't even know your favourite colour, and you're going to be asking me everything from my first pet to most embarrassing moment. Turnabout is fair play, I was taught. Maybe you could fill out one of those 'all about me' memes, or something. Then I'd at least know if you prefer bacon bits or croutons."

Sarah's throat tightened again. Was he finally making his play, trying to guilt her into giving personal information that he could use against her later? She studied his face and saw only teasing good humour. She thought about replying the same way she always had with Craig, playing the game to make sure she didn't lose any ground. But Steve was nothing like Craig. And he deserved to be treated with the same honesty he was willing to give her.

"I'm sorry, Steve. I want to believe that you are the nice, helpful guy that you seem to be, I really do. And my head does. But when it comes to making friends, I have good reason to be a little cautious. I want to trust you, but it might take time." She bit her lip. "I hope you can accept that."

He studied her, then covered the hand she had wrapped around the crook of his left elbow with his own. "You know what? That's fine by me. You take all the time you need."

Steve peered over the heads of the middle-aged couple in front of them, trying to see if progress was being made. They were nearly to the foyer, which meant that Sarah could soon sit down.

"Both, by the way," Sarah said, eyes front.

Steve tilted his head at her. "Excuse me?"

"You asked if I prefer bacon bits or croutons." She glanced at him with a small smile. "The best salads have both. Don't you think?"

Steve's eyes crinkled in that deep grin of his. "Definitely."

They were only a few steps from the front door of the restaurant. Sarah shifted her feet, trying to alleviate the discomfort she felt, glancing around at the lineup that now trailed down the sidewalk behind them.

She froze, eyes riveted to a couple several metres in back of them.

Steve must have felt her stiffen. "What's wrong?"

"Craig. And Erica."

Steve twisted, simultaneously catching the hand that fell from his arm with his other one as he glanced behind them. He opened his mouth, probably to ask for a description, when Craig's eyes locked on Sarah and his face hardened. Erica glanced questioningly at Craig, then followed his line of sight. When her eyes met Sarah's, her skin faded to an ashy colour.

Sarah tugged at Steve's hand. "Let's go. We need to go now."

Steve nodded and they stepped off the curb toward Sarah's RAV4.

"Sarah," Craig called. His voice sounded like iron.

Sarah kept walking, eyes forward.

"Sarah!" It was a shout this time.

Sarah's step faltered.

"You don't have to talk to him," Steve said quietly. "He's not even supposed to be talking to you."

Sarah knew that. The police officer had made it clear that there would be no restraining order on Craig unless charges were laid, but that he would be strongly discouraged from making contact with her until a decision was made one way or the other. She had hoped his understanding of the justice system would be all the deterrent he needed to prevent him from doing so. Apparently not—not when she was right in front of him.

She nodded, tight-lipped, and kept going. Her heart pounded so hard she feared a rib might break.

She heard footsteps behind her, and Erica trying to convince Craig to walk away and not make a scene. A hand grabbed her arm and stopped her short. She whirled.

"What, Craig?" She hoped she sounded angry, not terrified.

Sarah felt Steve place a steadying hand on her back. She could have kissed him right then.

"Is that him? The pimp?" Craig's voice was low and threatening. He was probably trying to keep his words contained, but he was still loud enough to be plainly heard by the lineup of onlookers. His handsome features were made ugly by anger. "Are you two together, now?"

Sarah gave an angry shrug. "And if we were, what difference does it make to you?"

Craig's eyes bulged. "A helluvalot! You're my wife, in case you've forgotten!"

Sarah gaped. The blatant hypocrisy of this man, who had her former best friend glued to his shadow, seemed beyond what even she thought possible. She had no idea how to respond to that.

Steve stepped forward and held out a placating hand. "Hey, man. We don't want any trouble. Why don't you go back to the line and we'll get in our car and leave?"

Craig's face reddened as he looked up at Steve, batting his hand away. All efforts at restraining his volume seemed abandoned. "'Your' car! *My* money paid for that car, you assclown. You've got some nerve, dating my wife. And you." He turned back to Sarah. "How dare you cheat on me, you bitch! First you get me arrested, then you hook up with this douche bag?" His eyes narrowed and he pointed at her. "I'm going to enjoy what's going to happen next, you slut. And trust me, you won't. I'm going to take every penny that belongs to me. And I haven't forgotten what your dog did to me, either."

Erica pulled on Craig's arm, her voice pleading. "C'mon, Craig. Let's go."

Craig didn't back down, his feet firmly planted and his hands curled into fists at his sides.

Steve wedged his body between Craig and Sarah. He stood several inches taller than Craig, and it seemed he was trying to accentuate the difference. He raised his hands in a placating gesture—or perhaps he was ready for action.

"Hey, back off, okay?" His tone was quiet, but hard. "Just walk away."

Craig glared at the taller man, then finally moved back a step. He whirled and marched past the lineup of staring people toward his car, wrenching his arm from Erica's grasp.

Erica cast a concerned frown first at Sarah, then Craig. Finally, she started after her boyfriend.

Steve turned toward Sarah, but kept a wary eye on his reluctantly retreating adversary. "Ignore him, Sarah. Let's just get in the car and go. This isn't helping."

Sarah didn't move. She was trembling so hard she worried she wouldn't be able to remain erect. The familiar icicle of fear sliced through her gut. She wrapped her arms around herself.

What did Craig intend to do? He'd already locked her out of their accounts—thank goodness she had started one of her own and socked enough money away to help her float for a few months. Could he really do something to Nelson?

The thought of her dog being hurt made panic start to bubble up into her throat. Maybe she could fix this, at least a little.

"Craig!"

Sarah's soon-to-be-ex-husband turned to face her, lips in a thin line. A step behind him, Erica stopped moving, but kept her eyes on the asphalt.

Sarah tried to look defiant and strong. "Nelson didn't do anything except protect me from you. And Steve and I aren't together. He's gay, remember?"

Craig glared. He didn't say anything, just whirled again and stomped away. Erica struggled to keep up on her high-heeled shoes.

The couples in line, many of whom looked like they had just gotten out of church, shifted uncomfortably and whispered and pointed while trying not to look like they were pointing. Sarah took them all in, then turned and got into the car through the door Steve was holding open for her.

He got in behind the wheel and started it up. She was breathing so hard, she felt like she'd run a race. She watched Craig and Erica get into his Audi and peel out of the parking lot. Erica glanced up at Sarah on the way by, then quickly looked away.

Sarah took several long, deep breaths, trying to slow her heart, and wished for a glass of wine. Steve grabbed her hand and squeezed. She looked up at him gratefully, squeezing back.

"Thanks for sticking up for me," she said.

He smiled. "My pleasure." He cleared his throat, and she noticed that he seemed a little stiff and his face was red.

"Is something wrong?" She worried that he might have gotten more than he bargained for this morning and was regretting that he'd asked her to come.

He looked straight ahead out the window. "Um, Sarah, I'm not gay."

It took a moment for that to sink in. Sarah's jaw dropped. "You—you're not? I thought you told me you were! In San Francisco!"

He shook his head, his jaw muscles tight. "I only went along with what you seemed to think. You were completely, um, sloshed. Correcting you didn't seem worthwhile, especially when you didn't seem likely to remember any of it and I didn't expect to see you again."

Sarah was thunderstruck. Heat rushed up her face until it felt like she could fry an egg on it.

He looked at her, a puzzled frown on his face. "If you don't mind me asking, why on earth did you assume I was?"

Sarah stuttered. Why *did* she? "Well, you are so good-looking and nice, but you didn't seem interested in me romantically at all, even though you kept stalking me around San Francisco. Or anyone else, even that waitress who kept flirting with you at the Canuck Cafe. And you said that your partner's name was Paul—"

"Paul? My 'partner'?" Steve interjected incredulously. He sounded like he was choking. "You thought I meant we were together as a couple?"

"Well, yeah. That's how it sounded."

Steve's face was flaming red. He looked like he didn't know if he should laugh or be outraged.

"Paul is my ministry partner. His wife's name is Aparna. And I'm completely heterosexual."

"Oh."

Sarah felt like an idiot. She had always prided herself on her gay-dar being foolproof, yet she had been hanging around with this very sexy, very *straight* man for two weeks now and hadn't had a clue—or hadn't wanted to. She realized she had relaxed around him because she thought he *was* gay—that he was "safe."

She gasped. If Steve were straight, that meant her warm feelings toward him were suddenly one more source of danger. She stiffened and pulled her hand out of his, tucking it inside her other hand on her lap. It still radiated the heat it had absorbed from his. She rubbed it as though to massage away the memory of how safe she had felt with it in his grasp only a moment ago.

"Are you okay?" Steve asked, concerned eyes searching her face.

Sarah nodded stiffly and forced a smile.

"I'm fine. But I don't think I'm all that hungry now. Do you think we could just go home?"

"You sure?"

Sarah couldn't tear her eyes from Steve's searching gaze.

"Yep. As long as you don't mind waiting that long to eat."

He nodded. "I'll be fine. It's only an hour. You're sure you'll be okay?"

She nodded again. "I'm a little shaken up, that's all. Just give me some time and I'll be okay."

That seemed to satisfy him, and he put the car into gear, but didn't pull ahead. "One more thing—we should probably report that incident to the police."

Sarah's heart deflated further, but she knew he was right. She looked at him and nodded. He squeezed her forearm with an encouraging smile, then turned his attention to driving.

On the way to the station, and all the way home afterward, Sarah kept her eyes fixed out the side window, scared to look at her companion. The vice grips of fear were clenched around her heart, but she didn't want him to see the change in her. He would keep pressing for the reason, and she didn't want him to know it was because every time she looked at him, she yearned for the warmth of his touch, his gentle smile to turn her way, or to hear his deep voice resonate through her. It had been so long since she had been treated with warmth, tenderness, or respect that her starving soul had been soaking it up like a cactus after the rain.

When she'd thought he was gay, those emotions seemed like a girlish crush, one that could never be indulged and was therefore harmless.

Now that she knew that Steve was just as straight and dangerous as every other red-blooded heterosexual male in the world, the thought of being with him terrified her. She had never been able to remain "just friends" with a guy, and the idea of romance set off all her alarms.

Wondering how he felt about her in return made her nauseous. As much as she longed for that human connection, she didn't think she could ever trust another man enough to let him into her life. She had already told Steve too much—he knew about her "mark," the one that broadcast that she was damaged goods, easy prey. It seemed like only a matter of time until he took advantage of that, no matter how trustworthy he had seemed to be up until now. Craig had been the picture of charm and sincerity until the day they were married, and look how that had turned out.

She had woken up that morning grieving that Steve would be leaving for the other side of the globe in two days.

Now, his departure couldn't come fast enough.

twenty-five

SARAH LAY ON THE COUCH IN THE LARSONS' LIVING ROOM, A SOFT THROW WRAPPED AROUND HER legs and her laptop screen staring blankly at her.

Her hosts, including Steve, had been invited out to dinner by a couple at the Larsons' church. Being the gracious people they were, they had invited her to come along. She had begged off due to exhaustion, which was no exaggeration. The confrontation with Craig on top of the rather active morning had pretty much done her in. She had actually been relieved to be left alone for the evening.

The police officer who had taken their statements had commended them for coming in right away.

"Will she be able to get a restraining order now?" Steve had asked before they left.

The husky ginger-haired man in navy blue had tipped his head to the side. "I can't say for sure, but it is likely. I'll call you tomorrow to let you know."

Sarah had nodded, still shell-shocked. "Thank you."

Nelson stirred on the floor beside her, and Sarah reached down to give his soft head a pat. She had snuck him into the house to spend time with her, moving his pillow from the garage to the floor by the couch and making sure he stayed put on it. She respected her host's wishes to not have him near Sophie, but she had missed having her faithful shadow with her during the past week—yet one more reason she was going to have to find another place to stay soon.

After taking some pain meds, changing into her yoga pants and getting settled on the couch with some tea, she had felt sufficiently recovered from the afternoon's ordeal to entertain the idea of getting some work done on her book. Becky might have said to take whatever time she needed, but Sarah didn't want to push her agent's—and her editor's—good graces too far. And now, she finally felt like she knew where to begin.

Or so she had thought. The blank word processor mocked her, and she smacked the keyboard in frustration, leaving a string of nonsense letters on the screen.

"Why is this so hard?"

Nelson lifted his head and looked at her as though he wished he could give her the answer. Sarah sighed, feeling guilty for distressing him.

"It's okay, boy. Lay down."

He gave a small whine in the back of his throat and obeyed.

Sarah chewed her lip and rested her wrists on the laptop, fingers poised in readiness.

She had managed to avoid Steve for most of the afternoon by pretending to sleep, though avoiding thoughts of him was a different matter. She had dozed a bit, but never truly rested. The reason why was still preventing her from getting any writing done—much more than Steve McGuire, she couldn't stop thinking about Craig and Erica.

Erica, who had been her best friend for six years. Erica, who had apparently broken up her own marriage, as well as Sarah's, over this affair. Sarah wondered if John, Erica's ex-husband, had known she was having an affair, and if so, who it was with. Maybe he had. Sarah couldn't remember the last time Craig had gotten together with him.

No wonder. Apparently, Sarah had been the only one too blind to see what was going on. All this time, she thought that if she only loved Craig enough, was good enough, did the right things, he would treat her better.

Well, maybe she had been losing hope in that regard. In fact, as things had gotten worse and worse, she had felt more and more like she must somehow deserve the treatment she was getting, and that she would never be "good enough." Just like she had idolized her father and believed for years that she had deserved the abuse he gave her, as Craig's violence escalated she had believed him when he had pinned his behaviour on her.

Maybe Craig was right about how lousy of a wife she was. After all, she didn't always listen to him or spend money the way he wanted. As much as she enjoyed cooking, she knew she wasn't that great at it. And she knew that other women were more passionate in bed than her—the woman who faked love more than she made it.

But dammit, when Craig had married her, he had given her his word to honour and respect her to the exclusion of all others. And he had lied.

The brand of that lie seared her soul. She smacked her leg this time, which was quieter than the keyboard. Nelson gave her an enquiring look and laid his head on the spot she had just hit. She began petting the soft fur and felt her anger ease with every stroke.

In the past six days, she had been treated with completely undeserved respect and kindness by strangers. She bit her lip again. She realized that part of her had been on constant alert, waiting for the other shoe to drop. How long before they, too, realized that she didn't deserve to be treated that way? How long before she wore out her welcome?

How long before they showed their true colours?

Sarah knew that wasn't fair. In the short time she had known Steve, he had already seen her at some fairly low points, and he knew more about the dark parts of her past than anyone else alive. Yet he accepted her, never wavering in showing her respect. He also must have kept her secrets, because Joanna and Derek had been nothing but gracious and never hinted that they thought she might be a bad influence on their daughter or unsafe to have in the house. Or maybe Steve *had* told them something, and they didn't care about that.

But if that was the case, why were they helping her? Why were *any* of them helping her? Would their religion have guilted them into doing it? What were they getting out of this?

Remember the boy and the ball. Sarah sighed. Some people really did help because they simply wanted to help. And maybe these people helped more than others would because, well, she didn't know. It still made no sense to her.

Steve wasn't gay. The thought hadn't left her mind all day, ever since he'd told her. She had reviewed every interaction they had ever had, trying to decide if he was looking for something more than friendship, but all the evidence would suggest he wanted nothing from her physically. The realization left her feeling ugly and unattractive, which she realized made no sense—she would have felt the same if he had made a pass at her.

No wonder he hadn't. Steve wasn't the kind of guy to get involved with someone as messed up as her. He probably didn't want to touch her with a ten foot pole, and she couldn't blame him. Which meant that he was still safe, right?

Sarah frowned. No matter how gentlemanly Steve had behaved up to this point, she no longer felt the same ease and comfort when she thought of him.

How could she trust him? If he was as decent as he seemed, why was such an attractive catch as Steve still single?

Derek and Joanna had insisted she stay as long as she needed to until she could get on her feet again, and had blown her off when she offered to pay for room and board. But between her sudden fear of getting too close to Steve—or his family, which would only strengthen the ties indirectly—and hating to feel like a freeloader, she knew she was going to have to move on soon.

On a whim, she began searching the Internet for apartments in Edmonton. She wrinkled her nose at what came up with her original price range and adjusted her search terms, hoping she could find a way to afford it. Within an hour, she had contacted several management companies and even set up a couple of viewings for later in the week.

That was all great, but she knew her savings would disappear fast if she was living on her own again. Too fast. She was going to be paying a divorce lawyer soon for a battle that Craig promised would not be quick and easy, and who knows what other expenses might come up in that process? Until her advance came in for *Her Father's Daughter*, she needed to conserve every penny.

There was no way she could live here that long. It didn't seem right to take advantage of the Larsons for several more weeks, or maybe months. The fact that Derek and Joanna wouldn't let her pay them made her feel indebted to them. She hated that feeling.

But that left only one person she could go to—her mother. Her stomach flipped at the thought. Besides a couple of texts, she hadn't spoken to Ellen since she had been tossed so unceremoniously into the night last Monday. Anger crawled under her skin and danced along her veins as she thought of how, even when told the blatant truth, her mother had still sided with Everett. Would she even let Sarah stay with her?

And if she did, could Sarah handle being there?

The voicemail messages Ellen had left had been typical—she sounded vacantly worried, as though she had nothing to do with the reason that Sarah was staying with strangers and had had to rely on them, not family, to help her get to her medical appointment. The very lack of acknowledgement of Ellen's role in Sarah's predicament infuriated Sarah even further. It was just like her mother. Living in a dream world of Ellen's own making, exactly like she had all through Sarah's childhood.

Of course, that also meant that if Sarah wanted to go back, Ellen would probably pretend that nothing had even happened. Could Sarah live with that?

Headlights pulled into the driveway, nearly blinding Sarah as they swept over her face. She glanced at the time. Nine o'clock already? She jumped up and coaxed Nelson to his feet, grabbing his pillow and dashing down the stairs with him in tow. She had barely managed to get him into the garage and closed the door behind her when the front door opened.

She dodged out of the way of the swinging door on the small landing, jumping onto the bottom stair of the ascending flight, and there stood Steve. His cheeks were ruddy under a grey toque he had borrowed from Derek. She was close enough to feel the chilly air clinging to his denim jacket. He smelled of frost with hints of evergreen.

Steve started when he looked up and saw her standing so close. Still off balance from her jump onto her good leg and trying to avoid contact, Sarah swayed backward and sat down on the stairs hard. His face broke into a grin.

"You didn't have to greet me at the door." He chuckled as he offered a hand to help her up. She accepted it, and the inertia of his heave landed her directly in front of him on the landing, staring up into his face. Through the open door, she could hear quiet conversation and the van doors closing as Derek and Joanna collected Sophie and all the gear babies required.

"I was, um, getting ready to walk Nelson." She was intensely aware of his hand around hers, warm and rough. His eyes were crinkled from his easy grin, and twinkling with that joke that always hid behind them.

His grin didn't fade as he met her gaze. Neither one of them broke contact.

"'Scuse us," whispered Derek as his form filled the door, diaper bag slung over his shoulder and a blanket-covered infant carrier over his arm.

"Oh!"

Sarah tried to pull away from Steve to dash up the stairs, but he stepped back to the other edge of the landing against the wide-open door, pulling Sarah with him. Her shoulder pressed against Steve's chest as she huddled out of the way, letting first the baby-laden Derek kick off his boots and head upstairs, then Joanna, who was close behind. Joanna mouthed a greeting with a bright smile as she went by. Sophie must be asleep.

As soon as the quiet flurry passed, Sarah realized how near to Steve she stood and jumped away as if burned. Her arm felt cold where it had been pressed against him. He gave her elbow a gentle squeeze, a warm smile on his face, and closed the door.

Her emotions were like scrambled eggs—she felt tingly and alive and afraid. There was a knot in her throat, either of excitement or terror, she wasn't sure.

"Do you want company?" Steve asked.

"Huh?" Sarah stared blankly.

"On the walk. Would you like me to come?"

Sarah tried to shake her head, but found herself nodding instead.

"Okay."

Sarah walked with her hands tucked into her armpits, Nelson's leash looped around one hand. With her coat, hat, and gloves on, she wasn't cold, but the posture felt safer somehow. She might have agreed to have Steve along, but now that he was here she didn't know what to say to him.

The walking path they had taken yesterday was transformed by darkness and the magic of the frozen night. Orange light from the street lamps on the other side of the houses refracted a million times through crystallized fog hanging in the air, making the path much brighter than it would otherwise have been.

Sarah loved October nights like this. It always felt like she was walking through a movie set. With the occasional exception of a lighted window blinking at them from a house's angular silhouette, it felt like she and Nelson and Steve were the only living creatures awake in all of Miller.

Steve broke the blanketing silence.

"Did you get much writing done?" He strolled beside her with his hands in his pockets, his long legs making his strides seem relaxed compared to her quick, irregular pace.

"No. But I managed to book some apartment viewings." Saying it aloud, she realized that she was truly going to be moving on with her life soon. The thought of living somewhere without Craig—without anyone—made her catch her breath.

Steve nodded. "That's great!" He caught her expression and frowned. "Isn't it?"

She offered a weak smile. "Yeah, it's good. It's just—I've never lived alone before. There was always family, or roommates, or boyfriends, or Craig.

Now, it's only going to be us." She indicated Nelson, who was trotting happily beside her, occasionally investigating an interesting smell at the walking path's grassy edge.

Steve kicked at a stone on the path and sent it skittering into the dried grass. "My dad once told me that you can never be truly happy with someone else until you learn to be happy with yourself." He pressed his lips together in a rueful grin. "Seems like he was right."

Sarah's jaw clenched. The words had the weight of truth, like a wisdom saying that would appear on an Internet meme in beautiful calligraphy superimposed on a picture of the ocean shore. But if it was true, she didn't know how she would ever find happiness—of all the people in her life that she was unsatisfied with, she found the most fault with herself. However, after so many years of pain at the hands of others, she was willing to give the idea of trying to be happy alone a try. Even being unhappy alone had to be better than the misery her life had been so far. Didn't it?

Steve's face had clouded over and he was gazing, unseeing, into the ethereal mist that billowed around them with every step. Sarah wondered at his somber look.

"Everything all right?"

Steve jolted and focused on her. "Hmm? Yeah. I was thinking about when my dad gave me that bit of advice. I was deeply in love, and sure she was the answer to all the things that were wrong with me. I didn't want to believe him. But time has proven him right."

Sarah's head snapped up in surprise. Steve had been in love? It obviously hadn't worked out. Was that the reason he was still single? A broken heart? She burned with questions, but wasn't sure whether it was her place to ask. She bit her lip and decided to venture a tentative enquiry.

"What happened with you and her, if you don't mind me asking?"

Steve's face closed for the first time since she had known him. "She . . . wasn't the person I thought she was. And I guess it went both ways."

Sarah nodded and decided to leave it alone. "I don't remember you mentioning your dad before. Where are your parents?"

Steve's expression brightened. "South America, in Brazil. They are missionaries down there."

"Really? How long have they been there?"

Steve looked thoughtful. "Almost fifteen years, I guess."

"What?" Sarah was dumbfounded by this piece of information, mostly because she had never imagined anyone being a missionary for even a short amount of time, let alone making a vocation of it. "Has it been that long since you've seen them?"

Steve chuckled. "Oh, no. They come home on furlough every few years. They'll be here again next spring, but I'll be in India and won't get to see them until I get home a few months later. They'll be glad to get to meet Sophie at last, though."

Sarah digested what she had just learned. She had never met such a bizarre, backward family in all her life. Steve gave up a career as a lawyer to work with prostitutes in India. Joanna and Derek took in complete strangers who needed help. And their parents were career missionaries in South America, despite having a new grandchild in Canada. She shook her head in puzzlement.

"What?" asked Steve with a laugh.

"I can't decide if your parents being missionaries explains everything or if I'm even more confused by it. I mean, have they always been missionaries? Even when you were a kid?"

Steve shook his head. "Nope. Well, not really. We did one short-term mission trip to Mexico, but mostly, we stayed in Miller. My parents always treated this as their mission field, though, and never passed up the opportunity to help someone if they could give it."

"That must be where you get it from."

Steve tilted his head at her. "I try. But I was quite selfish for a lot of years. Selfish and miserable. My parents fostered." He paused, as if this was all the explanation she needed. After a moment, he continued. "I couldn't understand why my parents were constantly taking in 'stray' kids. I always felt like I didn't truly belong, that I was just another charity case that they had taken on. I was angry."

Sarah frowned. "Why would you feel that way?"

"Well, I guess it's because I was adopted."

Sarah blinked. Another shock. "You were?"

Steve nodded and kicked the pavement. "When I was eighteen months old. Six months, if you count the time they fostered me. I didn't know anything about my birth family, but I always imagined how much better my life might have been if only they hadn't given me up. I wouldn't have to wear hand-me-down clothes and share my room with the foster kid of the month. It was the little fantasy I fed myself whenever I was angry at my parents, when I felt like they didn't really care about me." Steve shook his head. "I was such an idiot."

Sarah wasn't sure how to respond. "What changed?"

"Well, at camp one summer, our cabin did this skit that was based on one of Jesus' parables. You know what a parable is?"

Sarah nodded, hearing her Sunday School teacher's voice in her head. "Parables are stories that have lessons, like a fable, except parables might be true, right? In other words, no talking animals?"

Steve gave a slight nod of acknowledgement and continued. "It was about this rich man who was throwing a party, and he wanted to invite all his friends. So he had his servants go around town giving out invitations, but they all came back with dumb excuses about why the friends wouldn't make the party. It was completely insulting. So the rich man got angry about how ungrateful they all were, and told his servants to go find absolutely anyone on the street and bring them in to this feast. He had prepared his table with the best that money could buy and he wanted someone to enjoy it, so he opened his home to the people who would truly appreciate it. I got the part of the rich man's head servant, which was a speaking role. Felt pretty important."

Sarah chuckled at the image of a young Steve dressed in a butler's tuxedo, puffed up with pride. The most difficult part was picturing him as prideful. It was so opposite of the man she knew.

Steve shook his head. "I remember that we were performing this the last night of camp. Everyone was watching, and I was so nervous. Everything went fairly well until I had to deliver my last line. It was after all the beggars and lame and poor people had been seated at the banquet table. I had thought hard about how to deliver this line. I thought that this servant was looking at all those lowlifes in his house—the house he'd spent all afternoon cleaning— and was probably not impressed. Maybe he thought that if the riffraff could eat the banquet, why hadn't the servants been invited to join in? So I crossed the stage and bowed to the rich master, and told him how all the bums had been brought in, but that there was still room—but I did it like I was hoping for a reward, you know?"

Sarah laughed. "Was that how the line went? 'We brought in all the bums?'"

Steve laughed, too. "No, it was much more polite. I was far too well-trained of a servant to use that kind of language to my master."

Sarah was still chuckling. "Okay."

"Anyway, the next thing the master does is tells the servant—tells me—to go out into the country and just keep inviting people, dragging them in if necessary until the banquet table is full, because there is so much room and food. I stomped off the stage, acting like I thought this angry, jealous servant would act in that situation. The script didn't say to do it, I just did. Except I was truly angry, it wasn't only an act. You should have seen the other kids' eyes. One girl asked me what my problem was. My counsellor came to talk to me about it after and everything. And it was like thunder struck my fifteen-year-old brain."

"What happened?" Sarah held her breath.

"I realized that I was like that jealous servant, angry at the generosity of my parents, even though my mom and dad had never neglected any of my needs. Sure, I might have to wear second-hand shirts and didn't always get to go on the cool field trips. But they always made time for me. Every Saturday morning that he wasn't on a business trip, my dad would take me out for pancakes and we would hash out our week. Joanna got her own thing with Dad, but that was mine. But he did special stuff like that for the other kids, too. I used to get mad that I 'didn't get treated any differently than the fosters,' as I saw it then. But that night of the play, I realized what a selfish jerk I was. My parents had lots of room at the table, and I had a permanent place at it. They didn't love me any less when they invited others to join us, too. They simply had so much love to give that they were spreading it around."

"Wow." Sarah wondered what it would be like to live somewhere that was safe not only for herself, but was a haven for others, too. She felt a little jealous of Steve, even though she understood why he might feel angry for being raised like that. "So were things better between you and your parents after that?"

"I wish I could say that everything was great between us from then on. Changing my attitude helped, but it was still many years before God truly got a hold of my heart and I let go of the rejection I felt from my birth family, realizing I had painted my adopted family with the same brush. And it probably wasn't until I went to India that I finally saw the needs all around me and began learning to love people the way God does. The way my parents do."

Sarah frowned and stared at the pavement. "The God you talk about is very different from the one that I was raised with."

Now it was Steve's turn to look interested. "Really? You went to church?"

"Oh, yeah, we went. Every time the door was open, we were there. My dad was an elder in our church—that little white one on the south side of town?"

Steve nodded.

"Everyone thought he was such a great guy. Others would come to him for advice. He led Bible studies and we always had to look perfect and act perfect so we wouldn't embarrass him and Mom. But at home, it was a completely different story. We were never perfect enough. We could never please him. And Mom never gave me the time of day—she was always too busy with her friends, or her shows, or the house. The only time I ever felt special was when Dad . . . when he—" Sarah's voice broke. A gasping sob clutched her throat.

Steve put a comforting hand on her shoulder. She wanted to shrug it away, but was so thankful for the connection that she didn't.

All at once, something in her crumbled—the dam made up of all the excuses she had made for the father she loved. The wall chinked with words—words she had used to protect herself from giving in to the anger that only led to more pain, from hating the father who was supposed to love *her*, but instead had only neglected and abused her—disintegrated in a heaving sob. A tidal wave of grief flowed through her.

"I *hate* him!" She balled her hand into a fist and smacked her leg, barely feeling the pain. The gaping wound in her soul hurt far more than any mere physical blow. And the hate that surged through her was for more than just her father.

"I hate them all! How could Craig do this to me?"

Her steps slowed, then stopped, as the floodgates of control burst and she began sobbing uncontrollably, spasms wracking her. She covered her face in her hands.

"It's okay. It's okay." Steve kept saying it like a mantra as he folded her into his arms.

She turned into them and buried her face in his chest. "What did I do to deserve this?"

"Nothing. None of it was your fault. None."

She nodded, but the words were so obviously untrue that they slid off of her like water on oil. If she hadn't deserved it, why had it happened? Her father was a respected man—everyone said so. And he was her *dad*. She must have been a terrible daughter, or why had he treated her that way?

And Craig. Why would he go from so wonderful to so horrible unless she had done something to disappoint him? Conflicting feelings of desperate love and bitter hate for the men she constantly strove to please and perpetually disappointed rushed through her veins.

Steve kept holding her and rubbing her arms until the outpouring of emotion subsided and she was able to regain control. His chin rested on her head, and the seeping warmth comforted her.

She was suddenly very aware of his musky, piney scent, the cold, stiff denim of his coat beneath her cheek, the heat of his hands rubbing her arms. She pulled back, wiping her wet face on her glove and sniffling slightly. He handed her a crumpled but unused tissue he'd dug out of his coat pocket, which she accepted, eyes averted.

"Thank you," she murmured as she dabbed at her face. She mentally kicked herself for once again playing the weak fool in front of Steve.

Nelson was lying on the ground looking up at her, small whining sounds escaping his throat. She removed one glove, squatted down, and patted his head, ignoring the sharp pain the motion sent through her injured ankle.

"It's okay, boy. Mama's okay."

Nelson licked her hand. She felt herself become more grounded as she comforted him. He sat up and wagged his tail, his tongue lolling out as he gave her a doggy grin, and her heart warmed. Her breathing returned to normal.

She wondered if this same feeling of compassion and protectiveness was what prompted Steve's constant kindness to her. The thought of someone feeling protective toward her warmed her. Then she frowned.

You're protecting yourself now, fool girl. Slow learner much? She didn't want to depend on protection from Steve, or her mother, or anyone, ever again.

But she knew his kindness wasn't only for her. She had seen how he was with Sophie and Joanna. She had seen his face as he talked about Sita, Priya, and the other women he worked with. This man truly did seem unique among men—selfless to the point of exhaustion, only he rarely seemed exhausted.

Sarah thought about the "God of love" she had been told about as a kid, but had always equated with the torturing, condemning, twisted "love" her father had given her. In a moment of clarity, she realized why she had married Craig—he had controlled and manipulated her life the same way her father had. It was what she'd thought love looked like, and it had made her feel like they cared. But the kind of love she had known from her father and Craig couldn't be any more different from the sacrificial love that Steve and his family lived out every single day. How could they both be called the same thing?

She shifted her weight to stand up and gasped as her ankle betrayed her. Steve's hand extended into her line of sight. She grasped it and he pulled her to her feet. For the second time in an hour, she stood staring up into his face from close proximity. She could feel her pulse quicken, but didn't step away.

"Ready to go back?" His gentle smile held no demands, only concern.

Looking up into his open face, with its five o'clock shadow and blue eyes edged with laugh lines, Sarah knew that this man was the real deal. He had no hidden agenda. What she had seen was exactly who he was.

Never before had she been so desperate to be liked by someone, to be found worthy. But standing before the brightness of Steve's genuineness and authenticity, she wanted to cringe and hide. There were far too many ugly, hideous things about herself that she hoped would never be exposed to the light of day. And the inner light he radiated seemed destined to expose her dark places eventually. What would he do if he knew how he affected her? What if he rejected her like everyone else in her life had? The familiar icicle tore through her gut, and frost formed on her heart. Better not to give him the chance.

She nodded and pulled her hand from his. "Okay."

Turning, she limped with determination back toward the house, barely glancing at her companion in case he saw the emotions surging through her.

How could she taint this man by even being friends with him, let alone yearn for him to put his arms around her again? She couldn't afford to wait until Steve left on Tuesday morning. She needed to put a safe distance between her and Steve now, no matter the cost. For his sake.

And for hers.

twenty-six

STEVE POURED HIMSELF A CUP OF COFFEE, STIRRED IN SEVERAL HEAPING SPOONS FULL OF SUGAR and a large dollop of cream, and settled himself at the dining room table next to his niece's high chair. She gurgled at him, one saliva-covered finger stuck into the corner of her dimpled grin.

"Morning, Sophe." He pinched her cheek and she smacked the tray happily. Sophie's breakfast was over, but Joanna let her daughter play in the chair while she went about prepping everyone else's.

Sarah entered the kitchen and sat down across the table next to the wall.

"You look nice." Joanna poured her a cup of coffee. "Big plans today?"

"I guess." Sarah shrugged shyly. "I, um, called my mom last night and we worked stuff out a bit. She told me I could stay with her until I get my own place. So, I'm going to be leaving after breakfast. Thank you so much for extending your hospitality to me this long."

"Oh! You know you are welcome to stay longer, right?" Joanna arched a brow at Sarah, who dropped her gaze. "But I'm glad to hear you talked to your mom. I hope staying there will be good for you two."

Sarah nodded and reached for the sugar. "Me, too."

Sophie smacked a teething rattle on the plastic tray and squealed in loud delight at the noise she produced. Sarah cast a regretful smile at the cherubic girl Steve knew had been both a reminder of her shattered life and a balm for her broken heart. Sophie grinned back, still chewing on her finger.

Steve cleared his throat. "Well, that's good to hear. By 'worked things out,' does that mean she believes you now?"

Sarah glanced furtively at Joanna, who was busy wiping spit-up off of Sophie's face with a wet cloth.

"Well, no, probably not. I think as long as I don't mention 'it' again, she won't, either." She finished doctoring her coffee and took a sip, changing the subject with a firm tone. "The coffee's good, Joanna."

Joanna smiled brightly in thanks at the compliment.

Steve nodded, keeping his face even, but the hint that Sarah was done talking about her mother right now was not lost on him. His gut clenched. He couldn't help but wonder if this was the best move for Sarah. He worried that Craig would have much easier access to her at her mother's house, and so would her brother. Thinking about the men who had taken advantage of his friend made his blood boil, as it always did when he was confronted with abusers of any kind.

Safety concerns aside, Steve wondered if living with her mother and pretending that nothing had gone wrong between them might make it easier for Sarah to slip back into old patterns—patterns he had seen hints of as he had been getting to know her. Patterns from which she was just beginning to free herself.

God, protect her.

He took a bite of his toast, contemplating the situation. He had been avoiding the thought of the goodbyes, which he hated. He told himself he was simply worried about what would happen to Sarah after he left for India tomorrow. Now he was going to have to say goodbye much sooner than he'd been prepared for.

He had to keep reminding himself that his concern was completely platonic, that he cared for her only as a friend, and that Joanna could do just as good of a job checking in on Sarah as he could.

Glancing up, he caught Sarah looking at him. She smiled, blushing, then dropped her gaze to the plate of scrambled eggs Joanna was setting before her. The sun coming in the front window made her forget-me-not eyes seem to glow from within. Even from under her lashes, he could see their iridescent shine and resisted the urge to reach out and lift her chin so she would make eye contact.

Sarah had been strangely awkward since yesterday. He was trying not to let that bother him. At first, he had thought it odd that she would feel more comfortable around him when she believed he was gay, but then realized that, with her history, that might not be so odd after all. Every man she had ever known had taken advantage of her. She must be waiting for him to do the same. Still, it bothered him that she might believe he could.

Not that Steve ever would. He couldn't deny his attraction to her—a man would *have* to be gay, and possibly blind, not to appreciate such a beautiful woman—but he also knew that it was almost the worst timing possible for a romantic relationship, on both their parts. She had been separated from her abusive husband for less than a week and was only beginning to work through the mountain of baggage she had brought with her from childhood. He was about to leave the country for six months. If he made a move on her—not that he wanted to, but if he did—he would only be living down to her expectations.

Sarah needed support and space, not romance. He told himself again that his feelings were *strictly* platonic. Strictly. And it had nothing to do with Vanessa, or what she had done to him.

Sarah was not Vanessa. In fact, no two women could be more opposite. Vanessa had been a wild ride, the kind of woman who intoxicates you with her live-in-the-moment tenacious approach to life. But she had left both his heart and life in ruins. Sarah was cautious, careful, gentle, and kind. She expressed nothing but admiration for his work, respect for his family, gratitude for his friendship and a desire to help him in the best way she could—by writing about him. He shook his head. The idea of having a book written about him still boggled his mind.

Sarah amazed him. She had endured so much, and still kept trying for something better. More than that, she kept a kind heart. Despite all that she'd been through, she didn't seem to have a spiteful bone in her body. There had been no cries of "I'll make him pay," when she had decided to report Craig, only a conscious decision to stop living in an abusive situation.

In fact, the more he found out about her, the more he admired her. Her upbringing made his seem like a trip through Candyland by comparison. As he watched her struggle to find her bravery, he sometimes felt ashamed at how shallow his past injuries seemed, and how long he had let them rule his life.

But no matter how much he liked her, that didn't change the fact that right now, what she needed was a friend—and nothing else.

Steve felt a sharp pang of sadness at the thought of her imminent goodbye, which he had hoped would be the last one he would have to say when he departed tomorrow.

"What's wrong?" asked Sarah, catching the look on his face.

He glanced up, startled from his reverie, to see concern in her eyes. He covered his lapse by taking a sip of his coffee, grimacing at the sharp flavour.

"I should have made myself tea instead of settling for this swamp water."

Sarah chuckled. "You aren't a coffee guy, are you?"

Steve shook his head. "Nope."

Joanna gave an exaggerated sigh and put on a longsuffering expression. "Well, nobody's perfect, big brother."

Steve pasted on an aghast expression. "What are you saying?"

Joanna rolled her eyes. "Someone had to break the news to you eventually. As your sister, I guess it was bound to be me."

Steve laughed. He would miss Joanna, as he always did. He turned back to Sarah, who was still laughing at the sibling banter. Was it possible that he would miss Sarah more? He was closer to the emotional line than he'd realized. Maybe it was for the best that she was leaving this morning.

"I'll help you pack up the RAV after breakfast." His tone was too cheerful, and he knew it.

She didn't seem to notice.

"Thank you." She smiled again and reached for a few sausages and orange slices to go with her eggs.

"You're okay to drive today?" He indicated her ankle with a jerk of his hand.

Sarah flexed it slightly and her lips pressed together. It obviously still hurt. "Yeah, I'll be fine. It's only across town."

"Okay." He grinned at her. "Can't keep a good woman down, right? Not with a mere skydiving injury. Or abdominal surgery. Or—just who are you, Wonder Woman?"

She chuckled, and the smile made her whole face radiate.

Steve found he cracked jokes far more often when she was around, just so he could see the transformation rendered by her smile. It was magical. And addicting.

He realized he had been smiling and staring a little too long and grabbed a newspaper that sat on the other end of the table. It was open to the financial section. Derek must have been reading it before he left for work.

Sophie gurgled and banged. Joanna cooed to Sophie and took up the conversation with Sarah. Steve buried his nose in the newspaper and tried to ignore the debate between his head and his heart.

Man, that smile was amazing.

Good thing she's just a friend.

Steve folded another shirt and tucked it into his suitcase, which lay on the neatly-made guest bed. By this time tomorrow night, he would be on a plane back to Mumbai. Well, London, then Mumbai. He could hardly believe it was already time to return. But he was only nominally focused on the packing—an activity he could probably do in his sleep, he travelled so much. Images of Sarah kept creeping into his thoughts.

He had hoped that once the goodbyes were over and she was out of sight that he would also be able to put her out of mind. From now on, they would be communicating professionally about the biography from either side of the world's largest ocean. He could focus on his work and being a helpful friend without any ridiculous infatuation to distract him.

A subtle hint of her perfume wafted up from the quilt, and the memory of comforting her in his arms on last night's walk flashed into his mind. He closed his eyes and sighed with the memory of her silky hair under his chin and her soft curves against his chest.

He pressed his lips together. It might take a few more days to "put her out of mind."

"Should I leave you and the hairbrush alone?" Joanna stood inside the open door, a teasing smile on her face.

Steve realized he had been staring at a hairbrush in his hand, but not actually seeing it. What thoughts had shown on his face? He laughed to cover his embarrassment.

"We have some good memories together, this brush and I." He tossed it into his shaving kit and turned. "What's up?"

"Oh, just wanted to hang out. You know. The last day before goodbye."

She came over to the bed, moved a shirt to make room, and sat down.

Steve gave her a crooked smile. "What, you're not counting down the seconds until you get rid of me? Until you and Derek have your house all to yourselves? Who *are* you?"

Joanna chucked a pillow at him, which he caught with a laugh and returned. She tucked it behind her back against the wall and leaned on it.

Steve picked up the shaving kit and zipped it closed.

Joanna glanced at it with a musing look on her face.

"Do you remember Alison?"

Steve looked up, startled, then focused on his task with an intensity that should have lit his clothes on fire.

"Yep."

"She came to stay with us when I was about twelve, so you were, what, fourteen?"

He hadn't thought about Alison in years, but now her face popped to mind as though he had said goodbye yesterday.

He'd always remember her face.

Alison had been thirteen when she had come to live with them. She had tried to intervene in a beating her father was giving her mother, which only resulted in him putting both of them into the hospital.

Of all the foster kids that had come through the McGuire home, Alison was the only one Steve had felt an immediate connection with. She had seemed so tough, but he soon saw through the brave act. They discovered a shared love of The Simpsons and Red Hot Chili Peppers, and spent hours analyzing the finer points of tattoo art in the magazines stashed in his secret cubby in the wall of the furnace room. He had quickly grown as protective of her as he was of Joanna. Not surprising that he'd developed a crush.

After Alison's mother had recovered, she had left Ali's father and completed all the courses and requirements of Family Services so she could get her daughter back. But Steve couldn't accept that Alison would be better off with her mom. He was convinced that her mother would go back to her father and Alison would be worse off than ever. He knew it had happened to some of the other foster kids they had had, because the McGuires were often not a child's first placement.

Of course, Steve had no say in the matter. Alison had returned to her mother's and he hadn't ever seen her again.

He had called Ali a couple of times, but she sounded distant, and things weren't the same between them. Eventually, her number was no longer in service. After he graduated, he went looking for her, hoping to reconnect. His hunt fizzled at a dead end when he found out she had run away at sixteen and hadn't been heard from since.

He had never felt so miserable being right.

After Ali went home, Steve had maintained a safe distance from their other foster kids, although there hadn't been many more. His parents gave up fostering soon after—probably thanks to his tumultuous teen tantrums.

Steve glanced at his sister, then back at the shirt he was refolding to fit better into his suitcase. He affected a casual tone, as though the memory Joanna had evoked no longer bit deeply with the bitter taste of his own impotence. "That sounds right."

"Sarah isn't her."

Steve frowned and stopped his busy work, staring at his sister.

"Why would you say that?"

Joanna cocked her head and raised an eyebrow.

"Really? You think I don't see how attached you are becoming to her or noticed that worried look you've had for days when you thought no one was watching?"

Steve grunted, the comment about Alison putting him on guard. "I've been worried about the care centre, nothing more."

Joanna's skeptical eyes bored through his pretence.

Steve growled. "Fine! Of course I'm attached. Sarah's a great person. Don't you like her?"

Joanna sighed. "Yes, you know I do. But I don't want you to go overboard with worrying about her. She'll be fine. She's a big girl and she's taking some positive steps."

Steve frowned. "But this is such a crucial stage for her. She is beginning to change, but it would be too easy to slip back to the way things were." Back to Craig. Anger stabbed his gut at the thought. "Her mother isn't going to help, that much is obvious."

"You don't know that for sure. This could be Sarah's mother's chance to change, too."

"Because that happens so often."

Joanna shook her head. "You know it does happen."

Steve said nothing, tucking the last few items into his luggage.

"You know, I'm pretty sure Superman's secret identity is Clark Kent, not Steve McGuire. But even he couldn't save everyone."

"I'm not trying to be Superman, Jo." His voice was much colder than he'd intended.

"Aren't you?"

Steve zipped his bag shut and rested his hands on it.

"Joanna, it is my mission in life to help abused women and children. That's what my entire life's work is about. God put Sarah in my path and told me to help her, so I did. He gave me this job for a reason. And it's okay for me to like her and worry about her. So I'd appreciate it if you would back off a little."

Joanna closed her mouth and stared at him, forehead furrowed.

"Fine." She crossed her arms. "I was only trying to tell you that you aren't the only one God can use to help her, Steve. Maybe you've done your part. Go back to India, run your school, and leave Sarah in God's hands. You don't have to try to control the outcome. You're not the Lone Ranger, you know."

How ironic that she chose the same erroneous analogy he had used with Sarah yesterday. But he was too upset to point it out. Steve mashed his lips together. "Thanks. I'll keep it in mind."

He stepped back toward the wall, making a clear path between the bed and the door. Joanna took the hint, got up and gave him a hard stare, then turned away.

"Joanna—"

She stopped at the door and turned to face him.

He ran a hand through his hair, gathering his thoughts.

"You know, I often feel like that little Dutch boy in the story with his finger stuck in a hole in the dike, trying to prevent inevitable disaster. I know the problem is bigger than me. I know I can't do it all. But I also know I can't simply sit and do nothing. I have to at least try."

Joanna's face softened. She stepped toward him and placed a cool hand on his arm.

"I know." She gave him an understanding smile. Then she turned and went upstairs.

Steve stood there watching only one of his many Tontos as she walked away. In his anger, he had momentarily forgotten that he wasn't the only one with his finger in a hole. There was a whole group of people who were working with him to repair the dike—people who had joined him, not because of anything he did, but because God had told them to. Joanna was right. He was only one tool in God's tool set. After snapping at his sister, he *felt* a bit like a tool, and not the useful kind.

No, he wasn't alone. And neither was Sarah.

He turned off the light and followed his sister to apologize.

twenty-seven

SARAH PULLED UP TO THE CURB IN FRONT OF HER MOTHER'S HOUSE AND PUT THE RAV INTO PARK, but didn't turn off the engine. She chewed her lip as she stared at the snow-dusted vehicle in the driveway. Everett's.

What is he doing here?

She had spent the day in Edmonton, first with her divorce lawyer, then picking up the keys to her new apartment, and finally at Kathy's support group. She had hoped that she had come home late enough that her mother would be in bed and she'd be able to avoid conversation of any kind. After three weeks of tiptoeing around her mother's epic denial, she was only a night's sleep away from freedom. It couldn't come soon enough.

Her stomach clenched. She hadn't counted on having to face Everett before making her escape.

How ironic that tonight's group session had been about creating safety from abusers and here was one of them, seemingly lying in wait. She pondered driving back to the city and sleeping on the floor in her new place, but then thought of Nelson—she couldn't leave him here. Besides, Ellen would probably be calling the police by midnight if Sarah hadn't at least checked in.

She sighed and turned off the vehicle.

The house seemed mostly dark, but a small, soft light glowed through the front drapes. Everett and Ellen were probably visiting in the kitchen. She decided to try to sneak in the front door and up the stairs without them noticing her.

As soon as her key rattled in the lock, the entrance light came on and Ellen opened the door. Her mother stepped outside and closed the door behind her, wrapping her cabled cardigan around herself against the frigid air.

"Mom! What are you doing up?"

Ellen gave her a look. "You know very well that your brother is here." Her voice was hushed. "He's sleeping on the couch tonight. I didn't want you to disturb him when you came in."

"Me disturb *him*? Mom, what the hell? I don't want to sleep in the same house as him! Tell him to go home!"

Ellen looked stunned for a moment, then her face darkened. Her voice rose in quiet anger, but still low so as not to be heard inside. "Sarah Victoria! You will *not* use that tone with me. This is my house, and you have no right to tell me who may or may not sleep here. What is your problem, anyway?"

Sarah's jaw dropped. "You can't be serious. You know exactly what my 'problem' is. It's *him* and what he did to me. How he still treats me!"

"Don't you start with that again. You will not ever bring that up with me again, do you understand?"

Sarah saw the warning look in her eye, and decided to try another tack. If she could sleep in a warm bed instead of on a bare apartment floor tonight, that would be her preference.

"Why isn't he sleeping at home? It's not like there's a blizzard. I just drove in from Edmonton and the roads are fine."

Ellen's mouth opened, then closed. She looked away. "Jill kicked him out."

Outrage exploded in Sarah's chest. "So Jill kicks him out and you put him up on the couch, but I come to you beaten and bruised after leaving Craig and you send me packing? That's how it is?"

"He has nowhere else to go."

"And you think I did?"

"Well, you did, didn't you?"

"No, Mom. I didn't. It was sheer luck that I didn't end up sleeping in my car for the next week."

"Sheer luck" was the only answer she would let herself accept, Steve's divine directives notwithstanding.

Ellen frowned and put her hand on the door handle. "I'm done talking about this, and I'm done talking out here. I'm freezing. If you don't want to sleep in the same house as your brother, you are welcome to leave." She began to open the door.

Sarah shook her head in disgust. "You're unbelievable, you know that? Un-friggin'-believable. I can't believe that I thought it would help for me to be here, that you might actually care. What a joke."

Ellen stepped back and closed the door but didn't take her hand away from the knob. She frowned up at her daughter. "Why do you always twist things around? Why do you always make me out to be the bad guy?"

"You think that's what I'm doing? Mom, Everett abused me for over ten years and he still acts like a complete jerk to me. I don't even want to see him, let alone sleep in an unlocked room in the same house as him. How can you not get that?"

"I *told* you not to bring that up again."

"Yeah, well, not hearing it doesn't change the fact that it happened. And you can't tell me what to do anymore, *Mom*. I'm all grown up now, remember?"

"Really." Ellen crossed her arms. "Well, you're living under my roof, aren't you, oh wise and adult daughter of mine? So as long as you do, you will stop spouting lies and behave like a civilized human being to me *and* your brother. Do you understand?"

Sarah gave her mother a hard look. What was the point of arguing in the face of such adamant denial?

"You can hide your head up your butt for the rest of your life if you want, Mom. It seems to have worked for you so far." Sarah gritted her teeth. "And you might as well give Everett the guest bed. I'll grab my bags and my dog and then I won't ever be 'under your roof' again."

Ellen blinked, but didn't back down. "Fine, if that's the way you feel."

"It is the way I feel."

"Fine."

"Fine."

Ellen clamped her mouth together and frowned even deeper, then whirled and opened the door, leaving it open for Sarah to follow her inside but quietly stomping toward the kitchen without even glancing back at her daughter.

Sarah stepped in the door and glanced at the bulky form beneath a blanket on the couch. She wanted to slam the door to spite her mother and "Special Everett." Instead, she closed the door without a sound and quietly climbed the stairs.

She realized with chagrin that fear of her brother still outweighed anger at her mother by a long shot.

As she threw her clothes into her suitcase, she wondered if there were any twenty-four-hour Bed, Bath, and Beyond stores in Edmonton. But even if she couldn't find a pillow and a blanket anywhere before she got back to her apartment, she knew without a doubt that she would sleep far more soundly on the bare carpet under her winter coat than she would under the queen-sized duvet of her mother's guest bed as long as Everett was in the house.

Tonight, her "safe space" was anywhere but here.

As she drove away, she glanced at Nelson in the rear-view mirror. He sat in the middle of the back seat and panted quietly, looking at her with a steady swamp-brown gaze.

"We'll make our own safe space, won't we boy?"

Nelson stretched his neck and licked her cheek. She reached back and scratched behind his ear, keeping her hand entwined in his long mane to enjoy the warmth and remind herself that she wasn't completely alone. Thank God for Nelson.

She gave a sardonic snort as she realized what thought had just gone through her head, wanting to push it away in anger. Glancing into the mirror at those brown eyes, though, she knew that if there was a god somewhere who had any interest in her at all and who had bestowed anything good on her miserable life, Nelson was it—the one good thing. She honestly didn't know what she would do without him. A surge of gratitude filled her heart to the brim and her eyes stung. She swiped at the tears to clear her vision.

"God, do you exist?"

Nelson kept looking at her with that steady gaze. Other than his panting, the only answer was the hum of the tires on asphalt.

Sarah waited for a few minutes, then shook her head angrily at herself.

Now was no time to begin believing in fairy tales.

twenty-eight

STEVE STOOD IN THE DINING ROOM AT THE REAR OF PRAKAASH HOUSE, STARING THROUGH THE window at the building's small courtyard with his arms wrapped across his chest. The modest space was shaded from the morning sun by the building itself. In a few hours, it would be baking in the afternoon heat.

At present, the courtyard was occupied by twenty-odd grade school children arranged in a rough grid. Paul's nephew Ajay was leading them through the forms of a traditional dance, and they were mimicking the graceful movements with varying degrees of success. From a plastic chair in the shade of a Plumeria tree on the far side of the yard, Paul's energetic beating of the small tabla drum between his knees kept time for the group. Every single child seemed to be giving it their best effort, fully committed to learning the motions.

Steve mulled over that morning's encounter with the building's landlord. He had managed to negotiate yet another extension of their lease, but Vijay Paresh had been none too pleased by it. Steve had even tried, once again, to persuade Paresh to let them buy the property. The man had been even less receptive to that idea.

If they weren't able to find another appropriate building soon, Steve was afraid that all the hard work they had done with Prakaash House would be nullified by the project becoming homeless. What would happen to these children then?

Steve felt a presence beside him and turned to see Sita's round face watching through the window, also.

"She does well, no?" Sita asked, indicating her daughter with a flick of her chin.

Steve turned back to the courtyard and singled out Aashi, her black hair pulled back into a thick, short pony tail to keep it out of her face. She dipped and swayed in time to the drumbeat.

"They are all doing well, I think. I have rarely seen them all so focused. And look at little Pushpa. Have you ever seen her so carefree?"

The little girl who normally seemed to carry the weight of the world on her shoulders twirled in a wild pirouette and landed with her foot just *so*, gyrating her hips in time to the music, a rare smile on her lips.

"This was a good idea, Uncle Steve. You were right to hire Ajay to teach the children to dance." After all these years of knowing him, and now working with him, she still used the familiar honourific of "uncle" at times.

Steve chuckled, embarrassed. "I got tired of breaking up brawls, that's all. Needed to give these kids a safe way to blow off some steam."

Sita turned to him, smiling warmly. "God show you this, I think." Her accent turned "this" into "dis." It was one of the easier Indian accents for his Canadian ears to understand. "He give you wisdom to know what to do, and you turn a bad thing into a good thing."

Steve smiled down at the petite woman. She was no taller than some of the girls in the courtyard. "Perhaps you are right. I sometimes wish I could always find the answers to my problems so easily."

Sita nodded, her good eye twinkling. "Pray to God, Steve. He provide answers."

Steve smiled. It figured that this woman he had mentored would now become the teacher. "You are right. Thank you for the reminder. Perhaps I also need to pray for faith as big as a mustard seed."

Sita's eyes twinkled as she realized he was referring to Jesus saying that a person with faith the size of a mustard seed could move mountains. "You have already moved some mountains, no?" She indicated the dining hall, encompassing the whole building—and their whole history together—in her gesture. "Why you worry?"

Steve crossed one arm across his chest and cupped the other elbow, rubbing his chin with his hand and looking out the window—but not at the children. His thoughts were with Sarah.

He hadn't heard from her in over a month, and before that, their communications had been perfunctory, at best. Apparently, he hadn't imagined the awkwardness he had felt from her on their final day together. At first, he had thought that it might be for the best that he'd had a chance to distance himself. But as the weeks passed, he found that he was becoming desperate for news of her. He'd hoped Joanna would be able to keep tabs on her, at least, but his sister had been silent on the subject. Not that he could blame her—she was a very busy woman. But still, he worried that Sarah was potentially fighting through her battles unsupported.

"When I was in Canada last year, I made a new friend. She was going through a very difficult time. It is for her that I worry."

Sita nodded, a knowing look on her face. "I am no surprise. You always worrying for others. She is a believer?"

"No, she isn't. But she was trying to do better in her life when I left."

"So why you worry?" Sita eyed him sharply, her dark eye flashing.

Steve frowned. "Since I came back here, I have hardly talked to her. I want to know how she is doing. I am worried that she may need help."

"How you meet her?"

"I—" Steve faltered as he thought of trying to explain all the circumstances surrounding his meeting with Sarah. He decided to focus on the most important factor. "God told me to talk to her, so I did."

Sita's gaze became intense as she stared hard into Steve's eyes with her one good one. It made her seem taller than she was, and with her eye patch, she reminded him of a fierce and adorable pirate. "Then, why you worry?"

Steve opened his mouth to answer, then paused.

God told me to talk to her. Did I think he would abandon her because I left? He knew my itinerary.

"You know what? I don't know." He laughed to cover his embarrassment. "Trying to do too much again, I suppose." He narrowed his eyes in mock censure. "When did you become so wise, sister?"

Sita's eye twinkled up at him. "I had a wise *guruji* and he teach me well."

Steve laughed.

"The student has become the teacher." He pressed his palms together in front of his chest and bowed to his friend in jest.

She laughed, too, flushing slightly at the true complement hidden in the joke.

Priya, the cook's helper, appeared at the door to the adjoining kitchen. "You are here to talk to me, auntie?"

Sita turned. "Yes, Priya, it is your appointment time. We go to primary classroom, okay?"

The women exited through the door to the courtyard and Steve watched them pass the window on their way to the stairs leading to the second-floor classrooms around the corner of the building. He paused, musing about the purpose of Sita's visit to Prakaash House today.

Priya had left the red light district two years ago at the age of sixteen and had impressed many of the staff with her dedication to her schooling and recovery. A year ago, she had begun vocational training as a seamstress. Shortly after, she'd begun working as a maid and cook's helper at Prakaash House to earn some extra income. But two years after leaving her traumatic past behind, she still had regular counselling appointments with Sita.

Was it so unreasonable to want to check in on Sarah when she had begun working through her own difficult past so recently? All he wanted was some assurance that she was still moving forward, that she hadn't regressed after he'd left and perhaps even gone back to Craig. The last thought seemed to darken the room with a sickly shade of jealousy.

Steve batted the idea away. *I'm not jealous, I'm concerned.*

Even still, he couldn't deny that he hoped she would not go back to Craig until her husband had undergone months, maybe years, of treatment for his personal issues. Steve didn't believe in lost causes. But people like Craig made him question how firmly he held that belief.

He ran his fingers through his hair, watching the children perform the routine again. They were trying for synchronization with their movements, but failing in the way of awkward fawns still learning their bodies' capabilities. It would be years before they accomplished the fluidity of motion that Ajay made look so easy. Still, the young man patiently worked with each child, correcting an elbow here, a posture there, showing movements over and over again, exactly like he had every day for the last two months.

If it could take two months of dedicated practise to only begin to retrain a child's nimble body to learn how to dance, it would take at least that long, and longer, for Sarah to learn how to break her old ways of doing things. He knew she was trying, but perhaps she needed a *guruji* to check in on her, just to make sure she was keeping to the path she had begun walking.

Yes. That was wise. But he didn't want to seem to push her into a relationship with him before she was ready. He understood where her mistrust came from—that it had nothing to do with him. As much as he wished it were otherwise, he also knew better than to force her to accept his friendship before she was comfortable. But he also knew a way to work around that.

I trust you, God. But I need to know.

Reaching a decision, he pulled out his phone to call Joanna.

twenty-nine

SARAH PULLED BACK HER BEDROOM CURTAIN, EXPECTING TO SEE THE MUD AND GRIME THAT THE New Year's mild temperatures had left behind. Instead, the view revealed a world transformed by a fresh layer of snow. Amazing what a little snow could cover. It was like the city was getting a fresh start.

Sarah grunted. *How long until the shine wears off your fresh start, too, Edmonton?*

She turned away from the window to get dressed, the thought of fresh starts tasting bitter on her tongue. Two months ago, she had left Miller sure that she was beginning a better phase of her life. She would be happier and more successful than ever before, determined that she was finally on the road to happiness.

The first few weeks had been amazing. She had finally broken through her mental block on her book and pounded out the chapters and synopsis that Becky wanted. Her agent had liked what she had seen, and so had her editor, and Sarah's advance cheque soon came in the mail. Between that and the money that Craig had turned over to her from their joint account—thanks to a keen move by Sarah's divorce attorney—she had managed to create a little haven for herself here.

Outfitting her new home without having to bow to anyone else's tastes had been exhilarating. She wanted lime green towels? No one objected. Bright yellow paint in the kitchen? No problem. Watermelon accent pillows in the living room? The whole decorating committee gave unanimous approval.

It was empowering. She had never known this kind of freedom, and knew that she had done the right thing by striking out on her own.

But now, the glamour of making all her own decisions was getting a little tarnished. She wanted to order Chinese for supper for the third night in a row? Of course she could. No one cared what she chose.

And therein lay the problem. No one cared what she chose. As she'd always feared, independence was a terribly lonely freedom.

She sat in her cheery kitchen and sipped her coffee, watching the flakes drift by outside the balcony doors. The grey skies managed to dampen even the citrusy interior with melancholy, as though sadness was the price the city had to pay to cover its previous ugly patina.

Nelson whined, sitting patiently by the apartment door. Even he looked gloomy. Perhaps he sensed her mood.

Sarah gave a sardonic snort. At least someone would miss her if she was gone—even if it was only her dog.

Sarah had finished *Her Father's Daughter* and sent it to Becky and Yolanda only yesterday. She thought she would feel elated to finally be nearing the end of that writing contract. But instead she felt a little lost, like there was something else she should be doing, if only she could remember what. Steve's face flashed through her mind, and she pushed it aside. This had nothing to do with him, or the voicemail from Joanna she had yet to return. Definitely not.

She finished her coffee, rinsed the cup in the sink, then got dressed to go outside. Nelson perked up, realizing that his patience was about to be rewarded.

Sarah's melancholy lifted a little as it always did when she saw the joy in her canine friend's eyes. As she clipped on his leash and they headed out into the fresh air, she took a moment to be grateful for Nelson. The thought wasn't addressed to anyone in particular, but she was still thankful for him. Simply focusing on being grateful for something in her messed up life for a few moments made her feel better.

Snow crunched under their feet as they headed toward the dog park, and the fresh air nipped at her cheeks. She huddled into her winter gear and kept her head down, oblivious to the sparkling beauty around her.

As Sarah had developed her new routine and the luster had worn off of being free, she had increasingly isolated herself. That hadn't been difficult, as so very few people even cared enough to check in on her at all. Except her mother. And she never picked up the phone when Ellen called anymore.

Sarah's gut twisted in guilt and anger. Since their fight in November, things between Sarah and her mother had only gotten worse. Sarah hadn't even gone home for Christmas dinner. Ellen refused to understand why and Sarah was sure that her mother blamed her for the rift in their relationship.

Ellen blaming Sarah for everything? *And is the sky still blue somewhere above those clouds?*

When they reached the park, Sarah let Nelson off leash and wandered. She could see the river from here, its centre still running freely. The park was remarkably peaceful, despite the traffic noise drifting through the air. It was a marked contrast to the anxious, angry boil of her bubbling thoughts.

She'd been avoiding more than just her mother recently. Besides Ellen, she had yet to return the call from Joanna. That Kathy woman had been making a bit of a nuisance of herself. And she hadn't been in contact with Steve for over a month. A sharp pang of sadness and regret made her pull in on herself. She jammed her hands into her pockets.

I seem to be getting good at avoiding people.

Sarah hadn't even talked to Jill since Everett had moved back in. Somehow, Jill had gotten Everett to agree to go to counselling, and Everett had convinced Jill to let him come home.

Sarah frowned. How could Jill have let Everett move back so soon? Then she thought of how long she had clung to her relationship with Craig and her anger turned inward. Could she honestly sit in judgement of her sister-in-law? At least Everett was going to counselling, which was more than Craig would ever have done.

Thinking of Craig sent the familiar spike of fear through her gut. She lived in constant dread that she would run into him somewhere, or that he would show up at her house unexpectedly. She hadn't told him where she lived, but she knew that someone like him would be able to track her down in a heartbeat if he tried. Would his position as a lawyer be enough to keep him from becoming a crazed stalker, especially now that he had been suspended until the charges against him were resolved?

Sarah called Nelson to her and clipped the leash back onto his collar. She had stayed at the park for as long as she could bear the cold, not eager to return to a house devoid of both company and purpose. But she could feel her toes going numb and the tips of her fingers burning in icy pain. Nelson didn't object to being leashed, however, and when she told him to heel, he fell into place at her left side.

Another dog owner with a small black terrier approached. Sarah moved to the edge of the walking path and told Nelson to sit so that the strangers could pass unobstructed. The woman gave her a friendly greeting and Sarah forced a cheerful tone into her reply, then watched with relief as the woman and her dog passed without further conversation. With reluctant steps, Sarah turned Nelson toward home.

As they walked, Nelson turned his head in curiosity to watch the scenery, his tongue lolling from a contented doggy grin. Sarah smiled at him, feeling slightly envious of his simple life.

She still couldn't believe that Craig had filed for custody of Nelson in the divorce. She knew he was trying to manipulate her, but her heart froze thinking about what would have happened had he been successful. What would he do to Nelson out of spite for her? She gave a shiver that had nothing to do with the cold and reached down and patted the dog's soft head, as though to reassure herself he was still there.

Nelson looked up at her and whined.

"It's okay, boy." She petted his head, then straightened so they could continue. "I'll always look after you."

Nelson wagged his tail and barked at her, then went back to peering curiously at their surroundings, floppy ears alert.

When they got back to the house, Sarah brewed herself another cup of coffee and leaned against the counter, cupping it in her hands to absorb the heat. She noticed a collection of dust bunnies in the corner of the room with dismay. Well, housework hadn't exactly been a priority lately, what with her single-minded focus on finishing the book.

I have time now, don't I?

She set the cup on the kitchen table to let it cool for a few minutes and began tidying the various piles of clutter in the living space in preparation for vacuuming and dusting. While straightening the stack of reference books in the corner of her desk, she noticed the book she had borrowed from that church library in October.

She had never done more than thumb through it. She kept meaning to take it back, but something had stopped her—fear. If she was honest, she was afraid of running into Kathy and having to explain why she had never returned to the support group or returned any of the woman's calls about it.

The two support group sessions she had attended in the fall had been revealing—and terrifying. They had stirred memories and feelings that she hadn't been ready to deal with, especially with all the other upheaval in her life at the time.

When she had moved into her apartment in November, spurned once again by her own mother, she told herself it was better to try to work things out on her own than rely on anyone else, so she had stopped attending. The other group members didn't know why she was really there, after all. They simply thought she was doing research for her book.

Apparently, she hadn't fooled everyone. Either that, or Kathy was extraordinarily persistent in helping her with her "research." She had called Sarah at the end of December to tell her about a more structured support group beginning mid-January and invited her to join, explaining that it would walk the attendees from being victims to survivors to thrivers. Sarah had blown her off, but the idea of the scale of recovery had stuck with her.

Where am I on that scale? Was she a victim? She didn't think so. In fact, she was trying her best to make sure she would never be a victim again. She had joined a karate class at a local dojo. The twice-weekly sessions were the highlight of her week. Even small things she learned made her feel empowered, like she would never have to be a victim again. Did that make her a survivor? And what was a "thriver"?

Sarah picked up the book about CSA, setting the other books from the pile back on her desk. She chewed her lip as she read the back cover blurb, remembering the day she had picked it up off the shelf in the first place. What had changed since then?

Since leaving her mother's two months ago, she had tried to do everything on her own, and yes, she had made some positive steps. But the nightmares hadn't stopped. She still lived every day in fear. She had told herself that the isolation with which she buffered her life would protect her. But in reality, it was just another mask.

So many masks.

She might have exposed her crappy personal life to public scrutiny, but she was still hiding. When the cashier at the grocery store asked how she was doing, she would put on a bright smile and reply with "fine." She couldn't even be honest with a stranger.

But she was so not fine. Finishing *Her Father's Daughter* had not given her the satisfaction she had hoped for. The days blended in a hazy progression of loneliness. And the future that had seemed so bright in October was now obscured in grey fog, like the view outside her window. She tried to move forward, but could always feel the black hole of her past dragging at her. It pulled in all the light from every good thing she accomplished. More and more all she wanted to do was give up. Life was simply too hard. How did she ever think she could make it better than it was?

She looked at the book in her hands and frowned. What if progress was possible? Maybe there was a way to escape the crushing pull of the black hole. Ignoring her past hadn't worked. Maybe what she needed to do was finally deal with it.

Sarah grabbed her coffee mug from the table, took it and the book over to the couch and began to read.

Half an hour later, she put the book down, her body shaking with uncontrollable sobs.

Maybe I'm not ready for this, she thought, eyeing the cover warily and swiping at her wet cheeks with her sleeve.

She dried her face with a tissue and then got up to get a drink of water. Her phone vibrated, creeping along her desk. Curious, she strode over to check who was calling.

Kathy again?

Sarah's first instinct was not to answer, as per usual. But perhaps she was feeling vulnerable after reading the book. Perhaps she yearned for the distraction another person would give her from her melancholy mood. At any rate, she put the phone to her ear.

She immediately regretted it.

"Hi, it's Sarah."

"Hi, Sarah! Kathy here," came the chipper voice on the phone.

Sarah repressed a sigh. She didn't have the energy for this. "Hi, Kathy. What's up?"

"Oh, I only wanted to remind you that the next session of The Paths of Healing begins tonight. Have you thought about whether you would like to join us? I would be happy to pick you up if transportation is an issue."

Sarah pressed her fingers against her temple with her free hand, her heart still pounding from the feelings the book had awakened only moments ago. *And I barely got past the introduction.*

"I—I think I'm going to pass this time. Thank you so much for thinking of me, though." It never hurt to be polite.

Kathy sounded like she was trying to hide disappointment. "No problem. Maybe next time."

"Maybe next time," Sarah agreed, ready to end the call.

"Sarah—"

Something in Kathy's voice made Sarah pause.

"Yeah?"

"I want you to know that I've been praying for you. I don't know what's going on in your life, but after we met I felt very strongly that God was telling me to pray for you, and I do, every day. If you ever need anyone to talk to or . . . whatever, call me."

Sarah was speechless. Once upon a time, she might have been offended that a stranger had decided she was so pathetic as to need constant prayer, like her life was any of their business, and like they were somehow better than her and could deign to offer that to her. She almost went there now, but her experience with Steve and Joanna had taught her something—there truly were people who cared in the world. And sometimes, those people cared enough to help you when you didn't even know you needed it.

Sarah didn't believe in God, but she knew that people like Steve and Joanna and Kathy did, in a way that she had never seen anyone else believe—like he was a real person that they could have conversations with. The fact that this woman would take time to have those conversations about her touched her already-tender heart. She sniffled.

"Th-thank you. I appreciate that."

Kathy was silent for a moment. "Do you want to talk about something now?"

Sarah's throat clenched. "No, thanks. I, uh, better go. Thanks for calling. Talk to you later, okay?"

"Okay, goodbye."

Sarah stared at her phone for a minute as Kathy's number faded to a black screen. She almost changed her mind right then and called her back. *Yes, I need to talk!* she screamed to herself. She desperately wanted to connect with someone, but she didn't want to have to explain the whole situation to anyone. It needed to be someone she already knew and trusted.

That left a fairly short list.

Sarah glanced at the time—eleven fifteen—and did some quick math. It would be the middle of the night for Steve. Despite her need to connect with someone, she breathed a sigh of relief at the excuse not to call him.

What about Joanna? She hesitated. Joanna wanted to go for coffee, but in Sarah's current mood what she needed was to blow off some steam, go out dancing or something—and she needed to feel safe with whomever she was with.

In the old days, she would have called Erica.

Thinking of Erica left a bitter taste in her mouth and reminded her about Craig's criminal trial hearing in a few weeks. Her anxiety jumped even higher. Between the impending hearing, at which she would be required to make a statement, and her follow-up oncologist's appointment tomorrow, she definitely needed to get out and forget about it all for a while.

She felt an old familiar thirst and suddenly realized that the idea of "blowing off steam" at a club had less to do with dancing than alcohol. Perhaps a quiet coffee date might be a better idea, after all.

She was about to dial Joanna when the phone rang, startling her, and she dropped it. It landed with a thud on the carpet. She snatched it up in alarm at the accidental abuse, its back side toward her, then stood and turned the phone over to check the caller ID.

"Hello?" A woman's voice emanated faintly from the phone's ear speaker. In Sarah's mad scramble, she had accidentally answered the call. "Sarah? Are you there?"

Crap. It was her mother.

thirty

SARAH SCRUNCHED UP HER FACE, SILENTLY TOSSED HER HEAD AND MOUTHED SOME CHOICE WORDS for herself and technology in general, then put the phone to her ear.

"Hi, Mom! What's up?"

"Oh, you *are* there. I wondered if I dialled the wrong number."

"No, I dropped the phone while I was trying to answer. Nothing broke, though, so it's fine."

"Oh, thank heavens. Well, I'm glad that's all it was. However, it's been so long since I heard from you that I thought maybe your phone *was* broken."

Sarah drew a frustrated breath, trapped between guilt and anger at her mother's implication that the silence between them was all her own fault.

"I'm sorry," she said sullenly. She *was* sorry, but not for not calling. *I'm sorry you don't want to acknowledge how you've hurt me. I'm sorry we can't seem to get past this.*

"So, what's been keeping you so busy?" Ellen grumped.

Sarah frowned, peeved.

"Oh, you know, only a divorce, medical treatments, karate, my *job*." She felt guilty for the sarcasm, but not too guilty. How like her mother to call her up and start guilt-tripping her for not calling as though nothing whatsoever was wrong between them. Perhaps the sarcasm would help her take the hint.

"Are you finished that book yet?"

Sarah sighed. Sarcasm and subtlety were lost on Ellen. Trust her to ask about the least controversial topic on the list.

"Yeah, I finished it yesterday."

"Do I get to read it this time?"

"Um, okay. If you want to. I'm not sure you would like it."

"Why not?"

Sarah held her breath for a moment. Should she be completely honest, or only tell enough of the truth to put Ellen off the scent, as per usual? A half-truth would be easier. But how could she expect Ellen to acknowledge the truth if Sarah wasn't willing to tell it? If this was to be her only opportunity, she didn't want to waste it.

Her heart began beating a staccato rhythm against her ribs. She felt like she was standing on top of the high diving board at the swimming pool trying to decide if she truly wanted to take the plunge.

No more masks.

"Mom, there's something I need to tell you. I'm sorry for not telling you before, but . . ." She trailed off, reticent to insert the excuse she was about to use. No excuses. Only truth. "I write erotica. Under a pen name. Dad's name. The books you saw on the shelf at Walmart were mine."

The silence stretched. Several times, it sounded like Ellen drew in her breath to say something, but it wasn't until the third try that she succeeded.

Sarah felt a twinge of perverse pleasure. This honesty thing was kinda fun.

"You write erotica?" Ellen's voice sounded a little strangled.

Sarah nodded as she replied, "Yeah."

"As Devon Sinclair?" Ellen's bewilderment was plain.

Sarah couldn't blame her. It *was* a little odd for a woman to use her father's name as a pseudonym, especially in the romance genre.

"Yeah."

Ellen paused. "Well, he always was your favourite."

Sarah frowned at the ludicrous idea that her abusive father could have been seen as her favourite parent, but Ellen's stung tone kept her silent.

Her mother mumbled a couple more things that didn't seem to be directed at Sarah, so she didn't ask for clarification. After a moment, Ellen said, "Well, since you wrote it, I want to read it."

"Really?"

Ellen blew into the phone. "I suppose so. Does it have sex scenes in it?"

"Mom, it's erotica. What do you think?"

"What on earth would your father think?"

Ellen's question may have been rhetorical, but Sarah felt a surge of anger.

"Who the hell cares what Dad would think? He's dead!"

"Sarah, watch your tone. Is that how you show respect to your father?"

"Respect? Respect needs to be earned. You know, I can't wait for you to read my book, because then—"

Sarah froze as a thought occurred to her.

Ellen wouldn't let Sarah say a word about what had happened to her as a child, would never even acknowledge the abuse as a possibility. But if she read Sarah's book, she would hear it all without realizing that the story was about her own daughter. Sarah would tell her the truth—but afterward, when she could force her mother to admit to it. Maybe this was how she could finally get some closure on her horrific childhood.

"'Because then' what?" Ellen demanded.

"Never mind. I'll mail you a copy tomorrow."

"If you have something on your mind, you can tell me."

"Since when?" Sarah stopped herself before she spat more venom, but finished the thought in her mind. *You've never listened before.*

"That hurts, Sarah. Really, sometimes I don't know why I bother calling. I keep wanting you to be like Everett, I guess, and come by for a cup of coffee once in a while."

"The road goes both ways, Mom. I haven't seen you on my doorstep."

"Maybe if I felt welcome. Or knew where you lived."

Sarah bit her tongue on her next comment. She'd said too much in anger already, and guilt pricked her.

"Okay, Mom, I'm sorry." She took a deep breath. "I didn't tell you the address before because I was afraid you would tell Everett. I do *not* want him knowing where to find me."

"Oh, Sarah, honestly! I don't know what's gotten into you, but you need to get over this whole fight with your brother. He was quite hurt when I told him those terrible things you said about him. He couldn't believe you would say such things, either." She paused. "You know he's only jealous of you, right?"

"What?" Sarah blinked. Ellen had *told* Everett? After a moment, she realized it didn't matter. "He is not. If he told you that, he's trying to manipulate you. Don't listen to what he says."

"He didn't tell me any such thing. I used the two eyes that God gave me, but which *you* seem to think I don't have. He was always jealous of you, ever since you were young, because you were your father's favourite. Didn't you know that?"

Sarah stared at the wall in shock, phone to ear. She doubted very much that Everett was hurt by anything that Sarah had accused him of. He had obviously been bluffing so their mother wouldn't suspect the truth, knowing she'd believe whatever he said.

But could it be true that Everett was jealous? Because of the extra attention their father had given her? What a horrible, disgusting reason to be resentful of her—because their father had singled her out as his sexual plaything. Could that be why Everett had become a bully and abuser, too—to try to impress their father? The thought made her stomach heave, but in some sick, twisted way, it actually made sense. "Sick and twisted" described how her family interacted to a "t".

"Um, no. I never thought of it that way." The air seemed thick, and she sat down on the couch.

"I know you two haven't always gotten along, but he wouldn't hurt you. You should tell him where you live, in case you ever have an emergency. Family should stick together, Sarah."

When Sarah didn't respond, Ellen continued. "Why don't I have Jill and Everett bring me up for coffee next week, and we can have a little family house-warming for you?"

Sarah scowled. The new insight into her brother's behaviour notwithstanding, she still didn't want him to know where she lived. And she didn't trust her mother not to tell him, even if she asked her not to.

She cleared her throat. "I'm sorry, Mom. I appreciate the thought, but I don't trust Everett. You don't have to understand why, but I don't want him to know where I live. If you want to have coffee, I'll meet you at a coffee shop. I'll even come to Miller to see you."

"Huh." Ellen was obviously displeased. "Never mind, Sarah. If you don't want to be part of this family, I can't force you. I just hope you realize sooner or later that we love you and only want what's best for you."

Sarah gave a quiet snort and shook her head. No sense arguing the point.

"If you say so, Mom." She paused. "I love you, too, you know."

"'If you say so, Sarah.'"

Sarah guessed she had that coming. She bit her lip.

"Look, I'm sorry for not calling more often. I will come see you soon, okay? And I'll send you the manuscript to read."

After a heavy pause, Ellen spoke. It sounded like she might be trying not to cry. "Fine. Bye."

Sarah hung up the phone feeling guilty for being so rude. Maybe Ellen truly was trying, in her own dysfunctional way—whereas Sarah had acted like a bratty teenager. She should call her mother back to apologize.

A huge part of her didn't want to, wanting Ellen to have to endure this taste of her own medicine.

But was that the kind of person Sarah wanted to be?

She thought of Steve, about how many times he had shown her grace in the face of her own stupidity. Couldn't she be even a little bit gracious with her own mother?

She stared at the phone, wrestling with herself. Finally, she dialled her mother back and put the phone to her ear.

It rang until it finally went to voicemail.

Sarah frowned. *Now who's being a bratty teenager?* She hung up without leaving a message.

Now what?

She stared at Nelson, who blinked at her from his blanket near her desk. The book about CSA still rested on the couch where she had been sitting when Kathy called, and her stomach twisted. Between the book and the talk with her mother, she was in such a state of agitation that she wanted to scream.

She had to go do something before she exploded. But she couldn't go sky-diving in January. There was no karate today. It seemed the only thing left was another vigorous walk.

As though he sensed her thoughts, Nelson stood and wagged his tail.

"You're always ready for a walk, aren't you, boy?"

At the word "walk," Nelson bounced a little and barked.

Sarah smiled and bent down to give him a good scratch. He licked her face and she knelt and stroked his soft fur, relishing the connection.

Connection. That was what she needed. Connection with someone who would listen to her as she tried to exorcise the abused girl in her past. She knew someone who would be willing to take on the job—but did she want to let him?

She glanced at the clock again. It was now 1 a.m. in Mumbai. No way was she calling him now.

Standing, she scrolled through the contacts on her phone until she found Kathy's number. She pressed the call button.

"Hello?" came Kathy's voice on the line.

"Hi, Kathy. It's Sarah. I changed my mind. I would love to come to your support group. For . . . for myself, not for my book."

No more masks.

Kathy paused. When she spoke, her voice was suffused with warmth. "I'm *so* glad."

Sarah took down the pertinent details and they ended the call. She felt slightly better for having taken a positive step but now hummed with nervous energy in anticipation of the night's session.

Nelson stood in front of her and barked.

She put her hands on her hips and mock-scolded him. "No barking. I'm right here."

He padded a couple steps toward the door, then looked back at her over his shoulder as though to say, "Aren't you coming?"

Sarah smiled and gave an exaggerated sigh. "Fine, we'll go for another walk."

Nelson barked again, then panted and smiled, his tongue hanging from the side of his mouth.

It was impossible to stay angry with that face. For the second time that morning, Sarah put on her winter gear and she and Nelson headed out the door, her phone in hand.

She could call Joanna from the dog park. And maybe later she would send an email to Steve.

Despite the clouds that still hung over the city, the valley seemed much brighter than when she and Nelson had visited the park that morning. Just then, a beam of sunlight pierced the grey mantle and set the frosted treetops dancing with sparkling white diamonds.

Sarah smiled. It was going to be a beautiful day, after all.

Steve plunked himself into the molded plastic chair he used as a desk chair with a sigh. The morning had been busy, as always. He was looking forward to the excuse of answering emails for the next half an hour as a reason to sit before having to rush off again to take Sita to the doctor.

Outside, the sun had been baking Mumbai for hours, or would have been if the smog hadn't provided such a thick covering layer. The pollution had been especially bad since New Year's celebrations had added the smoke of millions of firecrackers to the normal pollution output in the city of twenty-two million.

Smog or no smog, the city—which was surrounded on three sides by ocean—had already reached the equivalent temperature of a hot summer's day in Alberta, and the humidity made Steve glad for the cooler, dryer air in his office.

Technically, the office didn't belong only to him. His little desk—which also saw little use—was tucked into a corner against two white plastered cement walls. The surface not required to support his laptop was obscured in random piles of paperwork he kept meaning to get to.

Paul claimed that the piles were random, anyway. To Steve, everything had a specific place, and he had forbidden Paul's wife, Aparna, from tidying it up at all. The last time she had done that, he hadn't been able to find anything for three weeks.

Steve glanced at Paul Ramanshankar's larger desk beneath the window, kitty-corner to his own, which dominated the small room on the ground floor at the front of Prakaash House. The tidiness bordered on compulsiveness, with its neat containers of office supplies lined up in a straight row beside an aging tube-style computer monitor. Paul was out. He'd said something about going to the bank on his way to the vocational centre, which meant that he was probably standing in line somewhere. Steve sighed. He had waited in his fair share of lines in India, and was glad that Paul was handling this one. Sometimes it seemed that half of Steve's time in this country was spent waiting.

He had just flipped open his laptop and woken up the screen when someone rapped on the open door. He glanced up to see Ajay stick his head into the room, his thick shock of black hair framing a baby-face with an attempt at a moustache.

"Steve? You have minute?"

Steve nodded and waved him in. "Of course, Ajay. Come, sit down."

When Steve had first hired Ajay, he had been skeptical. They needed a way for the kids to get exercise, sure, but dancing? However, it hadn't taken him long to see the wisdom of Paul's idea. The kids got so much more than exercise in Ajay's dance class. They found a way to express themselves, and the many unnamed fears they had already been exposed to, in a healthy manner.

Not only did the children love dancing, they also seemed to like Ajay. He always had a small swarm of them following him around between classes, and he never appeared bothered by it. That's why Steve was only slightly surprised to see him come into the room leading ten-year-old Geeta by the hand.

Steve frowned. Public touching between males and females was not culturally acceptable, and in a place like Love Mumbai, where they worked with the sexually exploited, they had to be extra careful about appearances. Those rules were relaxed somewhat with children, but Ajay should have had one of the female staff members with him to help Geeta, not be leading her around himself. Steve made a note to talk to him about it later, mildly surprised that it was even necessary.

The small man brought the girl to stand in front of the desk. She hung back shyly, playing with her braids with her free hand.

Ajay sat on a plastic chair in front of the desk, exactly like the one Steve was using. Geeta tried to pull her hand from Ajay's and step back, but he held on and positioned her facing Steve.

"Geeta is not feel well. I think she need see a doctor." Ajay turned to the little girl. "Tell Uncle Steve what you tell me."

Geeta tugged on her hand again, pulling it from Ajay's grasp. Steve thought he saw Ajay frown, but the look was so fleeting that he dismissed it. Geeta looked up at Steve from under her lashes, then glanced at Ajay fearfully. Ajay wobbled his head in the gesture for "yes" and said in Hindi, "Tell him."

"It's okay, Geeta," Steve said in Hindi, his voice gentle. Then in English, "What's wrong? You can tell me."

Geeta worked up her courage. "When I use toilet, it . . . it is paining. Passing water. It . . . burns." She dipped her chin again, refusing to look at either of the men.

Steve stood up and moved around the desk. "I'm going to feel your forehead, okay, Geeta?"

Geeta trembled, but waggled her head sideways in the Indian gesture of consent.

Steve heard Aparna's desk chair move as the receptionist in the outer room sat down. "Aparna, come in here, please."

A moment later, Paul's wife, a petite woman in a peach-coloured *salwar kameez* and black hair that trailed down her back from a gold clip, came through the door. When she saw that Steve had one of the girl children in the room, she waggled her head and stood to the side, fulfilling her job as chaperone without question.

Steve cupped Geeta's chin to steady her head and laid his other hand on her forehead. It was warmer than usual, enough to confirm his suspicions that she may have a urinary tract infection or something similar. That happened occasionally, as many of the children did not drink sufficient water without being reminded and were often eating substandard food when not in the child care centre. However, it was the second case in a month. Steve frowned. Maybe they needed to be more diligent about ensuring the children took water breaks.

Steve released Geeta's head and braced his hands on his knees to meet her eye level.

"I think you might have an infection. I am going to the doctor soon to take Auntie Sita. I'm going to take you, too, okay?"

Geeta's eyes grew wide and she wobbled her loose fist frantically in the gesture for no, backing away. "No, no! Mama would never let me go to doctor. We no have money."

Steve laid a calming hand on her shoulder, and she flinched slightly but stopped retreating. He withdrew his hand and tried to look in her eyes, which she kept downcast—a reflex from years on the street, where eye contact was seen as a challenge, or an invitation. At a glance from Steve, Aparna stepped up and laid her arm across the girl's shoulders instead.

"Your mama gave us permission to take you to the doctor if we need to," Aparna assured her.

Steve crouched down in front of Geeta. "She will not have to pay, I will pay. We need to get you some medicine or you will get very sick, and we must see the doctor to get it. I promise, you will be back here before your mama comes to get you this evening."

After a moment, Geeta gave a reluctant nod, and Steve stood.

"Aparna, would you take her out to the sofa and get her some water to drink? I need a few more minutes before I am ready to leave. And please find Priya to accompany us to the doctor." Steve guessed that Geeta would feel more comfortable if the older teen girl came along.

"Of course." Aparna moved to usher Geeta out.

Before she could, Ajay caught the girl's hand again and turned her to look at him. "You remember what we talked about, right?" he said in Hindi. "You listen to Uncle Steve and the doctor and you'll be fine."

Geeta gave a single sideways nod, but was clearly still frightened.

Steve felt sorry for her. When a child had lived on the streets their whole life, there were so many experiences that they found terrifying, at which most children wouldn't even blink. As Aparna guided her out to the lounge, Steve heard the woman assuring Geeta that all would be well and she would soon feel better after getting the medicine.

"Thanks, Ajay." Steve gave the young man a curt nod. "Odd that she felt comfortable enough to talk to you about this. The poor thing seems scared stiff. I'm glad she talked to someone, though. That's a sign of progress for her."

Ajay looked startled for a fleeting second, then his lips split into a wide smile under his sparse moustache. Steve wondered why the kid insisted on growing it when it looked so atrocious. He was probably trying to look older than his twenty years.

"Yes, yes, I am glad to help." Ajay nodded his head sideways. "What I can say? The kids trust me, yes?"

"That's not a gift to be used lightly." Steve reached out to shake Ajay's hand. "That's why we value you as part of the team."

Ajay pumped Steve's hand and grinned. "Thanks, Steve. Well, I, uh, better get back. I am supposed to help Meera Auntie teach the primary children Maths."

"Go, go." Steve waved him off and then sat down in his chair.

As Ajay left, Steve glanced at the clock and noticed that it was already later than he had realized. His laptop chimed to let him know that a new email had arrived, but he closed the machine and tucked it into the safe in the opposite corner. Whatever it was, it would have to wait until tonight. He had to get Geeta and Sita to the doctor.

thirty-one

SARAH PULLED INTO DEREK AND JOANNA'S DRIVEWAY AND PUT THE RAV INTO PARK. SINCE SHE HAD left in mid-October, she hadn't been back here. It all looked a little different, softened from yesterday's fresh snowfall. A lump formed in her throat as memories of her stay washed over her. She had never felt so safe anywhere before or since.

Swallowing, she gathered up her packages and purse from the passenger seat and paused, staring at the manila envelope beneath that contained the manuscript for her mother, already addressed to mail. She had intended to post it on the way home, but the thought occurred to her that she could deliver it in person. She brushed the idea aside as a familiar rush of resentment filled her.

The last thing I'll have energy for today is a session with Mom.

Especially after the text she'd received from Becky as she'd left the oncologist's that morning. *Latest book was a little wild. Still no takers on the bio. What else do you have for me? Erotica, please.*

For the first time, Sarah was beginning to question if Becky Sun really was the best agent for her. She resolved to call Becky as soon as possible to voice her frustration. No sense ending their relationship before at least trying to work out their differences.

She shook her head dismissively, got out of the car and headed for the stoop.

Joanna opened the door before she could ring the bell.

"Hi," Joanna whispered and embraced Sarah, packages and all. "Sophie surprised me with an extra-long morning nap. Sorry. She must be growing." She backed up to let Sarah inside.

Sarah smiled, genuinely happy to see the petite woman. She hadn't realized how much she had missed Joanna until she saw her familiar face.

"No problem. We'll be quiet."

Joanna took the paper shopping bags from her hands so Sarah could take off her things.

"What's all this?" Joanna asked, peeping at the brand names in curiosity.

"Oh, well. It's nothing much. I just wanted to say 'thank you' for all you did for me when, you know, when I stayed here a few months ago."

Joanna looked at her with a bemused smile. "That's very sweet of you. You know you didn't have to."

"I know. But I wanted to. Plus, I got something for Sophie. Shopping for babies is about the most fun ever."

Joanna laughed quietly. "Definitely."

Sarah's boots and coat now in the closet, the two women made their way upstairs. Joanna set the packages on the kitchen peninsula and grabbed the coffee pot to fill the drip maker up with water.

"You can look at them now, if you want." Sarah settled herself at the kitchen table.

"Oh!" Joanna put the glass pot down and began pulling items out of packages, exclaiming in delight about the cute baby outfit for Sophie and the lovely pillar candle, stand, and wreath centrepiece Sarah had purchased for Joanna's and Derek's home.

"Sorry for something so generic." Sarah bit her lip in embarrassment. "I wasn't sure what you would like. Buying art for others is always so tricky, and I didn't know which house plants were poisonous, so I—"

Joanna cut her off by coming around the table and wrapping her shoulders in a hug. "I love them. Honestly. Thank you."

Surprised, Sarah awkwardly returned her hug as well as she could. "Well, okay. You're welcome."

Joanna left the gifts on the counter and finished putting the coffee on.

Sarah watched her from the dining room table. At the first support group session she had attended last night, Kathy had urged the group members to cultivate relationships with people who would help them on their healing journey. She compared attempting to heal from the trauma of abuse alone to trying to remove your own appendix. *It might be possible, but why risk it?*

Sarah had gone through her short list of possible supporters and landed on Steve and Joanna. Heart in her throat, she had sent Joanna a text and Steve an email—just a silly Internet meme of personal trivia with the subject line "Bacon Bits or Croutons?" She hoped he would get the reference to their conversation at

Cora's a few months ago and see the apology she had written between the lines. Joanna's response had come like lightning, and Sarah had agreed to come see her in Miller after her morning check-up. She still hadn't heard back from Steve.

Now that she was back in the Larson home, it felt strange knowing that Steve wasn't even in the country, let alone the house. She kept expecting him to walk up the stairs or something.

As Joanna bustled around the kitchen gathering supplies, Sarah remembered the golden feeling of belonging she'd had not so long ago while in this chair. She knew she had been relegated back to guest status, but she still felt completely welcomed by this woman. She suspected that Joanna would have treated her just as warmly even if Sarah and Steve had never met.

Sarah pondered Joanna's and her family's willing service to her and felt undeserving, like she had taken advantage of them. Shame wicked through her like water through paper as she realized she had rewarded their open generosity with three months of silence. Suddenly, her gifts felt like cheap apologies instead of the thank yous she had intended. She squirmed, and her face began to grow warm.

She checked her phone again, but Steve still hadn't replied to her email. What if he hadn't replied because he was upset with her for snubbing him? She fidgeted with the edge of the table, heart heavy. If that were so, she deserved it. She put a hand in front of her mouth in an effort to hide her feelings.

"So, what's been keeping you busy lately?" Joanna asked, breaking in on Sarah's thoughts as she sat down at the table across from her. She set a plate of chocolate chip oatmeal cookies between them while sliding into her chair. When she noticed Sarah's expression, she gave her a quizzical look, but didn't say anything more.

"Um. Well . . ." Sarah groped for a topic to cover her embarrassment. Mentioning her book seemed too on-the-nose with Joanna, who would already know how much time she dedicated to her writing. She thought of the next activity on today's itinerary. "I joined a karate class back in November. That's been fun."

Joanna perked up. "Karate. Really?" She nodded approvingly. "Good for you. I bet it's great exercise. Maybe I should look into it." She pinched her midsection, which looked slim and trim to Sarah. "I'm starting to feel like I'll never lose the baby flab."

"Not that you need to lose weight, but yes, I have really enjoyed the exercise. It's also nice to get out of the house and talk to people—even if it's only learning to count in Japanese while I do *katas.*"

Joanna grinned. "It's not that I feel overweight, just *soft*. Getting out of the house sounds great, too. Sophie is a doll, but she is becoming so demanding. I think Derek is exhausted from being my sole source of adult conversation in a day. I should look into some kind of evening exercise class to give the poor guy a break."

Sarah chuckled. "I thought you got out of the house a few times a week."

The coffee maker finished and Joanna jumped up to get them their drinks.

"I guess so, if you count going to the grocery store." She grabbed a couple of mugs from a cupboard and put them and the beverage fixings on the table as she spoke. "I have a few friends I see on occasion, but we are all so busy that it doesn't happen as often as we'd like. And with Sophie getting so active, meeting in public is becoming out of the question."

Sarah nodded as though she understood perfectly, but it was more wistful than empathetic. However, the thought of Sophie—and babies in general—reminded her of the results from her follow-up appointment that morning. She smiled. Dr. Strickland had sounded more optimistic than ever and told Sarah that as long as things kept going this way, she could see no reason why Sarah could not bear children someday.

Not that Sarah had any immediate expectation of doing so. She knew there were options available if she wanted a child that badly—but there was no way she would get pregnant right now, what with her life in chaos. Not to mention being a single mother was not exactly what she had in mind. The bubbling, ever-constant resentment in her spirit grew as she thought of the reason for her disturbed hopes—Craig. She frowned.

Joanna set a steaming mug of coffee in front of Sarah and settled herself at the table again with her own. "I might even get to drink this while it's hot today." A baby's moan emanated from the white plastic receiver on the counter, and Joanna caught her breath in alarm. She dropped her voice. "If I didn't just jinx it."

She cocked her head and listened for a moment, but nothing but the sound of Sophie breathing came through the baby monitor. Joanna smiled and took a sip, then caught the pensive look on Sarah's face.

"What's up?" asked Joanna, concern etched between her eyes.

Sarah gave her head a small shake and began fixing her coffee. "Not much. I had my three month follow-up with the oncologist this morning, and she said everything was clear."

Joanna grinned. "That's wonderful! I bet your family will be so glad to hear that."

Sarah glanced up sharply. She thought Steve would have told his sister about Sarah's family history, but it would appear that he hadn't—at least not all of it. She was grateful, but surprised. He and Joanna seemed very close, and she had been the outsider.

"I'm—I'm not sure they care." Sarah frowned. "My sister-in-law might, but she's got her own issues to deal with right now." Between dealing with Everett and her own difficult pregnancy, Sarah guessed that Jill had barely spared a thought for Sarah's health since last fall.

"I'm sure they care more than you realize." Joanna paused. "Hey, let me know if I'm intruding, but how are things going with your mom?"

Intruding?

The resentment surged in her gut—not for Joanna's question, but for the answer she felt her mother had forced her into. For having to admit to one more area of her life that was a total mess.

"They could be better. We haven't been on the best terms since I moved to Edmonton in November."

"Would you like to talk about it?"

Sarah thought about that for a moment, taking a cookie and chewing slowly. She didn't know Joanna very well—not as well as she knew Steve—but Sarah believed her to be someone she could trust. Joanna had always listened without judgement before. Besides, the anxiety in Sarah's gut threatened to boil out of her at any second unless she did something about it. She decided to take a risk.

"Maybe. I think—" she broke off and bit her lip. "I'm angry with her. Like, really angry. So angry that it frightens me." Her voice cracked on the last, and she blinked moisture from her eyes.

Joanna nodded, considering. "Did something happen?"

Sarah snorted and stared at her cup, watching the cream swirl around as she stirred it in. *My whole life happened.*

She knew that Joanna meant since she had seen Sarah last, though.

"Things were okay with my mom for a few weeks. And then I came home one night and Everett—my brother—was sleeping on the couch. Mom wouldn't listen to me when I told her that I didn't want to be there when he was there. She treated me like a rebellious teenager who wouldn't see reason, so I left."

She dared a look at Joanna. The other woman was listening intently, her face open and concerned, her hands holding her mug in the air in front of her—poised for sipping, but unmoving.

Sarah gulped. "Did—did Steve tell you about my past?"

Joanna set down the mug. "He mentioned that you had had a rough background. He didn't go into details." She met Sarah's eyes. "You don't have to share anything with me you don't want to, okay? But if you do want to, I'll listen."

Sarah knew her words to be truth and felt a surge of gratitude. Is this how a real friend behaved—interested in what upsets you for your own benefit, not trying to twist your words to gain leverage against you? Why had she been holding Joanna at bay? She honestly couldn't remember.

That didn't mean talking about this stuff was easy, even with Joanna. She knew this was an opportunity to strip away another mask, but she was terrified about how Joanna would react when she saw the ugliness inside her.

Sarah gulped, unshed tears stinging her eyes. She stared at her mug, which had a painted picture of a black-and-white kitten on it. She noticed the excellent detail the artist had used to depict the fur, the red collar, the shiny little bell. When she had regained control, she spoke.

"My dad started sexually abusing me when I was four. Everett is four years older than me. He started abusing me a few years later. They didn't stop until I moved away from home when I was eighteen. Dad died a week later." The kitten stared at her with eyes too blue for real life. "Mom never did a thing about it. Last fall was the first time I stayed at home since I moved out to go to college. And once again, Mom put me into that dangerous situation and blamed *me* for causing trouble. It's what she always does."

After the constantly roiling emotion she had felt since her mother's call yesterday, Sarah felt strangely detached from the words she spoke, as though she were actually talking about someone else.

The kitten was very cute. Maybe she should get a kitten. She wondered if Nelson would get along with cats.

Sarah looked up to see Joanna's eyes brimming with moisture. *Great.* Maybe she shouldn't have said anything. The detachment trickled away and tears pressed against the back of her eyes. She had shocked Joanna, and now she would have to deal with the consequences. So much for her new friendship.

The kitten.

Nelson.

Red collar with a bell.

Bubbling rage. Snaking fear.

Sipping coffee.

Joanna blinked a few times, but no tears streamed down her cheeks.

Sarah gulped in relief as she reined in her own emotions.

"I'm sorry that you and your mom are having such a hard time." Joanna shifted in her chair and tucked one leg under the other. "It sounds like you've got some fairly deep wounds there. It won't be easy to resolve issues like that."

That was it? No shock, no horror or disgust, only a few tears of sympathy?

Sarah frowned, the numbness trickling away. "Deep wounds. You could say that. Whenever I think of her right now, all I can feel is blind rage." Her voice cracked again and she swallowed. She could see the rage hovering, red and angry, around the edges of her vision. She focused on the kitten's blue eyes in desperation. Perhaps it had been a mistake to talk about this with Joanna after all.

Joanna sipped her tea, her dark brows drawn together. "Have you considered trying to forgive her?"

The rage exploded in front of the kitten in a blood-red splatter.

"She doesn't deserve to be forgiven!" Hot tears tracked down Sarah's cheeks. She blinked furiously but her composure was fracturing. Her heart felt like it was doubling in on itself and her shoulders hunched together around the soul-deep pain that drenched her veins.

Joanna got up and grabbed a box of tissues from the counter top. She placed them in front of Sarah, then sat down.

Regaining control, Sarah grabbed one and kept her eyes averted as she dabbed at the moisture on her face. "Thanks," she said when she trusted her voice again. "Sorry about that. You must think I'm a horrible person."

"Don't be," Joanna said gently. "You were only being honest. It's perfectly natural to feel that way when you've been hurt." She swallowed and stared at her mug for a long moment. "Can I share something with you?"

Sarah looked up through her wet lashes, curious. Joanna looked troubled. Sarah nodded.

"I—I was raped once," Joanna began, and now it was her voice that had cracked. She looked like she was fighting tears again.

Sarah blinked. That was the last thing she had expected to hear.

Joanna's voice regained its strength as she continued. "In college. It was date rape, and I was so embarrassed by the whole thing and afraid of what people would say that I never told anyone, not for years."

Joanna looked up, her face covered in concern, her hand extended as though to ward off some unexpected consequence. "I know you've been through some truly horrific things, and I'm not trying to compare our stories or make less of what happened to you. This is simply what happened to me."

Sarah blinked again. Even in sharing her own trauma, Joanna's concern was for someone else.

Sometimes Sarah wondered if this woman was even real.

thirty-two

SARAH SWALLOWED AROUND THE LUMP IN HER THROAT, STUNNED.

Raped?

So Joanna *did* have a small idea of what Sarah had gone through, but Sarah could hardly believe it. Joanna's life seemed so perfect, and she was so happy. How could she have achieved that, when every relationship Sarah had had seemed to self-destruct? Maybe the effect of a one-time rape was much different than the lifetime of abuse she had endured. Uncertain of how to respond, she chewed her lip and nodded, encouraging Joanna to continue.

Joanna looked down, hesitating. "The rape changed me in ways that are difficult to explain. I was afraid all the time. I felt powerless and worthless. I didn't trust men, not for a very long time. It's a wonder that Derek ever got me to agree to go on a date."

Sarah felt cold. It was as though Joanna was describing her own state of mind. She thought of the rape in her own recent history, and how devastating that had been for her. Craig raping her had not only ripped open memories of her childhood abuse but had also left new scars on her soul. She still had nightmares about it, but they were all so mixed up with her other nightmares and flashbacks that she had no idea what was caused by which experience.

Joanna's eyes were looking into the past. "Obviously, I did eventually say yes, but Derek couldn't figure out why I shied away whenever he tried to touch me, even to hold my hand. Eventually, I told him what had happened. He was the one who encouraged me to go to counselling."

Sarah's hands shook, angry at the men who had taken advantage of Joanna and herself. She wrapped her hands around her mug and gripped hard to still them.

Joanna glanced at her with a concerned frown. "Are you okay with me telling you this?"

Sarah nodded, guessing she was as white as a sheet. "Yes. Please." It was all she could manage to squeak out around the lump in her throat.

Joanna tilted her head in acknowledgement and continued. "Counselling helped. I was able to deal with the trauma, at least somewhat. But much more difficult than that was forgiving the boy who had raped me." Joanna gulped. "After he had done that to me, he had gone on to live his life like nothing had changed. He dated other girls, and I wondered if he had done the same to them or if I was the only one so cheap as to deserve such treatment. He even got engaged. While I was walking around jumping at my own shadow, he was winning achievement awards and graduating with honours. And as far as he was concerned, it was like I didn't exist."

Joanna took a deep breath. "Once I acknowledged that the rape was not my fault, but his, I became terribly angry. My counsellor told me how important it was that I forgive him—not for his sake, and not because he deserved it, but because *I* did. He explained how bitterness and anger are like acids that eat us from the inside out. They have very little effect on the person that hurt us, if any. But they can change our own lives forever."

Sarah frowned, considering.

"I could see the counsellor's point, and I tried to forgive, but I simply couldn't. He didn't *deserve* to be forgiven, and I deserved some kind of justice for what had happened to me. Derek and I nearly broke up because of all the anger I carried around inside me. It began to tear our relationship apart."

Joanna stopped to take a sip of her coffee.

Sarah's knuckles were white on her mug. There had been so many people in her life who had done her wrong, and she had always felt powerless to do anything about it. Outbursts had usually only brought more retribution from her abusers. So she kept it tightly contained, rarely letting the heat escape, choosing instead to accept the blame for their actions.

Since living on her own, her anger had become more and more difficult to ignore. She no longer wanted to accept responsibility for what had been done to her. But what else could she do? Her father was dead. Neither her mother nor Erica had done anything illegal. She didn't know if she could even legally do anything against Everett, nor did she want to pay the emotional price of doing so.

At least I'm fighting Craig.

But she had been told that even if Craig were found guilty, his sentence could be extremely light. The injustice of it all made her want to explode.

"What if anger is all you have?" Sarah asked into her mug.

Joanna looked at her with compassion. "Consider who will be hurt by it the most."

Sarah could see how the acid of anger and bitterness had etched an indelible mark on the fabric of her soul, leaving it puckered and scarred and ugly. Sarah closed her eyes in revulsion. If she couldn't forgive, and the acid remained, what kind of person was she destined to become?

Would she hurt others to make her feel better about herself, too? Just like her father? And Everett?

And Craig?

Should she try to forgive them? Thinking about that, she realized that she didn't have the first idea how to begin.

She lifted her gaze to meet Joanna's. "How did you get past all that?"

Joanna gave a small smile. "I prayed. Constantly."

Sarah frowned. She didn't want to hear that.

Joanna continued as though she hadn't noticed. "At first, it was too hard to ask that God help me forgive that boy. It felt hypocritical to ask for forgiveness for someone I hated so much. I didn't want to forgive him, and I didn't want God to forgive him, either. So I asked him to help me *want* to forgive him."

Joanna paused and took a sip of her coffee.

Sarah didn't trust herself to speak, so she simply waited.

"A few months later, I woke up one morning and realized my prayer had been answered. It felt like a miracle, like a massive burden that had been hanging on me was gone. That's how I noticed it—not only did I want to forgive him, I realized I already had. I wanted the best for him and for him to know the kind of peace that I was finally experiencing." Joanna gulped. "Unfortunately, not long after that I found out that he had committed suicide."

"Oh!" Sarah exclaimed. The revelation seemed like the justified ending for such a detestable person. The universe had rewarded that jerk for what he had done to Joanna. The satisfied sense of fairness that permeated her was much like the cold righteousness she had felt when her father had died. Both men had gotten what they deserved. *Better late than never.*

Joanna's face, however, was blanketed in sadness. *She even feels empathy for her attacker.* Shame and confusion wrapped tentacles around Sarah's heart.

Joanna continued. "It made me see him differently. What he had done to me was still wrong. But I also realized that the way he acted was because of the deep wounds he carried. Only his had never healed."

What Joanna said reminded Sarah of something that Steve had said last October. *We all have wounds, Sarah. Mine might be different than yours, but they were deep enough to enlarge my heart.* She wondered again what Steve's wounds might be.

She also saw, in Joanna's story, the different potential outcomes of deep wounds. Do they turn us into bullies or beauties? Blessings or curses? People like Joanna and Steve, with happy, productive lives, or the sad story of the rapist who killed himself?

Craig had wounds, she knew he did. And according to her mother, Everett was jealous of her. She knew their father had never shown him any special attention and had taken his anger out on Everett's flesh in a different way from hers—she still shuddered as she remembered the strap made from tire rubber that left welts on the skin that lasted for days. Sometimes, Everett couldn't sit properly for a week after one of their father's "lectures."

What about her father? And her mother? Did they have wounds? Sarah knew very little about her parents' upbringings. She supposed it was logical that her dad's father had beaten him growing up. But what about her mom? She had no idea. Her maternal grandparents had always seemed like kind, decent people, and Sarah had considered it a blessing to escape to their house for even short periods of time as a child.

She gulped. Her abusers might have their own wounds, but that didn't make what they had done to her excusable. And right now, she didn't even want to *want* to forgive them. None of them. The anger felt like it was choking her.

"That's fine for you, Joanna. But I'm not like you. And I don't believe that there is some spirit in the sky that's going to help me heal. I'm all on my own, here."

Joanna looked at her sharply. "On your own? You know that's not true."

Sarah blinked, then dropped her gaze, her cheeks hot.

"You're right. I . . . I owe so much to Steve, and to you. Thank you."

Joanna shifted toward her. "You don't owe us anything. But I want you to know that we are here for you. You are *not* alone. And haven't you considered that it was quite the striking coincidence how you met Steve right when you were about to need someone like him in your life?"

Sarah couldn't look at her. Of course she had. That day in San Francisco when he'd offered her hope for the first time in years. A week later, when he rescued her at the gas station. All that he had done for her before he left for India. She fiddled with her mug handle. "What are you saying?"

When Joanna didn't answer immediately, Sarah looked up. Her friend's face was covered with compassion and understanding. "God is watching over you, Sarah. To him, you are a 'pearl of great price.' He loves you, and you are worth so much to him that he came and took the punishment for every wrong in the world that ever has happened, or ever will happen. He did it for all of us, but he would have done it all just for you, because that is the only way that you could be with him. He *loves* you, and wants to help you. And I think that somewhere inside of you, you know it."

Sarah felt another small crack open inside the icy fortress of her heart. But instead of the red glow of rage, a sliver of white light shone through from the other side. The crack wasn't big enough to see through, but Sarah recognized the warmth of hope. It was like she desperately wanted to believe that Joanna's words were true, and if she could force that crack open she would see something truly beautiful beyond the wall.

But she simply couldn't.

The crack iced over and the light faded.

She couldn't believe in a God that would ignore the desperate cries of the little girl she once was, while those meant to protect her had used her up. She *wouldn't*.

Sarah shook her head. "No. I'm sorry, but I don't. I wish I could, though." She wondered if Joanna had noticed the quiver in her voice.

Steve had intended to get back into his email as soon as he returned to the office, especially after he noticed on his phone that Sarah had written to him at last—it was one of those "getting to know you" chain letters, and the subject line of "Bacon Bits or Croutons?" let him see it for the olive branch he was sure it was. He had read it at the doctor's office while waiting with Sita and Geeta, chuckling more than once at her witty, self-deprecating responses. At the end, she had typed, "Your turn . . . ?"

As it turned out, that was to be the last slow moment he had for the rest of the day.

When they left the doctor's office, Steve sent Priya and Geeta back to Prakaash House in their own rickshaw to make sure Geeta got back to the centre before her mother arrived. He and Sita took another rickshaw to the women's shelter. The return journey was much roomier without all four of them squeezed onto one narrow seat.

"There." Steve pointed at the beauty parlour that camouflaged the shelter.

The rickshaw driver waggled his head in acknowledgement. Steve's gut clenched as the rickshaw shot through a small opening between two other vehicles in the moving line of traffic, then stopped abruptly beside the broken sidewalk.

Despite the driver's expert manoeuvring, he'd overshot by one building. The smell of pizza emanating from the Domino's stand beside them made Steve's stomach gurgle. He hadn't had much Western food in the last three months. Sometimes, he could really go for some melted cheese—but the high prices in the Western chains usually changed his mind as he tried to stretch his donated dollars as far as they would go.

Sita stepped out of the rickshaw into the shade of the building.

"Goodbye, Steve. See you tomorrow?"

Steve smiled. "I wouldn't miss it."

Suddenly, a ragged, gaunt-looking girl of about fifteen stood up from behind a rack of scooters crowding the sidewalk. She held her *pallu* wrapped around her lowered head and mouth as she hurried up to the rickshaw.

Sita stepped back in surprise and watched the girl as she peered at Steve in the shade of the vehicle's cab.

She must have recognized him, for her eyes widened in excitement. "Is you! I find you," she breathed. "I look you since morning time. They catch me almost!"

Steve recognized the girl from his rescue mission into the red light district several weeks ago. Lohini had offered him her services, enticing him to join her in a cubicle fronting the street that was barely wide enough for her bed. He had played along, but once inside he had used the privacy to tell her of the women's shelter and of Prakaash House.

She had been frightened when she realized that he had no intentions of having intercourse, fearfully glancing at the privacy curtain across the cubicle's entrance every few moments. After giving her a card with the building's address in hopes that she could read, he left several hundred rupees for her time—and to hopefully prevent her from getting in trouble from her owner—and made his escape.

He had done something similar many times, but not frequently. He had to be careful—with his distinctive foreign face, he had become somewhat known in the district after so many years of doing this work, so he only made these kinds of forays himself occasionally, never frequenting the same location more than once a year. Sometimes he felt guilty—Sita was much bolder in her efforts to reach these women than he was, making frequent trips into the area to hand out condoms and feminine hygiene supplies as an excuse to get close enough to talk to the workers for a few moments.

Steve glanced past Lohini's wide-eyed face. He could see a man at the other end of the street moving slowly toward them, looking this way and that.

Steve turned to the girl. "Come."

Lohini backed up as he clambered out. Sita closed ranks with Steve between Lohini and her pursuer, placing a hand on the girl's arm and ushering her into the building.

Steve tilted his head at the security guard, Aaron, as they moved past him. Aaron dipped his chin in acknowledgement, then positioned himself against the doorpost facing the street so his frame blocked the door as much as possible. Ratna, one of their rescued women who now managed the beauty parlour, glanced up from a haircut as they swept by, nodded at them, and kept talking to her client as though nothing had even happened. Aaron's wife, Joy, who had no clients at the moment, sauntered toward the front door to chat with her husband, casually blocking the entrance from curious observers—or searchers.

Steve and Sita led Lohini through the parlour to a small room where it was quiet. Since it was a Hindu festival, the workers building the new floor above had the day off. The other girls who lived at the shelter were down the street at the vocational centre. Steve could hear the shelter's cook making noise in the kitchen down the hall, the faint clanging of metal on stone punctuating the silence. The domestic sounds were comforting.

Once inside the dark interior, Lohini let her *pallu* drop and looked around doubtfully. "This is place you say me? 'Woman shelter?'"

Steve gave a sideways Indian nod. "Yes. You are safe now. *Surakshit*," he added in Hindi to make sure she understood the word "safe."

Sita took Lohini's hand. "*Aapka naam kya hai?* What is your name?" she asked.

Lohini only stared at her, like she had forgotten how to speak. Steve recognized the signs—she was thinking of changing her mind, like a rabbit who wonders if she has chosen a safe hole in which to hide or has run straight into the fox's den.

"It's okay, Lohini. Sita knows exactly what you have gone through. She once worked in a brothel only a few streets over from yours. Those women you saw up there"—Steve indicated the parlour—"used to work on the streets, too. Everyone here can be trusted."

Lohini blinked at Sita, who smiled at her warmly and continued speaking to her in Hindi.

"Are you hungry? I will have the cook get you some tea and food and then we can get you settled. Later, we can talk about what you would like to do next."

Lohini waggled her head and allowed Sita to begin leading her toward the kitchen. After a few steps, she paused and looked up at Steve with dark, serious eyes touched with sadness. "She not come. I try get Anjuna to come, but she not want leave. She say I crazy, but I no can take any more!"

Steve pressed his lips together. "I am sorry, Lohini. Perhaps your friend will change her mind later."

Lohini's eyes filmed with tears. "They never let her leave."

Steve glanced over her, taking note of injuries of varying freshness. They didn't look life-threatening, but he was sure they were painful. After a cursory assessment, he looked away before he made the girl uncomfortable—not because he couldn't handle the ugly bruises on her face or bare midriff, but because he didn't want to subject Lohini to the same treatment she had received from other men for so long. She was not a commodity or a piece of flesh to ogle. She was a precious daughter of God.

Most likely, however, the injuries had been inflicted by her madam, not a customer, which implied that she had not yet become well acclimated to her new life. She was still in "training."

Sita saw the injuries, too. She exchanged a knowing look with Steve.

"I will go get Chaitra," he said. "I'll be back in half an hour."

Sita murmured acknowledgement before turning back to the girl and leading her away.

The shelter's cook would be able to produce the required food, but Prakaash House's head cook Chaitra had knowledge of several teas and traditional

Ayurvedic remedies that were often helpful to soothe away injuries such as these. Not to mention that her motherly presence was comforting to these frightened rabbits. Later, they would take Lohini to get a proper medical exam—once she had been reassured of her safety.

After a quick stop at the front to check in with the staff, Steve headed back into the sweltering heat of the afternoon. He didn't see Lohini's pursuer anywhere. He surveyed the length of the street for several minutes to be sure, then began walking toward the rickshaw stand a block or so away.

As he thought of what Lohini had been through and the fate of the girl she had attempted to convince to join her, his heart broke as it always did. It didn't surprise Steve that the other girl had refused. It was dangerous to try to sneak out of the red light district. The pimps and madams had plenty of security measures in place to protect their assets.

But the most binding chains were the invisible ones—many of the girls were so brainwashed after years of torture and abuse that they no longer wanted to leave. Many of them had even "earned" their freedom and continued to do sex work because it was all they knew how to do—they felt it was too late to begin a different life. Most of them didn't even know what their other options were, and didn't want to find out.

Steve wondered if Anjuna was one of these, or if she had simply been too afraid to run. If the latter, there might be hope of rescuing her. If the former, their best option was to try to convince her to send her children to Prakaash House, to break the cycle and keep the younger ones out of the trade. Even career sex workers usually didn't want their children to follow in their footsteps. Given the option, they would give their kids a chance at a different life.

Not that Steve ever gave up on trying to help their mothers, either. He didn't believe in lost causes.

The rest of the day was a blur of activity, and he was on the verge of falling asleep that night when he realized that he still had not responded to Sarah's email. He thought about getting up to do it right then, but exhaustion changed his mind.

He lay spread-eagle on the bed, sticky despite the small air conditioning unit cranking away in the window. He stared at the ceiling and thought about Sarah's email. She had tried to keep it lighthearted, but in between the lines, he could see how tired, sad, and angry she was. Once more, he felt guilty that he had had to leave her right when it seemed she was at her most vulnerable.

He wondered if Sarah and Joanna had managed to have their coffee date yet—although, now that Sarah had reached out to him, he could ask her himself for the news he craved.

So why don't I?

He propped himself up against the wall and grabbed his phone. The call went to voicemail. He hung up before the beep.

After all this time, he didn't want to leave a message. He wanted to connect with her in person.

Eventually, he fell into an exhausted but fitful sleep.

thirty-three

SARAH DROVE AWAY FROM JOANNA'S IN DISTRESS. SHE FELT LIKE THE GIRL IN THE PICTURE KATHY had shown them at last night's support group meeting—a small figure dwarfed by the sleeping dragon of the "past" that prevented each of them from escaping their dungeon.

Mom. Dad. Everett. Craig. Erica. Even the man who had raped Joanna.

Images roiled like inky clouds through her thoughts, coalescing into lizard-like shapes before dissolving into another cameo.

How could Joanna have forgiven the man who took her worth? The very idea seemed impossible to Sarah right now. Yet she couldn't deny the difference in Joanna's life compared to her own, and it seemed to stem from one thing—Joanna was at peace. Unlike Sarah, whose innards felt like the staging field for a never-ending war.

Sarah wondered how she could achieve that peace. How could she be free of her abusers so she could move on with her life? Was forgiveness truly the answer?

The manila envelope caught her eye, distracting her. She had forgotten all about her intention to mail it. If she waited until she got back to Edmonton to mail the manuscript, the postmark wouldn't be until the following day, and she hated not keeping her word. She chewed her lip, debating what to do next.

It wasn't too late to turn around. She peeled into the gas station at the edge of town—the very one Steve had rescued her from—circled the lot, and headed back toward the post office downtown.

As she drove, thoughts of wounds and forgiveness and God circled around her brain. She couldn't help but wonder what her mother's wounds might be. And whether Ellen's phone call yesterday had been her way of trying to reach out to her angry daughter. They had never had a great relationship, but Sarah had rarely been openly hostile to her mother before, not even in her teen years. Ellen might be hurt and angry, too.

Good. Let her suffer.

Guilt wound its familiar fingers around her heart. *I'm sorry, Mom. I didn't mean it.*

Joanna had said that God saw her as a pearl of great price. She frowned. Had God been helping her somehow that she hadn't noticed? How *was* it that Steve had just "happened" to be at the gas station that night, right when she needed him most? Could it be that Steve's and Joanna's God was somehow real and looking out for the likes of her?

No. Her life was way too broken for that. There were too many other nights when she had needed a rescuer, and none had appeared. Quite beside her destroyed childhood, why wait until Craig had beaten her up before sending help? And where was help when he had raped her only days before that? If that was the protection of God, she didn't want it.

Thinking of Steve reminded her that she still hadn't heard back from him. Of course, it was the middle of the night again in Mumbai. *Damn this time difference.*

Now that *Her Father's Daughter* was complete, she had a decision to make— would she write Steve's biography, or wouldn't she? If she didn't, what were her other options? She thought about that for a few minutes, and the longer she did, the more she knew she still desperately wanted to work on the project she had conceived in October—the one that gave her hope of a new start on her career. The question was, was it worth the risk of getting close to Steve in order to get the information she needed to write the book? What if he took things too far? What if she did?

That was silly, she realized. She was a professional, and writers wrote biographies all the time without having love affairs with their subjects. Besides, he had never given her any indication that he wanted to be more than friends. That should have made her feel relieved, but for some reason, it made her feel unsettled.

Of course, the whole debate might be moot if he had been so offended by her behaviour that he wouldn't even talk to her anymore. She sighed. She sure had a knack for messing up her life.

When she had been with Craig, it had been easy to blame her lack of friends on him—after all, he was the one who had made it so uncomfortable to maintain those friendships that she had simply let them fade away. But now, she saw how the fault wasn't his, it was hers. She had chosen to let them go. Just like she had let Craig take over so many other areas of her life, *she* had made the choice to let him dominate her relationships, too. And now she was paying the penalty for letting him, and the fear of inter-gender relationships he and her father and brother had instilled in her, dominate her decisions. But if it weren't for them, she wouldn't be so messed up and alone in the first place.

She could see what was happening clearly enough, but she had no idea what to do about it. Even when she tried to break free of her past patterns, they held her captive. Maybe this was simply one more area of her life which would remain permanently broken.

She slammed her palm on the steering wheel.

Well, at least I've got Joanna. She feared holding the thought too tightly, in case by claiming Joanna as her friend the universe—or whatever hostile force seemed so bent on destroying her life—deemed her unworthy and tore that relationship away, too.

But next time, I won't let it.

She pulled into the angled parking space in front of the square, pale-brick building that housed the post office. When she got in the door, there was a short line at the counter, so she stood at the end to wait.

A few moments later, the door behind her opened again. Out of instinct and curiosity, she turned to see who had entered—

And came face-to-face with Everett.

Her mouth went dry.

"Sarah!" He looked as surprised as she felt. His face grew red under his crew cut and he stood opening and closing his hands. He peered at the package in her arms with interest, and she clasped it more tightly to her chest.

She looked at him for a moment, then moved around him to leave.

He caught her arm to stop her, and when she froze and looked at his hand on her arm, he dropped it. He almost seemed embarrassed.

Sarah didn't care. She took another step toward the door.

"Sarah, wait."

She stopped, but didn't look up. "What do you want, Everett?"

"What are you doing in town? Were you here to visit Mom?"

She frowned. "No, just a friend, if it's any of your business."

He glanced at the bulky envelope in her arms and narrowed his eyes. "What are you mailing?"

Sarah glared at him, emboldened by the public setting. "Why do you want to know?"

"Mom told me you were sending her a copy of your book. I'm here picking up her mail for her. If that's it, you could save yourself a couple of bucks and give it to me."

Sarah's jaw dropped and she floundered for a response. "No, that's not what it is." *That lie couldn't have been much more obvious.*

Everett looked skeptical. "It's not?"

"Well, it is a manuscript, but I'm sending this one to my, um, editor." What was wrong with her today? She was normally much better at this.

"From here? Miller? Why?"

"It had to be done today and the post office will be closed by the time I get back to Edmonton." At least that part was true.

"Why didn't you just email it to your editor? Do you usually send him a hard copy?"

"*Her.* And . . . yes. Yes, I do. She's old-school that way."

Everett's eyes showed that he didn't believe a word of what she said.

"So how did you give Mom a copy of your book today if you didn't see her and you aren't mailing it to her?"

Sarah gulped. "I didn't say I didn't see her."

"So you did see her?"

"I, um, stopped by."

"And you gave her the manuscript?"

Something in Everett's tone told her that he was laying a trap of some kind for her, but she didn't know what it might be. Was Mom even home today? Everett seemed to know something she didn't. She decided that ambiguity was the best course. *Never lie about something that can be checked.*

"No, I didn't see her. She didn't come to the door. Maybe she was out for a walk or something. Anyway, I left the manuscript in the mailbox for her." *Or I will right after this, anyway.*

"So," Everett crossed his arms, "you were there but didn't go in. It sounds like you didn't *want* to see her. Not that you could have, anyway. Mom has been out at our place all morning helping Jill paint the nursery. But I'll have to tell her what a wonderful daughter you are when I get home. Maybe I'll pick up the manuscript from her place on the way. She sounded so anxious to read it."

Everett's eyes glittered. He had called her bluff, and she knew the truth must be written all over her face.

"Excuse me," said an old man behind them. "Are you two in line?"

Sarah glanced around and noticed that the lady at the counter was waiting for her expectantly. Several sets of eyes behind them held varying degrees of expectation and annoyance at having to wait and be unwilling witnesses to hers and Everett's exchange in the small space.

"No, I've changed my mind," Sarah said to the postal worker and the old man at once. She whirled out of line to leave, leaning close to Everett and stretching to get into his face. "You bastard," she hissed and stormed away.

"What, now you're not mailing it to your editor, either?" Everett called after her mockingly.

His sneering chuckle was cut off as the glass foyer doors soft-closed behind her.

Forgive him? She hurled herself into the RAV. The slamming door shook the entire vehicle. *That'll be a cold day in hell.*

She left town by way of her mother's, using the spare key to take the manuscript right into the house and leave it on the kitchen counter. She looked at it sitting next to the stove, shook her head, and moved it to under her mother's bedroom pillow. She didn't want Everett to come by and make it "disappear." She wasn't sure he would, but he had seemed to be up to something. Sarah would text her mother about its location later, when she thought it likely that Ellen would be home.

Working through her *katas* at karate that evening, her energy had never been so focused. With every movement, she centred her rage. Her hands were only connecting with air, but in her mind, she saw the faces of all those that had betrayed and abused her, and she was wreaking her revenge.

No, she didn't want to forgive them. She didn't even *want* to want it.

She wanted to show that dragon who was boss.

"Well done, Sarah. Nice and strong," said the *sensei* as he walked by.

Sarah frowned. She didn't feel strong, but she was determined to become that way. The next time she saw Everett, she didn't want to go running with her tail between her legs. She wanted to smack that arrogant smile right off his face.

The *sensei* counted the next form, and she punched her dragon in the face with an explosive, "Ha!"

The sunlight in Steve's eyes and a horn honking loudly on the street outside jolted him out of sleep. Despite his sudden awakening, he felt good. Snippets of images from his dream floated through his mind and he smiled as Sarah's face floated with them. Then he started upright, blushing as he remembered what his dream-self had been doing with her. They were far, far away from doing *that*.

Steve pressed his fingers against his eyelids. Just when he thought he had finally left that part of his past behind . . .

How could I think of her that way? She needs me as a friend, not one more lecherous—

The phone rang. The sound was coming from somewhere beneath the covers. He flopped his hand around on the bed, looking for the source of the noise, finally pulling it out from a tangle of sheets. By the time he had answered the call, the ringing had stopped.

It had been Sarah.

Of course.

He waited a few seconds in case she was leaving him a voicemail, then dialled her back. She answered on the first ring.

"Hi, Steve. That was fast."

"Bacon."

"Excuse me?"

"Bacon over croutons, every time. In bits or not, I'll take bacon any way I can get it."

Sarah laughed, and it was the sound of rainbow bubbles or autumn wheat fields in the sun. Steve closed his eyes. He'd missed her.

"Well, that's good to know, I suppose." She paused. "I saw you called me earlier today. It must have been while I was at your sister's. It didn't ring for some reason, and I didn't notice it until it was too late to call. Man, that must have been the middle of the night for you." She gasped. "Oh, no! Did I just wake you up?"

Steve glanced at the clock. It was just after six thirty in the morning. "No, you didn't." *Not exactly*, he thought, remembering his dream, his face flushing with heat. "A truck did."

"Whew!" She laughed again, and the effervescent bubbles danced up his spine. "You just made me glad to be awake."

Sarah hesitated. "Really?"

Steve gulped. He didn't want to sound like a creep. But it was so good to hear her voice. "Yeah. So how are you?"

"Um . . . good, I guess. Joanna and I had a good visit this afternoon."

"Oh? That's good to hear. What else is new? You seem better than the last time we spoke. Happier." He was surprised. That certainly had not been the impression he'd gotten from her email.

"I suppose I am. Did I tell you I joined karate? I just got home, actually."

Steve shifted to a more comfortable position. "No, I don't think so. Good for you."

"And I finished the book."

"Already? Wow, that was fast. What did your editor think?"

"I don't know yet. I only sent it to her a couple of days ago. My agent seemed to like it, but that's no surprise."

Something in her tone perked up his ears.

"Why do you say it like that?"

Sarah sighed. "I think you might be right about Becky. She still hasn't found anyone to take the bio project. I'm beginning to think she hasn't really been trying. And she's made it clear that she wants my next pitch to be more of what I've already been doing." She paused. "Maybe it *is* time for me to move on."

Steve cleared his throat. "And how do you feel about that?"

"Terrified." Her soft laugh sounded nervous.

Steve smiled at her unselfconscious admission. "Sometimes God closes doors on things we are comfortable with so we can finally see the even better thing that's been waiting for us."

"I've never been good at jumping into the unknown."

"Says the woman who skydives for fun." Steve chuckled. "If you can do that, changing agents should be a snap."

"Skydiving is different, though."

"Obviously. With skydiving, you could only lose your life, not just an opportunity to improve it."

Sarah laughed. "Well, when you put it *that* way."

Steve chuckled. "When do you expect to hear back from your editor?"

"It usually only takes a couple of weeks max, but I think Yolanda might be in Mexico or something right now. I was way ahead of schedule." She sighed. "I wish I were in Mexico. Or India."

Steve's heart leapt. "Well, when are you coming? You said you were going to come see the project. My friends Sam and Kallie show up in a couple of days, too." He glanced around the small room, already working on logistics. "I only have two bedrooms in my flat, which is where we put up foreign visitors, so if you came while they were here we'd have to get creative with sleeping arrangements. But I'm sure we could work something out. I'll sleep on the couch or something."

"You've already slept on the couch for me enough, Steve. Seriously. That's what hotels are for. But I don't think I'll be able to come right away anyway. I, um, just started attending a support group, and I really think it's going to help. I committed to attend to the end of the session, so that's a couple of months. Besides, I've got to be at Craig's hearing in February, and if—*when*—I come see you, I want to be able to stay for a while."

Steve shifted position on the hard mattress and smiled to himself. *When?* He liked the sound of that.

"Well, keep me posted. My current visa expires in April, which means I'll be doing some travelling at that point. So plan to come before then, okay?"

"Sure."

Why did his heart stutter when she said that?

"So how have *you* been?" Sarah asked. "You sound exhausted."

"Thanks."

"Sorry." She sounded embarrassed. "I don't know why I can hold my tongue around everyone else, but with you it's like I say the first thing that flies into my head."

"It's okay. I like it."

Awkward silence.

"—when you lip me off," Steve added, cursing himself under his breath. Trust him to make this weird. Maybe he wasn't quite awake yet. "Someone's got to keep me honest."

Sarah chuckled. "Well, I've got plenty more where that came from. But tell me about what's going on there. I'm ready to tackle your book, and I need some material."

Her tone was lighthearted. It was good to hear, though he wondered if she was wearing a mask for his benefit. Even still, it was nice to have someone to talk to about his day—a Westerner, someone who understood his mindset. As much as he loved his co-labourers at Love Mumbai, there were things that he could never share with them, sure that they would never understand.

He hoped Sarah would.

"Yesterday was one of the good days," he said. "We helped a girl escape the streets."

"Why don't you sound happier about it?"

Steve sighed. "I am happy. Ecstatic, actually. It's just, my work here . . . it can be pretty hard. Yes, we had a victory. But for every girl like Lohini that escapes from slavery, there are dozens, maybe hundreds, more being brought in. It is sometimes difficult to feel like our work is a success when we are always so far behind the problem."

"I suppose. But if it weren't for Love Mumbai, that girl would never have escaped, right?"

"I don't know. We aren't the only ones doing this, thank God. But there are few enough." He ran his hand over his stubble. "Don't worry, I'm not thinking of quitting or anything. That's not in my wheelhouse. Just sometimes, I need to vent a little. The pressure gets to me, I guess."

"Really?" Sarah sounded genuinely surprised. "I didn't think anything ever got to you. You always seem so calm."

Steve laughed. "No, that's my partner, Paul."

Sarah chuckled. "Your 'partner' Paul? Be careful who you say that to, or you'll never get a girl."

Steve blinked, then laughed with her from deep in his belly. Their laughter fed from each other's and rose on a swell until they were no longer laughing at the joke but for the joy of laughing. Finally, their mirth began to abate. Steve wiped moisture away from the corner of his eye. "I'll—I'll keep that in mind," he said between gasps.

"Hey, just 'keeping you honest.'"

"I knew you would."

"You should try skydiving. That's how I work off steam."

"Skydiving. Hmm. I'm not sure that's an option around here."

"Huh. All that beautiful weather, going to waste?"

"Maybe Indians are far too sensible to jump out of perfectly good airplanes."

Sarah groaned at the old joke. "Next time you're in Canada, I'll take you. It'll be fun."

"I'd like that."

Steve glanced regretfully at the sun hitting the wall of the building outside his window. He had emails to write, decisions to make, projects to inspect,

people to reach out to—there was always so much to do. Then he thought of
Lohini, and Aashi, and the dozens of other precious faces that he did all of it for.

Worth it.

"I guess I better get going." He wished he didn't have to. "I have a long list
today, and it's not getting any shorter."

"I know you're busy. Um, thanks for taking the time to talk to me."

"This might be my new favourite way to start the day."

He regretted it as soon as he'd said it.

"O-kay."

Crap. He'd made it weird again. But he'd meant every word.

"Hey, Sarah, before you go . . ." He gulped.

"Yes?"

Her gentle prompt reassured him.

"I just want to say thank you."

"For what?"

"For writing. For listening. I missed you. Let's do this more often, okay?"

Sarah hesitated. "I'd like that. Tomorrow night? That would be tomorrow
morning for you, I guess."

Steve grinned. He caught himself before he jokingly said *It's a date.* One
less foot to take out of his mouth later.

"Sure. Tomorrow. Good morning, Sunshine."

"Good night, Steve."

thirty-four

SARAH APPLIED A DEMURE BERRY LIPSTICK AS THE FINISHING TOUCH TO HER MAKEUP AND PURSED her lips at herself in her bathroom mirror. She had brightened her complexion with foundation and blush, but knew that under all the cosmetics, she was pale.

She had been dreading this day for months, and it was finally here. In an hour, she would be sitting in a court room, testifying at Craig's preliminary hearing about what he had done to her. And he would be sitting right there, watching her.

Surveying her finished look, she wished she could have used a punchy red lipstick instead, but had gone with Doug Fenway's advice of looking earnest and trustworthy for the judge over her own defiant desire to prove she still 'had it'—to look more like a sexy dragon hunter than the whipped puppy that she was sure Craig saw her as.

Not that she felt much like slaying dragons this morning.

She hadn't seen Craig since that day at the restaurant. After that, the restraining order that had been issued against him had been enough to keep him away, thankfully. She had even managed to avoid meeting him in person throughout their painfully slow divorce proceedings so far.

But today, she would see Craig in the flesh. She would look him in the eyes as she publicly relayed what she had suffered at his hands.

And she would do it alone.

Sarah felt shaky all of a sudden and sat down on the closed toilet. How she wished that Steve were here. They had been communicating regularly via phone calls and email for the last month, and it had been wonderful in a way she hadn't expected. She had forgotten what it was like to have someone to talk to in the evenings, someone who was interested in her day or with whom she could discuss ideas. Ostensibly, they were conducting interviews for the biography, but other topics always worked their way in. She found that a day without talking to Steve felt incomplete somehow.

As fulfilling as it was to have a real connection with someone again, this morning she would have given anything for a warm body to hold her for even a few minutes. She closed her eyes and remembered how it felt when Steve had comforted her, his arms holding her tight, the scent of pine and crisp air clinging to the cold denim of his jacket beneath her cheek. She knew that she was forming the very emotional attachment to the man that she had feared—and was startled to realize that she didn't care. He wasn't going to take advantage of her, unlike most of the men she'd had experience with. And as long as he never knew how she felt about him, she wouldn't be taking advantage of him, either.

But on a day like today, it was difficult not to wish that she could have the kind of life that she yearned for—with a happy marriage and a bright future, instead of the dismal ruins she was trying to patch together into something that resembled a decent existence. Or at least a safe one.

Nelson padded into the bathroom and she patted his soft head. Not so long ago, she would have told herself that his gentle presence was support enough. Only three weeks ago, she'd managed to fire her agent—it had turned out that the differences were irreconcilable—and celebrated by beginning a blog in her own name. Her first post had been a defiant coming-out as the "real Devon Sinclair" and a rant about how she was stronger alone.

Today, it wasn't possible to lie to herself like that.

She had thought about asking Kathy from the support group to come with her today, but she didn't know her all that well and didn't want to impose. Joanna might have come—they had seen each other a couple of times since that coffee date in Miller a few weeks ago—but Sarah felt bad asking Joanna to take the trouble to find a sitter and go out of her way to help her. So she had bucked up, sucked it up, and decided that she could do it on her own.

Well, that's what she'd told herself to do last night when it had felt too daunting to ask one of the ladies at the group session. This morning, she wasn't sure she could stand up off this toilet, let alone make it to the front of that court room to relive her rape and abuse in front of its perpetrator and who-knew-how-many strangers. Just thinking about it caused blood to start rushing through her ears.

What if she froze when she saw Craig? She hated that she was still so afraid of him. In her nightmare last night, he had tortured and maimed her in another creatively horrific way before finally trying to kill her. She knew it was only a dream, but it revealed in no uncertain terms the effect he had on her.

But today is my chance to fight back.

A surge of burning liquid scorched up her throat. She scrambled to turn herself around and lift the toilet seat in time to heave into the bowl. She hadn't eaten yet, so all that came out was acrid yellow bile.

This didn't bode well.

So much for 'bucking up.' The only thing bucking is my stomach.

Doug Fenway had prepared her with what she needed to say. Sarah took grim comfort from the fact that he had insisted on being so thorough. Either he had noticed Craig flirting with his wife after all or Christine had told him about it later. He'd had definite satisfaction in his voice when he had called to inform her that he was the Crown Prosecutor on the case. Sarah certainly felt better knowing that the prosecutor wasn't one of Craig's cronies. But this morning, her racing heart and seasick stomach belied all the prep and drilling Doug had done with her.

"Steve, why do you have to be on the other side of the planet?" She stared at the wall, wishing that magic wishes were a real thing.

She should have asked Joanna. Or Jill. At this point, she even wished she'd asked her mother. *Which goes to show how desperate I am.*

Shakily, she pulled herself to her feet using the vanity for support and began cleaning up the mess she had made of her lipstick, cursing her prior stubborn determination to get through this on her own. She finished and stared at her ashen face.

At times like this, she almost envied those who could believe in the God that Steve and Joanna talked about. It was certainly tempting to imagine a big strong protector at her side rather than feeling abandoned and alone. It was even more tempting to ask someone—*anyone*—for help when her own strength seemed non-existent.

On impulse, she closed her eyes.

"God, if you exist, I could use some help today."

The words seemed to echo in the tiny room. She opened her eyes and stared at herself, feeling foolish. May as well have asked the Genie of the Mirror for her first wish.

"Sarah Daniels, you're an idi—"

Her phone rang.

Sarah frowned. It was seven thirty in the morning. Who would be calling her now?

She hurried to grab her phone from the kitchen counter. The caller ID showed Steve's face. She took a breath to regain some composure, then put the phone to her ear.

"Hello? Steve?"

"Good morning, Sunshine."

Sarah gave a weak laugh. "It's evening there."

"But it's morning for you."

Steve's warm chuckle comforted Sarah like syrup on pancakes. She sat on a dining room chair, her legs still trembling.

"Why are you calling? Is everything okay?"

"I wanted to ask you that very question. Today's the big day, isn't it? Craig's hearing?"

He remembered. She hadn't mentioned it to him except in passing a few weeks ago, bound and determined to soldier through on her own and not wanting him to worry. But if he'd shown up at her door that morning with a bagel, a coffee, and a free hug, she couldn't have felt more like kissing him than she did right then.

"Yeah. It is."

"How are you holding up?"

"I threw up."

"Oooh. That's not good."

"I know."

"Who's going with you?"

"I, um, no one. I didn't ask anyone." She hesitated, studying the linoleum. "I wish you were here."

"Weeell," he said, drawing it out. "I can't be there, as much as I wish I could. But I kinda figured you might try to pull a stunt like this and wish you hadn't, Miss Independent. So I called Joanna. She's on her way to Edmonton and she'll meet you in front of the courthouse at eight thirty."

"You—you did what?" Sarah gulped around the sudden lump in her throat. How did he do it? Even from the other side of the planet, he was still rescuing her. This time, it was from herself. She should probably be outraged at his presumption, but all she could muster was deep and profound gratitude.

"You're okay with that, right? I could probably still call her off if you truly want to do this alone."

Sarah shook her head, charmed by his uncertainty. She finally found her voice. "No, no, it's okay. I—I don't want to do this alone."

Steve blew out air.

"Was that a sigh of relief?"

"Maybe. I didn't know how you would feel about me jumping into your affairs like that. I just felt so helpless and I wanted to do something to let you know that you are not alone."

Sarah's sinuses prickled and she blinked back moisture. "Thank you, Steve. You didn't have to do that. But I'm really glad you did."

His voice was tender. "I know. But I wanted to. And you're welcome."

There was an awkward pause. Sarah bit her lip. "I—I better go if I'm going to get there on time."

"Call me later if you want to talk about it. Even if it's the middle of the night here. If I hear the phone, I'll answer."

"Okay. Thank you."

"Promise?"

Sarah laughed shakily. "Promise."

"And Sarah?"

"Yeah?"

"I'll be praying for you."

Sarah paused. Coming from Steve, that was more than a polite gesture, something he said to make himself sound good. She knew it was the best remaining service he could offer her, and he offered it from the bottom of his heart.

"Thanks."

"Bye."

"Bye."

Sarah stared at her phone for a moment in regret.

He'd rescued her again. From the other side of the freakin' planet. The cavalry had been called by Steve McGuire, right when she had needed him most.

And right after Sarah had asked for help.

Sarah froze, wondering about the timing of that call. Then she shook her head at herself, threw on her coat and grabbed her purse and keys.

Pull yourself together, woman, she berated herself as she locked her apartment door behind her. *You're reading way too much into this. Steve would already have been dialling the phone. Joanna's been on the road for twenty minutes, I bet. His call had nothing to do with that silly little prayer.*

Of course it didn't.

Did it?

Sarah fidgeted with her purse strap. Joanna sat next to her in the sparsely populated gallery of a small court room. Sarah glanced at her friend, who gave her an encouraging smile.

"You'll be fine." Joanna's voice was soothing.

Sarah gave a tight-lipped smile in return. "Uh-huh."

She had already thanked Joanna for doing this three times until Joanna had hushed her with an exasperated tone. "I am *glad* to do it. If you had told me about this, I would have volunteered."

Chastened, Sarah hadn't mentioned it again.

Craig sat behind the defendant's bench at the front of the room. From her place across the aisle behind him, she could see his strong profile as he whispered with his lawyer. He caught her looking at him and smiled—like a lion might smile at a gazelle—then whispered something else to his lawyer and laughed. His lawyer only nodded, cast a quick glance in her direction, and then turned his eyes expectantly to the front of the room.

Sarah's heartbeat thundered in her chest, and her breath started coming in shallow gasps. She wished she could get up and walk around, but instead she gripped her purse strap so tightly that her fingers started to go numb. *Should have gone with the red lipstick.*

Glancing around, she saw Erica slip in through the back door and sit directly across the aisle from her. The other woman didn't seem to notice Sarah sitting there.

Joanna leaned toward her. "Remember to breathe."

Sarah blinked and focused on her friend's face. She gave a tight nod.

"Do this with me," Joanna said. "Long deep breath in through the nose, like this." She used her hands to illustrate the opening of her diaphragm as she took a deep breath.

Sarah mimicked Joanna's slow intake of air, controlling her breathing with difficulty. It felt like every muscle in her body had contracted.

Joanna nodded encouragingly. "Now out through your mouth."

They exhaled. Then they did it again.

Sarah felt her heart rate slow and looked at her friend in amazement. "That actually worked!"

Joanna smiled. "My piano teacher taught me that trick for calming nerves before a performance when I was a kid. It works for other things, too, I discovered."

Doug Fenway entered and made his way to the prosecutor's bench.

Though she no longer felt like bolting, Sarah tried to calm her still-shaking fingers by running through the facts again in her mind. She took another deep, controlled breath for good measure.

"Stick to the facts, and you'll be fine," Doug had said to her yesterday in his office.

The facts. Stick to the facts. She inhaled. *Craig hit me. He choked me. He tried to rape me.* Exhale. *Nelson saved me. That time.*

Doug pulled some papers out of his briefcase and arranged them on the bench, then turned to her and smiled.

Sarah felt her breathing grow more erratic again and rummaged in her purse for a breath mint for something to do. Her hands shook, and she gripped the edges of the bag tightly to still them.

Inhale. Exhale.

Better.

A bailiff entered the room from the front side door.

"All rise for the Honourable Judge Mayhew," he intoned.

Sarah and Joanna stood, along with everyone else in the room, as a small woman with silvering close-cut hair entered and made her way to the judge's bench. From her vantage behind the prosecutor's bench, Sarah noticed Craig's face darken and a harsh exchange between him and his lawyer, and now it was Doug's turn to look smug as he, too, glanced at them. She remembered Doug saying something about the original judge having to recuse himself because of a conflict of interest.

With Craig's history in this city, Sarah found it a wonder that there was a judge who *didn't* have a conflict of interest. Then again, Craig had made a few enemies—not least of whom was the Crown Prosecutor handling this case.

Inhale.

Doug had warned her that with Craig's position, and since this was a first offence, it was possible that he would walk away from this with nothing but a slap on the wrist. Or maybe he would be suspended from the bar. The chances of jail time were slim.

Sarah had wavered when he'd told her that. Did she really want to go through this agony if Craig wouldn't even be punished for what he had done?

That was when she had been informed that it was no longer up to her. It was the Crown that laid the charges, and the Crown would be prosecuting Craig, not Sarah. She was the key witness, however, and she could tell that Doug wanted to be absolutely sure she wasn't going to crumble on the stand. Without her, the case pretty much didn't exist.

Exhale.

She could do this. She was stronger now. This was her chance to prove it.

The bailiff read the charges and court was underway. After some preliminaries, Sarah was called to the stand.

In that moment, all the terror returned. She stood and swayed. Joanna squeezed her hand and she glanced at her friend.

"Breathe," Joanna mouthed.

Sarah nodded. Knees trembling, she made her way to the stand. She sat and Craig's green eyes nailed her to her chair. She felt like a rabbit caught in a snare, and barely squeaked out an "I do" for her swearing-in.

I can't do this! Her thoughts scrambled every direction, trying to escape. Her gaze jumped from Erica's accusing face to Joanna's encouraging one and back to Craig's hard eyes. Panic stabbed her chest in frozen shards like icicles falling into snow in a sudden wind.

I can't do this I can't do this I can't—

Doug stood to prompt her through her statement. His voice came to her like she was underwater, trapped and drowning in the venom in those green eyes.

Sarah tore her gaze from Craig's and stared at a knot in the wood bench in front of her. The dark stain beautifully defined each curving line of the grain. She could imagine the craftsman moving his brush in masterful strokes along the length of the beam, taking pride in—

"Ms. Daniels?" prompted Doug.

Sarah's focus snapped back and she blinked at him. She vaguely remembered that he had asked her to give her version of the events that led to the charges.

Craig stared at her, a small, confident smile curling his lips.

He thinks he's won. He thinks I won't do this.

She could feel her dragon breathing hot fire over her neck, pinning her with its baleful, gloating stare. The flames seemed to dance in Craig's eyes.

Something Steve had said to her last week popped into her mind. "The only power he has over you is the power you give him. So don't give him any. Remember, you have the power now. The law is on your side, not his."

She saw Joanna over Doug's shoulder, her hands again mimicking the action of opening her diaphragm to deep-breathe. Sarah took one more long, steadying breath.

"Ms. Daniels?" Doug prompted again. "What happened on the night in question?"

Sarah glanced at Doug. His eyebrows were raised, like he wanted to prompt her with the words to begin. She stared at him, trying to think of a single coherent thought.

Finding Craig's face again, it came. In a rush of heat and rage, it came.

You're not going to win, you damn lizard.

"I arrived home at about seven thirty p.m. My husband, Craig, was already home . . ."

Once she began, continuing became easier. She stared straight at Doug as she continued reciting her statement, and with every word, her voice became stronger. When she'd finished, she glanced back at Craig. His confident smile had vanished.

Doug asked her a few questions to help her fill in details. The photos the police had taken when Sarah filed her report were displayed on a screen. Then Craig's lawyer, a barrel of a man with greying temples, a charcoal suit, and a blue-striped tie, stood and approached the bench. The serious look on his face made Sarah's palms begin to sweat.

"Ms. Daniels, were there any witnesses to the events you spoke of? Anyone who could corroborate what you said was true?"

Sarah gulped. "No one was in the room with us except my dog. However, there were neighbours in the hallway when I left. They had definitely heard something."

"But no one actually saw your husband strike you?"

"Um, no."

The man paced a few steps and glanced at Craig before continuing. "Is it true that you arrived home that day with a sprained ankle?"

Sarah blinked. Of course, Craig would have told him that. "Yes, I did."

"And how did that happen?"

Sarah's throat closed in panic. She gulped, trying to work up moisture into her mouth, and her glance skittered from the lawyer to Craig, then Doug, and then Joanna. "Skydiving," she said, barely above a whisper.

"Pardon me?"

Sarah took a breath and injected confidence into her voice. "Skydiving."

Craig's eyebrows shot up and his eyes narrowed. But the smile was back.

Craig's lawyer tilted his head at the screen showing her injured face and neck. "Could these injuries have been caused during the same 'skydiving' incident?"

Sarah shook her head. "No. I made no attempt to attribute my skydiving injury to my husband. I sprained my ankle because of a botched landing. The rest of the injuries occurred as I stated earlier. You can ask Bernie at the skydiving club—he treated my ankle."

The man nodded. "I see. Thank you. No further questions, your Honour."

He returned to the bench and sat down, and Sarah stepped down from the witness stand.

As Sarah passed Doug on her way back to the gallery, she caught an approving glint in his eye. She had done well.

She glanced across the aisle when she sat down and spotted Erica staring at her, looking somewhat stunned. Erica seemed to realize that she was staring and glanced away. Sarah wondered what Craig had told Erica about what had happened between the two of them—whatever it was didn't appear to be true.

Judge Mayhew cleared her throat. "Thank you, Ms. Daniels." She looked at Doug, then her eyes rested on Craig and his lawyer at the defendant's bench. "I believe there to be enough evidence here to proceed to a trial. The date is set for May third. Court adjourned."

She rose and left the courtroom in a swish of robes.

Sarah and Joanna stood and worked their way to the aisle. Sarah glanced at Erica again, managing to catch her ex-friend's eye. This time, Erica did not look away. Her dark brown eyes were clouded with confusion and, as she glanced at Craig, a glimmer of fear.

Sarah registered the woman's emotions and felt a twinge of compassion for her. No, Erica didn't deserve mercy or forgiveness. But she didn't deserve to be treated the way Sarah had been, either.

Sarah took a step into the aisle, toward the woman who stood frozen on the other side. Erica looked at her as though she was afraid of what she might do next.

"Now you know," Sarah said quietly. "Be careful, okay?"

Erica's eyes widened. She opened her mouth, but it was a few seconds before she could say, "I will."

Sarah nodded in acknowledgement, then walked out of the courtroom.

For some reason she couldn't possibly fathom, she actually felt okay.

thirty-five

SARAH FIDGETED WITH THE CLOTH NAPKIN IN HER LAP WHILE YOLANDA PRATTLED ON ABOUT HER two weeks in Mexico. Yolanda's thick, chin-length grey hair swung around her angular face as she regaled Sarah with the virtues of the cuisine at her resort. Sarah couldn't fathom how the best menu feature of a five-star resort could be the salad bar, but she nodded politely.

Sarah glanced around the Chilton's dining room, her gaze resting on the table she and Craig had shared with the Fenways the last time they were there. If it had been up to her, they would have been at almost any other restaurant in the city. However, Yolanda had chosen this one and Sarah didn't feel she was in a position to rock the boat at the moment.

It had been nearly five weeks since Sarah had submitted the manuscript for *Her Father's Daughter* to her editor, and she was sure that the delay meant some imminent doom for her career, regardless of Yolanda's Mexican vacation. She knew Yolanda would have brought her work with her to the beach and been reading manuscripts while sipping Mai Tais under a palm tree. So why had it taken so long for her to set up this appointment?

They made small talk while they ordered their meals and ate, discussing Sarah's divorce, Yolanda's cats and grandchildren, Mexican men, and even the benefits of karate—basically everything but the one topic burning in Sarah's mind—did Yolanda like the book? Not only did she want to know Yolanda's reaction to her novel, she was also hoping to work in an opportunity to give her the synopsis for Steve's bio, which was tucked into her laptop case. She'd been querying agents with it but had received no bites so far. Despite the odds against Steampressed taking on the project, she figured it couldn't hurt to try.

Finally, Sarah could take it no longer. When Yolanda had ordered coffee and dessert, still with no mention of the manuscript, she decided to bring up the topic herself.

"So, what—" she said, at the same time Yolanda began with "I suppose you—"

They both stopped, awkwardly trying to let the other person speak first. After several "no, you go ahead"s from each of them, Yolanda continued.

"I was going to say that I suppose you are anxious to know about the status of your book."

Sarah nodded, trying not to appear *too* anxious, despite her roiling gut. She couldn't remember the last time it had taken Yolanda so long to follow up on one of her submissions. As the weeks passed and her tension rose, she had begun to wonder if it might even have gotten lost in her editor's email inbox. But Yolanda was usually so organized that that didn't seem likely. Maybe Becky had been disgruntled enough with her dismissal that she'd managed to sabotage the project somehow—though that didn't make sense, either, since the agent would be damaged by the loss, too.

Now, as Yolanda hesitated, the frozen cord that tightened around Sarah's stomach convinced her of impending disaster. She folded her hands in her lap to keep them from shaking, anxiety flowing through each clenched finger.

Yolanda's face seemed a mask of carefully controlled nothingness, like one might use when about to break bad news.

Uh, oh.

Sarah steeled herself for the worst. She hadn't been this certain of rejection since very early in her career. She had taken so many risks with this manuscript, and it was so far out of her normal parameters—would the book even be publishable?

"How do you feel about a trip out to Toronto?" Yolanda asked, her face still unreadable.

Sarah frowned. "Why do you ask?"

"Because Toronto is where we launch the A-list books."

Sarah was still confused, hardly daring to believe the implications of the words when Yolanda's body language was so ambiguous. "A-list?" she asked dumbly.

"This manuscript," began Yolanda, then coughed. "This manuscript is probably some of the best writing I have ever seen from you. Or seen, period."

Sarah blinked. "Really?"

Yolanda relaxed, her face breaking into a broad smile. She leaned forward in excitement and her blunt-cut hair swayed like an iron curtain. It was the closest to giddy that Sarah had ever seen her. "Really. Sarah, this is *amazing* work. It might be the best book our press has ever produced. It's going to be the next *Fifty Shades*, I bet—except better. So much better. We're going to do the whole shebang on this one—big budget advertising, launch, you name it. We need to get you to the Toronto office so we can introduce . . ."

Sarah's head spun. She barely followed Yolanda's train of thought as the editor outlined her plan. It was like a dream come true.

My book, "A-list"?

Suddenly, some of Yolanda's words pierced through the fog.

". . . going to make Devon Sinclair a household name. This could launch a whole new franchise, and *you*. You could be the next E.L. James!"

The waitress brought their dessert and beverages, and Yolanda paused her excited speech to take a sip of steaming coffee.

Sarah picked up her spoon and studied it, not yet prepping her own drink. "No," she said softly.

Yolanda's head jerked up and she blinked at Sarah. "No? What do you mean?"

"No. My name is not Devon Sinclair. It is Sarah. I want to publish this book as Sarah Daniels."

Yolanda's jaw dropped slightly.

"But, why? You've already got an established brand under Devon Sinclair. And aren't you going to change your surname soon, anyway? Back to Sinclair? If only half your name is going to be correct regardless, why bother changing your pen name at all?"

Sarah thought about it. She'd considered changing her surname, despite the hassle. Who needed the constant reminder of her failed life every time she had to sign something? Not that her maiden name would be much better—they each signified failure and anguish in one way or another.

At that moment, she realized that she didn't want to change her name. The name "Daniels" seemed more like a badge of honour than a symbol of past pain and failure. She had become who she was while wearing that name. And for the first time in her life, she was beginning to like herself.

At last, she understood what Kathy had meant when she had told the support group that their dragons—their pasts—could become their allies. The things Sarah had gone through had become part of who she was, and she was stronger because of it. She didn't want to forget the pain and fire that had forged her. And she didn't want to hide behind a pseudonym.

She had written a book full of angst, pain, and heartache, but for the first time, her character had found joy and healing at the end of the story. That was a piece of work she was proud to own.

She met Yolanda's eye. "No, I will not be changing my name. I'm going to remain Sarah Daniels. And that is the only name I want to publish under from now on. If this book is truly the blockbuster you believe it to be, then publishing under my own name shouldn't hinder sales. There's nothing in my contract to prevent it. I checked."

She paused to spoon sugar into her coffee.

Yolanda's brow furrowed slightly. "Have you asked Becky for her opinion on all this?"

Sarah cleared her throat. "Repeatedly. And she always tried to keep me from changing anything I had ever done, which is why I had to let Becky go a few weeks ago."

Yolanda blinked. "That explains why she's been so slow to respond on this. Do you have another agent already?"

Sarah shook her head. "I'm in the market. But I'll be much choosier this time around."

Yolanda tilted her head. "You're not the first author I've heard say they had problems with Becky. I don't want to gossip, but I will say that it's so important for agents to be on the same page as their authors."

Sarah snorted. "I'd be happy with being in the same book at this point."

Yolanda laughed. "Okay, well, I don't want to try to hammer you into that box, but have you considered that your established fan base—"

She cut off at Sarah's headshake.

"I started a blog a month ago and already went public about my alter ego of Devon Sinclair. If we announce to my current fans that I am now publishing under my own name, they'll read this book. They won't care that I dropped the pseudonym. I think they may even appreciate getting to know the 'real Devon Sinclair.'"

Sarah smiled as she thought about the women she met at book signings, the ones she used to see as desperately in need of escape through titillation. She wondered now if, rather than a cheap thrill, what they were truly looking for was a connection with something real, just like she was.

She liked that. For the first time in her career, she found herself looking forward to talking to her fans at her next promotional event—as Sarah Daniels. As herself.

All this passed through her mind in a moment. She continued.

"As for the rest—the marketing, the franchise, more books—no. I'll fulfill my contract and do whatever you need me to do for this book. But I have decided that I want to write other things, and I know your house only publishes erotica. I already have my next book outlined, a biography of a friend of mine."

Sarah let go of the foolish idea that she could have Steampressed publish the bio. That was never going to happen—they didn't do nonfiction. But for the first time, she wasn't worried about finding a publisher. Whether she found one to take the book or not, she was determined to see the project into print.

Yolanda seemed to be processing everything Sarah had just said.

Sarah took a sip of coffee and set the mug back into the saucer, then faced her editor with a confidence she had never felt before. "From now on, I am going to decide what I write, and no one else. Maybe I'll come back to erotica one day. But first I need to figure out what I like."

Yolanda nodded thoughtfully. "I had no idea you felt so strongly about this. And I can respect your reasons. I think you're right—there should be no problem with fans finding your work under your new name, especially if you have gone public about the pseudonym. We should definitely be able to work something out." She paused and tapped her fingernail on the tablecloth. "Of course, it truly is a shame that you don't want another contract with us. However, our loss will be another imprint's gain."

Yolanda cocked her head at Sarah as though something had just occurred to her. She rummaged through her bag for a moment and pulled out a pen and notepad, ripped out a blank page and then scribbled a name and email address on it.

"Here." She pushed the paper toward Sarah. "This is Scott Segel's email address. He's an agent I know and respect at Lamarque. He specializes in non-fiction like your new project. I'll let him know to expect your synopsis."

Sarah took the piece of paper, stunned. She could feel tears pricking the backs of her eyes and her sinuses smarted. "Thank you, Yolanda. You have no idea how much this means to me."

Yolanda smiled. "Absolutely." She clicked her pen and turned to a different page in her notebook—one already filled with lines of blue ink in her neat cursive. "Now, let's talk logistics . . ."

thirty-six

STEVE STARED GLUMLY OUT THE CAB WINDOW AT THE BUILDINGS THAT LINED MARINE DRIVE. IN THIS part of town, upscale condos and hotels that advertised an ocean view alternated with shopping malls, ritzy coffee shops, and office buildings. The streets were lined with manicured palm trees, and the sidewalks crowded with well-groomed citizens in everything from traditional saris and lungis to jeans and designer brand-name T-shirts. Mumbai was a very cosmopolitan city, and for many foreigners, areas like this were all they would ever see. Any slums they noticed would be from the interior of air-conditioned cabs like the one Steve currently shared with Paul.

The cab was in the centre of an immobile press of vehicles, sitting firmly astride one of the dotted white lines intended to herd vehicles into lanes. Steve was almost surprised that the red light was even nominally successful at imposing structure on the traffic chaos. Traffic engineers in India were ever the optimists.

But why have a three-lane road of free-flowing traffic when there could be five-and-a-half vehicles abreast jammed into the same space, moving at a snail's pace?

Normally, Steve found Indian driving habits amusing. At the moment, all he could think about was that Prakaash House would soon be homeless.

Beyond the traffic jam, early afternoon sunlight glinted off of what was visible of the Indian Ocean through the hazy cloud of smog. From here, the entire length of the bay known as the "Queen's Necklace"—named for the miles-long glittering string of streetlights visible after dark—should have been visible, but a brown haze obscured everything farther away than a kilometre or so. It felt like some kind of fitting analogy for the care centre's future outlook. Or, at the very least, his mood.

"Perhaps it is for the best that he refused us." Paul shifted in the seat beside Steve. "We could never have afforded the rent for that place, anyway."

Steve made some kind of affirmative noise, watching two men on a scooter wedge into the space between their cab and the one beside them, the riders' elbows nearly touching the rear-view mirrors of the two vehicles.

Make that six abreast.

"Perhaps we should reconsider our new 'full disclosure' policy." Steve raised a quizzical brow at Paul, who raised an askance one in reply. Steve sighed. "No, you're right. We don't want to have to go through this again."

They had just looked at yet another property as a potential new location for Prakaash House. It was beautiful, clean, and spacious, but also too far away from the children's homes, and too expensive to be used for long. However, after a dozen other potential locations had fallen through, Steve and Paul were getting desperate. They had hoped only to use the location short-term while they looked for a more suitable property to purchase.

When they had begun searching for a new home for Prakaash House, they had decided to make sure that all their potential landlords knew to what use they would be putting the space, hoping to avoid a repeat situation. The landlords were always fine with a boarding school—until they were informed that the students were children of sex workers. Suddenly, there were all kinds of creative reasons why they couldn't possibly rent to Love Mumbai. The more honest ones just said no.

"Perhaps we could share space with the vocational centre," said Paul, bringing up an old idea.

Steve glanced at him, reconsidering it. They had already been through the pros and cons of this solution several times, but in a week, the cons may not matter. Vijay Paresh had given them until the end of February to be out of their current building, no more extensions. It now appeared that repurposing their existing spaces may be their only option.

"I think we may have to, my friend." Steve sighed and adjusted his long legs in the cramped space. "When we get back to the office, we will make a plan, okay? We will need to begin the transition immediately."

Paul waggled his head. "Yes, yes. Okay."

Steve cupped his hands over his knees, which were bare due to the option of wearing shorts, something his foreigner status gave him. "Do you think that God is trying to tell us something about Prakaash House, Paul? Is it something we are still supposed to be doing?"

Paul regarded him with steady brown eyes. "God has always come through for us before. I have to believe that there is a reason why he has closed so many doors this time. But it is not because we should close the school down. Have faith, brother. You will see."

Steve nodded and turned back to the window. Not for the first time, Paul's childlike faith left Steve wondering why such simple belief was so difficult for him.

Steve had met Paul when he and Sam had backpacked through the country almost nine years ago. Steve's pastor in Miller was friends with Paul's father, as they had both attended Bible College in British Columbia together. Pastor Eric had put Steve in touch with the Ramashankars, and Paul, who spoke excellent English, had served as Sam and Steve's guide while they visited Mumbai.

That friendship had been the jumping-off point for everything that followed.

When they met, Paul had recently graduated with a Bachelor of Social Work and a passion to make a difference in his city. One day, Paul had shown them the Kamathipura red light district. What they saw there completely horrified the two Canadian men—children playing in refuse unattended while johns victimized women who were no more than children themselves. Or worse, drugged children under the very beds their mothers were "working" on.

Calming their nerves over chai afterward, Paul had shared what he felt was his calling to work to break the cycle of sex trafficking in Mumbai. All he needed was a source of funding.

After leaving Mumbai, the things that Steve had experienced there wouldn't let him go. A new passion had been birthed in his spirit.

A year later, he and Paul had set up the first phase of the Love Mumbai project—a women's shelter a mere five-minute walk from the centre of the Kamathipura district. Last year, they had opened Prakaash House.

The current location of the care centre had many advantages, but at times, it already felt overcrowded. They were often filled to capacity, and some days they had to turn children away, which did not make Steve happy. However, the Government of India kept close tabs on an organization like theirs, and they didn't want to risk being shut down because they were over their allowed maximum. They had offered to purchase the building several times, thinking that if they owned the building they could easily add another floor to ease the space restrictions, just as they were doing at the women's shelter right now.

The problem was, Vijay Paresh had adamantly refused every offer they had made him. He said that the school would bring down all of the property values in the area, including the other buildings he owned there. And while they had managed to eventually convince him to fulfill his end of the current lease, he wouldn't hear of renewing. Which meant that in eight days, they had to be out.

Paul directed the cab driver through the back roads of their residential subdivision to avoid the busy streets of the bazaar near Prakaash House. When Steve got out in front of the squared brick building that was Love Mumbai's twenty-four-hour child care centre, the heat hit him like a sauna. Sometimes he wondered if air conditioning were truly a blessing, or if he had been better off in his early days in India—before AC was so widely available, and when his body seemed to acclimate much better to the heat without the constant fluctuations of temperature.

Steve followed Paul through the black iron gate that guarded the care centre. He nodded at Ragin, their daytime security guard, who was sitting in the three-foot-square air-conditioned security hut that stood directly behind the gatepost—one distinguishing feature from the other homes on the street. A flagstone walkway several feet wide skirted the tall, blocky main building. Deep-set square windows with scrolled painted-metal grates blinked at him from each of the three levels, and several potted peppers and other plants snuggled next to the wall, in shadow now but thriving from their daily dose of morning sunlight. Paul's small scooter motorcycle occupied the space between the house and the front fence, tucked behind Ragin's hut.

When Ragin saw them, the barrel-shaped man stepped out to greet them with a respectful *namaste*, his uniform crisp and clean as though he had just come on shift, despite having been there for six hours already. Ragin took his job very seriously, much like everything else in life. Steve could count on one hand the number of times he had seen the middle-aged man smile. But Ragin was a trustworthy and conscientious employee who treated everyone who came in the door with respect, so Steve couldn't fault him for his demeanour.

Steve and Paul both pressed their palms together and returned Ragin's greeting.

"Vijay Paresh is waiting for you inside, sirs," said Ragin.

"*Deniwada*," said Paul in acknowledgement.

Paul exchanged quizzical glances with Steve as they headed toward the door. Steve knew neither of them were looking forward to another encounter with their bullish landlord. *What could Paresh want now?*

The front room of the house had been a small living room which they had converted into a lounge area and receptionist's office. Aparna sat at her desk working on a computer. She glanced up and greeted them with a smile, tipping her chin toward the man waiting on the wicker sofa next to the window. Paresh sipped chai from a small stainless steel tumbler and regarded them coolly.

Paul gave the landlord a wide, genuine smile. "Greetings, sir. Please, come into our office."

Paul gestured toward the doorway behind Aparna's desk.

Paresh stood and exchanged polite greetings with Steve, then led the way as directed.

As Paul passed Aparna's desk, he leaned over slightly. "Tea?"

She waggled her head. They went into the office and closed the door.

"Please, sit." Paul indicated the extra chair in front of his desk while taking his own seat.

Paresh waggled his head politely and obliged. Steve pulled his own chair out from behind his desk to sit near Paresh.

"How can we help you today?" Steve asked after they were all settled. His gut clenched in preparation for whatever new demands Paresh might have for them.

Paresh set his empty tumbler on Paul's desk, then eyed them both for a moment before he spoke.

"I have decided that I will sell you this building, for the right price."

Paul and Steve blinked at each other, then turned back to their guest.

"And what would that be?" Paul asked.

Paresh named a figure three times higher than anything they had offered him before.

Steve knew that it was an outrageous asking price for this property, but he was still so stunned at the sudden turn of events that he remained silent.

Not Paul, for whom haggling was as natural as breathing. He immediately counter-offered, but the only response was a stoic stare from Paresh.

Paul frowned. "Surely you do not believe we can pay so much for this building, sir? That is very high. Will you not be reasonable?"

Paresh clamped his lips together and stood. "You have heard my price. And the offer is only good until the end of March. I will expect my regular rent until the deal is closed. And if it is not, then you will once again be required to evacuate the premises."

Priya appeared at the door holding a tray with three more tumblers of steaming chai. Paresh strode toward the door and she backed into the wall, wide-eyed, to clear his path.

Just before he reached the doorway, Paresh turned to face them. "I will let you think about it. You know how to reach me. *Namaste*, sirs."

And with that, he showed himself out, leaving Paul and Steve staring at each other in slack-jawed amazement.

Steve could hardly believe it. Prakaash House might have a home, right where it was already located. But at that price, it still seemed impossible to achieve. *What on earth made Paresh change his mind?*

"You were right again, brother," said Steve. "God does seem to be making a way. I am not sure how we will find the money, but if God could change Paresh's marble heart to limestone, perhaps the Almighty can soften it again so we can afford to accept."

Paul beamed. "I will keep praying for that. Or whatever outcome he deems best."

Priya set a cup in front of each of them. Paul thanked her, and she smiled and left.

Steve took a sip of the tea and then glanced at the clock on the wall.

"Excuse me." He set the cup of scalding liquid down on his desk, pulled out his phone, and headed outside. It was still early enough that he should be able to catch Sarah before she fell asleep, night owl that she was.

He couldn't wait to tell her the good news.

thirty-seven

"HI, IS THIS PASTOR ERIC?" SARAH SAID INTO THE PHONE. SHE BIT HER LIP.

"This is he." He sounded like an older gentleman. His voice was pleasant and comforting.

Sarah relaxed, reassured by his kind demeanour.

"My name is Sarah Daniels. I'm a friend of Steven McGuire and his sister Joanna Larson."

"Sarah? Right, right. Steve has mentioned you."

"He has?" Sarah blinked, taken aback. Why would Steve talk about her with his pastor, whom he hadn't seen since right after the two of them met?

"Yes, of course. What can I do for you?"

Sarah swallowed, wondering what this man knew about her. She forged ahead. "I was wondering if I could ask a favour of you."

Pastor Eric chuckled. "You can ask. I'll help if I can."

"Okay, well . . . has Steve told you about the opportunity they have to purchase the building for Prakaash House?"

"I knew that they had been looking for a new home. I didn't know they had found one."

"Well, I think the offer might have only come in yesterday. Steve called me about it late last night. Apparently, their current landlord has offered to sell them the building they are already in."

"Really? Praise God! What an answer to prayer."

Sarah smiled uncertainly. After the months of struggle she knew Steve had gone through searching for a new location, she still had a hard time believing the sudden development. It almost seemed as though a deity *had* been involved.

"Yes, it is definitely a reason to celebrate. However, there's a catch—the asking price is much higher than Steve expected. They do not have enough money to purchase the building. The landlord has put a time limit on his offer, too—five or six weeks, I think."

Eric blew out air. "Whew. That is unexpected on many levels. However, if God managed to change the landlord's mind once, who's to say he won't do it again?"

"Funny, Steve said pretty much the same thing."

Eric chuckled. "You're not a believer, are you, Ms. Daniels?"

Sarah froze, startled. "You mean, in God? I, um, no, I guess not."

"Oh? You 'guess not?' Does that mean you haven't thought about it, or you are currently reconsidering your position?"

Sarah floundered for an answer. "The—the second one, I guess. After seeing how the God my parents told me about ran things, I was an atheist for most of my life. But lately, I've been wondering if they maybe got it wrong and so did I. I don't know, though. I don't see how this world could be such an awful place if what Steve says about God is, um, true."

She petered out on the last sentence and bit her lip, realizing that the man she was speaking to probably held a position on God much like her friend's. Had she just shot herself in the foot? But the pastor only chuckled again.

"If you were God, what do you think you would do differently?"

Sarah frowned. That was an interesting tack. "I'm not God, though. That's my point. I don't think that a god could exist and allow all the terrible things in the world to exist at the same time—not unless he was a selfish bas—um, jerk."

"Humour me. What would you do to correct all the horrible things in the world?"

"Well, I'd just, I'd . . . hmm. Stop them, I guess. I'd make all the bad people not be bad anymore, so no one would hurt anyone else. I'd make sure there were no more accidents or disease, or even natural disasters, so people wouldn't lose those they cared about most. If an innocent were suffering, I'd intervene to save them."

"Really? How would you do that? Lock all wrongdoers in a giant vault so that they could only do what you allowed them to? Or would you use mind-control to change the world and protect the innocent? Or is there another option I haven't considered? This is a serious question. I have a certain clinical curiosity about these things."

Sarah did not like the turn this conversation had taken. How did they get talking about religion?

"No, I—I don't know. I'd just do something."

"Ms. Daniels, have you considered that it is precisely because God loves us so much that all these bad things happen?"

Sarah snorted. "That makes no sense at all."

"Doesn't it? God takes no pleasure in the suffering on earth. And he did make a plan to deal with it, but it involves *using*, not *removing*, the gift he gave man at Creation—free will."

Sarah frowned. "I don't understand."

"God didn't want automatons to serve him. He didn't create humankind as slaves, but as companions. He wanted friendship with us. He wanted us to love him as much as he loves us. But love cannot be forced. It is a choice. That's why he gave us the power to choose. He wants us to choose him and his ways over our own."

"I—I suppose that makes sense. But can't he change people's minds? Make sure that no one is killed or hurt? Supernaturally intervene when a—a child is being abused, for instance?" Sarah's face felt hot. She was glad they were speaking on the phone.

"He could. But if he simply flipped a switch in our brains every time we made a wrong choice, that isn't truly a choice at all, is it? That's the downside of having such a power—when we have the ability to choose, we can choose the wrong thing. And removing the consequences of our wrong choices means we have no opportunity to learn. Tell me, Ms. Daniels, would you be willing to give up your own power to choose if it meant you would never hurt anyone again? Would you give up your ability to feel love in order to never feel pain?"

Sarah thought about how Craig had tried to force her to obey him implicitly. He had wanted an automaton for a wife. It had never occurred to her that expecting a deity to prevent the kind of pain she had experienced as a child or in her marriage would essentially be asserting that same kind of power.

She closed her eyes. The concepts that Pastor Eric was presenting were so new to her, she had no idea what to say. She wanted time to think them over. "I don't know. But that's not why I called."

"Right, right. Prakaash House might have a home, but they need the money to pay for it. What were you hoping I could do about that?"

"Well . . ." She wondered if she had stacked the deck against herself by rudely cutting him off. She hoped not. If there was a God, and he was on Steve's side, then surely Pastor Eric would see the benefit of what she was asking, too. "I want to raise the money for Prakaash House, but I don't want Steve to know who did it. I was hoping that your church might be willing to send the money to Love Mumbai so I can remain anonymous, handle all the charitable donation receipts and such."

"I'm fairly sure we can do that."

Sarah blinked. Just like that? "Oh. Okay, great. Thank you so much." Flooded with relief, she thought she'd best end the call before they touched on any more uncomfortable topics. "Well—"

"You know, Steve was right about you."

Sarah's heart leapt. "He was? Um, what did he say about me?"

"That you were kind and generous and had a good heart. And a sharp mind, I might add. I can see why he likes you so much."

Heat rose from her gut and up her neck, and her stomach immediately tangled into knots. "I, um, like him, too. As a friend. He's shown me what true friendship is all about. I'm simply trying to return the favour."

"Well, I'm glad to see you using *your* power of choice to benefit so many others. And I'm happy to help. Let me know when your donation is ready or if there is anything else I can do."

Sarah gulped. "I will. Th-thanks again. Have a great day."

"God bless you, Sarah."

Sarah hung up the phone and set it on the dining room table, then sank down onto a nearby chair. Why had Steve said so much about her to Pastor Eric? She knew he cared for her a great deal, but this sounded like more, like he had feelings for her.

She squirmed. It was probably nothing. But if it were true, what was she going to do about it?

Especially when the deepest part of her soul hoped that he did?

"Guess what?" Sarah all but squealed with excitement into the phone as soon as Steve picked up. "I'm coming to India."

"What? That's great. You booked your ticket?"

"Yup, ten minutes ago." She sat on her bed with her laptop in front of her, Nelson snoozing beside her and a cup of chamomile tea on the bedside stand. Despite being surrounded by all the things that normally calmed her, she had basically been running on adrenaline all day, ever since she had decided to do the fundraiser.

She'd spent the day trying to brainstorm about how to raise the money, and the pile of crumpled papers in her wastebasket attested to the fruitlessness of her efforts. She knew she could write an email campaign, but the amount of money to raise was so massive—it was going to take something much bigger, and much more involved, than that. She'd almost wondered if she had bitten off more than she could chew.

When she'd told the ladies at the support group about it tonight, they had been nothing but encouraging. Maryanne and Kathy had even volunteered to help. Now she only had to decide what they were helping her do.

She desperately wanted to talk to Steve about it, just to bounce ideas off of him. But that would totally ruin the surprise.

Not only that, then I would truly feel committed. She hated the idea of telling him about what she was doing when the results might potentially be so disappointing.

"So, when will you arrive?" Steve asked, snapping her back to the topic at hand.

"Um . . ." She double-checked her ticket. "March twenty-third. I planned for three weeks there before coming home. That should be enough time, right?"

"Should be. Sounds like you'll be leaving the country right around the same time I am. We should arrange to fly home together."

Sarah smiled, pleased at the idea. She hated travelling alone. "That would be fabulous." Her text notification chimed. "Just a sec." She took her phone away from her ear to check who the text was from. *Jill.* She read it and groaned.

"What's up?" Steve asked.

"Oh, nothing. Something. Argh."

At her growl, Nelson lifted his head to peer at her in curiosity. Sarah scratched behind his ears to reassure him, but inside she was boiling with frustration. "Jill and I are going to go shopping for the baby on Friday. I was really looking forward to it. But she just texted to tell me that my mother will be joining us."

"Hmm. Is that a bad thing?"

"Well, we're still not on the best terms. I haven't even talked to her since I left her my manuscript. I'm not so sure that I want to have the next conversation

I need to have with her in front of Jill. And I'm not so sure she wants to talk to me, period."

"What conversation is that?"

"Well . . ." Sarah fidgeted with Nelson's soft, floppy ear, feeling her face flush with heat. "I confess, I gave her the manuscript as a way of making her see what I went through as a kid. I wanted to talk to her about it after she read it." *Not ambush. Talk.* "That might not have been the most mature thing to do, but I didn't know how else to approach it."

Steve paused. "Okay, it is definitely important for you to get some closure on your past. But you're right, that might not have been the best method. You want her to acknowledge what happened to you because you think it will help you. But what if she's not ready to deal with her own wounds? Could you move past this without her participation?"

"What wounds would she have about this? I'm the one who was raped by my father."

"And do you know for a fact that the same thing didn't happen to her?"

Sarah paused, flummoxed. "No, I guess not. But Pop-pop was a fairly gentle man. I can't see him doing anything like that."

"Maybe it wasn't him. She might have been abused by someone else, maybe even your dad. Or maybe she wasn't abused at all and simply couldn't handle the fact that her husband was choosing her daughter over her."

"Steve, that's sick. What mother would stand by and knowingly let her daughter be abused?"

"Sadly, it happens all the time, and for all kinds of reasons. You'll never know why your mother did it unless she tells you."

Sarah thought of some of the stories that the other women in the support group had shared about their pasts. What Steve said was true—there could be all kinds of reasons her mother may not have intervened in the abuse, even if she'd known.

Had she known?

Sarah wasn't sure she could forgive her mother if she had. She punched her thigh. It was so frustrating trying to work through this with someone who didn't even want to talk about it.

"Well, the first step is to get her to snap out of her denial about the whole thing." She rubbed the sore spot on her leg. "Giving her the book might not have been mature, but it still might work."

"No, that's not the first step." Steve's voice was gentle. "The first step is to approach her in love, and remember that she is a pearl of great price, the same as you."

Sarah frowned. "I don't know what you mean. Joanna mentioned that phrase 'pearl of great price,' too. What is that referring to?"

"It's from one of Jesus' parables. He compared the kingdom of heaven to a merchant looking for fine pearls. The merchant finds one of great value, so he sells everything else he has to buy it."

"O-kay. Not seeing how this applies."

Steve cleared his throat. "I see this parable as multi-layered. Not only is it talking about the value of the gospel—that we can choose eternal life because of what Jesus did for us—but also the value of those Jesus came to save with it. Much like the merchant, he sacrificed everything—his position, power, and even his life—to purchase the thing that was most valuable to him—us."

"But why would God need to do that, anyway? If he made the world, and everything in it, including us, wouldn't we already all belong to him?"

"Do you belong to him, Sarah?"

Sarah snorted. "No. I don't 'belong' to anyone. I won't ever be owned again."

"Exactly. God would never force you to choose him—but everything he does is an invitation to do so. As soon as humans chose their own way over God's, they were separated from him. Jesus' sacrifice of a flawless life, completely surrendered to his Father's will, was what bridged that divide. He was the merchant, all right, but the price he paid for us was his own blood."

Sarah's throat felt too thick to speak. She hadn't been able to get what Pastor Eric had told her this morning out of her head. She'd never thought about how God might love humans so much he let them choose, even if it was wrong. Now, the idea that he let them choose the wrong thing, and still saw them as valuable enough to die for them and *still* let them choose—that was too much to wrap her head around. It made absolutely no sense.

"When I say that you are a 'pearl of great price,' and so is Ellen, that's because the King of Heaven paid the ultimate price for you. And her. And Craig. But unlike the pearl, we also need to choose him. He loves us all, and offers us all the same gift, the same hope. It's up to us whether or not we accept it."

Sarah had a momentary vision of an image of Christ on the cross—not the twisted, scrawny sculptures she saw so often in childhood, but a kind, gentle man of strength looking right at her, eyes conveying that he was doing all of it for her. Because he loved her.

"But I'm not worthy of that kind of sacrifice," she whispered.

Steve's voice was steel and velvet all at the same time. "Yes, Sarah. You are. You are worth every sacrifice."

Sarah caught her breath. He hadn't said it in the same way that he talked about her mother, or Craig, or Sita. In that moment, Sarah sensed how deep his care for her ran. She could hear his love in his voice, could almost feel it reaching through the receiver and wrapping itself around her. Did he love her as more than a friend? The thought terrified and thrilled her at once. She couldn't deny that she cared for him deeply, but could never imagine the two of them being together. How would she ever be worthy of sharing her life with someone like Steve McGuire?

Tears dripped silently down her face. She didn't want Steve to hear her cry, and she didn't want him to know about the emotional maelstrom inside of her. As quickly and politely as she could, she ended the call.

Then she buried her face in her hands and wept.

When Sarah woke up the next morning, it was with new clarity and purpose. Inspiration had struck in her sleep, and she knew exactly what she wanted to do for a fundraiser. As soon as it was socially acceptable to do so, she called Yolanda.

"Good morning, Sarah. Are you all ready for your photo shoot today? You don't have to cancel, do you?"

Since Sarah was publishing under her own name, they had decided to do some profile shots of her for the book jacket and the launch party.

"No, no. I'm good to go. I just wanted to talk to you about something in private before we get there."

"Oh? What can I do for you?"

Sarah took a deep breath and dove in. She hated asking people for things, but she knew this wouldn't be the last favour she'd have to ask if she was going to pull this off. *The worst she can do is say no*, she reminded herself.

"I'm organizing a fundraiser for my friend's charity, and I was wondering if we could combine the launch with it somehow? I'd like to donate all my profits from this book, too. And I think we should do it here, in Edmonton."

"Hmm. It won't be nearly as effective here. And I'm not sure whether the higher-ups will go for a fundraiser launch."

"Why not? It will make them look great. My friend is an Alberta boy, and the book is set here. I have a gut instinct that we'll get a great show of support from local businesses for both the book and my friend's charity. Or maybe we could do one here and another one in Toronto? I need the fundraiser to happen soon, within the next four weeks."

Yolanda made a choking sound. "There's no way we will be ready to publish that soon, Sarah. You know how these things work."

"Hmm." Sarah chewed her lip and studied her morning cup of coffee. Yolanda was right. Expecting Steampressed to be ready to publish and organize a launch party here in Edmonton within that time frame was akin to asking for a miracle.

But wasn't the fact that the building was even for sale already a bit of a miracle?

Yolanda broke into her thoughts, and her tone was musing. "Is this the same friend whose story you are writing?"

"Yes. He runs an organization in India called Love Mumbai that works with victims of sex trafficking. They have a rare opportunity to purchase a building for one of their projects, but the asking price and the time frame both seem to be a little beyond the realm of feasibility. I'm doing my best to help them achieve it."

"That sounds amazing. Hmm." She paused for a few moments, and Sarah let her think.

"If I push it, we might be ready to launch your book in two months. It would take a lot of 'ifs' falling perfectly into place. But maybe we could do some kind of prelaunch fundraiser here in Edmonton, sell special edition copies to benefit the charity or something," Yolanda said. Sarah could almost hear the woman's gears turning. "Do a ritzy gala, charge a hundred dollars a plate, and announce you to the local community under your real name at the same time. I went to something like that last year. I don't think it would be that difficult to pull together. I bet I could even get some of our other authors on board to donate copies of their books for the cause."

Sarah's heart had lightened with every word from Yolanda's mouth. She was hit with one final bit of inspiration. "A gala would be perfect. And the theme is going to be 'Pearls of Great Price.'"

"I love it."

"So, you'll help me? We can do it?"

Yolanda hesitated. "I must admit that the idea of an erotica imprint benefiting a charity that helps the sexually exploited has a certain delightful irony to it." She didn't sound a hundred percent convinced yet. "The trickiest thing will be getting people to show up. It's pretty last-minute."

Sarah thought about the extensive contacts she had made in Edmonton's high society through her years of being married to Craig. She knew judges, lawyers, and business people all over the city. She was pretty sure that Christine Fenway might even be convinced to get on board—Sarah remembered her saying something about being passionate about similar causes—and maybe even provide them with some affordable live music. And thanks to her dusty marketing degree, Sarah certainly knew she could write a convincing pitch. Maybe her college education and failed marriage would both be of some use after all.

For the first time, she felt confident that she could actually pull this off.

"You arrange the venue and talk to the other authors," she said. "Leave filling the seats to me."

thirty-eight

STEVE STRODE DOWN THE DUSTY STREET OF THE BAZAAR, AVOIDING THE POTHOLES, BROKEN RED bricks, and piles of refuse that littered the jagged sidewalk. Tiny shops and storefronts crowded together along the side like washing strung on a line. Scooters tried to find a path through the crowd of foot traffic. Vendors brave enough to venture out into the February afternoon's sweltering heat called out to passersby, determined to drum up business—especially from the white "tourist," which was how many of them still saw him after a year of working in their neighbourhood.

Steve swiped at the sweat trickling down his forehead and kept his eyes forward, gently turning away sample-laden vendors who pushed into his path with a "*Nahi, deniwada,*"—*no, thank you*—and stepping around them. After a dozen such encounters, he began to regret choosing to walk back to work after lunch instead of taking an auto rickshaw, no matter how good the smog index was today.

Normally, he could handle the constant barrage, but not after the news Sarah had given him that morning. His head wasn't in the game, and the walk through the bazaar was doing nothing to clear it.

Sarah was coming to India? It was actually happening?

Steve had been running on adrenaline since she'd told him. He'd always hoped she would eventually decide to come, but he hadn't dared believe it.

Thank you, Lord, he prayed for the fifteenth time that day. Then he dared an addendum. *Let her love it as much as I do.*

He turned down the side street connecting the bazaar to their subdivision. At the far end of the block on the left, the pale, plastered-brick face of Prakaash House was quite innocuous amongst look-alike neighbours—which made it perfect for what they used it for.

Just around the corner from the busy thoroughfare, a small open clothing stall claimed space on the edge of the dusty road. It was quieter on this street, but close enough to the action to attract some customers. A small, round man in a white buttoned shirt and faded mint-green lungi sat on a plastic lawn chair. He had tucked his perch inside the meagre shade offered by a sagging red awning that did little to keep the sun and grime out of the shop. Children's and ladies' blouses, shirts, and skirts hung on plastic hangers on a rope strung under the lip of the awning, their inert state bearing witness to the complete lack of breeze today.

Despite its proximity to the bazaar, Padmesh's shop never seemed particularly busy, so as usual, the little man was watching the action on the busy street corner. He recognized Steve, and his face broke into a smile.

"Ah, Mr. Steve, you have good lunch?"

Steve smiled, speaking in simplified English so his neighbour would understand the words. "Yes, very good *dosas*. Now I am sooo fat," he added, patting his belly. "How are you today, Padmesh?"

"Fine, fine, Mr. Steve." He patted his belly, also. "I think my wife make better *dosas* than Vishnu's Darbar, no?"

Steve waggled his head sideways in agreement. "Your wife is a fine cook, but she is too busy to cook for me. You are a lucky man. She must make you very happy."

Padmesh beamed. "Yes, she is good wife. You come anytime to have *dosas*, okay?"

Steve waggled his head again. "Okay, okay. Sometime I will."

The vendor turned and cast a glance at the woman in question, who hovered behind the counter inside the shop, and began speaking in fast Hindi. Steve understood enough to realize that Padmesh was relaying the conversation they had just had. Manavi smiled shyly and nodded at Steve from the shadows. Steve smiled back, pressed his hands together in front of his face and bowed slightly. "*Namaste*, Manavi." He twisted to face the man in the chair and made the same gesture. "Padmesh."

Padmesh pressed his hands together and bowed his head in return. "*Namaste*, Mr. Steve. Happy digesting." He patted his belly again with a twinkle in his eye.

Steve laughed, then unlatched the gate and stepped into the relative peace behind the high stone barrier fence. A raucous outburst of children's laughter greeted him, and he smiled—he would take the noise of happy children over the honking, dusty cacophony of a Mumbai street any day of the week.

Ragin greeted him with pressed palms.

"*Namaste*, sir. Mr. Paul would like to see you right away." Ragin's serious face and growly voice made him sound like the harbinger of doom. Steve smiled internally at the sudden feeling of being called to the principal's office.

"Thank you, Ragin. Has Sam returned yet?"

"No, sir."

"Okay, thanks."

Ragin nodded respectfully, and Steve headed down the walkway toward the door, which was slightly recessed into the building. The sound of children's voices shouting in Hindi and heavily accented English from the back courtyard got louder, punctuated by good-natured English commands in a woman's voice. Ajay's voice echoed the commands in Hindi for those who didn't understand English as well.

Steve smiled to himself. Kallie was teaching the children how to play Red Rover.

His friends, Sam and Kallie, were already a month into their planned two-month working vacation. Steve could hardly believe how quickly the time had flown.

Kallie had dived right in to working with the children, putting her teaching skills to good use and giving their staff much-needed support. Sam had made himself useful with overseeing construction of the women's shelter addition. He wasn't familiar with Indian methods of construction, which were very different from what he typically employed as a general contractor and carpenter in Alberta. However, Steve knew he could count on Sam to handle any issues that arose and Sam could rely on the contractors for construction expertise. Sam had actually jumped at the chance to participate in the project and learn how things were done here. And having Sam as the project manager freed Steve up to deal with other things. Like the future of Prakaash House.

He had written an email campaign about their need, and had begun spending most of his time at the office reaching out individually to their supporters. He had begun to wonder if he should cut his six-month stint in India short so he could travel and raise the needed funds in person. It was rare for an email request to generate the kind of cash that Love Mumbai needed if they were to purchase this building.

He ducked through the wooden door into the building's cool interior and pulled his sticky shirt away from his body in relief. Aparna glanced up from her monitor when he entered.

"Hello, Aparna. Is Paul in there?" Steve indicated the closed office door behind her desk.

Aparna smiled up at him in greeting. "No, Paul is washing dishes. He said to send you back there."

Steve frowned. "I thought Saturday was Paul's day on dishes, not Friday."

Aparna dropped her voice and leaned closer. Her English was good, with the gentle rolling "r"s and singsong lilt of someone well-educated. "Priya was sent home, so Paul is covering for her."

"Is she sick again?"

Aparna looked uncomfortable. "It's best that Paul explains."

"Ah. Okay. Thanks."

Odd.

Steve headed down the hallway toward the back of the oblong building, brow furrowed. This was the third time in the last couple of weeks that Priya had been sent home by mid-day. The other two times were due to illness. What was going on?

The washing area was in the left side yard, right off the kitchen at the back of the building. Steve greeted Chaitra on his way through the kitchen. She glanced up from the vegetables she was chopping for the early evening meal group and returned his greeting with a jowly smile, then went back to work, her sari's *pallu* draped around her midriff and tucked into the waistband of her petticoat on the opposite side to keep it out of the way. The chopping sound reverberated off the stainless steel dishes lining the open shelves and hard stone surfaces of the high-ceilinged, narrow room.

Steve stepped outside into the courtyard and blinked to let his eyes adjust. The dish-washing area was protected from the sun by a thatch roof, but light reflected off the pale red flagstones beyond and made the scullery much brighter than the building's interior. To his right, he could see the group of elementary school children gleefully calling Tiya over, Kallie's blond head right in there with them. He grinned.

Paul was bent over a large metal pot in the deep cement sink, his clothes protected by a plain white lap apron, the sleeves of his pale blue button-down rolled up past his elbows. Sweat beaded on his forehead as he scoured the pot with steel wool. A lovely girl in her early teens with the distinctive mongoloid features of Northeast India stood next to him, drying the stack of clean dishes with a faded cotton towel. She was concentrating on buffing a stainless-steel plate. When Steve came up beside her, she glanced up and flashed him a bright smile that shone from her almond-shaped eyes.

"Hello, Uncle Steve!"

"Hi, Khambi. You're on dish duty today, eh?"

"Yes, but I don't mind. If everyone helps, the house runs smoothly. Correct, Uncle Paul?"

Paul glanced at Khambi with a wry grin and then exchanged an amused glance with Steve. "Correct."

Khambi's words were an echo of something Paul often said in his efforts to instill an all-for-one work ethic in the children—and staff—that were under their care. Drying dishes was one of several rotating duties that children could help with, and everyone took their turn. When it came to communal chores, there were no exceptions on the duty roster. Not even for staff.

Steve chuckled, grabbed a dry towel from a bin inside the kitchen door, and joined in.

In a hierarchical society like India's, seeing the men help with the dishes—especially the heads of the organization—was often one of the first surprises visitors and new students received. But Steve and Paul were in complete agreement that one of their goals in how they "raised" these children was to show them that no one is better than anyone else—everyone serves everyone else to make the facility run smoothly, and the leaders most of all.

It was one of Paul's more counter-cultural attitudes, and one of the reasons their partnership worked so well.

Paul finished scouring the pot and rinsed it out, handed it to Khambi to dry, then drained the water and wiped everything down. The sounds of the herd of children playing in the back yard abruptly amplified as they reverberated into the dining room beyond the kitchen, then faded as they retreated into the second-story classrooms for the afternoon.

Steve glanced at the wall clock he could see through the kitchen door. "Khambi, your class is starting now. Give that to me and you run upstairs so you can get there on time."

Khambi smiled. "Okay, Uncle Steve, thank you so much. Auntie Meera gets so cross when we are late."

The girl wiped her hands and dashed off toward the stairs on the other side of the house. Steve watched her go, thinking of how shy and reserved she had been when she had first come to them a year ago. Now she was one of their most diligent and outgoing students, and often helped other new children settle into the routines of the care centre. Khambi was one of the permanent residents of Prakaash House, though her mother often came to see her. Success stories like Khambi were what kept him going.

Paul took off his apron and hung it to dry, then glanced at Steve, his face grim.

Steve took a step toward his friend and dropped his voice. "What's wrong?"

Paul gestured for Steve to follow him and silently lead the way into the house.

When they reached the converted bedroom they used as an office, Paul gestured Aparna inside ahead of them and closed the door behind her.

Steve grabbed the chairs by his desk and pulled them over in front of Paul's—one for himself and the other for Aparna. The plastic legs stuttered loudly on the gritty tile floor. Aparna, whose pregnancy was barely beginning to show, thanked him and sat, and Steve plunked himself down next to her. Paul sat in his office chair and folded his hands on his desk, the troubled expression still pinching his features.

Paul surprised Steve by asking about him first. "You looked disturbed when you first arrived from lunch break. What is wrong?"

Steve waved it off. "Oh, I was thinking about Paresh's deal. I'm a little worried that we will not be able to raise the money he is demanding. But that isn't the most pressing issue, I think. Priya's sick again?" Steve prompted.

Paul waggled his head, eyes darker than usual. "Yes, in a manner of speaking. That is what I wanted to see you about. Her stomach was paining her again this morning, so I had Aparna take her to the doctor and then home to the shelter." He paused, his face serious. He cleared his throat. "It seems that monsoon has come early this year, brother."

Monsoon? That was dramatic, especially for Paul.

"Hey, man. What's up?" Steve asked, bracing himself for the worst.

Paul glanced at Aparna, who looked at Steve.

"Priya is pregnant." Her lips were set in a grim line.

Steve rocked back in stunned confusion.

Pregnant? How was that possible?

Priya had fled from a brothel to Love Mumbai's women's shelter two years ago when she was sixteen, where she still lived for the pittance of rent they charged long-term residents to help them learn fiscal responsibility. The only men allowed in the shelter were their security guards, Steve, and Paul—all men they trusted implicitly, and none of whom were allowed beyond the rooms associated with the beauty parlour at the front of the building. For the last year, Priya had been working at Prakaash House to earn extra income while she went through vocational training to be a seamstress. As far as Steve knew, Priya's whole life revolved around the training centre, Prakaash House, and the shelter.

"Was she raped? Or has she been seeing anyone? Who is the father?"

"She won't say." Aparna's tone revealed exactly what she thought of *that*.

"Could it be someone from the bazaar?"

Priya often went to the market for Chaitra to purchase supplies, so it was possible she had been maintaining a relationship there. However, it didn't seem likely that Priya would do that, especially as one of the conditions of her employment by Love Mumbai was that she not have any illicit relationships. It was a contractual caveat meant to protect the women if they needed a way of deterring an unwanted suitor, as well as to ensure they gave themselves the necessary time to heal from psychological trauma without distraction. It also protected Love Mumbai from allegations of trafficking themselves. Rescued women usually had very little difficulty complying—they were often deeply mistrustful of men, even Paul and Steve.

"If that were the case, why wouldn't she tell us?" Aparna looked more bewildered than disapproving. This was certainly not the first time one of their "clients" had run into trouble. "She's already been found out. She wouldn't get into any worse trouble than she is already in."

Steve glanced at Paul. "Then whoever it is, she must be protecting him."

Paul nodded, and his frown deepened. "Which means it is most likely a staff member. Or a volunteer."

Steve ran a hand over his stubble as the full implications hit him. "You know that Aaron would never do that. Nor Sam. And it wasn't you or I. Who does that even leave?"

They had very few male staff, and the list of those that Priya could have interacted with was exceedingly short.

Paul cocked his head, studying his beige-painted metal desk as though it would hold the answers. "It couldn't be Ragin or any of the other guards. Perhaps Jai?"

Both Ragin and Jai Sharma—the administrative head of the vocational centre—were married men, as were their other guards, and Steve's mind boggled at the thought that any of them would cheat on their wives or abuse their positions of trust within the organization. In fact, other than himself, Love Mumbai only had one other unmarried male employee.

Dread settled in Steve's stomach. Ajay was young, fairly handsome, charming, and single. When Steve had cautioned him about taking extra care to touch the children appropriately due to their backgrounds, Ajay had been most compliant. Other than that minor indiscretion with Geeta, Steve had never seen him behave inappropriately toward anyone at Love Mumbai. However, Ajay and Priya had been seen spending time together on several occasions. And it would make sense that Priya would not want to expose him, as it would mean he would also lose his job. Perhaps he had even made promises to her.

Steve and Paul shared a glance.

"Ajay." Steve set his mouth in a grim line.

Paul's pained expression revealed that he had come to the same conclusion about his nephew that Steve had.

"And him with a decent engagement, too." Paul shook his head in stunned denial, staring at the wall like it would provide an answer to the conundrum in which they had just been placed. Then he focused on Steve. "I will do the needful. Please do not say anything to Ajay until I get the chance to talk to him."

"And what are we going to do about Priya?" asked Aparna.

Steve sighed. Unless it turned out that Priya had indeed been coerced, the evidence suggested that she had broken her employment contract, which gave her grounds for termination. The thought rankled. After all that they had done for her, it was heartbreaking that she had still made such a poor decision, but not surprising. Steve, of all people, knew how humanity got the best of everyone at times. And those were the times when they often needed the most support.

Steve braced his hands on his legs and met his companion's eyes. "Perhaps we should ask her what she wants us to do. I'll talk to her. Aparna, will you accompany me when I do?"

His friends waggled their heads in grim assent. Priya's choices may have put them into a difficult position. But there was no way they would abandon her.

Paul perked up, folding his hands on his desk and giving them a wry smile. "As far as Paresh and his incredible, awe-inspiring price," he chuckled at his own joke, "we shall continue to pray. We shall keep working to raise the money. Our God 'owns the cattle on a thousand hills,' so if he wants us to remain here"—he indicated the building with a small gesture—"I'm sure he can send some 'cattle' to us. This is the land of holy cows, yes?" Paul's eyes twinkled. "And perhaps Paresh will even discover he doesn't want quite so much after all."

Steve smiled. "Why does it sound so much more likely when you say it?"

Paul's smile widened to a grin. "Because I don't have a funny accent."

Steve chuckled, inspired once again by his friend's simple faith. Despite nearly a decade working together, Steve often felt the shame of his Western self-reliance that tended to trust God only as far as he could do the work himself. Paul had a simple way of reminding Steve that no matter what they did, their true provision came not by their own hand, but by the Heavenly Overseer of their operation. That being said, he hadn't ever shirked his own responsibility to the mission before, and he wasn't about to start now.

He still couldn't help but burn with curiosity at Vijay Paresh's sudden change of heart. He wondered if he dared ask the man, or whether it was better not to look a gift horse in the mouth.

Either way, this new drama with Priya had added to his workload.

"Okay." Steve rose. "Let's get to work."

thirty-nine

SARAH PARKED THE RAV4 IN ONE OF WEST EDMONTON MALL'S PARKADES. SHE SAT IN THE QUIET vehicle for a moment, steeling herself against the ordeal of a day spent with her mother. After the conversation with Steve the other night, she had decided that if Ellen was willing to come, it must mean she was willing to try, and in that case, so was Sarah.

That didn't mean she was looking forward to it.

Sighing, she grabbed her purse and got out into the frigid air to head inside.

As she approached the coffee shop they had set as a meeting place in the enormous mall, she scanned tables, looking for the two women. A waving hand caught her eye, and she turned to see a cluster of people around one of the small round tables—the back of her mother's greying blond head, Jill with her hand raised, and—

Sarah froze. Beside Jill, Everett sat drinking a coffee. He lifted his gaze to meet hers and stared with an implacable expression.

Sarah's stomach heaved slightly, and she fought the urge to spin on her heels and walk right back out to her car. She didn't know what to do. They'd already seen her, so she couldn't simply fade away and make up a legitimate-sounding excuse for not showing up.

Jill's brow furrowed slightly as Sarah hesitated. She didn't want to let Jill down, either. Finally, grudgingly, Sarah began moving forward again.

Jill stood to greet her, and Sarah gave her a quick, awkward hug around her baby bump as they exchanged hellos, then scooted behind her to reach the only remaining empty chair, which was mercifully opposite of her brother's.

"I hope you don't mind that Everett came." Jill wiped her mouth with a napkin. "I want to buy some furniture for the nursery today, and I need him to help carry everything."

Everett and Sarah locked gazes. She was surprised that he looked nearly as uncomfortable as she felt.

"No, of course not. As long as he doesn't mind hanging out on a 'girls' day,' why would I mind?"

Jill smiled, but it seemed strained as she glanced between them.

Ellen broke in. "Well, I'm glad to have all my kids here today. We're going to have so much fun. Sarah, I hope you brought your walking shoes, because we are going to 'own' this mall today. Isn't that how you kids say it nowadays?"

Sarah stared at her mother, wondering if her brain had been swapped by aliens. It wasn't the attempt at modern jargon that threw Sarah off—it was Ellen acting like there was nothing whatsoever wrong between any of them.

She shook her head. *And why does that surprise me?*

Despite her misgivings, the morning went better than Sarah would have expected. They wandered in and out of shops with Everett trailing awkwardly along beside Jill, and Ellen peppering the conversation with comments like, "I'm so *thrilled* to have a little one to shop for. Too bad you didn't find out the gender. I hope it's a girl!" and "Sarah and Everett, do you remember when we came here to the water park with your father when you were kids? Oh, if only he could see you both now."

Sarah tried to keep up polite conversation with Jill, but felt constrained by her brother's proximity to shallow topics like the baby preparations and comments about products they saw.

By lunchtime, Sarah's entire body ached from the tension of constantly keeping half an eye on Everett wherever she went. He seemed to be as wary of her as she was of him, like they were two muzzled dogs on best behaviour for their owners' benefit. She shook her head at herself, frowning at the packages in the new baby stroller she was pushing for Jill. Surely she was imagining things. Everett had never been afraid of her in his life.

"So, when does your book come out?" Jill asked when they had settled themselves at a table in the food court at last.

Ellen sat across from Sarah, trying to open her cutlery package so she could eat the Chinese food piled on the Styrofoam plate in front of her. The stroller and a shopping cart overflowing with a boxed crib kit and other loot were parked around their table like a protective wall.

At the mention of the book, Everett stared ferociously at his hamburger, his jaw tight.

Sarah gulped. It was the opening she'd been waiting for—time to put her plan into action. She slowly unwrapped her pita and glanced at her mother. Was she listening? "I'm not exactly sure yet. I hit a snag."

Everett peered at her in curiosity.

"What kind of snag?" asked Jill between sips of high-vitamin green smoothie.

"Well, I met with my editor on Monday, and she loved the book. She said that it was the best writing she had ever seen from me."

Ellen harrumphed and stabbed at a piece of ginger beef.

Jill ignored her, eyes on Sarah. "But?"

Sarah swallowed. "But she said that they can't publish it. Not as an erotica title, anyway. Apparently, there are limits to what even that genre will allow."

Ellen's face darkened for the first time that day. "I'm not surprised. I couldn't even get past the fourth chapter of that book. Why did you think anyone would ever want to read that? It isn't natural, the way those two carried on in the bedroom. And the flashbacks! Honestly! Where did you come up with such appalling images? I felt dirty just reading about it."

Sarah crowed internally that her mother had fallen for the bait. So, Ellen *had* read the book, or at least some of it. She frowned as she remembered something she had shared at Wednesday night's support group session. *I know the words to write to make other women feel aroused during a sex scene. I know how I should feel, but I have seldom felt that way myself. I often wonder if I will ever feel "normal."*

It seemed the apple didn't fall far from the tree when it came to sex. Maybe her mother *had* been abused.

"Not everyone feels the same way about sex as you, Mom. Some women actually enjoy it." *That's the rumour, anyway.* She refolded the wrapper around her pita to avoid her mother's glare. "And the flashbacks aren't meant to be enjoyable."

Ellen glanced at Everett uncomfortably and leaned closer to Sarah, dropping her voice. Despite the noisy food court, Sarah was sure that her brother heard every word.

"I enjoyed *sex* just fine, thank you. Your father was a very considerate . . . man."

Sarah was sure that Ellen had been about to say "lover" and had changed her mind.

"Oh? Was he like that with you? Hmmph."

Sarah kept her voice light, putting only slight emphasis on the word "you." She stared hard at her mother to gauge her reaction. Would Ellen follow Sarah down the Yellow Brick Road or stay in her pretty little Kansas farmhouse of denial?

Either way, Sarah refused to pretend for her mother's sake anymore. She was determined that Ellen finally admit the truth about what her father had done to her, and if it had to be now, in the food court, in front of Jill and Everett, so be it.

Ellen glared at her, then focused on her plate.

Jill cleared her throat. "So, what is the plan with your book now? I read the copy you gave Ellen, and it doesn't seem like it would fit into any other genre very well."

Sarah refocused on Jill, but kept glancing at her mother as she continued speaking. Jill hadn't even known Sarah's plan, but she kept helping her out. If there was a God, maybe he was on her side today.

"I'm going to tweak it a bit—remove some of the erotic elements and the few things I made up—then publish it as a memoir. Maybe even self-publish. I'm hoping to have it ready to go in another month or so."

Ellen frowned in confusion, then the horror registered on her face.

Everett stared at Sarah, his face ashen, his Adam's apple bobbing convulsively. He seemed to shrink in on himself—a strange illusion for someone so burly.

Even Jill's eyes were as wide as saucers. She glanced between Sarah, Ellen, and her husband, finally settling on Everett. "A *memoir*?" Emotions flitted across her face like the shadows of fleeing birds. She looked like she was having a hard time believing the implications of what Sarah had just said.

Ellen's face was a summer thunderstorm. "Sarah, how *dare* you?" she hissed. "Bad enough that you try to make me believe your lies. Now you are going to spread them to the world? Drag Everett—our family—through the mud, and for what? Your own vainglorious purpose? Do you truly hate me that much?"

Ellen's voice had risen in pitch throughout the diatribe, and others in the food court were glancing at them uncomfortably. Ellen didn't seem to notice. Her eyes were brimming with tears and she was huffing like a steam engine. In her bubble-gum pantsuit, she looked like a furious pink dragon.

Sarah's heart thumped like a kettle drum in her ears. Now that she had committed to her path, she fought the urge to flee. But this was what she had wanted to do all along, right? Force her mother into the truth, kicking and screaming? Now that it was upon her, Sarah wished there had been a less traumatic way.

Suddenly, she remembered what Steve had said. *Mom is a pearl of great price, too.*

She looked at her mother again, but it was like reality had shifted. Instead of seeing only the mother who had ignored Sarah's lifetime of pain and abuse, she saw a woman trying to cope with the loss of a husband for whom she still grieved, fourteen years later. She saw her trying to hold her fracturing reality together. And she saw the hurt and confusion in her mother's eyes. For the first time, she realized that her mother bore her own pain, and she was dealing with it the only way she knew how.

Damn. She'd really messed this up.

"Mom, I—"

"Don't 'Mom' me. You're not my daughter. My daughter would never do this to me, to our family. You need help, Sarah. You really do." She jabbed the air with her plastic fork. "If you publish this book, so help me, I will scrounge every last penny I have to sue you for libel. You can live in your own little fantasy world if you want, but you will *not* make the rest of us suffer for it."

Sarah stared at her mother in shock. So it was the Kansas farmhouse, then. Her mother's capacity to live in denial topped even Sarah's jaded expectations. What would she do if Ellen never admitted to the truth? No matter what Sarah said, or did, Ellen seemed determined to stake her flag in her fictional, sanitized view of the world. She was even up in arms, ready to defend it. Perhaps it would never be possible to break through that barrier.

"Don't," said Everett.

Three sets of eyes turned to stare at the hulking man. He trembled as he looked at Sarah, his face white. The untouched burger was forgotten in his shaking hand.

"'Don't' what?" asked Jill, her face hard.

Everett glanced at his wife, his mother, and at last, met his sister's gaze with an imploring look. "Don't publish that book, Sarah. Please. You have no right." He gulped. "If you won't do it for me, do it for Dad."

Jill stared at her husband, jaw agape. She closed her mouth as colour rose through her face, then abruptly stood up and waddled away down the hall as fast as she could.

Everett looked after her helplessly, then glanced back at his mother's near-catatonic face. He set down his burger, stood and hurried after his wife. Sarah couldn't hear them, but she watched their tense discussion until they were blocked from view by a kiosk. She glanced back at her mother, who sat staring at her with crossed arms. The thunderstorm had become a hurricane.

"I hope you're happy, Sarah," Ellen said. "They say that misery loves company. Was it worth it?" She indicated the retreating couple with her head.

Sarah studied her hands. What about Everett? Was he a pearl, too? Or Jill? *I'm sorry, Jill.*

"No, Mom. I'm not happy. Most of the time, I'm depressed, angry, and sad. You say I need help? You're right. I'm getting it. And I'm healing. But our family is sick, full of pus and poison, and the only way we are going to get better is if we lance the wound. I'm sorry that the truth is so hard to hear, but that doesn't change it."

"What truth? All I hear is my delusional failure of a daughter spouting her lies and causing problems for the rest of the family. The only sick one around here is you!"

Sarah stared at her mother, frustration threatening to swamp her. "You heard Everett, Mom. He practically admitted what happened. Do you still not believe me?"

"He did no such thing. He knows what's in that book. Do you expect him to be happy that you want to spread that kind of filth about him?"

"Of course not! Especially because it actually happened!"

Ellen glared at her, nostrils flaring. "Sarah, I think you'd better go."

Sarah felt tears threatening. Talking to her mother was like talking to a brick wall. She was getting absolutely nowhere. She wanted to apologize to Jill before she left, but she wasn't sure how long it would take Jill and Everett to work through their spat.

She stood and slung her purse over her shoulder, giving her mother one last pleading look. Ellen's gaze held only ice.

Sarah turned and walked away, blinking back tears long enough to make it into a toilet stall in the nearby restroom. For several long minutes, she shook with uncontrollable sobs, stifling the sound with her coat sleeve.

When she finally got herself under control, she stood up off the closed toilet lid, dabbed the moisture off her face with toilet paper, and unlocked the stall to fix the rest of the mess in the mirror. She kept her eyes averted from the washroom's other tenants, hoping to avoid idle chitchat about the weather.

"Sarah?"

Sarah lifted her head toward the familiar voice, the lead weight in her stomach becoming a hundred pounds heavier. She met the woman's gaze in the mirror.

"Erica? What—what are you doing here?"

Erica stood at the sink next to her, washing her hands. She gave Sarah a cool look. "Craig and I are looking at engagement rings today."

Sarah's throat closed. She held onto the counter for support as her knees wobbled. She took a deep breath and swallowed the lump in her throat. Her voice came out surprisingly clear. "Oh? That's interesting, since he refuses to make the divorce official."

Erica finished patting her hands dry on a paper towel, tossed it into the trash and turned toward Sarah, hands on her hips. "He told me that you were the one causing all the delay."

Sarah shook her head. "No, not technically. Everything would be fairly clear-cut except he keeps trying to get custody of Nelson. And that's not going to happen."

Erica snorted. "Yeah, right. He hates dogs. He would never do that." She took a step toward Sarah. "Just let him go, okay? You lost. He's mine now, and dragging out the divorce isn't going to bring him back."

Sarah was getting very tired of not being believed. First her mother, now her ex-best friend. They had been all too happy to believe her when she had lied all the time. Now that she was being honest, they insisted on the fantasy.

She sighed. "Believe what you want. I'm telling the truth. He probably wants to manipulate me, and he doesn't have much leverage anymore. And he's manipulating you with the divorce, too, I bet. Be careful how much leverage you give him, Erica, or this will be you in two years, standing in a bathroom telling some other woman to be careful. Or wishing you could break free."

Erica blinked at her, then frowned.

Sarah tossed her paper towel into the trash and swept past the other woman's disapproving glare and out of the bathroom. She kept a watchful eye out for Craig as she exited—the last thing she needed was to bump into him, too.

She didn't wish Erica ill any more than she did Jill or even her mother. In that moment when she had seen the confusion register in Erica's eyes, she realized that the other woman was being duped, just as she had been. They had all been duped—herself, her mother, Jill, and Erica. They were all victims of liars. And sometimes the chocolate-covered lie was easier to swallow than to taste the bitter truth.

Sarah had been where Erica and her mother both were. But she was there no longer. With gratitude, she let another mask slip through her fingers and shatter on the floor of the food court. Thanks to a man who saw a pearl of great price where others only saw a broken and used-up vessel, she was willing to admit the truth.

And only the truth, so help me . . .

She couldn't finish the thought. Where the word "God" would normally be inserted in that phrase, all she saw was a question mark. But she knew what Steve would want her to do.

She strode up to the table her mother still occupied. Jill and Everett had returned and were sitting there in silence, Jill fiddling with her smoothie cup and Everett slouched with his arms crossed. Ellen sat erect, clutching her purse on her lap like a shield. As Sarah approached, the others stared at her with varying shades of fear and misgiving.

I caused this.

Guilt pricked her. But so did compassion.

"I'm not going to publish the book as a memoir." Sarah stared down at the table. "That was a lie. And I have decided that I will not lie anymore. Not to me or to anyone else." She paused. "There are things in that book that aren't real, that I made up to tell a story that others would want to read. But the book is based on my life. I left out and watered down far more truth than I invented. Mom, Everett knows. You ask him which parts are true and which parts aren't."

Ellen blinked at Everett fearfully. He frowned and ducked his head, studying the table.

Sarah looked at Jill, who was fidgeting with the hem of her t-shirt. "I'm sorry for ruining our shopping day, and for any pain that my revelation may cause you. You are a good person, Jill, and a good friend, and you deserve better than this. But I couldn't pretend any more. I'm done with pretending."

She turned to her mother, whose knuckles were white on her bag. "If you would rather disown me than admit to the truth, then I pity you, Mom. The lie might seem like it protects us, but in the end it only turns us into victims. 'The truth will set you free.' Isn't that what your Bible says? I refuse to be a victim anymore. I hope that one day you get to this point. I love you."

She turned away from the table to leave and saw Erica standing a few feet from her, watching the exchange wide-eyed. Craig came up behind her and locked eyes with Sarah. She stared at him until Erica grabbed his hand and pulled him away, glancing back over her shoulder.

Sarah clamped her jaw and took a step toward the exit.

"Sarah, wait," said Jill.

Sarah paused and looked back at her sister-in-law.

Jill frowned. "Thank you."

A look of understanding passed between them. Sarah gave her a small smile, and then turned and walked out of the mall.

forty

PRIYA SET THE TRAY WITH THE STEAMING CUPS OF CHAI ON PAUL'S DESK. SHE PLACED ONE OF THE stainless steel demitasse tumblers of tea in front of Paul's keyboard and carried the other over to Steve.

Steve exchanged a glance with Paul, who stood.

"Thank you, Priya." Paul smiled at the girl and moved toward the door. "There is something I must do right now. Aparna may drink my tea."

"Okay, Uncle." She bent to pick up the tumbler again, then paused in confusion as Aparna entered the room.

"Simply leave it there, please." Aparna indicated the desk, then stepped aside to let her husband pass in the narrow space. She and Paul exchanged meaningful looks as he exited.

Priya set the cup back down, dipped her head slightly toward Steve, and then picked up her tray to leave.

"Wait, Priya." He put his cup down in a small clearing in the chaos beside his laptop.

Priya hesitated, glancing from Steve to Aparna in concern.

"Don't worry, you're not in trouble." Steve gave her a reassuring smile. "Please sit."

Aparna took the tray from Priya and guided her to the chair in front of Steve's desk. She sat down, looking nervous. Aparna placed the tray on Paul's desk, pulled over her husband's chair, and sat beside the young woman.

Steve decided to try to put her at ease first. "I'm glad to see you have been well enough to work for the last few days. Has the nausea subsided?"

Priya quirked her mouth and rotated her loose fist from side to side in the Indian gesture for "no." "It still comes, but the doctor gave me medicine, which helps. Also, Chaitra has been making me ginger tea, which helps more."

Aparna smiled and placed a hand on her own bulging abdomen. "Yes, Chaitra's ginger tea is amazing."

Priya smiled weakly at Aparna, then turned back to Steve, waiting. She looked no less nervous.

Steve sighed. May as well get right to it.

"Priya, we need to talk about what is going to happen now. You do not make enough money to pay for the expenses of a pregnancy, let alone a child. You know this is true."

Priya frowned. "I am keeping this baby," she said, steel in her voice.

Steve sat back, shocked. "Of—of course, you—did you think I was going to tell you to get an abortion?"

Priya's eyes widened in confusion, her back erect. "At the brothel, Vini—the madam—she give me a pill when she think I pregnant. It make me lose baby. One time only, I am too much pregnant, like this, and she make me have abortion. It was horrible."

The girl's body shook with tension and her face contorted in remembered pain. Aparna laid a comforting hand on her arm. Priya turned to the other woman and clasped her hands, and kept holding them.

Steve had recovered from the shock, but his gut roiled from the reminder of the atrocities these girls had to endure.

"Priya, I believe abortion is wrong. I would never ask you to do that. And if you want to raise this baby yourself, we will help you make that work in any way we can. I only wanted to talk to you about how we can best help you."

Priya stared at him for a moment. Suddenly, she let forth an avalanche of words.

"I so sorry, Uncle Steve! I not want this to happen. I want only to . . . He tell me he will marry me if I . . ." She broke down sobbing.

Aparna rubbed her back in a circular motion and shushed her.

"He?" Steve asked gently. "Do you mean Ajay?"

Priya's eyes snapped up to Steve's. She didn't have to say anything for him to see that she knew he knew.

"You—you going to put him out?" Her voice trembled and he could see her grip on Aparna's hand tighten. "You going to put me out?"

"No, we will not put you out," Aparna assured her.

Steve ran a hand over his stubble and gave a heavy sigh. "As Aparna said, we are not going to put you out. I would very much like to see you complete your vocational training. Do you think you could do that?"

Priya waggled her head, looking like she wasn't sure if she should trust Steve. "And what you do with Ajay?"

"Well, that depends on him. Did he tell you he still wants to marry you?"

Steve had to tread carefully. Ajay's fate rested mostly in the hands of his family, especially where marriage was concerned. He had no idea if what the boy said to Priya had any basis of truth to it, or if he was merely manipulating her. However, engagement or no, he knew that the chances of convincing Ajay to marry the ex-prostitute he had impregnated were slim to none. At the least, Steve hoped he could be made to take responsibility for the child somehow.

"I—I not know." Priya dropped her eyes and fiddled with her *dupatta*, smoothing the scarf across her lap with her free hand. "I not tell him yet."

Steve leaned back. "I see."

Priya glanced up and back down, as though afraid to meet Steve's eyes, much like she had behaved when she first left the brothel. "I afraid, Uncle Steve. He does not talk to me for so long. I think he not want to see me now, especially if I tell him about the baby."

"Well, he will soon know. Paul is speaking to him right now."

Priya looked up at Steve in alarm. She pulled her hand from Aparna's and covered her mouth, tears welling in her eyes once more.

Steve felt compassion stir for this young woman. She was barely eighteen, but she had stopped being a child many years before, forced into an adult world against her choosing. Yet she still had so little idea of how to handle it. Like many of the women they rescued, she was a strange combination of selfish naiveté and brazen crassness that would make a sailor blush. She was used to doing whatever she could to gain a little power for herself, and for many years, she did that through sexual acts. Was it any wonder she had done it again, grasping for some form of security?

"Priya, I want to assure you that whatever happens, we will help you and your baby. You must keep learning so you can help support yourself. We will not abandon you to the streets. You will not have to go back to Vini to survive."

Priya gave a sideways nod, looking overwhelmed with relief. "Thank you, Uncle Steve. *Deniwada.*"

The office door opened, and Paul stepped inside. He glanced at Priya, who stared back at him like a frightened bird. Then he raised his eyebrows in a question at Steve and Aparna.

"It's okay," Steve said. "We were just finishing."

Paul waggled his head once in acknowledgement. "I could not find Ajay. I wondered if Priya might know where he is."

Priya's lip quivered. "Sorry, Uncle. I do not know."

Aparna took the girl's hand again.

Steve stood. "I'll help you look. Priya, please stay here with Aparna. Aparna, if Ajay shows up, have him wait in the lounge until we come back."

"Yes, okay." Aparna gave Priya a sympathetic glance.

Steve and Paul stepped out to the lounge and conferred. Paul decided to take his scooter to the bazaar in case Ajay had stepped out to get a Thums Up cola or something. Steve headed to the top floor to begin his search.

He checked the dorm rooms, but they were nearly empty at this time of day—most of the children were in class. There was a young child sleeping on one of the pallets, her small form covered by a thin sheet. Steve recognized her as one of the newer "night shift babies"—her mother would have dropped her off last evening and would be coming by in an hour or so to pick her up. He smiled and nodded at Taluja, the house warden, who sat quietly hand-stitching nearby as she supervised the girl.

A sweep of the second floor rooms was equally fruitless. The classrooms on that floor were in use, and a quick investigation revealed that Ajay was not present. Steve smiled and returned the children's greetings. Meera, the grade-school teacher, glared at him in consternation. He dipped his chin apologetically at her and then closed the door.

He knew he was retracing steps that Paul had already made, but they had agreed it was best to be thorough.

When he got down to the main floor and entered the dining hall, several children sat at a table near the far wall playing checkers.

Steve wove his way through the two lines of tables until he reached them. There were two girls and a boy, all around eight to eleven years old. When he approached, they looked up at him but did not greet him and smile as he was used to the children doing. Instead, they looked guilty.

"*Namaste*, Ravi, Pushpa, Jala. Aren't you supposed to be in class?" asked Steve.

The boy, Ravi, spoke up. "No, we have break now. So we play checkers." He flashed Steve a disarming smile that revealed two missing teeth among new neighbours that looked too large for his face.

"I already beat Ravi twice." Jala's dark eyes flashed in triumph. By the look of the board, she was about to make it a triple crown.

Steve gave a look of mock consternation. "Ravi, I think you are pulling my leg. You are pulling it so hard it grows to the next street. All the other children are in class. Why are you three playing checkers?"

The children laughed, but Ravi looked a little nervous.

"Meera Auntie say it okay for us to come here for break. You check, okay? I promise. She say it." The little boy cocked his head, looking up at Steve with a crooked grin as though daring to be challenged. The other two regarded Steve with wide, earnest eyes.

If Steve hadn't been dealing with a much more pressing problem, he would have dragged Ravi to the office for a good talking-to about lying, and all three of them would have gotten an earful for skipping class. However, right now, he had a different mission. He could deal with the truant children later.

"Okay, okay, no problem. Have you seen Ajay come through here?"

The children sobered, and their earnestness became even more intense as they all denied having seen him. Even Ravi's false bravado melted away as he seemed desperate for Steve to believe him.

Steve frowned. That was odd.

He pulled over a metal folding chair from the next table and sat on it backward so he was facing them. They all watched him, bodies tense.

Steve studied each of them. They were truly frightened about something, and it must have something to do with Ajay. They were all among the children who had seemed to take a shine to the young man. Had they known about Ajay and Priya? Perhaps they had been sworn to secrecy and were afraid of betraying their friend in case it meant his job.

But Ajay wasn't with Priya right now, so why wouldn't they tell him if they had seen him?

"I need to ask you something," he said, following a hunch. "Have I ever treated you unkindly?"

The children exchanged glances, then looked back at him in confusion.

"No, Uncle Steve, never," said Ravi.

Little Pushpa looked at him with wide eyes and shook her loose fist in denial.

"Has Uncle Paul?"

Fist shakes.

"Or Auntie Meera? Or Auntie Aparna, or any of the other adults?"

The children had continued their emphatic denials as Steve ran through the list, until he got to the general grouping of "other adults." Then they dropped their gazes. Pushpa, who was no more than eight, played with a red checkers piece, turning it over and over in her hands and avoiding his gaze. She looked like she might cry.

"Pushpa?" Steve said gently. He had a knot in his stomach that was making him nauseous, but something told him that he was on the right track. He had to know.

The child looked at him.

"Has Ajay ever hurt you?"

Her eyes grew wide with fright, and tears started coursing down her cheeks. "He made me promise not to tell. He said he kill me if I tell." She flung herself into his arms. "Please, Uncle Steve, don't let him kill me."

Steve picked up the child, standing so he could hold her trembling frame without the chair in the way. She buried her face in his shoulder and sobbed. He bounced her like a toddler. She was much smaller than most eight-year-olds, and her weight was slight. He held her protectively, his jaw grinding as he tried to control his fury.

At that moment, Paul entered the room from the far side. Steve glanced at him questioningly, and Paul shook his head as he made his way toward them.

Steve turned to the other two, who still stared at him in obvious fright.

"Has Ajay done this to you, too? It's okay, you are not in trouble and we will keep you safe. But we need to find him so we can stop him from hurting anyone else."

Paul came up beside Steve and waited, watching the children.

Ravi looked between Paul and Pushpa, whose sobs had subsided to sniffles. Then he met Steve's eyes. "He is in the toilet. With Geeta." He pointed through the window to the shed on the far side of the back courtyard that housed an Indian-style toilet.

Steve felt rage and fear shoot through his system. Without another thought, he handed Pushpa to Paul and ran out the back door of the dining hall. He was at the shed within seconds. The door was locked, and he rattled it against the sliding bolt on the inside.

"Ajay, open up! I know you're in there!"

He heard a child whimper, and Ajay angrily shushing her. Another surge of rage flooded through Steve and he kicked the door. The wooden boards splintered from the hinges and deadbolt.

Steve grabbed the broken boards, ripping and cracking, heedless of the wooden needles spiking into his hands. He created a hole large enough to be able to reach in and slide back the bolt. When he ripped his hand out, the door swung askew, barely hanging on to its hinges.

Geeta huddled in the far corner on the other side of the squat toilet's hole, dark eyes wide. She was clothed, but her knees beneath the uniform's skirt showed imprinted red lines matching the pattern on the toilet's foot slabs, indicating that she had just been kneeling there.

Ajay stood at the other side of the toilet, scrambling to pull up his pants, his erection protruding from under his shirt.

Steve took it all in at a glance, then lost control. He lunged forward and swung his fist, sending Ajay sprawling back against the corner, moaning.

Steve stood panting. Geeta stared back and forth between him and Ajay in terror.

"It's okay, Geeta. He won't hurt you anymore. Come with me."

He helped her up and out of the toilet.

Kallie stood outside with questioning eyes. Several children trailed into the yard behind her, beginning to form a crowd. Kallie took one look at Steve's face and the trembling girl and bent to pick Geeta up.

Steve gestured toward the back door. "Take her to the dining hall. Paul is in there. He'll know what to do." He looked around the circle of frightened and curious eyes. "Have the other kids wait out here."

Kallie nodded and turned around, giving quick instructions to the assembling children to go begin a game on the other side of the yard, then carried the quaking girl into the building.

Steve turned abruptly and ducked his head behind the swinging shed door, tossing the remains of his breakfast and tea into the shrubs at the edge of the yard. He wiped his mouth with the back of his hand, then stood up and stared into the outhouse.

Ajay had sat up and was holding his head. He looked up at Steve, his face covered in horror and terror.

"You. Get dressed. You're coming with me."

Ajay mutely obeyed, and did not resist when Steve grabbed him roughly by the arm to make sure he didn't bolt on the way to the office.

Paul was right. Monsoon had come early this year. And it had brought a tsunami with it.

forty-one

STEVE ZIPPED HIS SUITCASE CLOSED, CHECKED HIS BEDROOM ONE LAST TIME FOR ANYTHING HE MAY have missed, and headed out to the common room of his flat.

Sam and Kallie were already up and waiting for him. When he appeared, they quit their hushed conversation and turned to face him. Their awkward postures and expressions of compassionate concern grated on his already-raw nerves.

"I made chai." Kallie indicated the tumblers on the small wooden table.

Steve smiled joylessly. Of course Kallie would think to do that.

"Thanks." He set his things by the door and came over to join them at the table.

"So, where are you going first?" Sam fidgeted with his cup, a frown on his normally-jovial face.

"I have a couple of speaking engagements in Tokyo. Then I'll be heading to California, and I even managed to set up a week of talks in the Bible Belt—Texas, Arkansas, Missouri. I have a few open slots, but for such short notice, I really can't complain."

His friends nodded, and they quietly sipped their tea. The early-morning sounds of birds and traffic drifted in the window, and sunlight dappled the world with a golden glow—but Steve saw everything through a grey filter, just as he had for the last five days.

He'd said his goodbyes to Sita yesterday. He almost couldn't stand to face her, but she had come to Prakaash House and practically cornered him alone in his office.

"Steve, I have something to say to you, and you will sit and listen to me, okay?"

Steve had forced himself to meet her eye. The fierceness in her one-eyed glare reminded him of his mother's when he'd been caught shoplifting from Duncan's as a kid. Aashi's face kept flashing through his mind, along with the four other children that had admitted to Ajay's abuse. *How many more are too afraid to speak?* Whatever Sita had to say to him, she'd earned the right. And he deserved to hear it.

Sita sat down in the chair across from him and folded her hands. She studied him for a moment in silence before she began.

"When you found me, I worth nothing. I have nothing, except small baby. I know nothing. But then, you help me. You take care of me and Aashi. You teach me to read, and help me get education. You tell me about Jesus, about how he heals inside. And I believe you."

She looked up and met his eyes. Steve refused to look away, as much as he wanted to. His shame was flaming from his face, anyway.

"Aashi was hurt by Ajay, not you. She will heal. I am so sad that my little girl was hurt, but it was not you who did the hurting, nor I. Jesus healed me. Jesus healed you. And Jesus will heal Aashi. So stop blaming yourself. This is not your load to bear."

Steve knew she was right. Intellectually, he knew that it was not his direct choices that had led to the pain these children bore. But he had still carried the shame of it every moment since he'd found Ajay with Geeta in the toilet. *If only I hadn't hired Ajay. If only I'd paid more attention to what was happening. If only . . . If only . . .*

The self-condemnation was endless.

He smiled at Sita through his pain. "Thank you, little sister. You speak wisdom. I will try."

Sita stood to her full height, not much taller than a child herself—but she was anything but vulnerable. Her good eye washed over him with love and compassion.

"You know I not angry with you, Steve. And Aashi is not. Please come back to us soon, okay?"

She had come over and, very un-Indian-like, given him a hug.

Sitting across the table from Sam and Kallie, Steve studied his tumbler, twirling it around by the rim as he avoided all he wished he didn't have to say to his friends.

At last, he looked up at them.

"Look, guys, I'm sorry to have to do this. I wish I could stay until your visit here was finished, but we really need to raise this money right now. I tried to think of another way to work this out, but I couldn't."

Sam raised a placating hand. "No worries, buddy. We totally understand. We only had one more week here anyway, remember? And I want to take Kallie up into North India before we head home."

Kallie put on a bright smile. "Can't come to India and not visit the Taj Mahal, right?"

Steve tried to laugh with them, but he only mustered a chuckle. "It's been done, but I'm glad you won't have to miss it."

He took the last swallow of his tea and glanced at his phone's Uber app. "Looks like my cab is only a minute away."

Sam and Kallie nodded in acknowledgement. Heart as heavy as lead, Steve stood. They followed him to the door.

He put on his ball cap, then turned to face his friends.

Sam offered him a hand. Steve grabbed it and his friend pulled him in close. "Hey, bud. It's going to be fine. You've been through worse before, right?"

Steve gave a curt nod, and they hugged and smacked each other's backs as guy friends do.

Kallie's hug was much more tender as she wrapped her arms around him. "Oh, Steve. I'm so sorry for what you're going through. But this, too, will pass."

Steve gave a tight-lipped smile, his arms around her shoulders. "Yes, it will."

Kallie stepped back and stood next to her husband, who put an affectionate arm around her as they watched Steve pick up his suitcase and travel pack.

"We'll be praying for you, buddy." Sam nodded in emphasis.

Kallie smiled and waved as he headed out the door. "We'll be fine. We love you! Bye!"

After Steve settled into his cab for the thirty-minute ride to the airport, his thoughts soon resumed travelling the well-worn rut they had gouged over the last five days.

Ajay had been sent to Delhi yesterday. Love Mumbai's board of directors and his father had decided that the best thing to do with him was to send him far away to Bible College in order to give him time to reflect, and also to dissipate the scandal as quickly as possible.

The children's mothers had been informed of what had happened, and counselling was offered for them and their children. All but one had accepted the offer, agreeing that their children were in a better place at Prakaash House than staying home with them. Little Pushpa's mother had dragged her daughter away in a cold fury, heedless of the child's cries to stay.

Steve couldn't blame the woman. In fact, he was mildly surprised that there had only been one.

Paul had few worries that anyone would report the incident to the police. Ajay wouldn't, obviously—he had far more to lose from reporting Steve's punch than he had to gain. The mothers wouldn't. They had received nothing but poor treatment from police for most of their lives, many of them having been fined multiple times after police raids of the brothels, only to be returned to their mistresses further in debt than before.

Steve had wanted to. It had been his first reaction, actually. He had dragged Ajay into the office and slammed him into a chair.

"Don't move," he'd growled.

Ajay rubbed his arm where Steve had gripped him. His face was sullen. "Steve, I—"

"And don't talk."

Steve paced the room, clenching and unclenching his fists as he walked. A few moments later the door opened and Paul entered and frowned at his nephew.

"We should have Aparna call the police," Steve said. "I would have done it already, but I thought I should calm down first."

"And what good would that do?" asked Paul, coming to lean against the corner of his desk. He cast a cool glance at Ajay, crossed his arms, and then looked at his friend.

"That's justice! Why wouldn't we do that?"

Paul looked thoughtful. And sad. "Ah, 'justice.' That is a difficult thing to pin down in India, my friend. You know this."

Steve glared at Ajay and crossed his arms, furious that Paul was right when he wanted so badly to do something.

Ajay looked alarmed. "Uncle Paul, I—"

"Quiet, son." Paul didn't raise his voice in the slightest, but the soft command cut through Ajay's bluster as effectively as a knife.

The boy closed his mouth, his face anxious.

Paul kept his eyes on Ajay, but spoke to Steve. "Words cannot express how upset and disappointed I am in my nephew, and I, more than anyone, want to see him corrected for what he has done."

Ajay gulped and leaned forward in his chair, but obeyed his uncle's imperative of silence.

Paul continued. "But for us to take this to the police would be inviting in devils who would expose the children to public guilt and shame and harass our organization until we could no longer minister effectively. We could go through the entire process, and Ajay would learn nothing and most likely walk free. And do you think the children's mothers would want them to testify? No, taking this to court would do far more harm to everyone than good." He pinned Steve with an unblinking stare. "I thought we were more interested in mercy than justice, anyway?"

Paul's words echoed in Steve's thoughts as he glared out of the cab window at an ocean swallowed up in haze.

Mercy. Justice. He'd thought his life was dictated by the first. He'd certainly known mercy beyond understanding more than once, and had been grateful. But standing on the other side of the equation, he was finding it difficult to extend mercy over justice, especially since it had been the innocents in his care that had paid the price for his sins.

The board had argued quite extensively about what to do with Priya. Ajay had agreed to the exile to Delhi—since the alternative was the threat of being dragged before the courts—but laughed at the idea of marrying the girl.

"You want me to marry a prostitute? Why would I do that?"

Steve had let the outrage seep into his voice. "She carries your child, Ajay. Does that mean nothing to you?"

"The bastard child of a whore? Why would it?"

Steve had lunged at him again, his fist itching to connect with Ajay's face. The other men in the room had jumped to prevent him, but he had restrained himself. With a cursory look at the men and women in the room, he stormed out.

He'd still been stalking the streets when Paul had called with the outcome of the meeting.

"Ajay is to be sent to Delhi to study. Everyone agreed it was the best path."

Steve grunted. "And what of Priya?"

"She will continue to work here. She will keep up her schooling. And we will help her with the baby if she needs it."

Two days later, Ajay's father had come by to offer Priya a position as a live-in maid in his household. They wanted to see their grandson grow up, he said, even if Ajay never laid claim to him. Despite Paul's misgivings, Priya had immediately agreed and had moved into their house on the same day that Ajay had been sent away.

Steve supposed it was the best outcome that could have realistically been hoped for, under the circumstances. Priya may not earn a lot as a domestic, but the position offered stability. Now all that remained was the guilt.

Steve had spent the next several days on the phone. They needed to raise money for Prakaash House, and the best way he could see to do that was a three-week speaking tour. Talking to people face-to-face, presenting an immediate need, was always the most effective way of sharing a cause. The only downside was that it meant leaving before his friends' trip was over.

That, and the hours of travel time with nothing to keep him company but his thoughts.

Sarah had noticed that he seemed down. When she'd asked why, he had told her only that there had been some trouble at Prakaash House, but it had been dealt with. He may have the entire event on a silent loop in his head, but he was not yet ready to lay out the grizzly details aloud.

If he was honest, he was afraid of her reaction. He knew she saw him as a virtuous example of what men should be. She'd never said those exact words, but she'd made him feel like a hero enough times that he was hesitant to remove the veil. Not for this. For stuff from his past, sure. Maybe. But this was too raw, too recent. He wasn't ready to let it go.

He was going to have to tell her eventually, of course. About this, about Vanessa, about everything. But not yet.

As he made his way through the boarding line at the airport and the plane took off for the first leg of his journey, there was one more face he couldn't get out of his mind.

It was the face of a woman in a porn magazine that he had purchased in his late teens. She was beautiful, and nubile, and had fired every passion that he had been too ashamed to show to the rest of his safe, molded-plastic world at the time.

It was only later—much later—that he would find out who she was.

Reaching into his wallet, he unfolded a well-worn piece of a magazine page with nothing more than the girl's face. For long moments, he stared into the eyes of his birth mother, then tucked it back into its hidey-hole.

He wiped away a tear and stared out the window as the haze of Mumbai faded away beneath him.

forty-two

THE MONTH LEADING UP TO THE GALA AND SARAH'S TRIP WAS A FLURRY OF PLANNING AND ORGA-
nization. Sarah had never been to a developing country before, and knew so little
about India that she felt compelled to do research at every possible opportunity.
With Steve's speaking itinerary, their daily phone calls dropped off to bi-weekly.
She couldn't tell him that most of her time was taken up with preparations for
the fundraiser, so when they did speak, she felt like she spent the entire time
peppering him with questions about India. She was glad to have that topic to
talk about, because otherwise, she was sure he would have become suspicious
that her life seemed so suddenly devoid of other activities.

Steve seemed exceptionally tired, which she supposed was understandable
with his whirlwind travel schedule. She wouldn't have thought it possible to fit
so many speaking engagements into one month, but it seemed that by the time
Steve had landed in San Francisco, his entire calendar had filled up. She knew
he must be thrilled underneath the exhaustion—she wished she could think of
a way to perk him up.

Maybe I should tell him about the fundraiser.

But something held her back. A fear of—what? Failure? No. The number
of people who had come on board to help plan, the donated services and goods,
the way the event was coming together, and the advance ticket sales all prophe-
sied a function that would not only meet her expectations, it would explosively
exceed them.

Still, she hesitated. Despite—or maybe because of—how close they had
become, she was afraid of how he would react. She was doing all of this for him,
to help him, but she was afraid that if he knew, it would only encourage whatever feelings he might have for her.

On the other hand, would that be such a bad thing? Lately, her dreams had been much less *Nightmare on Elm Street* and much more *When Harry Met Sally*, with Steve as the leading man. Recently, simply hearing his voice on the other end of the line had been enough to set her heart racing. She didn't know if she was falling in love or simply responding to the emotions he seemed to have for her. Until she did know, she didn't want to appear encouraging.

Besides, she couldn't be sure Steve did feel anything more for her than friendship. Maybe she was imagining the whole thing.

For once, I'm not going to rush headlong into something just because I think it's expected of me.

If Steve had known her reasoning, she was pretty sure he'd be proud of her.

In planning the gala, Sarah had tapped into skills she had almost forgotten she had, including her ability to reach out and network with others. The biggest risk she took was not in contacting Christine Fenway, who was delighted to help once Sarah explained the details.

It was when she called Abby.

After more than a year of not speaking, and having left their relationship on such poor terms, Sarah wasn't sure that her old friend would even be interested in hearing from her. So she was both surprised and delighted when her invitation to a coffee date was immediately accepted.

Sarah told Abby about Steve, his work in India, and how much he had influenced her life over the past five months. Abby's hazel eyes danced with amused delight as she teased Sarah about 'Steve the dreamboat.' When Sarah mentioned the fundraiser, Abby's immediate response was "Count me in!"

"Just like that? You don't need to do some research and check to see whether this is something you can get behind?"

Abby levelled a serious gaze at her, her chestnut curls falling softly around her freckled face. "Sarah, you are so different than the last time I saw you. You are stronger than you have been in years, or maybe ever. I can only credit that to this guy you're seeing."

"Um, we're not seeing each other. I'm still married."

"On paper. And you talk every day? Sounds like you're seeing him to me."

Sarah blushed. "Think what you want, I guess."

"Well, can you tell me you'd be where you are today if you hadn't met him?"

Sarah stared blankly at her friend. "No, I guess not. He gave me the initial push, anyway."

He had done much more than that, but she didn't want to feed Abby's overactive musings about the nature of their relationship.

"Potayto, potahto. I think any guy that can do that for you has a decent shot at changing the world. If you trust him, then so do I."

The day after her coffee with Abby, the divorce papers came in the mail. Craig had finally signed the most recent version of the contract, which said that he relinquished all rights to Nelson. Sarah read and re-read the letter from her lawyer as she let it sink in.

She was finally free of him. On paper. Why did she feel that his influence on her life would take exponentially longer to purge?

When Joanna called Sarah the Tuesday before the gala to invite her to Sophie's first birthday party that Friday afternoon, Sarah hemmed and hawed and told her friend she would call her back. But as she went through her checklists, she could see no reason not to go. Preparations for the event were complete—her team of helpers had knocked it out of the park, and she hardly felt like she could even take credit for what would happen at the Paradise Centre on Saturday night.

She was even mostly prepared for her flight on Monday. All her papers were in order, she'd had her travel vaccinations, and had even had an early six-month follow-up with the oncologist earlier in the week since she would be out of the country on the actual due date.

Other than a bit of last-minute packing, things were about as prepped and planned as they could be. She knew an afternoon alone would only be spent stressing over every last detail, with nothing that could be changed at that point, anyway. Why do that when she could spend the afternoon celebrating her favourite little girl's birthday?

"So, can you come tomorrow?" Joanna asked when Sarah called her back. Sarah smiled. "I wouldn't miss it."

Steve jumped out of another burpee, careful to avoid hitting the small motel room's TV with his arms. He dove back down for the squat, kicked his legs back for the push-up, back to the squat, then jumped as high as he could go for the jumping jack, his heart beating to the rhythm of self-condemnation's voice. The added strength it had gained from this morning's news had made it feel like a physical force in the room, taunting him in whispers every time he paused for even a moment to think.

. . . ninety-six . . .

I failed.

. . . ninety-seven . . .

I failed.

. . . ninety-eight . . .

He hit one hundred, then braced his hands on his knees to catch his breath. Sweat poured off of him in rivulets, and his legs felt like jelly after the intense body-resistance workout he'd just put them through. But when he looked up, self-condemnation was still sitting in the chair beside his bed, smiling wickedly.

Paul's words from this morning's conversation kept playing on a loop in his head.

Priya moved back into the women's shelter today. They forced her to have an abortion.

Steve had promised Priya she would not have to abort the baby. One more broken promise. One more failure. One more person he'd let down.

Lord, why do you give me tasks that I cannot complete?

He did not blame God for the abortion, just as he hadn't blamed him for Ajay's abuse of the children or Priya's unwanted pregnancy. He understood that it was man's selfishness that had caused the pain and sorrow in those situations, not God's negligence.

No, he didn't blame God—he blamed himself. He was the one appointed to protect those weak ones. It was his task, and he had failed. The truth bit into his spirit like the straps of the full duffel bag on his back bit into his shoulders as he began a hundred squats.

You said your yoke is easy, your burden light. So why am I being crushed by it?

. . . eighteen, nineteen . . .

There's not enough money for the building. That means more ways that the children will suffer.

. . . twenty-five, twenty-six . . .

How long before I fail the rest of them? Joanna? Sarah? Paul and Aparna? How long until I let them all down, too?

Sarah. What would she put in her book now? Would she still write it, so his failure would be known to the world?

. . . eighty-nine, ninety, ninety-one . . .

Should he wait to tell her until they both got to Mumbai next week? *Should I even go back?*

. . . one hundred.

He finished by sitting on an imaginary chair with his back pressed against the wall, held there by body tension alone. After several minutes, his legs began to tremble. When he hit five minutes, Steve collapsed on the floor.

He was fairly certain he could not put his body through one more set of anything, not even a set of stairs. He rolled onto his back and stared at the grungy ceiling. Breath began to return to his lungs while the weight of the world crushed it out of them.

There was no urgency to do anything or go anywhere today. After twenty-three days of non-stop travel and speaking engagements in both hemispheres, he had three days free before he headed back to Mumbai. He had tried to fill them several times, but nothing had ever worked out.

For the most part, the tour had been successful. People had been supportive and extremely generous, despite the current economic climate. Many had given sacrificially, and yet, when Steve had added up the total donations, they still fell far short of what Paresh was demanding.

"How long until I fail them again?" he asked the walls rhetorically. "How about March thirty-first when they are evicted?"

His heart rate finally dropped below audible levels and he heaved himself off of the floor to head for the shower. He'd just removed his shirt and thrown the sweaty ball of fabric into his laundry bag when the phone rang.

Steve glanced at the caller ID. *Pastor Eric.*

"Hello." He attempted to force cheer into his voice and was sure he failed miserably.

"Hello, my young friend. I hope I am not catching you at a bad time." Eric's voice was warm and reassuring, as usual. Steve smiled, his spirits lifting slightly.

"No, not at all. I just finished a workout. What can I do for you?"

"I was wondering whether I should be asking you that question instead."

"What do you mean?" Steve frowned, confused.

"Well, m'boy, I've had the strangest feeling all day, like maybe I should call you. Can you think why that might be?"

Steve wiped away some sweat that was dripping into his eyes and sank onto the chair. He leaned on his elbows, supporting his head in his hands.

"Yeah, I suppose I do. I've been . . . struggling lately. A lot."

"How so?"

Steve ran a hand over his chin. If there was anyone who would be able to give him helpful advice, it was Eric. "Not long ago, we found out that one of our staff members had gotten one of our rescued women pregnant, and had also sexually abused some of the children. This morning, I received word that his family forced the girl to have an abortion, even though she wanted to keep the baby."

"I see." His voice was somber. "That is definitely a lot of unfortunate news. Those poor souls." He paused. "But what is the nature of *your* struggle, exactly?"

"I—I just can't help feeling that I let everyone down. That somehow, it's all my fault."

"Why would you think that?"

"Because I was the one who hired the boy. I didn't pay close enough attention to the signs of abuse. And I told Priya she would not have to have an abortion. When she went to live with the family, I thought she would be safe there. They are supposedly Christians. Now, I have begun to wonder if there is any point in even fighting a war this big in a country where even the Christians have so little regard for human life." Steve hated how much that sounded like whining, but Pastor Eric had asked. And the truth was, Steve felt utterly defeated.

"Hmm. I see."

Pastor Eric was silent for a moment. Steve waited. His pastor always had a reason for his silences.

"I had an interesting visitor today. Ellen Sinclair. Isn't that your friend Sarah's mother?"

Steve blinked at the non-sequitur. Ellen had gone to see *his* pastor? "Yes. Why do you ask?"

"It seems that Ellen is looking for some counselling, trying to find a way to patch things up with her daughter. Normally, I wouldn't discuss a client with others, but I feel like you need to hear it. From what you've already told me, Ms. Daniels has been working through some fairly difficult trauma herself, hasn't she?"

"Yes." Steve hadn't revealed the nature of the trauma, but when he had first met Sarah he had asked Eric for some advice on how to counsel her.

"How is she doing, by the way?"

"Sarah? Very well. She seems to be getting to a really good place."

"That's good to hear. You sound very proud of her."

Steve sat up, considering. "I *am* proud of her, I guess. But not in a proprietary way. She has overcome a lot in a very short amount of time. She inspires me more than anything."

"You don't think you are responsible for that success in any way?"

Steve rubbed his chin. "No, not much. I have helped her and supported her as much as I can, but she has done all the hard work herself."

"But you told me that you felt God telling you to help her—that he couldn't have made it clearer with a flashing neon sign. You're sure you don't feel like her progress is at least partly your doing?"

Steve frowned. "I—I don't know. I provided friendship and support, but she could have rejected it. I didn't do anything for her that I wouldn't have done for anyone else."

He cringed at making light of his relationship with Sarah. She'd earned a place in his heart among his most precious of relationships. Still, what he had said was true in the strictest sense. Everything he'd done to help Sarah, he would have done for another.

"Hmm. And do you think that Ellen would be in here looking for help if you hadn't ever introduced yourself to Ms. Daniels?"

"Maybe. I don't know. Maybe not." Steve ran his fingers through his hair. He had no idea where Eric was going with this.

"Ah. The sanguine 'maybe.'" Pastor Eric chuckled. "I love 'maybe,' because it reminds me that nothing is set in stone. No one is beyond hope. The future is an open door, full of light and possibilities, regardless of whatever dungeon we might find ourselves in at any given moment."

"No such thing as a lost cause," Steve said, quoting his favourite mantra.

"Praise the Lord for his mercy, or we'd all be in trouble." Eric chuckled, then heaved a sigh. "Steve, I know you feel like your choices are what allowed these tragedies to happen. But have you considered the other wills involved in the situation?"

"Yes, of course." Steve frowned. This was an old discussion between the two of them. He still couldn't see where this was going, or how it related to Sarah. "I know that Ajay and Priya both made choices, too, as did Ajay's family, the children, and everyone else involved. But if I had been better at my job, they may never have made the choices they made."

His shoulders sank a little lower under the admission. "I failed in that I—I didn't protect them from making the wrong choices. And I especially failed the children and Priya's baby—" His voice cracked, and he swallowed the knot of emotion that choked him. The fact that innocents in his charge had been hurt was the toughest pill to swallow. "They had no say in what happened to them."

Eric's voice was full of compassion. "Do you feel that the young man and lady in question did not know which path was the right one, or that they were forced into making the choices they did because of a lack of options?"

Steve pondered. Both Ajay and Priya had known the potential consequences for the actions they took, but had taken them anyway.

"No, they weren't coerced, and both were aware of the right thing to do. Or, at the very least, what was expected of them."

"Ah. So, they chose sin with full knowledge of their wrongdoing. How does that make what happened your fault?"

Steve slumped back against the chair, not sure how to respond. Perhaps there was no response.

"I don't know. It's just the way I feel."

Pastor Eric sighed. "Steve, m'boy, working in ministry is a tricky business. It can be tempting to measure our success by the results we see. We want to know that what we are doing is making a difference, and rightfully so. After all, Jesus tells us that if our lives are not bearing the fruits of godliness, we do not have the Spirit of God in us."

"Yes. What are you getting at?"

"Sometimes we get so results-oriented that we forget that the results aren't ours to claim. We measure our campaigns by dollars raised, or souls baptized, or seats filled, when all we should be counting is the number of seeds we've sown."

Steve was beginning to understand. "'A farmer went out to sow his seed,'" he began, quoting the parable. He paraphrased the rest. "Some fell on rocky places, some was eaten by birds, some was choked by thorns, and some fell on good soil and bore a crop, a hundred times what was sown."

"Exactly. You are a sower, friend, as am I. And our only job is to plant seeds. We have absolutely no control over how the seeds grow. And it's not our job to force them to, either."

Steve knew this. He *knew* it, but it was like he was hearing it for the first time.

Eric continued. "You have an exceptional talent as a sower of seeds, Steve. You have sowed good seeds into the lives of a great many people. But just as you did not claim responsibility for the seeds that took hold, such as for Ms. Daniels, you cannot claim it when seeds take no root and the lives bear no fruit. We must leave the growing to God and claim no credit where it is not due, for good or for ill."

Conviction lay heavy on Steve's heart. His friend spoke the words that both condemned him and promised release. Tears ran down his cheeks as he repented for his pride—for trying to do a task that was never his to begin with.

"Thank you, Eric. That is exactly what I needed to hear." He swiped at his face with his free hand and sniffled. "Would—would you pray with me?"

He could hear the smile in Eric's voice. "It would be my pleasure."

Steve bowed his head and laid his pride before his God, repenting and asking for forgiveness for claiming a right that was not his. He thanked his Creator once again for his patience and love with an imperfect creation such as himself.

Cheated of its prize, Self-condemnation melted into the walls. It would have to find another victim to torment.

forty-three

"There is one more thing I wanted to talk to you about. It is regarding your friend, Ms. Daniels."

Steve smiled to himself. He should have expected this to come up with Eric eventually. "Yes?" he asked, prepared to weather a good-natured lecture about his intentions. But Eric surprised him.

"Where are you?"

Steve blinked. "Good question." He glanced around his motel room. "I'm at, uh—" He spotted the town's name on the nightstand's notepad. "Texarkana, Arkansas."

"Are you busy tomorrow night?"

"Nope. My schedule is wide open until I head back to India on Monday."

"Well, as a personal favour to me, get yourself on a plane to Edmonton. You're speaking at a gala tomorrow night."

"I am? What are you talking about?"

Eric sighed. "She asked me not to tell you, but that was before she asked me to speak. And before I was completely aware of what manner of book she is launching."

"Oh?" Steve frowned. "I'm sorry, but I'm not really following."

"Ms. Daniels. She has organized a fundraiser to benefit Love Mumbai. It is quite the high-brow affair, black tie, all that."

Steve's eyebrows climbed into his hairline. She'd done *what*? And why hadn't she told him?

His heart melted as he thought of the tremendous gift she had been preparing for him. Her, and God. A fundraiser gala, and he'd had nothing to do with it. Perhaps they would have enough money to purchase the—he caught himself. The results didn't matter. God would look after it.

"Okay, if she's got the whole thing planned, why do you need me?"

Pastor Eric sighed. "She asked me to speak at the event, but apparently, she and a half-dozen other erotica authors are the main sponsors. I don't want to pass up the opportunity to speak to a crowd of so many, uh, 'hungry ears,' but something tells me you would be a much better man for the job."

Steve chuckled. He so seldom saw Eric squeamish, he couldn't resist the opportunity to tease him a little. "You think so? I'm not even married. I'm hardly an expert on the subject at hand."

"Perhaps not, if the subject were sex."

Steve blinked. Maybe Eric was less squeamish than he'd believed.

Eric continued, his voice dry. "It appears that there will be quite a few manuals about bedroom activities already available. They don't need a speech about it, too."

Steve just about choked. "Uh, I suppose not." His tender gut muscles complained as he shook with barely-contained silent howls of laughter.

"At any rate, I would take it as a personal favour if you would take my place. I sense a case of sudden-onset laryngitis coming on."

"Well, we must protect your sensitive vocal cords. You have to speak from a pulpit the next morning, after all." Steve wiped moisture from his eye. "I'll see what I can do. It sounds like the perfect opportunity for 'sowing some seeds,' don't you think?"

"Yes, yes, qui—" Eric paused as the double entendre hit him. His tone held restrained amusement. "You can be quite the young scalawag at times, son."

"I couldn't resist. Sorry," said Steve, not feeling very sorry. It seemed that his pastor was much less stodgy than some would believe.

Eric justified that view by laughing. "Perhaps I *should* reconsider. Sending you might be more like the 'blind leading the blind.'" His voice took on a devilish tone. "We wouldn't want your Ms. Daniels to be disappointed in your performance."

Steve felt his face catch fire and he laughed out loud. *So, Eric can give it as well as take it.* He couldn't resist one more. "Well, now you've caught me with my pants down."

"Steven . . ." Eric's voice had a warning tone, but shook with restrained laughter.

Steve knew the growl was more for the sake of Eric's position than that he hadn't enjoyed the joke. Still, he bit off further quips. "I'll be good. I promise."

Eric chuckled. "Okay. And thank you."

After they hung up the phone, Steve collapsed onto the floor, rolling with laughter, letting a month of pent-up tension drain away.

"I wish I could have seen his face," he said to no one in particular, wiping away the tears.

When he'd caught his breath, he stood up with renewed purpose. He had a shower to take, a flight to book, and a tuxedo to find.

And tomorrow night, a beautiful blonde to thank for it.

Sarah parked the RAV4 in front of the Larsons' home with a heavy heart. Resting her elbows on the steering wheel, she cradled her head in her hands for a moment to collect herself.

She had been so looking forward to Sophie's party. She had spent the morning shopping for gifts, thinking wistfully of the day when she might be shopping for her own little girl. She'd been standing at the till, paying for her purchases, when she'd received the call from Dr. Strickland's office.

"Dr. Strickland has reviewed the results of Tuesday's biopsy, and she needs to see you as soon as possible. Can you come in on Monday morning, nine o'clock?"

Sarah's heart fell. That was never a good sign. "I'm flying out of the country for three weeks on Monday. Could I come in right now?"

The receptionist clicked some keys, muttering to herself. "I can squeeze you in at one fifteen. It shouldn't take very long."

"Okay, sounds great. Thanks." Sarah tried to keep a hint of cheer she didn't feel in her voice.

The icicle that had begun to form in her gut with the receptionist's call only grew. She skipped lunch, having lost her appetite. And Dr. Strickland's news was as bad as she had feared.

More evidence of cancer . . . much deeper in the uterus than I had realized . . . recommend total hysterectomy as soon as possible.

The joy that Sarah had anticipated sharing with her friends at their daughter's birthday was now permeated with a sense of loss. This could never be hers. Not with Steve, not with anyone.

She'd been right not to encourage his feelings for her by telling him about the gala. He deserved someone so much better than her.

She clenched her teeth. She would get through this. She *would* be happy for her friends. She could go home and weep later.

It was not Derek or Joanna that answered the door, but a middle-aged woman Sarah had only seen in photos before.

"Hi, I'm Sarah." She felt suddenly shy. "You must be Steve's and Joanna's mom."

The copper-haired woman with the piercing blue eyes beamed at her, then pulled her in for a hug. "Sarah. I have heard *so* much about you."

Sarah stiffened, unused to public displays of affection from strangers. "Nice to meet you, Mrs. McGuire." She returned the hug, her head awkwardly bowed over the petite woman's shoulder.

"Please, call me Gertrude."

"Okay, Gertrude."

Despite Sarah's graceless hug execution, Gertrude's warmth buoyed Sarah's flagging spirits, and she melted into the embrace for the moments that it lasted. When Sarah stepped back, the woman's blue eyes sparkled with instant affection and her smile looked like it would light up a subway tunnel in a blackout.

Adopted or no, Steve reminded Sarah very much of his mother.

Sarah was ushered up the stairs and her gift spirited away by Gertrude. Joanna introduced Sarah to her father, Angus, and Derek held Sophie out of the way until the baby gate could be closed again. Angus seemed much more reserved than his wife, but the laugh lines around his piercing grey eyes—so like Joanna's—and his firm but gentle handshake put Sarah at ease.

Steve's parents were exactly the sort of people she had expected them to be. She loved them immediately.

Sarah spent the next couple of hours laughing and listening to stories about the McGuires' adventures in Brazil, helping corral Sophie long enough so Joanna could take some one-year-old photos for posterity, and watching the littlest member of the household thoroughly annihilate a piece of chocolate cake. She almost forgot about the weight on her own heart until Gertrude turned the conversation toward Sarah.

Gertrude stood next to Sophie's high chair in the dining room with a wet facecloth in her hand. While attempting to clean up the chocolate facsimile of her granddaughter that Sophie had made of herself, Gertrude directed a question toward Sarah, who sat on the couch finishing her cake.

"So, I hear that you are hosting a fundraising gala for Love Mumbai tomorrow."

Sophie squealed and smacked the tray, and Gertrude swiped the cloth over Sophie's mouth.

"My goodness, little goose! How did you get chocolate up your nose?" She mopped the cloth around Sophie's chubby cheeks, finishing with a dab on the tot's nose.

Sophie giggled up at her grandmother and showed off four square little teeth.

Sarah's smile froze as she watched the vignette of joy. "Yes, I am. Joanna's been helping, too. It looks like we're going to be packed out."

Angus spoke up from his chair opposite of her. "How many people are you expecting?"

"Around five hundred, give or take. There are always a few no-shows at an event like this, I've been told, but I'm not worried. The tickets have been paid for either way, I guess." She was thankful that she was not the one in charge of the tickets—Kathy and Maryanne had graciously volunteered for the position. "Will you be coming?"

Angus blew out air. "Oh, I don't know. A hundred dollars a plate sounds a bit rich for my blood. I think we'll just give you the money to donate to the cause and save you the trouble and expense of feeding us."

Derek leaned toward his father-in-law from the other chair, his nearly-empty plate in hand. "Sorry, Angus. We got you tickets already."

Gertrude glanced up from her granddaughter's nearly-clean face and her free hand fluttered next to her throat. "You did what? But it's black-tie! We don't have anything to wear to something like that."

Joanna stood up from the couch and collected the men's cups in one hand, then paused to squeeze Gertrude's shoulders in a side-hug with her free hand as she buzzed past her mother on her way to the sink. "Gotcha covered, Mom. You can borrow a dress from me. And Derek's already got a tux on hold for Dad—they'll just have to pick them up in the morning."

"Well!" said Gertrude as Joanna began loading the dishwasher. Gertrude playfully swatted the air in her daughter's general direction. "It looks like we don't have a choice, do we?"

"Nope." Joanna smiled affectionately.

Joanna's mother put her hands on her hips in mock consternation and her father looked abashed but pleased.

Sarah gathered up the remaining dirty dishes from the men in the living room and took them to Joanna in the kitchen.

Joanna took them with a grateful smile that transformed into a concerned frown when she saw Sarah's face. "Hey, what's up?"

Sarah blinked and pasted on a cheerful expression. She hadn't meant to look glum. She didn't want to be the one to ruin the pleasant atmosphere in the house. Her news could wait.

"Uh, no big deal. Just tired. It's been a busy few weeks." A thought occurred to her. "Hey, I've been meaning to ask—do you have any of Steve's baby pictures, or mementos from his childhood? It might help with the book. Maybe there will even be something we can use at the gala tomorrow night."

Joanna tilted her head in thought. "I'm not sure. I think Steve might have left a couple of boxes in the storage room downstairs. We'll go take a look in a few minutes, okay?"

Sarah nodded and helped Joanna finish cleaning up.

Ten minutes later, Joanna hauled a couple of old fruit boxes out of the storage room under the stairs. Steve's name was scribbled on them in a fat black marker. They each opened one.

"Holy blast-from-the-past, Batman." Joanna grinned and pulled out a framed photo of the two of them, both with sunburned faces and cheesy grins. They looked like they were about eight and ten years old.

Sarah peered curiously into her box at the collection of trophies, awards, and even an old ball glove.

"Whatcha doing?" Gertrude hollered down the stairwell.

"Looking at Steve's photo albums," Joanna shouted back, barely even raising her chin. She began pulling old plaques and ribbons into view and piling them on the floor.

Sarah spotted a couple of binders in the bottom of her box. "Jackpot!"

She dove in and gently extricated them from beneath a signed Oilers jersey and hockey puck, then took them over to the couch and plunked them on the coffee table.

Gertrude had arrived at the bottom of the stairs. "Did you find them?"

Sarah carefully opened the first album, conscious of the brittle crackling of the plastic on the magnetic pages. "I think so."

Joanna and Gertrude sat on either side of her as she turned a few pages, but all the photos were from when Steve was quite young. She had actually been hoping to find something from a little later in life, perhaps unearth a story that would explain his altruistic drive to quit law school and begin Love Mumbai.

It was the one piece of Steve's puzzle that didn't quite make sense to her based on what she knew of him.

Sure, it might be enough to have missionary parents and an amazing upbringing, but there had to be something that sparked that trip to India in the first place. What could have caused that drastic of a life change?

There were no pictures of him before six months when the McGuires had begun fostering him, of course. She chuckled as she paged through the photo essay of the boy who'd become the man she knew, quietly absorbing Joanna's and Gertrude's giggles and anecdotes.

They began on the second album, which showed more promise. There was a picture of a teenage Steve with a nineties punk hairstyle, looking tough with his arm around a girl with a gothic look.

"Who's this?" Sarah asked, pointing at the girl.

Joanna glanced at the photo and sobered. "That was Alison. She was a foster kid that Steve took a shine to."

Gertrude leaned over the photo, studying it. "She was a firecracker, that one. Sometimes fostering was the most rewarding experience in the world, and sometimes it just broke your heart." Her face grew sad. "She had so much potential."

"What happened to her?" Sarah studied the girl's dyed black hair and dramatic makeup.

"Her mom got her back." Joanna turned the page, which showed more photos of Alison with the McGuire family. "We thought it would be a good thing, but the last we heard, she had run away from home. That was years ago. Who knows where she is now?"

"We just keep praying for her," Gertrude added.

Sarah blinked. "You do?"

Gertrude's eyes widened in earnestness. "Oh, yes. We pray for all of our foster kids to this day."

Sarah shook her head. This family could still amaze and surprise her.

Handing the album to Joanna to hold, Sarah extricated herself from between the ladies and went back over to the box, carefully rummaging through the remaining contents for clues. A magazine's ragged edges caught her eye, and she gently tugged at them to pull it free from the framed Bible school graduation certificate on top of it.

As the image on the cover came into view, a boulder lodged in Sarah's throat. A woman with grotesquely exaggerated curves in a barely-there bikini gazed seductively from the page. Flipping through a few pages, Sarah discovered that what had barely existed on the cover model was completely absent on the women inside. Nude women in sexually graphic and provocative poses filled the pages in between articles about how to pick up a girl in less than five minutes or seven ways to make any woman want you. Some of the pictures had even been cut out.

Sarah blinked back hot tears of rage and confusion. This was Steve's? How was that possible? But who else's would it be? Everything else in these boxes was clearly here for a reason. It hardly seemed that a well-worn porn magazine would have made it in by accident.

Using her body to hide her actions from the other women, Sarah stuffed the magazine back under the certificate and wiped her face.

"Thank you for everything, Joanna," she said over her shoulder. "I don't think this is what I was looking for. I . . . have to go. See you tomorrow."

She dashed up the stairs, grabbed her coat and purse from the closet, threw a hasty goodbye at the men, and was out the door before anyone could stop her.

Joanna exchanged confused looks with her mother.

"What on earth happened?" asked Gertrude, frowning.

"I have no idea."

Joanna set the photo album on the couch and went to inspect the box Sarah had been looking through. A magazine stuffed partially into the pile caught her eye, and she pulled it out, a lead weight pulling at her innards.

"I was wrong." She held up the magazine for her mother to see. "I know exactly what happened."

They exchanged looks of dismay. Outside, Sarah's vehicle engine revved to life and roared away.

Joanna dropped the magazine back into the box and went to find her phone. She had no idea why Steve had kept a porn magazine after all these years free from the addiction. Maybe he simply hadn't noticed it when he'd stashed his stuff before he moved to India all those years ago. Whatever the reason, it was time to do damage control.

forty-four

SARAH SPED OUT OF MILLER, DRIVING WITH ONLY HALF HER ATTENTION. HER THOUGHTS CIRCLED like buzzards over the corpse of the person she had thought Steve McGuire to be.

All his talk of the preciousness of women, and pearls of great price, and rescuing slaves, and he had a porn magazine in his box of keepsakes? How could he spend his life working with the sexually exploited and secretly be exploiting them himself?

Some part of her said that it was ridiculous to be angry that Steve had proven to be duplicitous. After all, who wasn't? Everyone had masks and hidden vices. Even herself. She should have expected this to happen eventually. As Kathy said, "these behaviours are how we learned to protect ourselves and normalize our pain."

But Steve had been the person who had convinced her that not everyone takes advantage of others, or thinks only of their own needs. She had *believed* in him, had believed that she could change because he said so. And now she was reeling from what felt like the most painful betrayal of all—the one man she had thought was the "real deal" had turned out to be Steve the Phony after all.

She had been duped. Again. Either she was the most gullible person in the history of the planet, or Steve was the most convincing actor she had ever met. Maybe Erica was right—he'd always had an angle. Maybe he was using Love Mumbai as a front for illicit activities. What did she truly know about his organization, anyway? Only what he'd told her and the pictures he'd shown her or what she'd read on the website. And anyone could make a website.

Her blood felt like ice in her veins. What if it had all been lies? Everything he had said? And like a blind schoolgirl with a teenage crush, she had not only believed him, but even volunteered to help with marketing. Oh, how he must have been laughing behind her back all this time, knowing that she was writing a book that would lend his "work" legitimacy and bring in even more funds to his profiteering scam.

She sniffled and swiped a hand at the moisture tracking down her face, slamming her palm against the steering wheel. Something about the whole idea of Steve being a fake felt wrong. Could she truly picture the kind, gentle man she knew running a prostitution ring, lying, and stealing from those who loved him? Would the son of Angus and Gertrude McGuire, career missionaries, be so callous and cold as to take advantage of so many people so unscrupulously?

She didn't want to believe it. Steve had always been anything but callous and cold toward her. Maybe she was blowing everything way out of proportion. But then the images of those women in the magazine blazed in her mind's eye and cast everything Steven McGuire was into a noxious yellow light. Even if what she thought she knew about him was completely legitimate, how could she ever see him the same way again, knowing what she knew now?

She should call Steve and see what he had to say for himself. But how could she believe anything he said? She thought of Craig, and all the times she had believed him when he'd told her he was different, that he'd changed, that he would never do it again. What if Steve told her that it was a misunderstanding, or that the magazine was from a long time ago and that he'd changed, or even that he didn't even know about the magazine or where it had come from? How on earth could she trust him?

How would she ever trust anyone again?

She thought of the fundraiser and felt nauseated. Should she cancel it? Could she go up on that stage tomorrow night and promote Love Mumbai while uncertainty ate at her gut like a cancer? She had given up lying, but right now, if she stood up on that stage, it would feel like the biggest lie of all.

Cancelling the gala would be disastrous. There was much more at stake than her reputation and career, though the scandal could prove devastating to both. What about Yolanda, who had staked her own credibility on Sarah's word about Steve? What about Sarah's publisher, and the bad press the last-minute cancellation would generate for them?

But which would be worse—going ahead with raising money for a potential scam, or dealing with all the inconvenience and embarrassment that would go along with cancelling?

Her phone rang and, in her distraction, she hit the Answer button on her hands-free device.

"Hello," she barked.

"Sarah? Are you all right?" It was Joanna.

"Fine. Never been better. Why do you ask?"

"You left in an awful rush. I thought it might have something to do with the magazine in Steve's things."

Sarah bit her lip. Silent tears began streaming down her cheeks. After a few moments, she found her voice.

"Do you know why he had that in there?"

"No, not exactly. I have my suspicions, but you should really ask him about it."

"I don't think I trust myself to speak to him right now."

"Hmm." Joanna sighed. "I can tell you that it is probably not what it seems. Steve isn't into porn. I'm mighty curious why that magazine was in there, but I don't believe that it was intentional."

"He's your brother. Of course you would see the best in him and defend him. That's how you two work."

Joanna's voice was firm. "He *is* my brother, and I probably know him better than just about anyone, including his flaws. And that's why I can tell you beyond doubt that Steve is not addicted to pornography. That is the kind of thing that breaks his heart. Frankly, I'm surprised that you don't know him well enough by now to see that yourself."

Sarah frowned. "I thought I did know him. But now I'm not so sure. Every person I've ever known has betrayed me—maybe Steve is simply the most recent mistake on my list. I obviously have no ability to judge character—look at the man I married and the woman I picked as my former best friend. How do I know whom I can believe?" She choked on a sob. "Maybe he's fooled you, too. You might not know him as well as you think. Or maybe you're trying to protect his reputation because you know I'm writing his biography."

"Sarah—"

Sarah bit her lip. "I'm sorry. I didn't mean that."

Joanna's voice was compassionate. "Oh, sweetie. I can't imagine what it's been like to walk in your shoes. And I don't know how to make you believe me. If you don't trust me by now, I guess I don't know what I could do to change your mind."

Sarah sniffled and her voice cracked. "I . . . I want to trust you, Joanna, and Steve, too. I want to get rid of this cloud of doubt and fear that invades every part of my life, every relationship I have. But I don't know how. I'm just . . .

very confused right now, and would like some time to think. I'll talk to you later, okay?"

"Okay. But call Steve and talk to him, too—"

Joanna's voice cut off when Sarah punched the button and ended the call, not trusting herself to say another word. She blinked away tears so she could see the road, pulled over to the edge of the highway and parked on the shoulder, then put on her flashers. Finally out of harm's way, she erupted into heaving sobs, shaking with fear and frustration and doubt.

Ten minutes later, the flow of tears had reduced to hiccups. She found a napkin left over from a fast food dinner and blew her nose.

Her phone rang. She picked it up to look at the caller ID.

Steve.

Frowning, she rejected the call. She needed more time to think than that.

Seconds later, the phone rang again. Annoyed and angry, she hit Answer.

"I don't want to talk right now, Steve. Don't you get it?"

"Who's 'Steve?' Sarah, is that you?"

"Mom?" Sarah pressed her hand against her forehead, trying to collect herself. "Sorry. I thought it was someone else."

"'Steve', by chance?"

"Yeah."

"Have you been seeing someone already, Sarah?" Ellen's voice sounded truly concerned.

Sarah sighed. "No, not really. It's . . . complicated. Everything is so complicated right now. I—" She cut off as another sob escaped.

"Sarah? My goodness, what's wrong?"

Sarah stared at cars passing her on the highway through a film of tears. The sunny day melting the remnants of snow huddled against the fence lines along the highway's margins belied the storm inside her. She wanted so badly to be able to talk to her mother about all the things that had gone wrong today. But she knew she couldn't.

"Why did you call, Mom?"

"What I called about doesn't matter. If you need to talk about something, let's talk about that."

Sarah gaped. Her mother wanted to let her talk? Ellen was *interested* in her? The surprise choked off the flow of tears as she tried to decide what to make of this new tactic.

"Uh . . . this morning, I found out I have to have a—a hysterectomy."

"Why?"

"The cancer. The doctor didn't get it all with the LEEP."

"Oh." Ellen's voice was quiet. "I'm so sorry, Buttercup."

At the use of her mother's childhood nickname for her, tears—silent ones this time—started sliding down Sarah's face. Her mother had called her that all the time as a small child. Sarah couldn't remember when she had stopped, but it was right around the time Ellen had cocooned herself against reality.

"Was that the only thing?"

Of all the times for her mother to take an acute interest in her life. Sarah almost lied, if only to get Ellen off her back, but she couldn't quite bring herself to do it. It wasn't because of Steve—after today's revelations, she no longer felt the need to be accountable to him. But lying at this point would have felt like a betrayal of herself.

"Partly. There's some other stuff going on, but I don't want to get into it."

"With Steve?"

Sarah pressed her lips together. "Yeah. With Steve." After a few moments of silence, Sarah repeated her question. "Why did you call?"

"Well." Ellen paused and took a breath. "I was going to ask if you would like to come over tomorrow. There are some things that I want to talk to you about. But if you'd like, we could do it tonight. Sounds like you could use someone to talk to. Where are you? Do you want to come for supper? I assume you still don't want me at your place."

Sarah blinked. Was this the same woman who had practically disowned her a month ago? It almost sounded like her mother wanted to work on some of their issues. And she was respecting Sarah's boundaries? *Who is this person?* Maybe Ellen's brain had been swapped by aliens for real this time.

"Um . . ." Sarah wavered, trying to decide what to do. But as much as she truly wanted to take advantage of what might be a fleeting opportunity, she decided that this turn of the sundial already had enough problems for her to face.

"I . . . I can't, Mom. I just came from Miller, and I have this thing tomorrow night, so I think I'd better go home and get ready." *And decide on the least painful way to commit professional suicide.* "Could we do brunch on Sunday morning?"

"I have church Sunday morning. And what 'thing'?"

"It's nothing, just this fundraiser I organized—"

Ellen broke in. "Are you talking on the phone while you're driving? You have your hands-free thingy, right?"

"No. Yes." Sarah was getting dizzy from keeping up with her mother's barrage of questions. She felt a familiar pain begin creeping up the back of her skull. "I'm not driving. I stopped on the side of the highway. Don't worry, I'm far off on the shoulder and I have my blinkers on."

"Good. But why have you stopped? Are you having car problems? I'll send Ev—" She cut herself off. "Would you like me to come get you or call a tow truck?"

Sarah shook her head. Her mother was behaving so oddly. But the headache on top of everything else was the final straw—she made no effort to curb the sharpness in her tongue. "No, I'm fine. My RAV is fine. And I have a phone, remember? I could call my own tow truck if I needed it."

"Oh. Right."

Sarah pinched the bridge of her nose and squeezed her eyes shut. Light was starting to become painful, and the sun wouldn't set for another hour or two. She scrounged around in her purse for painkillers. She hadn't had a migraine for so long that she hoped she still had some in there.

"Mom, I think I better just head home and rest."

There they are. She tapped a couple ibuprofen into her hand and swallowed them without water, then dropped the bottle back into her bag.

"Okay, but when can I see you? This is important."

Ellen's wheedling tone crawled into Sarah's ears like a parasite. She gripped the steering wheel in frustration. Why wouldn't her mother leave her alone? "Mom! I don't have time for this! You've ignored me for months—or for my entire life, depending on how you look at it—and now you want to see me right freakin' now? On one of the worst days of my entire life? No. Just no. I have more important things to think about than whatever 'emergency' you've concocted to manipulate me with. I'll call you next week when I have time."

"Oh." Ellen cleared her throat. "I see. Well, if that's how you feel about it."

Ellen's hurt tone stabbed Sarah's conscience, but she couldn't summon the emotional energy to deal with it right now. Not when everything she'd built her life on for the last six months seemed to be crumbling around her.

Sarah took a breath and squeezed her eyes shut. "Okay. I'll talk to you on Sunday."

She hung up before Ellen could say another word. Clenching her teeth, she picked up her phone and turned it off. She didn't want to talk to anyone else tonight.

She felt like a jerk for how she'd treated her mother. Ellen had been uncharacteristically lucid and civil for most of the conversation, and Sarah had snapped at her. And this was right after she'd called one of her few real friends a liar. Meanwhile, she was tormented by thoughts that the only man she had ever trusted—the man she had believed had shown her what love truly was—had betrayed her.

Shame washed over her like a flood. She should have known better than to believe she deserved the hope she had been chasing for the last six months. Craig had been right about her. She was weak. She'd done this to herself, seen only what she wanted to see, and gotten what she deserved, like always. Now the real mask was being stripped away, and she was becoming her true self again.

She had thought she could be a pearl when all she would ever be was an ugly, slime-covered troll.

Why had she thought she could be anyone else?

Steve sat in the Tulsa airport's departures area, tapping his toe with his cell phone pressed against his ear. He'd dialled Sarah's number the moment he'd received Joanna's text.

"C'mon, c'mon," he urged aloud as the phone rang. Why didn't she pick up? *Stupid.*

He knew why.

He was running out of time before his flight. He wouldn't be able to call her back for hours. Her voicemail beeped and he decided to leave a message.

"Hi, Sarah. Joanna told me about the magazine. I can't tell you enough how sorry I am that I kept that. I have a reason, though it suddenly doesn't seem that great. I—"

They called his zone for boarding, and passengers stood and began moving toward the line.

"I'm about to get on a plane. Please call me when you get this. Leave a message if I don't pick up. I'll call you back as soon as I can."

Steve ended the call, his heart heavy. *Please let her get the message, Lord.* He scooped up his duffel bag and joined the lake of passengers bottlenecking into the queue. Once there, the line seemed to crawl.

He tried Sarah again and it went straight to voicemail. Growling in frustration, he speed-dialled Joanna.

"Hello?"

"Sarah's not picking up, and my flight is boarding." He could hear the hint of desperation in his voice, and he didn't care. "I think she turned off her phone. I know it's a lot to ask, but would you please drive to her place and call me from there so I can have a chance to explain?"

He shuffled forward. The line was moving faster than he'd thought it would.

"Would you care to explain to me, first?"

"Jo-jo, I would, but I'm just about at the boarding counter. I'll call you from the Denver airport in an hour and a half during my layover. Is that enough time for you to get up there?"

"You seriously want me to drive to Edmonton tonight?"

"Please, Jo. With the crazy last-minute flights I found, I won't be up there until right before the gala tomorrow night. I can't let Sarah wonder that long. Not if she's as upset as you say."

"You know about the gala?"

"Eric asked me to speak."

"Oh." Joanna blew out air. "Yeah. I'll do it, because I really want to hear this. Sarah's not the only one who's upset, you know."

Steve handed his passport and ticket to the airline attendant. She scanned it, tore off the ticket stub, and handed it back without a word. He thanked her with a nod and entered the boarding tunnel.

"Thanks," he said into the phone. "You're the best. I owe you."

"Yes, you do."

"Talk to you soon."

"Fly safe."

He hung up the phone as he entered the plane, glanced at it to check the time, and shoved it into his pocket. He stowed his luggage in the overhead compartment and plunked into his aisle seat. His leg bounced, and he didn't bother trying to stop it.

He'd screwed up, big time. And this one actually was his fault.

What must Sarah be thinking about him right now? He closed his eyes at the answers his imagination supplied.

He pulled his phone out of his pocket to check the time again, only to discover that it had only been two minutes since he'd looked before.

It was going to be a long flight.

forty-five

WHEN SARAH STEPPED INTO HER APARTMENT, NELSON WAS SITTING AND WAITING FOR HER. HE jumped to his feet and barked at her happily in greeting. She gave a half-hearted smile.

"I suppose you would like a walk."

He barked in excitement, then went and stood by the door and panted, looking at her expectantly.

Not that she could blame him. He'd been cooped up all day.

"You sure you don't mind being seen with a troll?"

He barked again, oblivious to the meaning behind the words.

Sarah sighed. Even Nelson's guileless joy couldn't lift her spirits tonight. "Fine, just give me a moment."

She took a few minutes to use the facilities and to try to clean up the mess she'd made of her mascara, took a drink of water, found a pair of sunglasses to dull the effects of the sunlight on her migraine, and grabbed Nelson's leash.

"Okay, boy, let's go."

She clipped the leash onto his collar and they headed out the door to their favourite spot, the off-leash park along the river. Tonight, the calming effect of nature seemed to be nullified. Her thoughts continued their tornado path of destruction the entire time she let Nelson run around.

The sun was beginning to go down when Sarah finally called Nelson back to her. Spring was in the air, and he'd spent the half-hour of freedom gleefully chasing small critters that had been stirring in the underbrush. But he came obediently when called, smiling and happy, with his tongue flopping as he jogged toward her.

Sarah clipped the leash back onto his collar and they climbed the path up to the street. He still seemed to be full of repressed energy, but she knew she had none of her own left to give. The headache was raging through her skull, and all she wanted to do was to climb into a bubble bath and then her bed.

The sun cast long shadows along the street. It looked as though it was aiming to sit down on the pavement directly in front of her. Despite the sunglasses, water leaked down Sarah's cheeks from the painful assault. She kept her eyes directed at the sidewalk and a hand shielding her eyes to prevent being blinded.

A gold minivan materialized out of the glare next to the curb directly ahead of her. She startled as the driver's door of the parked vehicle opened and relaxed only slightly when Joanna got out, a cell phone pressed to her ear. Sarah stopped, and Nelson sat obediently beside her.

"Joanna? What are you doing here?"

Joanna spoke into the receiver. "Okay, here she is." She thrust the phone toward Sarah. "It's Steve. He wants to talk to you."

Sarah held up her palms in an exasperated shrug. "I told you I needed time to think! I don't want to talk to him right now."

"Sarah." Joanna's brows drew together like a curtain. "C'mon. After everything he's done for you, don't you think you can at least give him a chance to try to explain himself?"

Sarah stared at the offered phone, considering. Joanna was right. She did owe him that much.

She slid the loop of Nelson's leash loosely up her arm. But as she took the phone from Joanna's hand, Nelson's gaze snapped to the gutter near the curb and he bolted into the street.

The leash tore Joanna's phone from Sarah's outstretched hand and it clattered to the asphalt. She turned to yell at Nelson to come back.

In a fraction of a moment, she took in the squirrel scampering up onto the opposite curb, the red pickup speeding toward them from the east, the driver squinting into the setting sun, the dog gleefully chasing his prey. Panic split her chest as Nelson ran straight into the truck's path.

"Nelson, NO!" she screamed with every ounce of strength she could muster, knowing that it was already too late.

The driver saw the dog. Tires squealed on pavement and Sarah felt, rather than heard, the sickening crunch as Nelson disappeared under its shiny chrome bumper.

Her head felt like it was exploding, but she didn't care. She ran at the truck, waving her hands and shouting at the top of her lungs. The kid behind the wheel had slowed, almost stopping, but suddenly accelerated and disappeared into the setting sun.

Sarah swore and rushed toward the inert bundle of red-gold fur that lay in the road.

"Oh, God. Oh, no."

He was breathing. His eyes were open, and he was looking at her in bewilderment, as if she could explain what had just happened and why he hurt so much.

He's alive. Thank God!

She was dimly aware of Joanna running up behind her, helping her lift Nelson and get him out of harm's way.

"Quickly," Joanna ordered, "put him into the van."

She opened the hatch and helped Sarah slide the whimpering animal onto the floor of the generous cargo area. Sarah climbed in beside him and Joanna closed the door.

Sarah scooted herself to sit next to Nelson's head and stroked it gently to calm the trembling animal.

"It's okay, buddy. It's okay." She said it over and over, like a mantra, her shaking hand gently roving over his soft fur. She looked him over, but it was difficult to tell exactly what was wrong beneath his thick mat of hair. She was afraid to touch him anywhere other than his head in case she hurt him worse. His back leg seemed angled weirdly. Maybe it was broken?

Lord, let that be all it is.

"Is there an animal hospital near here?" Joanna demanded as she clambered into the driver's seat. She must have found her phone, because she held it in her hand and was swiping around, probably trying to answer her own question. A man's voice echoed faintly from the speaker, and she put it to her ear.

"Sorry, Steve, there's been an accident. Nelson's been hit. We'll call you later. Bye." She hung up without letting her brother say a word.

"Never mind. Got it."

Some part of Sarah's brain registered the van being put into gear, movement, and Joanna talking to someone at the emergency vet clinic over her hands-free speaker. But all she could think about was that her beautiful dog, her constant companion, her "one good thing," had been hurt, and Sarah hadn't been able to do a thing to prevent it.

All through that terrifying ride, admitting him to the clinic, and the tortuous waiting for him to be seen by the vet, Sarah prayed. She prayed like she hadn't ever prayed before in her life.

God, please be real. And if you ever loved me at all, please don't let my dog die.

Beside her on the floor, Nelson whimpered under her touch.

forty-six

AFTER JOANNA HUNG UP ON HIM, STEVE SPENT SEVERAL OF THE MOST HELLISH HOURS IN AN AIR-port he'd ever experienced. Given how many travel mishaps he'd been through in the past, he figured that was saying something.

First, he spent twenty minutes at an airline counter using all the charm he could muster to try to get moved to an earlier flight. But no, his last-minute booking from Tulsa to Edmonton had already put him on the earliest flights available. Discouraged, he had tried two other airlines and spent an hour trying to find deals on his phone, but apparently all of Denver needed to fly to Edmonton this weekend. There seemed to be absolutely no earlier flight available.

By ten thirty p.m., he had yet to hear back from Joanna. Cautious about intruding on the situation if they were still in emergency mode, he sent her a text instead of phoning. She texted back almost immediately to say that they were at a vet clinic, Nelson had a broken leg and some bumps and bruises but appeared fine otherwise, and she would be taking Sarah home soon. The vet was keeping Nelson overnight for observation.

Glad to hear. Should I talk to Sarah now?

A few moments later, Joanna replied.

Not a good time. Talk to her tomorrow.

Frustrated, he paced the length of the terminal for hours, sometimes taking the people mover belts, sometimes wandering aimlessly.

He'd made a mess. Why had he kept that stupid magazine all these years? He'd thrown most of his old stash away almost a decade ago, but he'd kept that one as a reminder. Never in a million years did he suspect that anyone would be hurt by the token of his own weakness. No one but him, anyway.

He'd tried to explain his reasoning to Joanna on the phone while she was on her way to Edmonton, and she said she understood, but he still wasn't certain she had. And now Sarah would go through the entire night wondering if he was a hypocrite. Maybe worse.

The selfish part of him kind of hoped that she would be too consumed with her worry for Nelson to give Steve much thought. Not that he was glad that Nelson had been injured—on the contrary, he'd been praying for the dog in regular rotation with his other concerns ever since the accident. But he didn't want Sarah to come to some kind of breaking point because of what she now knew about him.

He didn't want to be a stumbling block. Not when she had been doing so well.

After several hours of walking, he sat in a rest area, staring through the screen of a nearby television and trying to stay awake.

It occurred to him that he was doing it again. He was trying to control the outcome. Ever since Joanna had first texted him about what had happened, all he could think about was trying to keep Sarah from making a wrong decision because of a mistake he'd made, as though his transgression could be responsible for the direction Sarah's life took from this night forward.

Not that it couldn't have an impact. He knew that. If he could influence her life for the better, he could also influence it for the worse. And his explanation may not even help the situation. There would be no avoiding the truth about his past any longer—he would have to tell her everything. If she let him.

But, whether or not she did, her life was still her own, and her decisions were between her and God, not her and Steve. She had an inner strength and determination that he believed would carry her forward, regardless of what happened between the two of them. She had already set her foot on the path, and he didn't think something like this would derail her completely.

Then why does my heart ache so much?

He rested his elbows on his knees, hung his head and studied his hands to shield his emotions from prying eyes. He knew exactly why his heart felt like it was in a press.

He loved her. She was the first woman since Vanessa that he had cared about so deeply. But the feelings he had for Sarah were much deeper and richer than what he'd ever experienced before. And he was afraid that, once again, the truth about who he was would push away the woman with whom he wanted to share the rest of his life.

That's why he was afraid of the decision she might make. He wasn't sure his heart could take the rejection a second time.

He spent the rest of that sleepless night alternately sitting and walking along miles and miles of the concourse until he was finally allowed to make his way through customs and wait at the gate.

And through it all, he prayed.

It was nearly midnight by the time the gold minivan pulled up in front of Sarah's apartment building. Joanna put the vehicle into park and let it idle. Sarah was grateful for the warm heat that kept blowing into the cabin on such a chilly night.

Sarah's headache had subdued to a muted throb, thanks to the painkillers, but she knew that if she didn't get to bed soon that it could choose to stick around for another twenty-four hours or so, and the timing on that couldn't possibly be any worse. Still, she hesitated before saying her goodbyes.

She didn't know what she would have done tonight without Joanna. Her friend had kept her head through the entire emergency, while Sarah had basically gone numb with shock.

Of course, it never might have even happened if Joanna hadn't . . .

Sarah shook her head. That wasn't fair to her friend. This wasn't Joanna's fault. *Then whose fault is it? Nelson's? Mine? The driver's?*

"What are you thinking about over there?" Joanna's face was etched with concern.

Sarah took a deep breath and fidgeted with her gloves. "Do you think God did this to send me a message?"

Joanna frowned in confusion. "Did what? Let Nelson get hurt?"

Sarah met her friend's eyes and nodded.

Joanna shook her head. "That's not how God works at all. He doesn't inflict pain and suffering. And he doesn't send messages through it. He would never have orchestrated Nelson's injury in order to tell you something."

"But don't you Christians say that 'everything happens for a reason?'"

Joanna shook her head. "That has got to be the most overused and least understood phrase in common use. Yes, many Christians say it, but it is not scriptural. Not directly, anyway. If anything, it has more to do with the idea of fate."

Sarah bit her lip. She'd thought Nelson was safe when Craig had finally signed the divorce papers. She'd promised Nelson that she would look after him. But in the end, she could only watch while he had nearly been killed.

Had it been karma that he'd been run over by a truck tonight? Fate? Was it punishment for her own wrong choices? Or was it only a stupid accident?

She'd actually begun to believe in the God that Joanna and Steve talked about. But now she came back to the same argument of how an all-powerful, loving god could allow something like this to happen to an innocent?

She heard Pastor Eric's voice talking about the power to choose.

Why do the innocents always suffer because of others' choices?

Joanna turned toward Sarah. She looked thoughtful. "You want to know how God sends messages? He sends them through dreams. He sends them through his Spirit, speaking to our hearts or through a person's wise words at a key moment. Or his creation. The Bible says that 'every good and perfect gift is from above.' Nelson is a pretty good gift to you. If God is using him to show you anything, it is only how very much he loves you. He saved Nelson for you tonight, I think."

Sarah glanced down, remembering her frantic prayers on the way to the vet clinic. Maybe God had heard her. Or maybe there was nothing extraordinary about the fact that her dog had been run over and had no more serious injury than a broken leg.

Replaying the accident in her mind for the hundredth time, she couldn't believe that, though. She'd seen the tire crush Nelson's entire hind end. There's no way he should have only minor injuries after that collision. His insides should be damaged beyond repair.

Like hers.

"This morning, I found out I have to have a hysterectomy." Sarah thought she might start crying again when she told Joanna that, but her tear ducts seemed to be empty. After this day, there were no tears left.

Without warning, Joanna's arms enclosed her. Sarah stiffened in surprise, then relaxed. She wrapped her arms around her friend, drawing comfort from the embrace despite the awkward angle induced by the console between the seats. Sometimes, no words were the best words.

Sarah finally spoke aloud the thought that had haunted her since she'd been in the doctor's office that day. "I'm never going to have kids, Joanna," she said into the other woman's brown hair. "I'm never going to know what it's like to be a mom."

Her tear ducts started pumping out moisture again. She sniffled and withdrew, rummaging in her purse for a tissue. Joanna grabbed one from a box in the console and handed it to her.

Sarah accepted it, sniffling. "Thanks." As a mom of a tot, Joanna probably had good reason to keep that box handy.

Not that Sarah would ever have the chance to find out for herself.

Suddenly, the enormity of her losses hit her. It was like the last strap that had held the full weight of her burdens off of her had broken, and they hit her full force. Her marriage. Her future children. Her fairy tale life. She felt like she couldn't breathe, like she was being smothered by their crushing weight. She gulped for air between long, rasping howls.

Joanna laid a comforting hand on her shoulder and let her weep.

"I could have lost Nelson tonight," Sarah sobbed. "I could have lost him, and I couldn't have done a thing about it. He just ran out on that road before I—before I could even—*think*!"

She gave up attempting to stay ahead of the tears and buried her face in her hands.

In her mind's eye, she saw a little girl in a bathtub whose innocence had just been ripped away by her own father. At four years old, her childhood had ended. She had always hated that little girl, hated her for not running away, or screaming, or telling her mother. But for the first time, she saw the girl's inability to do any of that. She was only a kid trying to keep her daddy happy. She didn't know that she didn't have to do what he said or that he wouldn't really kill her mother if she told. She saw her father take her innocence and figuratively murder it—and there was nothing that young Sarah could have done about it.

She would never get her childhood back. And thanks to the damage done by the man who had stolen it from her, she would never have children of her own. Her dog was the only being on the entire planet who needed her—and tonight she had almost lost him.

She wept for it all.

But especially for that broken little girl.

"I'm never going to know what it's like to be a kid, either. I'm broken, Joanna. After today, I wonder if I can ever be fixed."

Joanna sucked in a breath. "I've got something to show you." She grabbed her phone and swiped around for a few moments, then handed it to Sarah.

The screen showed the image of a beautiful blue bowl. It had been broken into tiny pieces—none more than an inch across—and reconstructed with thin veins of gold binding the pieces together.

"This is an example of the Japanese art of Kintsugi. Artisans repair broken pieces of pottery with precious metals. According to Wikipedia, they treat the breakage and repair of an object as part of its history that should be revealed, not disguised."

Sarah scrolled through several more images of other pieces, wide-eyed. "It's stunning."

Joanna peeked over her shoulder at the screen. "I think many of the repaired pieces are more beautiful than the originals would have been, don't you?"

Sarah nodded. "If only I were a piece of pottery. Then I could be made beautiful again, too."

"But you are." Joanna's voice was soft.

Sarah glanced up in confusion.

"A common metaphor for God is that he is the master potter," Joanna explained. "He shapes and molds the clay, which is us, to create vessels for his own purpose. But I also like to think of him as a master Kintsugi artisan. The damaged vessels are the ones he can repair to be even more glorious than before. He is in the business of making the broken beautiful."

Sarah's eyes welled with tears. She wished she could stop crying today. But oh, how she longed to feel beautiful.

Steve had let her believe that her life could be repaired when he told her she could make a change. And she had made great progress since they'd met six months ago. But now that she had seen the magazine, she wondered if the man who'd kept it had even known what he was talking about.

She frowned as a thought occurred to her. Maybe that magazine was in Steve's box of keepsakes to remind him of his own brokenness. He'd always claimed to have been an unholy terror in his younger years—maybe the magazine was part of the wound he had never fully explained to her.

What mementos had she brought from her own past? What scars did that little girl bear that would never make it into a box of keepsakes, but would still advertise her brokenness to the world like a billboard?

Sarah buried her head in her hands. If she would always have these scars, she wanted them to be veins of gold. She thought of Sita, the ex-sex slave with the eye patch and the beatific smile. She thought of Steve, the man with the porn magazine and a heart for the sexually exploited. And she thought of Joanna, the woman whose life had been shattered by rape and restored by forgiveness.

Sarah knew what the common denominator was for each of these people—faith. They had each surrendered their brokenness to the Master Potter and let him put their pieces back together.

What if God's true work was not in preventing the pain and suffering on this earth, but in healing those to whom it occurred? Nelson could have died tonight, but he hadn't. And as damaged as her own life had been, she knew that it could have been so much worse. If Steve hadn't entered her life, it would have been.

In that moment, she saw God in a completely different light—not a lucky charm to be invoked in times of trouble, nor an absentee or abusive father whose only interaction with his offspring was to take and destroy, but a desperate, loving dad who sacrificed everything in a rescue mission to restore intimacy with the children he loved so much. She could hear him now, whispering to her heart until she thought it might burst—a story of love and truth and life from the dead.

In that moment, she decided that she was done fighting, and done running. She had already lived through hell on earth. Why not give heaven a try?

She turned to her beautiful, back-from-the-broken friend and swiped at her moist eyes.

"Okay." She sniffled. "I'm ready to meet this artisan. I've seen his work. If anyone can take my life and make it beautiful, I believe he can. What do I have to do?"

Inexplicably, Joanna began weeping, silent tears sliding down her cheeks past an enormous grin. "Tell him what you just told me. Give him all your broken pieces. Ask him to come and fix them. Let him take care of the rest."

Sarah nodded, suddenly shy. "Will . . . will you pray with me?"

Joanna slipped her hand into Sarah's and squeezed. "With all my heart."

When Sarah finally slipped through her front door, her headache had disappeared and her heart was full of wonder. She didn't exactly feel like the daughter of a king, as Joanna had told her she now was. But in the moment she had asked Jesus into her heart, a peace unlike anything she had ever known washed over her. For the first time, she felt free of the guilt that she had carried on her back for as long as she could remember. She hadn't known how heavy the weight was until it was gone.

I am forgiven.

Her brain kept wanting to deny it, but her heart knew it was true. The peace walked with her, enveloping her in its quiet but steady presence as she made her way to her apartment, got into her pyjamas, and brushed her teeth.

She stared into the mirror at the little girl she had spent most of her life hating. And for the first time, she *loved* her.

"I forgive you," she said.

The little girl gave her a small smile in return.

As Sarah drifted off to sleep, she felt gold dust on her heart.

forty-seven

STEVE ADJUSTED THE STRAP OF HIS LAPTOP BAG ON HIS SHOULDER AND WHEELED HIS SMALL SUIT-case out of the arrivals bay of Edmonton International Airport, scanning for Derek's face along the concourse. Instead, he saw his father sitting in one of the metal lounge chairs looking down the long hallway.

"Dad!"

Angus McGuire's attention snapped to the source of Steve's voice and his face broke into a wide grin. He stood to his full, diminutive height and met Steve halfway. They embraced, giving each other firm slaps on the back.

"It's good to see you, son. I think you're still growing, though. What are you, thirty-five now? Won't you ever stop?"

Angus' sharp grey eyes twinkled beneath thinning brown salt-and-pepper hair. Steve grinned down at his father, whose head only reached Steve's nose.

"I'll stop growing if you stop cracking jokes about it."

"It appears we are at an impasse, then. Life's way too important to be taken seriously, don't you think?"

"Something I learned from the best." He grabbed his suitcase handle and followed his father out of the airport. "I'm surprised to see you—I thought Joanna said Derek would be coming."

"Ah, yeah, but apparently there was some kind of decorating emergency for that shindig tonight, and all hands were needed on deck. Your mother is at home looking after Sophie, so I came to get you. What, aren't you happy to see me?"

Steve laughed. "Couldn't be more thrilled, Dad. It's been way too long."

Angus had brought Derek's little BMW. Steve threw his suitcase into the trunk and fished out his phone charger from an inside pocket. That morning after checking his luggage in Denver, he'd discovered that his phone had died and that he'd accidentally packed the charging cable in his suitcase. He plugged it in to the car's charging adapter, hoping that Sarah had heard the message he had left last night and had tried to respond.

"So," said Angus as he manoeuvred the vehicle out of the parkade, "what's going on between you and this Sarah Daniels? There seems to have been quite a bit of excitement involving her in the last twenty-four hours."

Steve felt heat creep up his face, but a point-blank question deserved a point-blank answer. That was his father's way—he didn't seem to have time for shallow things like weather or sports. He always went straight to the heart of the matter.

"Sarah is a friend. A good friend. And if the excitement settles down in my favour, I hope that she will become more." He watched the phone's battery indicator slowly blink, and decided to try turning it on.

Angus nodded, keeping an eye on the road. "What are the chances of that happening, do you think?"

Steve's phone notifications started chiming. His heart leapt as he saw that there was a text from Sarah.

Apology accepted. Explanation requested. I have news, but am too busy to talk today. Call you tomorrow.

Steve smiled, his heart humming with hope. He turned to his dad.

"All of a sudden, things are looking pretty good."

Angus glanced at his son and back at the road, a knowing smile on his face. He threw an Irish lilt into his speech, the one he always used when he was telling a story about Steve's great-grandfather. "Ye got it bad, don't ye, laddy?" He winked at Steve. "Well, son, I hope you're right."

Steve re-read the text and typed a quick reply. The anxiety that had propelled him through the night drained out of him and exhaustion threatened. He'd slept a couple of hours on the plane, and not well, but that was it.

"Hey, Dad? Any chance we could hit a coffee shop in the near future?"

Angus glanced at his son again and frowned. "You don't need caffeine, you need sleep."

"Yeah, but I don't have time. The gala is in only a few hours. And I want to talk with you."

"Lay yourself back and rest a spell, son. We can visit later."

Steve wanted to argue. It seemed he and his father never had enough time to catch up during their brief visits. But the warm car and his drooping eyelids coaxed him into agreeing.

He laid the seat back. Catching forty winks had never sounded so good.

His last thought before he dozed off was that as soon as he got to his sister's, he was going to burn that cursed magazine.

Sarah signed another copy of *Her Father's Daughter* and handed it to the taste-fully-attired woman on the other side of the table with a smile.

"Give my regards to your daughter," she said.

The woman clasped the two special-edition hardcovers she'd purchased on the way in—one for herself and one for her daughter—and smiled in gratitude.

"Thank you, Ms. Daniels. I can't wait to read this. I've read all of your other books, and simply loved them."

Sarah gave a wry grin. Justification was sweet. "My pleasure. I'm sure you'll enjoy this one, too. It's special."

After a few parting words, the woman turned and left. Sarah's eyes landed on the only remaining person in line, and her heart stopped.

Steve.

He looked more-than-usually handsome—clean-shaven, black tux, his wild blond curls tamed into something like a respectable condition. She sucked in air, thankful that she was already sitting. Her knees felt like jelly.

"You're here."

He smiled, and his expression reminded her of a schoolboy who has handed a girl a note with "Do you like me? Check yes or no" scrawled on it. He timidly stepped right up to the table, the question in his eyes.

"How's Nelson?" he asked.

"He's recovering. Laying low today, but the vet said he should make a full recovery before long." She felt a pang that she'd had to leave him home alone tonight, and hoped that he was doing okay.

"Are you angry?"

"About you being here? Or about the porn?"

"Yes."

Sarah glanced down, shock giving way to other emotions. "I'm . . . curious about the magazine. But I figure you must have a good explanation. Are you going to tell me?"

She looked up, studying him. His blue eyes held an unfathomable expression. After so long apart, she just wanted to drink him in. She wanted to rush around this table and melt into his arms, taste his lips at last, feel his heartbeat, maybe slap him for what he'd put her through . . . but she sat and watched him.

"Yes. But not right here."

She nodded. "I guess I can accept that. How did you find out about this?"

Steve gave a sheepish smile. "Pastor Eric asked me to speak in his place. Don't be angry with him, okay?" He gestured around the ballroom, filled to the brim with fancy dining tables and lined with other erotica authors signing books, exactly like she was. "Cut the old guy some slack. He has a congregation to answer to."

Sarah glanced around, and it occurred to her for the first time that the subject matter of this launch might not be in good taste for a man of the cloth. Perhaps she should have thought through her request to Eric a little more thoroughly before she'd asked. She bit her lip.

"Ah, I've missed seeing that." Steve grinned. He gestured toward her mouth, and she released her lip immediately. His smile softened. "I missed you."

Sarah's insides melted into a puddle at those words and the look in his eyes. She took a breath to respond, but was interrupted by Yolanda. The older woman flicked her eyes over Steve appreciatively, then turned to Sarah, all business.

"I'm about to go announce dinner. Where is your pastor friend? He's supposed to pray."

Sarah stood and moved around the table. "I, um, guess he's not coming. But he sent us a surprise replacement. Yolanda, this is Steve McGuire, the co-founder of Love Mumbai. Steve, this is my editor, Yolanda Hufnagel."

Yolanda's face registered surprise, but she quickly covered it and turned to Steve to shake hands. He returned it with his typical hunky grin, and Yolanda cast an approving glance at Sarah.

"Steve, m'boy, you made it!" A spry-looking elderly gentleman came up and clapped Steve on the shoulder, his wife beaming beside him.

Steve cocked his head in confusion. "Pastor Eric? I thought you said you didn't want to come."

"I never said that." Eric wagged a finger in Steve's face. "I just figured you'd be a much better choice as speaker than me. I take every opportunity to support your work. You should know that."

"Pastor Eric, I presume?" Yolanda asked, turning to the couple and extending her hand toward him.

"Yes, and this is my wife, Valerie."

Yolanda greeted them both, then asked them to follow her toward the podium on the raised stage at the front of the room so they could begin the dinner.

Sarah watched them leave. Turning, she found that Steve had extended an arm for her to take.

"May I accompany you to dinner, m'lady?"

She studied him for a moment, trying to read the emotions behind his eyes. *Who are you, Steven McGuire? Can I trust you?* But she already knew that, for tonight, that decision had been made, or she wouldn't have gone ahead with the gala. Whatever truth he had yet to share would be dealt with later. For now, he was the reason they were all here.

He raised an eyebrow, the schoolboy's question still in his eyes. She had no idea how to answer. Why did everything have to be so complicated?

She turned to the banquet tables to conceal her thoughts and put her hand through the crook of his elbow. "Where are you sitting?"

"Joanna snuck me into your table. Seems there was an odd number there, anyway."

"So she knew you were coming?"

"Oh. Uh . . ." Steve seemed to realize that he'd just incriminated his sister in the plot. "Not until last night, after, um, all hell broke loose. I didn't even know myself until yesterday morning."

"I see. Anyone else know?"

"Hmm. My parents and Derek, obviously. Other than that, no."

"Well, they did a fine job of keeping the secret for you. Better than Eric did at keeping mine." She kept her tone teasing. With her insides quivering like a taut-strung bow, it was difficult to be angry with the pastor for the surprise. Her thoughts were far more occupied with the firmness of Steve's arm under his jacket and all the unsaid things between them.

Steve glanced around the ballroom at the twinkling lights, the glints of silver and gold, and loads of white and pearlescent decorations around the room. "I can't believe you did all this. This is incredible, Sarah."

She dipped her chin, pleased, not wanting him to see her blush. "Thank you. I, um, only wanted to help. But I didn't do it alone. I *couldn't* have done it alone. The helpers I had . . ." She trailed off, still overwhelmed by the way people in her circle and beyond had rallied around this cause and made this event come together. "Let's just say, I'm humbled and grateful to have been a part of this. I guess I shouldn't have been surprised by how many people care about you and your work."

Steve glanced around at the crowded room and then down at her. "I'd say that most of these people are here because of you, not me."

Sarah smiled, unsure of how to respond.

They had reached their reserved table near the stage. Abby and her fiancé, Brendan, were already sitting there. Sarah introduced them to Steve, then sat beside Abby.

Steve cast an appraising glance at Sarah as he helped her into her chair, then seated himself beside her. Yolanda reached the podium and asked for everyone's attention so they could begin. Derek, Joanna, Angus, and Gertrude arrived at the table and found their seats, smiling and nodding their greetings at Sarah.

As people meandered through the room to their places, Yolanda thanked everyone for coming, went through a few other obligatory expressions of gratitude, explained how the meal would be served, and asked for silence so they could bless it. As she backed away to allow Pastor Eric to step forward, Steve leaned toward Sarah and whispered into her ear.

"You look amazing."

His warm breath tickled her ear and set a swarm of butterflies loose in her gut. She glanced at him and blushed, remembering how she had wistfully regretted that Steve wouldn't see her in the pearl-spangled black evening gown. His face was only inches from hers, and she was hit by the spicy scent of musk and man. She couldn't tear her gaze away from the icy blue depths of his eyes. Her pulse quickened, and her breath came in shallow gasps.

Then Pastor Eric began his prayer and the moment was broken. They bowed their heads.

During the meal, they made light-hearted conversation with the other members of the table, but Sarah kept glancing at Steve to find him looking at her, eyes full of unsaid words. Each time she broke eye contact she was a little more breathless than the last. She'd never felt this way before, not about anyone— not even Craig.

The warmth she felt toward him conflicted with the small serpent of doubt coiled around her heart after what she had seen in Steve's keepsake box yesterday. She wished she could have heard his explanation before having to go introduce him to five hundred people. As much as she was enjoying herself, she kept dreaming of taking Steve aside so they could finally have a few minutes alone to work things out. If only they'd had a chance to talk before the gala! Talk, and maybe—

Sarah gave her head a small shake. Frowning at her salad, she remembered her resolve not to allow her relationship with Steve to become romantic. That hadn't changed, despite the stuttering of her heart. Perhaps she was a "pearl of great price," as Joanna had said. She could believe that her past had been forgiven, and that she was supposedly the daughter of the King of Heaven. Perhaps she could even believe that she could find love someday—real love, like Steve had shown her, not the bogus imitations she'd always known before. But the fact remained that she would never have children. There was no way she was going to make Steve choose between her and being a dad. Not when he'd make such a good one.

The next time Steve cracked a joke and glanced her way, she dropped her gaze without smiling. Taking a sip of champagne, she leaned back a little and chewed her lip. Perhaps it was for the best that it would be several more hours before they could talk privately. All of a sudden, she wasn't anticipating that discussion much at all.

Christine Fenway and a half-dozen other members of the Edmonton Philharmonic sat on the stage in a semi-circle providing chamber music throughout the dinner. She could see Doug sitting at a table across the room from hers, the empty seat beside him evidence of his support of the project. She caught his eye and smiled her thanks, and he nodded back and then took a sip of wine.

They had finished dessert when Kristalee Summers, one of Sarah's fellow authors, stopped by their table and crouched between Steve's and Sarah's chairs. "Devon, this"—she indicated the room with her hand—"is fantastic. Oops, I guess I should say 'Sarah', now. I can't believe you got Michaels the Miser to agree to this."

Sarah glanced around in alarm to see if the head of their publishing house, Christopher Michaels, had been close enough to overhear the comment.

"Oh, don't worry, he's way over there." Kristalee waved her hand over her shoulder dismissively. "There's no way in a million years he would have forked over to launch one of my books like this."

Sarah felt her cheeks get hot and glanced nervously at Steve. "Actually, he didn't. My real book launch is late next month, in Toronto. His involvement was more for, um, credibility. He did agree to contribute the publisher's share on whatever books are sold this evening."

Kristalee's eyes were as big as the salad plates. "Then how did you pay for all this?"

Sarah glanced at Steve again, who was listening with interest, then focused on Kristalee. That had to be her pen name, but Sarah didn't know another. "Everyone contributed something. Like you, the other authors are donating their royalties for the books sold tonight. There were lots of other contributions, too. The musicians volunteered. The venue gave us their best rate. The organizers—we all pitched in. Most of us will be reimbursed from the ticket sales." She cleared her throat, uncomfortably aware of the intense way Steve was looking at her as she spoke. "Kristalee, may I introduce—"

Sarah's introduction of Steve was cut off when Kristalee stood abruptly and waved her hand at someone walking by a few tables over. "Arianna, so good to see you!"

As Kristalee bustled off, Sarah wondered if the other woman had even heard anything she'd said.

Steve leaned toward Sarah. "'Most' of you will be reimbursed?" He raised his eyebrow meaningfully.

Sarah pressed her lips together and stared at her fidgeting hands.

The squealing of feedback through the sound system pulled her head up. Yolanda stood at the podium, stooping over the microphone. She adjusted it to a more appropriate height, cleared her throat and glanced at the semicircle of musicians, who had just finished a piece of music and sat with bows and instruments erect, waiting.

"Excuse me." Yolanda paused to let the hubbub die down. "If I could have your attention please, we will begin the program."

The guests, who had been milling around since finishing their meals, returned to their seats as Yolanda continued. "In a moment, I will bring up our featured author to introduce tonight's speaker. But first, our musicians have a special treat for us. Didn't they play beautifully during dinner?"

She led the crowd in an enthusiastic round of applause. The musicians bowed their heads in acknowledgement, then turned once again to Yolanda.

"Before we let them go eat their own dinners, they have prepared a special number for tonight's event. I understand that this is an original piece of music written by Edmonton's own Christine Fenway. Tonight will be the first time it is performed."

Christine rose and bowed to the applauding audience, then resettled herself with her cello between her be-gowned legs.

Yolanda continued, reading from a small card. "The number is called, 'She Shines.' It is 'a celebration of the triumph of the indomitable human spirit.' Without further ado, please give your attention to the members of the Edmonton Philharmonic who have volunteered their time and talents to be with us this evening."

Yolanda stepped back into the shadows as the house lights went down and spotlights illuminated the group onstage. Sarah held her breath as the musicians poised their bows, exchanged looks, and began.

The music was the song of Sarah's soul. It began with a single cello line in a haunting melody of discordant intervals, jagged and rough, writhing in lonely anxiety. One by one, the other instruments joined in, building chord upon unexpected chord as though the instruments were fighting each other. The chaos and frenzy continued in a rising storm until it broke over the cello line. The throaty instrument sang out again, a single, sustained note that sounded like a declaration, or a promise. The melody was similar to the first, but this time, the music was smooth, soothing, and uplifting. As the other instruments came back in, the chords and rhythms solidified into an echo and amplification of the same, soothing line, perfectly in harmony, creating the effect of an anthem and rising to a triumphant climax.

By the time the last, haunting notes faded away, Sarah was weeping. She dabbed at her face with her napkin, knowing that she would be going onstage in a few moments.

The musicians bowed to hearty applause, then filed offstage. Yolanda was already standing at the microphone, clapping with a wide grin on her face. After the last musician descended to the floor of the banquet hall, she turned back to the mic.

"Next up, it is my pleasure to introduce you all to someone whose work you are probably quite familiar with, but whose name may be a mystery. She is the woman responsible for bringing all of us here together tonight. It was her vision that . . ."

Sarah bent toward Abby. "Is my mascara running?"

Abby flashed her a quick grin. "Nope. You look amazeballs. And may I say, since you are actually deigning to *speak* to me, Steve is a real catch!"

Sarah chuckled and rolled her eyes.

Yolanda was getting to the climax of her speech.

"You know her as Devon Sinclair, but it is my pleasure to introduce to you, for the first time, Ms. Sarah Daniels!"

The crowd began to applaud. Sarah stood and glanced at Steve, who gave her his most brilliant smile.

"Good luck," he said.

"You're up next, mister."

He grinned at her, blue eyes crinkling with the familiar look of mischief.

Sarah turned and climbed the stairs to the stage, her heart rattling her ribcage like a bird making a bid for freedom. She hoped she'd made the right decision about Steve. She hoped that this was all for a real cause, and that he wasn't leading them all down the garden path. *Especially me*. She also hoped that she could get through this speech without puking on her dress.

Jesus, help me.

Sarah stood behind the podium and scanned the crowd. With the spotlight in her eyes, she couldn't make out more than a few faces in the darkened room. But there at the front was the table of her closest friends—Joanna and Derek. Abby. Steve.

Steve winked at her. Joanna moved her hands in and out to simulate a deep breath in. Abby flashed her a bright and encouraging smile. The others waited expectantly. The room was quiet, only a few murmurs or clinks of glasses marring the silence.

Sarah swallowed and stared at the arrangement of flowers sitting on the edge of the stage. She focused on the way the twinkly lights filtered through the white tulle, the white lilies and gerbera daisies, the faux pearls—

No.

Tonight, she would be present.

Steve was watching her with a hint of a smile on his lips and an encouraging nod. In an instant, memories flowed through her mind. That first awkward meeting at Starbucks. Ice cream at Ghirardelli's. Him rescuing her at the hotel, then again after she had fled from Craig. A hundred phone conversations as they laughed late into the night. Him holding Sophie, or teasing Joanna. The affectionate way he spoke of Sita. The way he had been looking at her all night, like she was the only woman in the room.

Sarah glanced at Steve's vivacious mother, his strong and gentle father. Could this man, who had become such a rock for her, and whose very life spoke love, truly have betrayed her?

It couldn't be true. Whatever his reasons for having a porn magazine in with his treasured memories, she wouldn't believe that he had lied to her about Love Mumbai, or his work, or anything else. He'd stood by her through so much. He deserved for her to believe the best of him now.

She stared Steve firmly in the eyes and smiled. Then she took a deep breath, sent up a little prayer for her nerves, and faced the crowd.

"I am truly humbled that so many of you came out to be with us tonight. I look around, and I see many familiar faces—but most of you are friends to whom I have not yet been introduced."

She saw some polite nods, and felt five hundred attentive pairs of eyes.

"As we have prepared to launch *Her Father's Daughter*, several people have asked me why I have chosen to release it under my real name. Why not the pseudonym that has served me so well?"

She paused and glanced at the table with Kathy, Maryanne, and the other ladies from her support group. They nodded at her, and she tipped her chin in acknowledgement and gratitude.

"Writing this story has been deeply symbolic for me. This past year has been an extremely difficult one. Much like my book's character, I had come to a point where I was thoroughly discontent with my life. You see, the life I used to have, it was a lie. Everything about it was fake. I was ruled by the demons in my past. But as I wrote this book, I took my journey to authenticity, right along with my character."

She gulped, and the bird in her chest almost wedged in her throat. She glanced at Joanna, took another deep breath, and continued. "Writing this book helped me understand my own wounds—many of which my character shares—much better. I took risks this last year, both as a writer and in my life, that I would never have considered before. The gain from those risks has been more than I would have dreamed possible."

Sarah's glance found Abby's open face and her friend smiled and nodded. From the little bit of catching up they had managed to do, Sarah knew that her old friend could relate to some of what she said. It was encouraging to know that at least one person from her old life still stood by her. She smiled back at Abby, then glanced into the dark beyond her.

"So when you read my latest creation, know that you are not reading a book that I wrote only for a paycheque"—she found the table with Yolanda and Christopher Michaels at it—"though getting paid is my *preference* ..." The crowd, including her publisher, laughed good-naturedly in response to her joke. "You are reading a piece of my heart."

The audience clapped politely in response.

Sarah froze. She had spotted Pastor Eric and Valerie, and beside them sat her mother. She blinked to be sure she wasn't seeing things. No, that was definitely Ellen Sinclair.

What on earth?

She drew a shaky breath and continued, watching her mother. It was too difficult to read her expression in the dim light at this distance. "It is my dearest hope that as you read this book, this journal of hope, that you would not only be entertained, but that you, too, may be brought to a better place through the lessons my character learns. That I have learned."

She glanced once again at Steve. He was shaking his head with a wide grin on his face, as though he were in awe of her words. That couldn't be right, though. Why would he be amazed by *her*?

"However, this book, and my own personal journey, would have both looked very different if it were not for one man—a man who has become very important to me in the six months I've known him. Even though we both grew up in the same town, I had to go to San Francisco to meet him. His kindness, compassion, and mission have changed me, in ways I never would have expected.

"He is the one who encouraged me to write *Her Father's Daughter* the way I did. He has been a true friend during the most difficult year of my life. And he is also the man who co-founded the charity Love Mumbai nine years ago with a mission to work with victims of sex trafficking on the streets of Mumbai. His life is so inspiring and intriguing, I have made him the subject of my next book. Ladies and gentleman, I give you Alberta's own Mr. Steven McGuire!"

forty-eight

Then he stepped up to the podium and faced the crowded room. He took in their rapt faces. With Sarah's vulnerable introduction still echoing in his ears, he knew that he couldn't use his normal spiel. Not tonight.

He pulled the microphone out of the stand on the podium so he could pace with it, walked to the centre of the stage, and faced the dark.

"Sex."

He paused and looked around, and the audience tittered nervously.

Pastor Eric's eyebrows shot up, and he crossed his arms, leaning back and shaking his head. It looked like he was chuckling.

"Am I allowed to say that here? Anyone not sure what that is?" He raised his hand in jest, squinting at the room, and the audience laughed more heartily at his antics.

"Oh, good. We all attended eighth grade health class. Or at least eighth grade locker room." He was rewarded with another swell of laughter, and he relaxed, knowing that he had their full attention.

"Our culture idealizes sex, doesn't it? That's because, in the right context, there are few human experiences that are more gratifying. That is probably why we write about it, talk about it, advertise with it, and have so many ways to seek it. We have apps and websites and singles bars, all in the hopes of finding the elusive thrill that comes from an amazing sexual experience. If it weren't for this drive to experience out-of-this-world sex, and the connection that comes with it, my guess is that a few writers in this room might be out of a job." He shaded his eyes from the spotlight with his free hand and scanned the room. "Am I right?" he asked, and was met with a ripple of laughter and some nodding heads.

"In the right context, sex is a celebration and expression of love. In the wrong context, though . . ." He faded off, and his face grew serious. "In the wrong context, sex becomes a weapon that can break, destroy, and twist a person into a mere shadow of who they could have been. While consensual intimacy between sympathetic partners gives, non-consensual intercourse takes. And by 'consensual,' I mean a transaction where neither party was coerced by financial or other means.

"There is a reason that the word 'rape' holds connotations of pillage and plunder, because that is exactly what it does to the human spirit. It turns its victims into lanterns without light, shrouding the blessings they should have been to the world inside a dark veil of shame."

He paced a few steps, running his hand over his chin. Then he glanced up and found Sarah's face. She was looking at him with a mixture of bemusement and alarm. He wondered if he might have stepped over the line, but he had chosen his path. Nothing for it now but to continue.

Here's hoping I'm sowing some seeds.

"You might be looking at me up here, all purtied up in this shiny tux, and wondering what I know about any of this. Who am I to talk, right? Well, how about I tell you a little bit about myself?"

He glanced at his father, his hero, who gave him a sharp nod, the kind he used to give him before every baseball and soccer game. He could do this.

"I was raised in the sprawling metropolis of Miller, Alberta. I had a good family and a simple life and dreams not much different from many of yours—I wanted to help people and be as comfortable as possible while doing it. Since I get queasy at the sight of blood, that ruled out the medical profession, and I quickly decided that the best way to accomplish my goals was to become a lawyer."

The audience laughed appreciatively.

"My parents, who are wonderful people, adopted me when I was eighteen months old after fostering me for over a year. Driven by the need to answer some deeply bothersome questions about my past, in my final year of high school, I began a quest to find my birth mother. Little was known about her, as she had surrendered me to Family Services when I was only six months old, leaving contact details that were sketchy and no longer accurate.

"In my third year of law school, I finally made contact with my birth family. Unfortunately, my biological mother had recently passed away from a drug overdose. It was my biological grandmother who had agreed to see me."

Steve looked into his mother's eyes. Gertrude's eyes radiated kindness and encouragement. He swallowed his nervousness and continued.

"What my grandmother revealed to me was deeply disturbing and difficult to absorb. While she had agreed to see me, she was not particularly kind or gracious toward me. My very existence had been a surprise, and when she met me and did the math on my age, she no longer wanted to have me in her life at all."

Steve gulped and felt a surge of adrenaline spike through his body. He was about to cross the first hurdle. He licked his suddenly dry lips and continued.

"I will spare you the particulars about the run-around she gave me and how all of the sordid details were finally revealed. But what I learned was this—my mother had fled her abusive home at the age of sixteen, already pregnant with me. Despite my grandmother's attempts to deny it, it soon became obvious that my father and my grandfather were the same person."

He paused. You could have heard a pin drop in that room. Blood pulsed through his ears with a steady *whoosh, whoosh, whoosh*. It felt like he'd just completed the hardest workout of his life.

"My teenage mother had obviously tried to care for me for a while on her own, but had found the task beyond her. From what I could piece together, after she gave me up, she mostly lived on the streets until she got involved with a man who made underground porn flicks. Eventually, she even got a few jobs posing for some more 'reputable' gentleman's magazines. How do I know that?"

He paused and met Sarah's eyes. Her brows were drawn together, but it seemed to be a look of concern, not rejection. She flashed him a quick smile, and he continued, bolstered by her encouragement.

"When I was at my birth grandmother's house, she showed me a picture of my mother. I recognized her immediately—from one of the magazines I kept stashed between the mattresses in my dorm."

Memories flooded him, and he turned away from the crowd for a moment to collect himself. It was so long ago, but he remembered the shame of it as though he had seen that framed photo on his grandmother's wall yesterday— the nauseous understanding of who he was, the thunderstruck revulsion as he realized that he had used his own mother's image to arouse himself, bringing his grandfather's incest full circle.

Knees shaking, Steve sent up a quiet request for peace. He knew that he had been forgiven for the things he had done and was loved by God and his family for who he was, but the memories still left the taste of bile in the back of his throat.

The audience was becoming increasingly restless. He turned back toward them and made a point of making eye-contact throughout the room with those faces he could see as he continued.

"I had been raised in a God-fearing home, and supposedly, I was living an upright life. I had a fiancée that I loved, a mother and sister I adored, and many female friends. Yet I saw nothing wrong with my secret vice of pornography. As long as no one in my life found out, I figured I wasn't hurting anyone. I justified it to myself by saying that at least I didn't indulge in any higher-risk forms of self-gratification, such as drugs, alcohol, or gambling.

"But finding out the truth about my mother changed all that. Suddenly, I was no longer paying to be artificially satisfied by nameless faces—and bodies—whom I told myself had been compensated for their involvement. Not only did I feel the shame of my incestuous titillation, but I began to see every woman in those images in a different light. Had they chosen this for themselves? Were they happy doing what they were doing? Or were they, like my birth mother, simply trying to survive in a world that had repeatedly beaten them with the shortest and ugliest end of the stick by using the only asset they felt they had—their bodies?"

Steve paced a few steps, taking a steadying breath, then continued. "After learning who I was and how I had misused my own mother, I had thought that shame couldn't bring me any lower. But I was wrong. Rocked to my very core by what I had discovered, I confided in my fiancée, telling her everything. She couldn't handle the truth about who I was and what I'd done and rejected me, spreading the details of my past around the entire campus."

Two faces in the dimly-lit crowd came into crystal-clear focus. Sam and Kallie were here? They were listening as raptly as everyone else. Knowing that the friends who had stood by him throughout the most difficult trial of his life were in the crowd buoyed his spirits even further. He felt like he was doing a strip tease of his own soul up here, but with the two people who had never stopped seeing his dignity nodding their encouragement, he continued with renewed vigour.

"I became a pariah, and felt I couldn't even meet the eyes of someone I passed on the street, let alone at my university. Adrift, I decided that what I needed to do was go 'find myself' somewhere. India seemed like an ideal place to do that, what with the Taj Mahal, its culture steeped in spirituality, and being located on the other side of the planet and all. So a friend and I geared up and began backpacking around the country."

He took a breath, gaining momentum now that the difficult parts were past.

"As it turned out, I did find my purpose in India, but it was long before I reached the majestic white spires of the world's most famous monument to love. No, instead, I found it on the streets of Mumbai, in the face of a fourteen-year-old girl with a missing eye, an incurable disease, and a newborn child, whose madam had just cast her out onto the mercy of the fates. Sita was the first girl I rescued. But she would not be the last.

"My heart broke over and over again in Mumbai. There, I saw what misused sex could do. The shame and brokenness in the eyes of the women and children of Kamathipura were a mirror of my own heart. Everywhere I turned, I saw my birth mother's face." He gulped. "I knew that it was too late for her—she was beyond my reach. But I wondered if her life could have been different if someone had offered her help. And standing in the midst of all that need, I knew that I had to be that person for the broken-hearted of Mumbai. My life would never be the same again."

He stopped his pacing and scanned the faces of his family, his pastor, his friends, strangers in the crowd, and Sarah. Most of the women were crying, and not a few of the men. Tears streamed down Sarah's face, but she didn't look sad. She was biting her lip in that adorable way of hers and gazing at him as though she were seeing him for the first time.

"Every day for the last eight years, my fellow soldiers at Love Mumbai and I have gone into the trenches of a war on human dignity. We fight to break the chains of slavery for both the sex workers and their children. No, the chains are not usually literal, but they are there—in the layers upon layers of extortion and abuse that permeates the prostitution industry, in corrupt law enforcement that turns a blind eye to the atrocities committed against the innocent, and in the hearts and minds of the victims who, even if they escape the web of the sex industry, must still work for many years to rid themselves of the stigma, shame and disgrace of their pasts—if they ever succeed at all."

Steve resumed pacing, scanning the crowd as he delivered his closing statement.

"I hope that I have made you think tonight, friend. I hope you don't have to learn the hard way, as I did, that there are no winners in a non-consensual sexual transaction. Any time we use another's body for our own selfish pleasure, both parties have been stripped of dignity. Even if no one else ever finds out, the true price you pay is a piece of your own soul.

"That's what Love Mumbai is about—working to shine a light into the darkness of shame by showing those we work with what love truly is. These beautiful souls are not 'someone else's problem' or 'nameless faces' to us. They are someone's daughters, sons, and mothers. They are the casualties of mass destruction caused by the rape of the innocents. And they are not so different from our own daughters, mothers, sisters, brothers, sons, and fathers. Each one of them is a 'pearl of great price.'"

The expressions he could see ranged from discomfort to rapt attention. He prayed again that God would take his words and use them as seeds of hope for someone in the crowd tonight.

"You may not have been a victim of sexual violence, and I hope, for your sake, that this is true. But maybe you have been. Or maybe you have perpetrated it on someone else, directly or remotely, such as through a magazine or the Internet. Or maybe your wounds are completely different—but I know you have some. I want to tell you tonight that it is never too late to restore your dignity, or choose a different path. Yes, you have wounds, but so do we all. You no longer need to keep letting your scars inflict pain on others or yourself. Look around you."

He paused, and the crowd glanced uncomfortably around as they realized he had meant the directive literally. "Every person in this room tonight, no matter how beautifully dressed, is wounded. It's true. We are each broken in our own way. But just because we are broken doesn't mean we are without value. On the contrary, you, my friend, are a priceless pearl. I want you to turn to the person beside you and say, 'I am a priceless pearl.'"

He paused and heard the typical half-hearted mumbling from this type of instruction. "No, you can do better than that. C'mon, say it. 'I am a priceless pearl.'"

This time, the chorus came back loud and strong. Steve smiled.

"You've said it. Now go out and live like it. Thank you very much."

He laid the mic back on the podium and began to walk straight back to his seat. His abrupt departure seemed to have caught the audience by surprise. The applause was hesitant at first, then grew and swelled to fill the entire cavernous space. When he was halfway down the stairs, he looked up and noticed that people had begun standing as they clapped, more every second, until the entire room was giving him a standing ovation.

He had never felt so humbled. He nodded and waved, then made his way over to his table.

As he reached Sarah and they sat down, she grasped his hand.

"That. Was perfect."

He looked into eyes so full of emotion that, if he hadn't already been sitting, would have knocked him right over.

"The magazine," he said. "It was a reminder of my birth mother, and what I'd done to her."

"I know that now." Her gaze didn't waver.

"I'm sorry I hurt you. I never would have kept it if I had known that would happen."

"I know that, too."

He squeezed her hand and gazed into those forget-me-not eyes for long moments. His attention was pulled away at last by Yolanda's voice from the podium wrapping up the event.

Sarah's hand was soft and warm inside his own. She twined her fingers through his, and he dared a glance at her profile as she listened to Yolanda thank all those involved. She looked like a porcelain angel, with pearls pinned into her golden hair and her cheek flushed pink. She was the most stunning creature he had ever seen, but that wasn't why he felt a surge of warmth as he looked at her.

After baring the ugliness of his soul, she had taken his hand. He felt the curtain of shame that had shrouded his past fall away in the face of her loving acceptance.

Not until the lights came up, the congratulations had been said, and he was forced to stand to greet people coming up to meet him did Sarah let go.

forty-nine

SARAH SAW YOLANDA STAND AND WAVE AT HER FROM ACROSS THE CROWD OF PEOPLE SWARMING to meet Steve. She cast a regretful glance toward her book table at the back near the entrance, then gave his sleeve a tug and leaned toward his ear.

"I have to go sign books again."

As much as she would enjoy speaking to any fans who had not yet had their new book signed, she was loathe to leave Steve's side. She felt strangely protective of him now, like she should shield him in case anyone said or did anything inappropriate in the wake of his revelations.

She had seen the effort it had taken him to get through that speech—the heart-wrenching courage it had required to expose his only remaining secret. She now understood why he had felt so guarded about it, even with her. She'd been with a man for four years and had never told him about her own past. She could hardly fault Steve for being cautious about with whom he chose to share his secret. And now he'd shared it publicly. She wasn't sure why, but she suspected it was because of her.

Which meant she needed to speak to him alone at the earliest opportunity. She needed to make it clear that his future did not lie with her, no matter how difficult that would be for her to do.

He slipped his hand around hers and wrapped her with his gentle gaze. "I'll come back there with you. There will be more room, anyway."

He loves me.

Any remaining doubt she may have had fled in the tenderness of his expression. She gave a shy smile and nodded, then followed him as he led her through the maze of tables. She clutched the bittersweet feeling of being protected and loved close to her, knowing that it could only be temporary.

She knew how much he wanted to be a father. Once he knew he could never have that future with her, it would be over. She consoled herself by thinking how he would find another woman to love. Still, her sinuses smarted and she blinked back tears at the thought.

Pastor Eric and Valerie were the first ones to catch up with them before they got even halfway across the room.

"Well, m'boy, you never cease to surprise and amaze." The jovial older gentleman clapped Steve on the shoulder. "That's a speech that should have been recorded and included in high school curricula across the country."

Steve laughed. "Oh, dear God, please no. Perhaps a less mortifying version."

Gertrude came up behind them and tapped her son on the shoulder. When he turned around, she reached around his neck and gave him an enormous hug. Angus, only a step behind her, nodded with an approving glint in his eye.

"Aye, wee laddy, ye done good," Angus teased. "I thought you might be getting too big for those britches, but it would seem you've grown right down to size."

Gertrude tweaked her son's chin. Her eyes looked watery. "I am *so* proud of you."

Steve smiled at his parents. "Thanks, Mom. Dad. I love you guys."

Sarah saw Yolanda by the book table with a line-up of customers. She was making subtle gestures that Sarah should hurry.

"I'm sorry, I have to—" Sarah pointed, and everyone nodded and waved her off. Steve followed right on her heels.

Sarah seated herself, and Steve planted himself beside the table to speak to the guests converging to meet him.

Sarah picked up her pen and glanced at the first person in line, a pretty twenty-something woman in a sparkling blush gown. "Who do I make it out to?"

The woman smiled brightly. "Regina, please."

Sarah returned the smile and began inscribing her name, relishing the sweep and motions of her real signature.

Abby appeared beside the table on Brendan's arm. She flashed her copy of *Her Father's Daughter* and winked at Sarah.

"You were phenomenal, sweetie. I'll get you to sign mine later, okay? Gotta go clean up."

"Sounds good." Sarah smiled at her high-octane friend, who was already tugging Brendan away.

She turned back to the queue and greeted the next customer—a man who wanted the book endorsed to his wife. As she chatted with the fans, she kept half an eye on Steve, who hovered near her table chatting with the many people who wanted to talk to him about his work, or his speech, or simply to meet him. She smiled to herself. No one seemed appalled or condemning about what he'd shared—on the contrary, she heard only admiration for him and his work from the snippets of conversation that drifted toward her.

"Ms. Daniels," said a man's voice. Sarah glanced up at the next person in line, a clean-cut man with a hint of grey in his black hair. "Yolanda told me you were talented, but she never mentioned how pretty you are."

The man took her hand and kissed it before she even knew what was happening.

"I'm sorry, but who are you?"

"Pardon me. I'm Scott Segel. I believe you sent me a pitch for your latest project. Am I to understand that the Mr. McGuire who spoke tonight is the subject of the book?"

Steve turned from some departing guests when he heard his name and extended his hand to the man.

"Steve."

"Scott."

They shook hands, and then Scott turned to introduce another man who stood close behind his elbow. "This is my partner, Paul Anderson."

Steve caught Sarah's eye, and she clenched her teeth to keep from giggling out loud. *My partner Paul.*

Steve shook Paul's hand with nothing but sincerity and interest on his face, but Sarah felt like she would die from holding in the laughter about their shared joke. Explaining the reason for any released hilarity would be extremely awkward—especially as it was obvious that these two were partners in the romantic sense.

Paul stepped up to Sarah and handed her a book to sign while Steve and Scott continued chatting.

"Mr. McGuire is certainly quite charismatic, isn't he? I can understand why he does so well at this."

Sarah glanced at Steve—his easy stance, his arms crossed and his eyes twinkling as he and Scott joked about something to do with motorcycles. *Steve knows about motorcycles?* But unlike Craig, whose charm had always seemed designed to give him an advantage, Steve was completely without guile. Whether in a tuxedo or a denim jacket, with his family or a complete stranger, he was always the same person. He didn't flirt with the women, and he didn't schmooze with the men. And why would he? He was a man with nothing to hide.

She loved that about him.

She glanced up at Paul as she handed him back the book. "I don't know if he's 'charismatic.' I think people want to help him because he is always *himself.* What you see is what you get."

"And do you ever get a lot." He grinned appreciatively.

Sarah choked on a surprised snort.

"That man has got more guts than most people I've ever met." Paul opened the cover of the book to read what she'd written, then held it up and tapped the image of the broken-looking woman on the front. "Except, perhaps, you. You two must make a dynamite couple."

Sarah felt her face flush. "Oh, no, we—we're not . . ."

She glanced at Steve, who was looking right at her, a curious smile on his face. He had obviously heard the comment.

Sarah didn't know what to do. She looked back at Paul and Scott, who now stood behind his partner. "Would you excuse us?"

"Of course," Scott said.

Sarah stood and grabbed Steve's hand, then led him at a trot out through the double doors and away from the press of the crowds that lingered in the lobby. She spotted an empty hallway and made for it. When she felt they were in a private enough location, she turned to face him.

"I can't have kids," she blurted.

Steve blinked and frowned. "What are you talking about?"

"I found out yesterday. I need to have a hysterectomy. I'll never be able to bear children. I want you to know, because then you can stop looking at me that way."

"And how am I looking at you?"

Sarah stared up into his eyes. They were the blue of a summer sky, and right now their usual mischief was tempered by a look that made her insides disintegrate. He wasn't making this easy.

"Like . . . like that. Like you want to—"

His lips crushed hers. He tasted like chocolate, and sunshine, and the breeze off the San Francisco Bay. As they kissed, she felt her body respond in a way it never had before, not with anyone. He put one hand on the back of her neck and the other around her waist to pull her to him. She tangled her hands in his curls, wanting the kiss to last forever. Her gut throbbed with a pleasant ache, and every nerve in her body zinged with electricity.

So this was what it felt like to want someone. And she wasn't trying to use his attraction to make her feel better about herself. She wanted only to show him how much she loved him, how much she wanted to see him happy, every day for the rest—

She broke off the kiss, put a hand on his chest, and pushed him away.

"What's wrong?" He frowned. "Sarah, did I go too fast? I'm so sorry. I've just wanted to do that for so long."

She shook her head.

"No, that's not it at all. But didn't you hear me? If you're with me, you won't ever be a dad. And I refuse to be the one responsible for doing that to you."

Steve wrapped his arm around her waist once more and pulled her close, using his forefinger to trace her jaw and looking at her with an intensity that stoked the fire within her.

"Sarah, I already have kids. Like, forty of them. All I need now is you."

They kissed again, breathing a duet of raw need, his hands roving over her back. Suddenly, he broke off and pushed her away, holding her by the elbows.

"I—I have to stop. Sarah, I want to do this right with you. I hope you understand, but I will not sleep with you until we get married." He gulped. "If we get married."

Sarah nodded and laid a hand on his chest. "I understand. I want to do it right, too." She looked up at him shyly. "That's what God would want us to do."

He searched her face as if trying to discover the answer to a riddle. "God?"

She bit her lip. Excitement and nervousness twanged in her intestines. "That was my news. I asked Jesus into my heart last night. After everything I've seen and everything you've taught me, I couldn't doubt his love for me anymore."

Steve's face transformed from confusion to joy in an instant. "Oh, Sarah. That's the best news I've received all day." He kissed her again with a passion that made Sarah ache. He pulled away with a groan.

"God give me strength. He's finally found me the perfect woman. Now he's going to have to hold me back to keep me from ruining it."

Sarah dipped her chin and fidgeted with his lapel. Despite all the talk of pearls and what God had done for her, she still had a hard time accepting the way Steve talked about her.

"I'm not perfect."

He smiled, his face inches from hers. "Neither am I. But you're perfect for me." He sighed and kissed her forehead. "I suppose we should go help clean up, hey?"

Sarah regretted the necessity as much as he seemed to, but they would have plenty of time to catch up later. They were about to head to India together in a few days, after all. She let him lead her slowly back to the ballroom to join the fray.

When they came through the doors, Ellen Sinclair stood waiting on the other side.

Sarah stopped short. "Mom?"

"Sarah, can I talk to you?" She glanced up at Steve. "Alone?"

Sarah looked up at Steve, who nodded and left her to go help tear down decorations. Sarah led her mother to an unoccupied banquet table at the edge of the room. The dishes had been cleared, but it was still covered with a white tablecloth and the centrepiece.

They pulled out two chairs and sat.

Sarah let her hands rest in her lap. "I was surprised to see you here tonight. How did you get here?" She knew how much Ellen hated driving at night, especially in drizzly weather.

"I came with Eric and Valerie Stanton. He told me about it when I went to see him yesterday. I had no idea that this was your 'thing' until I got here."

"Oh." Sarah made no attempt to conceal her surprise. How did her mother know Pastor Eric?

Ellen hesitated, obviously trying to find words for something difficult to say.

Sarah studied her fingernails, thinking about how she had treated her mother on the phone. "Mom, I'm sorry for snapping at you last night. I'd had a rough day, but I shouldn't have taken it out on you."

Ellen laid a hand on her knee, and she looked up.

"No, Sarah. I'm the one who needs to apologize. There is so much . . ." she shook her head, holding back tears. ". . . so much we need to talk about. But first, I want to say how very sorry I am for the kind of mother I was. I—I was so focused on my own problems, my depression, that I completely ignored what was happening to you."

Sarah frowned. "What depression?"

Ellen folded her hands on her knees. "I've struggled with depression since you were a child."

Sarah tried to absorb this new information. Her mother struggled with depression? How could she not have known that? But then, she had always been so focused on herself, and her own pain, that it was no wonder she hadn't noticed her mother's. Looking back, Sarah could see the evidence that supported her mother's confession—the withdrawing, the frequent illnesses, the unexplained medications. Why had she never seen it before?

"Mom, why didn't you tell me?"

"When you were little, I didn't want you to know because I didn't want to burden you with adult problems. When you were older, you were so difficult to get along with that I didn't think you would care. Your father—"

She broke off, choking on tears that began to flow freely.

"I thought he was simply being a good dad and husband. When I had my spells, which was often, he was always so respectful of me and my needs and seemed to do great with you kids, stepping in and spending time with you, getting you off to school, all that. I—I had no idea he—" She swallowed. "I was in denial, I guess. I couldn't admit the truth to myself. And then he died."

Sarah covered her mother's hands with hers. "It's okay, Mom. I wish you would have told me about the depression. I wish a lot of things. But we can't change any of it now."

Ellen met her eye. "Everett is trying to get better, you know. He's still going to counselling. He finally told me everything, or enough of everything, anyway."

Sarah heard the hollowness in her mother's voice and wondered what facing the truth about her perfect son had cost her.

Ellen shook her head as though denying the thoughts that faced her. "There's no way to go back and fix the past, is there? I can't go back and undo all the damage that was done in our family. Oh, Buttercup, I wish I could."

Ellen reached out and stroked Sarah's cheek. Sarah leaned into her mother's gentle touch and tears began sliding down her face.

"No, we can't go back, Mom. But we can go forward. We can build something new, together. Okay?"

Ellen nodded, blinking back tears.

Sarah had an idea. "You know, I'm—going to need some help after my surgery. Apparently, I won't be able to do a whole lot for six weeks or so—"

"Yes." Ellen broke in, her face set.

"Are you sure? It will be after I get home from India in a few weeks, so right during farmer's market season. It's a pretty big commitment, what with Nelson and the post-op care. You don't want to think about it?"

"I said I'll do it. I want to do it. You can come stay with me . . . and Everett will only be allowed to come over if you agree to it. But I do hope you give him a chance."

Sarah could hardly believe her ears. It was what she'd been hoping for. Could it be possible that she and Ellen would be able to have a real relationship?

Her mother patted Sarah's hand, an amused smile on her face. "Besides, I want a chance to get to know this Steve fellow. I have a feeling that we might be seeing a lot of him from now on."

Sarah glanced across the room at Steve, who had stripped down to his tuxedo shirt and was carrying a pair of enormous candelabras out the door, his untied bow tie draped casually around his neck. She had no idea what his schedule looked like over the next couple of months—but something told her that seeing her would be a priority for him. Her heart sped up again, and she smiled.

"Yeah, I'd say that you're right."

fifty

SARAH SLIPPED HER LAPTOP INTO HER MESSENGER BAG AND SURVEYED HER ROOM TO MAKE SURE she had everything she needed for the day. She'd been staying at the Women's Shelter ever since arriving in Mumbai two days ago. She and Steve had decided that it was best—for both propriety's sake and their own willpower—that she not stay in his flat.

"Besides, this way I can get to know the girls and what it is like to be part of Love Mumbai," Sarah had said, trying to make them both feel better about the necessary arrangement.

Sita had put her into one of the rooms on the recently-completed third floor, so everything still had that new-paint smell and was remarkably clean. The furnishings might be sparse, but she had everything she needed. A bed, a small desk that doubled as a night stand, and a chair were the room's only furnishings. She zipped up her suitcase and tucked it under the bed to keep it out of the way.

She heard a quiet rapping on the door and stood. "Come in."

The wooden door swung open, revealing Aashi, already in her uniform and with her black hair brushed and oiled. She had her mother's sweet smile.

"Are you ready to go down, auntie?"

Sarah smiled and swung her bag over her shoulder. It was only seven o'clock, but thanks to jet lag, she'd been awake for three hours. "Ready."

She followed Aashi down the stairs, following the aroma of fried onions and spices, until they reached the sunny whitewashed dining room. Several other women were already sitting on the benches at the two wooden tables enjoying the spiced wheat-and-vegetable porridge—Sarah remembered that they had called it "upma"—and hot plain chai.

She collected her breakfast from the cafeteria-style buffet spread at the kitchen pass-through counter and sat down between Aashi and the teenage girl named Lohini, saying good morning to those nearest her as she lowered herself. Lohini didn't speak much English, and she seemed extraordinarily shy around Sarah, but this morning, she nodded and smiled in return to Sarah's cheery greeting.

With so many unusual names, foods, and words in general, Sarah's brain was working overtime trying to remember everything. Considering how exhausted she'd been since she'd arrived here, she thought she was doing fairly well.

The first day had pretty much been spent laying as low as possible to recover from jet lag, though she had been introduced to the staff and lodgers at the shelter, the staff and children at Prakaash House, and a completely new diet. She thought she would feel better by the second day, but if possible, she'd been more exhausted than the first. Neither she nor Steve had let the jet lag prevent them from getting out and about the city, though, and between her map app and yesterday's driving tour, she felt like she had a decent lay of the land already.

This morning, the plan was for her to shadow Steve throughout his day. One of the first items on the docket was a meeting with Prakaash House's landlord, Vijay Paresh.

Sita sat across the table from Sarah and flashed her a smile that would glow in the dark.

"Good morning, Miss Sarah. You sleep well?"

Sarah shook her head, then remembered that the Western gesture looked much more like the Indian head motion for "yes" than a negative answer in the other woman's eyes. She swallowed her mouthful of food and smiled.

"No, jet lag is still kicking my butt, but it was better than the night before."

Sita frowned slightly, and Sarah realized that the phrasing must have confused her. It was going to take a while to get used to dropping Canadian idioms and speaking with basic words and phrases her new companions would understand.

Sita turned to her daughter and rattled off a question in a language Sarah thought might be Nepali, which she had already learned was Sita's native tongue, or perhaps Hindi. Aashi looked confused, then laughed and replied in the same language. After a couple of sentences were passed back and forth between them, Aashi turned to Sarah.

"Mama wants to know what means this 'kick my butt.' What is 'butt?'"

Sarah felt her face flush. Why had she chosen that particular phrase?

"Um, 'butt' is short for 'buttocks' and means, um . . ." At a loss to find a polite word that Aashi might understand to replace 'butt,' she simply pointed at her own. "I was trying to say that being tired from the jet lag is like it is winning a fight against me."

The look of intense concentration on Aashi's face broke into a wide grin as she comprehended Sarah's meaning. "Ah, yes, yes, okay, okay!" She translated for her mother in jabbering syllables.

Sita listened intently, then smiled. She turned to Sarah and held up her tumbler of chai meaningfully.

"Maybe you need to kick back, yes?"

The women in the room all broke out in delighted laughter. Even Lohini, who had been listening quietly while eating her porridge, giggled into her spoon.

Aashi took a sip of chai, then turned to Sarah. "Auntie, you like it here in Mumbai?"

Sarah thought about it. She missed Nelson already, even though Joanna had assured her he was doing just fine at their place, despite Sophie's attentions. She was exhausted, and everything was new, and her intestines were already rebelling after the two days of non-stop travel to get here and the sudden switch in diet when she'd arrived. Her accommodations were spartan and the curfew at the shelter meant she and Steve would almost never have an evening out on the town. The traffic gave her heart palpitations— she'd actually screamed a couple of times—and the smog burned her lungs. She would never smell diesel exhaust again without thinking of this city. Steve had said he would bring her a breathing mask to wear today, which should help.

But on the other hand, much of what she'd seen of the country so far was gorgeous, the food was delicious, the culture was vibrant and exciting, and the people had been friendly and welcoming.

With concentration, she made a passable facsimile of the sideways head waggle that was an Indian affirmative. "Yes, I think so."

"You like it enough to come back?"

Sarah smiled and waggled again, doing a much better job this time. "Yes, I think so."

"You going to marry Uncle Steve?"

Sarah choked on her *upma* and her face immediately felt as hot as the chili pepper she had just swallowed, much to Aashi's delight, as well as several of the other women at the two breakfast tables.

"I, uh . . ."

Sita shushed her daughter. "Go brush your teeth, *nanu*. Leave Miss Sarah alone."

Sarah smiled, waving it away. "It's okay, really. She was only being curious."

Nevertheless, Aashi obediently took her empty dishes to the bus bin and retreated upstairs to brush her teeth. Sarah watched her leave, then turned back to the girl's mother.

"She is a very sweet girl. You must be so proud."

Sita smiled and dipped her head, pride shining from her face. "Yes, Miss Sarah. She is a good girl. She will be fine, by the grace of God."

Sarah blinked back a sudden tear as she remembered what Steve had told her about the recent occurrences with Ajay. She frowned and stared at her *upma*. Little Aashi seemed so happy for such recent trauma. Was she already learning how to put on masks? Sarah studied Sita. If anyone were equipped to help her daughter through the pain she'd experienced, Sita was.

Sita glanced at Sarah out of the corner of her good eye. "I know she should not say about you and Steve. But it is only that we never see Steve so happy. She is worry, if you and Steve get married, that you not to want to live here. You have a life in Canada, and maybe you not to want to leave it."

Sarah drew in her breath, then looked around at the other women in the room. They had all stopped eating and seemed to be listening intently for her answer—an answer to a question she hadn't even considered before now.

She turned back to Sita, choosing her words carefully.

"I am a writer, so I could do my work from anywhere. And if Steve and I do marry"—a notion that had already crossed their lips several times—"we will decide together where we will live. But I would never make him choose between me and his work here in India. And I promise that I will do my best to learn to feel comfortable here."

Sita waggled her head and smiled. "Yes, I think you will." Her caramel eye twinkled, and she bent her head back to her breakfast.

Aashi came pounding down the stairs and flew into the dining room. At the moment, she was the only child here, as she preferred to live with Sita than stay in the dorm at Prakaash House.

"Uncle Steve is here to take us to school. I saw him out the window. Come, auntie! Come, Priya! We must go!"

Sarah stood and deposited her dishes into the bus bin and stuck her head into the kitchen to thank the cook, whose name she still could not pronounce.

"*Deniwada*," she said, trying out one of her few Hindi words.

The apple-cheeked cook nodded and beamed in acknowledgement.

Smiling her goodbyes to the women, Sarah scooped up her bag and followed Aashi and the quiet Priya out to the parlour to meet Steve.

Steve accepted a tumbler of chai from Priya with a nod of thanks. The girl lowered her eyes in acknowledgement, then finished making the rounds of the guests seated in Prakaash House's lounge before retreating to the kitchen. Steve watched her go with a little prayer. Though she had resumed her duties, her every movement seemed to be permeated by a heavy sadness. He knew that Sita had been helping her through the grief of her most recent loss, but that for the most part, it would just take time. Nevertheless, his heart grieved with hers.

He glanced at Sarah, who sat near him in one of the white wicker chairs, gingerly holding the hot steel tumbler of tea by the rim. She blew across it and the surface skin crinkled.

He leaned toward her. "You can set it down and let it cool. It's okay."

She gave him a mischievous smile. "And let you think I can't handle it? That'll never do."

He winked at her, then set his own tumbler on the glass-and-wicker coffee table. She chuckled, then followed suit.

The wicker sofa squeaked as Vijay Paresh shifted his weight. He gave Sarah a lingering glance while taking a sip of chai, then turned toward Paul and Steve. Aparna, her midriff bulging, sat next to her husband on her desk chair, which she had pulled over to join the circle.

"So," said Paresh. "You have the money? Or are you going to try to convince me to give you another extension?" His gloating expression said he was sure of the latter.

Steve smiled to himself. Paresh was about to get a surprise.

Steve still experienced a flash of wonder every time he remembered the moment when Kathy had tallied up the income from the fundraiser—it was almost exactly what Paresh had demanded for the building's price. In that one event, God had provided for their need, and that was over and above what he had raised on his speaking tour.

When Steve had called Paul to tell him, his friend had taken the announcement in his typical even-keeled manner. "That is very good news, brother," he'd said on the phone. "God is good."

"All the time," Steve answered in the traditional response. "But couldn't you be at least a little bit excited about this?"

"You think I am not excited?"

Steve could picture him in his office, eyes twinkling and a big smile on his face. But Paul was not the type to jump for joy or yell his glee for the world to hear.

"Yeah, I guess you are, friend. I suppose we shall leave the happy dancing to me, then?"

"Okay. You dance. I will call Vijay Paresh and tell him we want to see him."

"Do you think we should try to haggle him down one more time? If we tell him we have the money in cash, perhaps he will be more reasonable."

Paul had chuckled. "Steve, I am Indian. Of course I will barter. It would be an insult not to."

Facing Paresh in the flesh now, Paul glanced at Steve before turning once more to the landlord.

"Paresh, we will buy this building, but for a fair price. We have the money in cash."

Paresh blinked at Paul, but gave no other indication of his thoughts.

Paul continued. "I compared the price of other buildings like this, and your asking price is almost four times as high as it should be. Will you not take this amount instead?"

Paul slid a piece of paper over the coffee table toward Paresh, the price he and Steve had agreed upon scribbled across it in pencil. Paresh didn't even glance down at it.

"You know my price. No money, no deal. And you will have six days to move to another location."

Paul looked at Steve and lifted his shoulders slightly as though to say, *I tried*. Steve sighed. He'd been praying that Paresh's heart would be softened again so they could afford to begin renovating right away, but perhaps they would have to part with all that money, anyway.

Steve braced his hands on his knees. "Okay, Paresh, you win. We will pay your asking price."

Paresh blinked at Steve, then Paul, holding his tumbler of chai frozen in midair halfway to his mouth. He looked like he was not quite sure he had heard correctly. Steve couldn't tell for sure, but he thought the man looked a little pale.

"You have it all?" Paresh looked agog. "All of the money I asked for?"

Paul waggled his head. "Yes, yes, sir. God has blessed us with it. So, do we still have a deal?"

Paresh looked back and forth in bewilderment, as if waiting for someone to jump in and expose the joke. For some reason, he gave Sarah a look as though she had just appeared out of thin air. Finally, he set down the tumbler on the table.

"No. I cannot sell you this building at that price."

Anger and frustration exploded through Steve's gut. Fortunately, it was Paul who spoke first.

"What is this, sir? You said—" Paul cut off as Paresh held up a hand.

Paresh stared straight ahead at the table, looking like he was trying to decide how to say something difficult.

"Six months ago," he said, "I had a dream. In it, a man came to me and told me that he was a messenger of God and that you would soon come to me and ask to purchase this building. I was to sell not only this building to you, but also the two buildings beside it, for a fair market price. I asked him which god had sent him, and he said the One God of the Jews and Christians."

Steve gulped. He could hardly believe what he was hearing.

Paresh continued. "I was very angry with this dream, thinking that I had only had a bad dinner and my mind was playing tricks on me. But every night for seven nights, I had the same dream. Then I found out that the school is for the children of prostitutes. I was so angry that when you offered to buy the building I instead told you that you must leave."

Paresh paused and took a sip of his chai, then dangled the cup between his knees and fidgeted with it as he continued. "The dream would not leave me alone. This guy kept coming back to me and telling me to sell you the buildings. I did not want to listen. 'Who is this god? And who are you?' I asked him. But he always said the same thing only."

He licked his lips. "I am a Hindu by birth, but was not very observant. After this dream started bothering me, I was worried that something bad might happen to me from your god, so I appealed to Lord Vishnu for protection. I set up the *paarad shivling* in my home. I invoked the name of Ram several times a day. But still, this dream would come.

"Eventually, I could no longer stand it. But I still did not want to sell you the building, so I decided to make you an offer you had to refuse. I would offer to sell you only this one building that you had asked for, but at the same price I would like to receive if I sold all three buildings at above market value. I thought you would tell me to get lost and would simply move on to a different place, and my problem would be solved.

"After I made you that offer, the dreams stopped. I was filled with relief, and thought that Lord Vishnu had had mercy on me and you would soon be gone.

"Then, on Monday, you called me." Paresh looked at Paul. "When you told me you were ready to make an offer to purchase, I thought it could not be true. But I decided that I would not lower my price, no matter what you offered me.

"That night, I had another dream. In it, a different man came to me. He was wearing white robes, and his hair was long and wild. His skin was like a North Indian's, and his eyes . . ." Paresh faded off, staring into nothingness. "He told me that he was Jesus, and that when I came to see you, his new sister would be with you. Then he showed me your face." Paresh turned to Sarah, and she gulped.

Steve felt like he'd forgotten how to breathe.

Paresh continued, looking at Sarah. "He said that you had raised the money for the buildings. Is this true?"

Sarah bit her lip and nodded, then seemed to remember the cultural difference. "Yes, it's true."

Paresh lowered his eyelids in acknowledgement, then turned back to the men. "He also said again that I was to sell you the buildings at a fair price." He leaned forward and tapped the paper Paul had set on the table. "Good sirs, you may have each of these three buildings for this cost, which will come to a total much lower than my asking price. Now please. Tell me about this god, Jesus."

Sarah listened as Steve and Paul shared the gospel with their landlord, the man who had seen her face in a dream. She could still hardly believe what she had heard, that God had intervened so directly on behalf of Love Mumbai— and that she had been a part of it. She watched in wonder as Vijay Paresh accepted Jesus on the spot, they prayed with him, and then made promises to get in contact with their lawyers to complete the legal details of the real estate transaction.

After he left, Sarah gazed wide-eyed around the circle of faces. "Does this kind of thing happen often here?"

Steve hesitated, but Paul beamed a wide smile. "Yes, sister. God is working in India. And in Canada, too, I think."

Aparna smiled, too. "Thank you, sister, for your blessing. All three buildings! Think what we can do with that."

Sarah shook her head. "But I had so little to do with any of it."

Aparna cocked her head, glanced at Steve, then back at her new Canadian friend. "God uses willing hearts. When we cast our bread—our efforts—on the waters, he returns it a hundred times."

Sarah looked at Steve, and he shrugged. "It's true. As I continue to learn." His mouth quirked in a grin, and he stood and moved toward the hallway. "Come, my job shadow. I must acquaint you with the other parts of my work."

She stood to follow him, collecting the tumblers from around the room.

"Please, sister," Aparna interrupted, trying to take them from her hands. "Let me do that."

Steve had warned Sarah that this may happen. She kept a firm grip and said as gently as she could, "You serve me, and I serve you. Treat me as staff, not a guest. Please let me do this."

Aparna smiled, and waggled her head. "Okay, okay."

Sarah followed Steve through the house to the dining room with the cups in her hand. As soon as they reached the kitchen door, Priya took them from her and disappeared through the kitchen to wash them outside. Through the door, Sarah could see the heavy-set cook industriously preparing the mid-day meal.

Steve grabbed Sarah's hand and led her out of the dining room to the courtyard behind the house. The sun was barely peeking around the building to warm the flagstones, and she enjoyed the beauty of the tropical plants and the stillness in the yard. It was already uncomfortably warm to her, and she knew that soon the sweltering summer heat would chase them all indoors for the afternoon.

Steve eyed the building, then manoeuvred her to a location against the wall where they would not be spotted from either indoors or from any of the neighbour's balconies. He pressed her back against the wall, planted his elbow beside her head, and kissed her like he was a man lost in the desert and she was the oasis.

After he broke away, Sarah looked up at him coquettishly. "Is this what you do with all your job shadows?"

He smiled. "Only the ones that help save the school."

She pulled his head down to kiss him again.

When he pulled back, his eyes danced with mischief. "Is this the way you treat all your biography subjects?"

She gazed up into those amazing blue eyes, crinkled with laugh lines, and her heart felt like it might burst. She hadn't thought such love could be possible. She could still hardly believe that of all the women in the world, Steve had chosen her, that she had somehow been blessed with this kind of happiness. She couldn't even find the words to describe how she was feeling, and all of her witty quips dissolved inside the intense, gentle love in his gaze.

"No." She tangled a hand in his wild curls. "Only you. It will always only be you."

He stroked her chin, his eyes roving over her face. "Good morning, Sunshine."

As they kissed again, Aashi giggled furiously from beyond the dining room window beside them.

They broke apart. Steve's face was as red as hers felt. He snuck over to the dining room door and popped his head inside.

"You little monkey!" Steve hollered in mock consternation.

Aashi squealed in delight and ran through the room and out the other door.

Sarah watched the exchange and chuckled. She already loved Aashi, and Sita, and Lohini, and Priya, though she had only just met them. It was strange that, though they came from opposite sides of the globe, they had so much in common.

We're not so different, are we?

As the dining hall began filling up with children coming in for lunch, she watched Steve joke and tease with them and the staff. Yeah, she was pretty sure she was going to like it here.

After wandering alone for so long, she felt like she'd finally come home.

epilogue

SARAH STOOD IN THE BELLY OF THE AIRPLANE, SUITED UP AND READY TO JUMP. STEVE STOOD NEXT to her in a matching outfit, his goggles sitting on top of his head.

Sarah looked at the love of her life and smiled to herself. Not all of the marks Craig had left on her had become scars. Skydiving had become a passion that Steve had embraced as fully as Sarah did.

They had tried to convince Joanna, Derek, and the rest of the bridal party to join them in making their grand entrance, but apparently, the thought of parachuting into the wedding was not as appealing to the others as it was to the two daredevil adventurers about to get hitched. Pastor Eric had seemed interested, but Sarah got the feeling he'd declined to save his wife's nerves.

The plane had almost reached jump height. Sarah turned to Steve and checked his straps. He'd been through this many times already, but she wanted to be sure everything was as it should be.

"I'll be fine." He grabbed her elbows. "I've got you with me." He bent and gave her a quick peck.

She smiled up at him. "I know. You'll be great."

"*We'll* be great," he corrected her with a wink.

The pilot announced the altitude, and they adjusted their goggles on their faces. Sarah glanced up at her partner for life.

"Wanna go get married?"

He grinned, arms braced against the sides of the open hatch. "I thought you'd never ask!"

He fell out the door, and she followed behind him seconds later.

Screaming toward the earth at one hundred twenty miles per hour, she whooped at the top of her lungs in delight. She manoeuvred closer to her husband-to-be and grabbed his hand. He met her eyes, grinning from ear to ear.

Sarah couldn't help but feel that she had flown over the rainbow and found the pot of gold. In moments, they would begin their new lives together. If that wasn't a fairy tale, Sarah didn't know what was. But instead of a "happily ever after," she was looking forward to the challenges that this new chapter would bring them—because for the first time, she would not face them alone. She had God, and Abby, and Joanna, and so many more people with her. Even her mom. But most of all, she had Steve.

She let out a final whoop as she pulled her chute.

Let the adventure begin!

Dear Reader,

THANK YOU FOR READING *FINDING HEAVEN*, A STORY THAT IS VERY SPECIAL TO ME.

Finding Heaven began as a simple question in 2012, when I heard about an author who hated her genre and her fans. "Why would she write about something she hates?" I wondered. In the process of answering that question, the ideas that formed the basis of this book were planted.

On June 3, 2015, at three o'clock a.m., I uploaded my first book, *The Friday Night Date Dress*, to my distributor for its release two weeks following. Five hours later, I lost my youngest son, who was three, in a traumatic vehicle accident. This changed my life forever.

As I grieved, God gave me the final pieces for this book. I could finally relate to the magnitude of the trauma and loss that Sarah experienced, and I could understand why survivors of childhood sexual abuse have such a difficult time trusting God. As I got to know Sarah and her story, God gave me a much more complete picture of himself and his heart's desire to heal all of my broken pieces.

Sarah's timeline of recovery has been accelerated to suit the pacing of this book. If you are struggling with the hurts of abuse, I pray that you don't compare yourself to Sarah's rapid progress. The process is different for everyone, but it can take years, decades, or a lifetime to overcome many of the patterns with which we have learned to protect ourselves since childhood. No matter where you may find yourself on the scale of recovery, please give yourself grace. Don't give up. Healing is possible, as long as you keep moving forward.

I would encourage you to invite God to help you in your healing journey. As the Master Potter who made you to begin with, he knows every part of you. Only he knows how to put your pieces back together, and he binds them with veins of gold.

For those who are interested in supporting organizations that work with at-risk children or victims of sex trafficking in India, here are several I recommend:

1. International Justice Mission (IJM, www.ijm.ca) is a global organization that works to free slaves and victims of human trafficking around the world. They partner with local authorities to provide justice for the poor. For information on their work in Mumbai, search their site (using the search term "Mumbai").

2. Prerana (www.preranaantitrafficking.org) works in Mumbai to end intergenerational prostitution. They have programs and facilities in place to provide care for and education the children of sex workers, drastically reducing the chances that these children will be trafficked.

3. Good Shepherd Agricultural Mission (indianorphanage.com) is an organization located far north of Mumbai, but every organization in India that gives poor and underprivileged children better opportunities is reducing the chances that those children will be trafficked or live out their lives on the streets. Sign up for GSAM's weekly newsletters to keep abreast of the work they do and get to know the children at the mission.

Sex trafficking is a global issue. I have focused on Mumbai in this book because India holds a special place in my heart. However, please become informed on how sex trafficking can happen anywhere, anytime—even to people you love. Learn how traffickers work and educate your children.

While researching this book, I found many helpful resources dealing with the issues of Childhood Sexual Abuse, Sex Trafficking, Domestic Violence, Emotional Abuse, and Grief. To access the most current list, see my Resources page at www.talenawinters.com/resources.

Lastly, I ask that if you read a free or pirated copy of this book and you enjoyed it, please purchase a copy (or, at the very least, leave a review on Amazon or Goodreads). As a self-published author, I pour vast amounts of time, love, and money into producing a quality product meant to bless and inspire my readers. The income I receive from this work allows me to help feed my family and produce even more work for you to enjoy. Thank you for being an important part of the free market for published works.

Word-of-mouth is an indie author's bread and butter, so please remember to review this book on Amazon, Goodreads, or the selling platform of your choice. (Just a single sentence makes a difference!) Also, I invite you to join my mailing list at www.talenawinters.com/contact to receive inspirational articles, updates about future projects, news of book giveaways, and more. You can also find me on Facebook: www.facebook.com/talenawinters.artist.

Do you want to extend the story? I have additional bonuses meant to accompany *Finding Heaven* on my website, including a playlist soundtrack inspired by the story. Check it out at www.talenawinters.com/finding-heaven.

I hope that *Finding Heaven* has blessed you in some way. I love hearing from my readers, especially about how my work has impacted you. Feel free to drop me a note at www.talenawinters.com/contact.

Until next time,

Talena Winters

Acknowledgements

WRITING THIS BOOK HAS BEEN A JOURNEY OF EPIC PROPORTIONS, AND IT NEVER WOULD HAVE COME to fruition without many key people in my life.

Firstly, thank you to my critique group. Sue Bergman and Jessica Jackson, without you this book would be a pitiful mess. Thank you for keeping me on track, calling it like it is, making me a better writer, and lovingly pointing out when I broke my story.

Colleen Hilman, you have been one of my best supports. Thank you for praying through this book with me and encouraging me when I wanted to give up. Guess what? I wrote all the words. :-)

To my other prayer warriors: my mom, Laurel Easton, and friends Larrissa Mundt and Laverna Stanley. Your prayers made all the difference.

I have made every effort to ensure accuracy in the many aspects of this book. That would not have been possible without experts in many fields willing to share their time, talents, and knowledge with me. While I take full responsibility for any errors that remain, I want to send a heartfelt "thank you" to the following people for your contributions: Dr. Erin Gregory, MD, Serena Burdick, RN, Peace River RCMP Staff Sgt. Brent Meyer, Brian Turpin of Peace River Victim Services Unit, Sharon Mailloux of Stepping Up (the North Peace Society for the Prevention of Domestic Violence), and Mark Mastel and James Brydon (Crown Prosecutors with Alberta Justice).

To the folks who gave me fast answers when I needed them most: George Lok, Janet Michaylow, Jacob Gregory, Melanie Kay and her lawyer cousin Dannelle Greig, Marla Forman, Chantelle Bentley, George Peters, Rohini Haldea, Aakanksha Chhikara, and Mauro Azzano.

To Tammy Cronin, whose inspirational love and cancer survival story was the final piece I needed to bring this book to life.

To Holly Lisle, who gave me the seed idea in an anecdote in one of her writing lessons about writing stories that matter.

To my beta readers: whether you read only a scene or the entire manuscript, your invaluable feedback helped make this story even better. Thank you to Colleen Hilman, Laurel Easton, Jason Winters, Michele Daub, Shaunna Dallyn, Jessica Jackson, Sue Bergman, Katrin Hilman, Laverna Stanley, George Peters, Melissa Keaster, Jamie Rath, and Lora Doncea.

Thank you to my editor, Kristin Dyck (familychatter.ca/copyediting), for saving me from many embarrassing mistakes (though I take full ownership of those that remain), Tamara Cribley (deliberatepage.com) for the beautiful print book formatting, and Fiona Jayde (fionajaydemedia.com) for the perfect book cover.

Thank you to my husband, Jason, who tirelessly lets me bounce ideas off of him, endures my many nights in front of the computer, and constantly shows me what true love is. You're why I know what it means to feel priceless.

Lastly, to the many, many women who have shared your personal stories of abuse and loss with me as I wrote this book: thank you for entrusting me with your scars. Your courage gave me courage.

Also by Talena Winters:

Historical Epic Young Adult Fantasy:

Rise of the Grigori Series:

The Waterboy (prequel)
The Undine's Tear
The Sphinx's Heart

Sweet Romance:

The Friday Night Date Dress

About the Author

Talena Winters is addicted to stories, tea, chocolate, yarn, and silver linings. She writes page-turning fiction for teens and adults in multiple genres, coaches other writers, has written several award-winning songs, designs knitting patterns under her label *My Secret Wish*, and is lead writer for *Move Up* magazine. She currently resides on an acreage in the Peace Country of northern Alberta, Canada, with her husband, three surviving boys, two dogs, and an assortment of farm cats. She would love to be a mermaid when she grows up.

You can find her on the web at www.talenawinters.com.